WEST AND EAST

"The novel most fully shines when the characters are allowed to strive for their full potential: Czech sniper Vaclav Jezek adopts an antitank rifle as his favorite weapon; German pilot Hans-Ulrich Rudel ingeniously modifies his aircraft; Soviet soldier Chaim Weinberg becomes a Party propagandist; and the Goldman family tries to achieve a semblance of normal life in Nazi-ruled Münster. The war is always present, though, and there's plenty to satisfy fans of military strategy, tactics, and armaments."

—*Publishers Weekly*

"And so it whirls on, the suspense building inexorably, thanks to two of Turtledove's gifts, in particular. One is for portraying so much of the action from the viewpoint of the grunts, or even civilians, who know little of what the Great Ones are up to until the consequences are all over them. The other proceeds from the first and is for envisioning WWII unraveling like an endless ball of yarn in the paws of an intelligent kitten. Keep reading or miss something exceedingly fine."

—*Booklist* (starred review)

"Turtledove is in top form as he traverses familiar and beloved terrain, the war years of the 20th century. The author's fans and lovers of military fiction and alternative history should welcome this addition to the genre."

—*Library Journal*

"As entertainment, this is as good as an alternative fiction, or historical novel, you are going to read this or any other year. But take a few deep breaths as you devour it with glee and ask yourself if the course of events and the Triumph of Good, we usually so happily take for granted is as secure or predictable, as we think. Reading Mr. Turtledove will make you wonder."

—*The Washington Times*

HITLER'S WAR

"Turtledove is always good, but this return to World War II, one of his favorite turfs, is genuinely brilliant."

—*Booklist*

"The author's mastery of the ever-widening ripples that small changes make in history is unchallenged, his storytelling always gripping, and his research impeccable."

—*Library Journal*

"One can rely on Turtledove. He writes well and with confidence. He develops strong plots. Delivers well considered storylines. Take the most recent entry, *Hitler's War*. The novel is predicated on a single question: What would have happened if Britain's Prime Minister Neville Chamberlain had refused to allow Hitler to annex the Sudetenland? Again, change one thing and, like a kaleidoscope, everything looks different. One piece falls another way and all things are altered. . . . [*Hitler's War*] is solid writing and classic Turtledove."

—*January Magazine*

"[Turtledove] brings the deprivations of war to life in this vision of a very different WWII. . . . American Peggy Druce, caught behind the lines, gets a firsthand look at the period military hardware and nationalistic mindsets that Turtledove so expertly describes."

—*Publishers Weekly*

"Not for the squeamish . . . *Hitler's War* would qualify as realistic war fiction except for the alt-history setting. No generals, strategists and such here, just regular people. . . . If you like 'real war' novels the book is for you."

—Fantasy Book Critic

Coup d'Etat

THE WAR THAT CAME EARLY

Coup d'Etat

HARRY TURTLEDOVE

BALLANTINE BOOKS | NEW YORK

2013 Del Rey Books Trade Paperback Edition

Copyright © 2012 by Harry Turtledove

Excerpt from *The War That Came Early: Two Fronts* by Harry Turtledove copyright © 2013 by Harry Turtledove

Published in the United States by Del Rey Books, an imprint of The Random House Publishing Group, a division of Random House, Inc., New York.

DEL REY is a registered trademark and the Del Rey colophon is a trademark of Random House, Inc.

Originally published in hardcover in the United States by Del Rey, an imprint of the Random House Publishing Group, a division of Random House, Inc., New York, in 2012.

This book contains an excerpt from the forthcoming book *The War That Came Early: Two Fronts* by Harry Turtledove. This excerpt has been set for this edition only and may not reflect the final content of the forthcoming edition.

Library of Congress Cataloging-in-Publication Data
Turtledove, Harry.
    Coup d'etat / Harry Turtledove.
      p.   cm. — (The war that came early ; 4)
    ISBN 978-0-345-52466-9 — ISBN 978-0-345-52467-6 (ebook)
1. World War, 1939–1945—Fiction.   I. Title.
    PS3570.U76C69 2012
    813'.54—dc23   2012009999

Printed in the United States of America on acid-free paper

www.delreybooks.com

9 8 7 6 5 4 3 2 1

Coup d'Etat

Chapter 1

anila harbor was a mess. Pete McGill hadn't expected it to be any-thing else. And the fierce Philippine sun beat down on him even though it was January. The past few years, he'd served in Peking and Shanghai. He was used to winter blowing straight down from Siberia. This muggy tropical heat, by contrast, seemed like too much of a good thing.

He still wasn't as steady on his pins as he wished he were, either. The bomb in Shanghai that killed his ladylove came much too close to fin-ishing him, too. The docs here did as good a job of patching him up as they could, and he'd had time to heal. All the same, an ankle ached and a shoulder twinged every time he took a step. His face was set in a per-manent grimace, not least so nobody would notice him wincing and try to send him back to the hospital.

Or maybe no one would bother any which way. It looked to Pete as if they'd take anybody with a pulse right now. A fireboat played streams of water on a burning barge. Whatever was going up didn't seem to care. Black, greasy, stinking smoke rose high into the sky.

That wasn't the only fire burning around here, either—nowhere close. Pete coughed harder than he usually did after his first morning cigarette. Jap bombing raids had hit the airports and the harbor hard. Now the only question was when the slant-eyed little monkeys would try to land an invasion force. Pete was sure it wouldn't be long.

Maybe all the smoke here would keep them from bombing accurately. Maybe . . .

"Out of the fucking way, Corporal, goddammit!" somebody bellowed behind Pete.

"Sorry." He sidestepped as fast as he could, which wasn't very. A petty officer went back to yelling at the Filipino gun crew manhandling an antiaircraft gun into place. The swab jockey must have served here for a while, because he was as fluently profane in Tagalog as he was in English.

Pete picked his way through the chaos toward the light cruiser *Boise*. The U.S. Asiatic Fleet wasn't very big. This part of the world was too close to Japanese waters for the USA to risk much around here. Chances were that meant the Philippines would fall, something the Marine tried hard not to think about.

Bomb fragments scarred and dented the *Boise*'s metalwork, but she hadn't taken any direct hits. If—no, when—Japanese planes came back . . . with luck, she wouldn't be here. Exhaust from her funnels meant she could get going in a hurry. She could, and she probably would.

But she hadn't yet. Mooring lines and a gangplank still tethered her to the wharf. Ignoring the pain in his leg, Pete strode up the gangplank and saluted the fresh-faced ensign standing at the far end of it. "Permission to come aboard, sir?" he asked the officer of the deck.

After returning the salute, the kid asked, "And you are . . . ?"

"Corporal Peter McGill, sir, reporting as ordered."

The ensign checked the papers in the clipboard he carried in his left hand. "McGill . . . Yes, here you are." He made a checkmark with a mechanical pencil he pulled from his breast pocket. The United States might be at war, but that didn't mean you didn't have to dot every *i* and cross every *t*. Not yet it didn't, anyhow. Once the sacred checkmark went into place, the youngster unbent enough to add, "Permission granted."

"Thank you, sir." As soon as Pete set foot on the ship, he turned and saluted the Stars and Stripes at the stern. The flag fluttered in the warm, moist breeze.

"Dalrymple!" the ensign called. As if by magic, a tall, redheaded able seaman appeared beside him. "Take Corporal, uh, McGill to the Marines' quarters. We'll let them decide how best to use him." As if catching himself at that, he asked Pete, "You *can* serve a five-inch gun, can't you?"

"Oh, yes, sir," Pete answered at once. Marines aboard battleships and cruisers often manned the big ships' secondary armament. The *Boise* fought other ships with half a dozen long six-inch guns mounted in three turrets. The stubbier five-inchers and a variety of smaller, quick-firing weapons tried to keep planes off her.

When they weren't serving the secondary armament, shipboard Marines also did duty as constables. Pete didn't look forward to that. He wanted to fight Japs, not his own countrymen. Along with everything Hirohito's bastards had done to him, he had Vera to pay them back for, too. A million slanties might be enough for that. Two would definitely be better, though.

"Come on with me, Corporal. I'll show you where you can stow your duffel and all," Dalrymple said.

"I'm coming," Pete said. The sailor took long, quick steps. Keeping up with him made Pete's ankle whimper, but he took no notice of it.

He knew about where he'd be going, but not exactly. He'd served aboard two destroyers and a battleship before going to Peking, but never a cruiser. Steps between decks might almost have been ladders: the treads were that narrow and steep. He managed to stay close to Dalrymple, anyhow.

Two corporals and two sergeants were playing pinochle in the cramped bunkroom to which the able seaman led him. They glanced up with no particular interest or liking. But one of the two-stripers looked vaguely familiar. "You're Joe Orsatti, aren't you?" Pete said.

"Yeah." The other guy's swarthy face scrunched up as he eyed Pete in a new way. "We were in the *Brooks* together, weren't we? Sorry, Mac, but screw me if I remember your handle." His New York City accent might have been even more clotted than Pete's.

"McGill," Pete said, and stuck out his hand. Orsatti reached for it. Their trial of strength was a push, or near enough. Pete chucked his duffel onto a top bunk. He wasn't surprised to run into somebody with whom he'd served before. The Marines were a small club, and noncoms in the Corps a smaller one.

Orsatti introduced Pete to the other card players. They switched from pinochle to poker. Pete lost a little, won a little, lost a little more. He was down five bucks when the general-quarters klaxon hooted. He hadn't heard that noise in years, but it still raised his hackles.

"What do I do? Where do I go?" he asked as they all sprang to their feet. "You guys are the only ones I've seen."

"C'mon with me," Orsatti said. "Our shell jerker's got a bad back. I bet you can feed us ammo faster'n him."

Pete hadn't said anything about his own injuries. He didn't say anything now, either. Instead, he followed Orsatti to a portside five-inch gun.

"Step aside, Jonesy," Orsatti snapped to the private standing next to the ammunition hoist. "We got a new guy here who ain't gonna keel over on us."

"I'm okay, goddammit," Jonesy said.

"Move," Orsatti told him, and the other Marine moved. Such was the power of two stripes.

Pete grabbed a shell and handed it to the loader. How much did it weigh? Fifty pounds? Seventy-five? He wasn't in anything like good hard shape. He'd have to do the best he could—that was all. He could hear planes overhead. The more they could knock down or scare off, the better.

The gun roared. The smaller antiaircraft guns were already stuttering out destruction. He seized the next shell and passed it on. Sweat was already springing out. Only dead men didn't sweat like pigs in the Philippines.

A plane with big red meatballs on the wings and fuselage plummeted into the harbor, trailing smoke and fire. The blast as its bombs exploded staggered Pete; water they kicked up drenched him. And a glistening metal fragment tore out Jonesy's throat. His cheers turned to horrible gobbling noises. He clutched at his neck with both hands, but blood sprayed and gushed all the same. His hands relaxed. He slumped to the deck. He couldn't hope to live, not with his head half cut off.

More bombs whistled down. In spite of blast and whining, screeching fragments—in spite of almost literally being scared shitless—Pete went on feeding the five-inch gun. Maybe the intense antiaircraft fire from the *Boise* did scare off some Japs. Maybe the light cruiser was just lucky. Any which way, she picked up a few new dents and dings, but no more. Some of the other gun crews also had men down, wounded or as dead as Jonesy. All the same, she remained a going concern.

Her skipper decided it was time for her to *get* going, too. As soon as the Japanese bombers droned off to the west—back toward Jap-owned Formosa, Pete supposed—he ordered the lines cast off and the gangplank raised. Then he took her out of the harbor as fast as she would go. Nobody aboard had a bad word or, Pete was sure, a bad thought about that. If she stayed where she was, odds were she wouldn't stay lucky a third time. All the old boring jokes about sitting ducks applied.

And Pete had more new buddies than Joe Orsatti. Go through a fight with a gun crew and you were all pals if you survived it. Jonesy—his first name was Elijah—went into the Pacific shrouded in cloth and weighed down by shell casings, along with half a dozen other dead men. The *Boise* raced south at upwards of thirty knots, looking for . . . Pete didn't exactly know what. Whatever it proved to be, he hoped he'd come out the other side again.

JANUARY 20, 1941, was a miserable, frigid day in Philadelphia. Sleet made the roads anywhere from dangerous to impossible. Ice clung to power lines, too, and its weight brought some of them down. Peggy Druce wouldn't have wanted to be without electricity in this weather. If you didn't use coal, if you had an oil-fired furnace that depended on a pump, losing power meant that before long you'd start chopping up your furniture and burning it so you didn't freeze to death.

Washington lay less than a hundred miles south, but it was conveniently on the other side of the cold front. Lowell Thomas assured his nationwide radio audience that it was in the forties, with clouds moving in front of the sun every now and then but no rain and certainly no sleet. Peggy, who hadn't seen the sun since last Friday, was bright green with envy.

"We are here on this historic occasion to observe the third inauguration of President Roosevelt," Thomas said in his ringing, sonorous tones. "This is, of course, the first time in the history of the United States that a President will be inaugurated for a third term. And, with the nation plunged into war little more than a week ago through the Empire of Japan's unprovoked attacks on Hawaii and the Philippines, the President surely has a lot on his mind."

Peggy wished Herb were sitting there beside her listening to the ceremony, too. Things weren't so easy between them as they had been before she got back from Europe. She wished like hell some of what had happened there hadn't happened. Those wishes did as much, or as little, good as ever. Still, she would have enjoyed what were sure to be his sarcastic comments about the ceremony farther south.

But her husband had taken the Packard in to his law office regardless of the slick, icy roads. He hadn't called with tales of accidents, and neither had the police or a hospital, so Peggy supposed he'd made it downtown in one piece.

He was bound to have the radio on if he wasn't with a client, and maybe if he was. Herb was always somebody who kept up with the news. Till Peggy got stuck in war-torn Europe, she'd wondered whether that had any point. She didn't any more.

Lowell Thomas dropped his voice a little: "Ladies and gentlemen, Chief Justice Hughes will administer the oath of office to President Roosevelt. With his robes and his white beard, the Chief Justice looks most distinguished, most distinguished indeed. He also gave the President the oath at his two previous inaugurations."

Only a few old men wore beards in these modern times. Well, Charles Evans Hughes was pushing eighty. He'd probably grown his before the turn of the century, decided he liked it, and kept it ever since. He'd come as close as a bad Republican turnout in California to unseating Woodrow Wilson in 1916. The world would be a different place if he had. Peggy wasn't sure how, but she was sure it would be.

"Are you ready to take the oath, Mr. President?" Hughes sounded younger than he was, even if rumor said he would step down from the Court before too long.

"I am, Mr. Chief Justice." No one who'd ever heard FDR's jaunty voice could mistake it.

"Repeat after me, then," Hughes said.

And the President—the third-term President—did: "I, Franklin Delano Roosevelt, do solemnly swear that I will faithfully execute the Office of President of the United States, and will to the best of my ability, preserve, protect and defend the Constitution of the United States."

"Congratulations, Mr. President," the Chief Justice said.

"They are shaking hands," Lowell Thomas said quietly.

In the background, applause rose like the sound of surging surf. "Thank you very much," Roosevelt said, and then again, a moment later, "Thank you."

"He is holding up his hands to still the clapping," Thomas noted. But the clapping didn't want to still. Back in 1933, FDR'd said we had nothing to fear but fear itself. Well, we had other things to fear now, starting with Japanese planes and carriers and battleships and soldiers.

"Thank you," Roosevelt said once more. Slowly, the applause ebbed. Very slowly: it was as if people didn't want the President to go on, because if he did they would have to look out across the sea at the big, dangerous world. Into something approaching quiet, FDR continued, "Believe me, I do thank you, from the bottom of my heart. What greater honor can any man claim than the continued confidence of the American people?"

That drew more applause and cheers. Now, though, they quickly died away. "I am going to tell you the plain truth," Roosevelt said, "and the plain truth is, things could be better. When I ran for reelection promising not to send American boys off to fight in a foreign war, I meant every word of it."

Peggy coughed as she inhaled cigarette smoke. Nobody in the United States played a deeper political game than FDR. When he started going on about what a plain, simple fellow he was, that was the time to hold on to your wallet.

"But we have had war delivered to us no matter how little we want it." The President let anger rise in his voice. "And our freedom is threatened not only in the Far East. Whoever wins the great European struggle, liberty will be the loser."

He was bound to be right about that. Whether Hitler beat Stalin or the other way around, the winner would be big trouble for the rest of the world. Right now, with France and England trailing along in his wake because he'd pulled German troops out of France, the Nazi seemed to have the edge on the Red. But there could be more big switches after the one Daladier and Chamberlain had pulled. Nobody would know under which shell the pea lurked till all the sliding around stopped.

Some people suspected Roosevelt's intentions, too. "No European war!" a man yelled, loud enough for Lowell Thomas' microphone to pick it up.

Hitler hadn't declared war on the United States. If he did, it would hurt his palsy-walsy relationship with the last two surviving Western European democracies. It wouldn't do the Third *Reich* any good, either. Peggy'd spent much more time in Nazi Germany than she ever wanted. The Germans didn't understand how strong the USA could be. But even the *Führer* seemed to want to take things one step at a time.

"I do not intend to get us involved in a European war," Roosevelt said firmly—so firmly, in fact, that Peggy got that wallet-clutching urge again. Did that yell come from a shill? Then the President proceeded to hedge: "I did not intend to get us involved in war against Japan, either. The only things I know for certain now are that the road ahead will be long and hard and dangerous, and that the United States of America will emerge triumphant at the end of that road."

He got another hand then. Peggy remembered that, back in the days of ancient Rome, people used to keep track of how many times the Senate applauded the Emperor when he addressed it. She didn't know how she knew that, but she did. Maybe Herb told her once upon a time—they'd rammed a big dose of Latin down his throat in high school and college. Somebody needed to keep track of the ovations in Washington today.

"We are going to become the arsenal of democracy, as I said in my Fireside Chat not long ago," the President continued. "We must be strong enough to defeat the enemy in the Far East and to ensure that no enemy anywhere in the world can possibly defeat us."

Yet again, people clapped and cheered. How many of those people had the faintest idea what war was like? Oh, some of the men would have gone Over There a generation before. They'd seen the elephant, as their grandfathers would have said in Civil War days. Most of FDR's audience, though, didn't really have any idea of what he was talking about.

Peggy did. She'd watched the Nazis storm into Czechoslovakia and promptly start tormenting Jews. She'd watched them march off freighters and into Copenhagen, ruining her chances to get back to the States for a while. She'd huddled against their bombs—and, while she was stuck in Germany, against English bombs, too, and maybe even against French and Russian bombs as well.

So she knew as much about what war was like these days as anyone who hadn't carried a rifle could. Some people cheering Roosevelt would find out just that way. And others would learn when young men they loved came back maimed or didn't come back at all. Would they still be cheering then?

The truly scary thing was, all the anguish and agony Roosevelt wouldn't talk about in an inaugural address were going to be needed. The horror Peggy had seen and gone through in Europe made her much too sure of that.

SARAH GOLDMAN EYED the clerk behind the barred window in the Münster *Rathaus* with nothing but dismay. She'd never faced this fellow before. It wasn't that he was gray-haired and had a hook where his left hand should have been. No one young and healthy would have sat behind that window. Young, healthy German men wore *Feldgrau* these days, not a baggy brown suit that reeked of mothballs.

But a button gleamed on the clerk's left lapel. It wasn't the ordinary swastika button that proved somebody belonged to the Nazi party. No: The gold rim on this button showed that the clerk was one of the first 100,000 Party members. He'd been a Nazi long before Hitler came to power, in other words. He'd like Jews even less than most National Socialists.

"You wish?" he said as Sarah came to the head of the queue. He sounded polite enough for the moment. Well, why not? She was a pretty girl—not beautiful, but pretty. And, with her light brown hair, hazel eyes, and fair skin, she didn't look especially Jewish.

"I need . . ." She had to nerve herself to speak louder than a whisper. "I need to arrange the paperwork for my wedding." There. She'd said it, and loud enough for him to hear it, too.

"You should be happy when you do that, dear." The clerk might be graying and mutilated, but he noticed a pretty girl, all right. Behind the reading glasses that magnified them, his own pale eyes seemed enormous as he studied her. He held out his good hand. "Let me have your identity booklet, and we'll begin."

"All right," Sarah said as she took the indispensable document out of her purse. It wasn't all right, and it wasn't going to be.

He held the document down with the hook and opened it with the fingers of his meat hand. He was no slower or clumsier than someone who hadn't got hurt. How many years of practice and repetition lay behind him?

"Oh," he said in a voice suddenly colder than the nasty weather outside. Of course the booklet bore the big stamp that said *Jude*. The Nazis had made all German Jews take the first names Moses or Sarah. Since Sarah already owned the one required for women, she'd briefly confused the bureaucracy. She didn't confuse the clerk now. She just irritated him, or more likely disgusted him. He shook his head. "*You* wish to . . . marry?"

"Yes, sir," she said. Staying polite wouldn't hurt, though it might not help, either. "It's not against the law for two Jews to marry each other, sir."

That was true—after a fashion. Law for Jews in Germany these days was whatever the Nazis said it was. Jews weren't even German citizens any more. They were only residents, forced to become strangers in what most of them still thought of as their *Vaterland*.

"Well . . ." the clerk said ominously. He pushed back his chair and stood up. He was shorter than Sarah expected; the chair let him look down on the people he was supposed to serve. Shaking his head, he went on, "I must consult with my supervisor."

The stout middle-aged woman behind Sarah in line groaned. "What's eating him?" she said.

Sarah only shrugged. She knew, all right, but she didn't think telling would do her any good. She waited as patiently as she could for the clerk to return. The woman and the people in the queue behind *her* grumbled louder and louder. Anything that made him leave his post obviously sprang from a plot to throw sand in the system's gear train.

He came back after three or four minutes that seemed like an hour. With him came another functionary, this one a little older, who also wore an *alter Kämpfer*'s gold-rimmed Party button on his lapel. The newcomer eyed Sarah as if he'd have to clean her off the bottom of his shoe.

"*You* want to get married?" he said, his voice full of even more revolted disbelief than his subordinate's had held.

"Yes, sir," Sarah repeated. Whatever she thought of him, she carefully didn't show.

"And your intended is also of Hebraic blood?"

"That's right." Sarah supposed her family had some Aryans in the woodpile. Isidor Bruck looked like what everybody's idea of looking Jewish looked like. He came by it honestly—so did his father and mother and younger brother.

"What is his name?" the senior bureaucrat asked. She gave it. The senior man sneered. "No, that is not correct. He is Moses Isidor Bruck, and will be so listed in our records."

"Sorry," said Sarah, who was anything but. She was mad at herself. She'd just been thinking about the forced name change, but she'd forgotten to use it. Nobody remembered . . . except people like the ones on the other side of the window.

"I see by your documents that you are twenty years old," the senior man said. "And what is the age of the other Hebrew?" It was as if he couldn't even bear to say the word *Jew*.

"He's, uh, twenty-two," Sarah answered.

"Why is he not here to speak for himself?" the bureaucrat demanded.

"He's working, sir. He's a baker, like his father." Bakers never starved. When rations for most German Jews were so miserable, that wasn't the smallest consideration in the world.

"Mrmp." The functionary was anything but impressed. He scribbled a note on a form, then glared out through the bars that made him look like a caged animal. But he and his kind were the ones who kept Jews in the enormous cage they'd made of the Third *Reich*. "And what is your father's occupation?"

"He's a laborer," Sarah said, as steadily as she could. "He used to be a university professor when Jews could still do that." Both Nazi bureaucrats scowled. To wipe those nasty expressions off their faces, Sarah added, "He's a wounded war veteran, too. Wounded and decorated."

Benjamin Goldman's Iron Cross Second Class and his limp did matter. Nazi laws mandated better treatment for Jews who'd fought at the front and their families. Not good treatment—nowhere near good treatment—but better.

Sarah almost told the clerk and his boss that her father and brother tried to volunteer for the *Wehrmacht* this time around. But she didn't want to remind them she was related to Saul Goldman, who was wanted for smashing in a labor gang boss' head after the other fellow hit him and rode him for being a Jew once too often. On the lam, Saul had stolen papers or got his hands on a forged set, so he was in the army now even though the Nazis didn't know it. The less they thought about him these days, the better Sarah liked it.

Both men with gold-rimmed Party badges went right on looking unhappy. No matter what Nazi laws said about Jewish frontline veterans, a Jew with a medal and a wound was plainly just another kike to them. "Laborer," the senior fellow said, and he wrote that down, too.

"When will Isidor—uh, Moses Isidor—and I hear about getting official permission to marry, sir?" Sarah asked. This wasn't her first trip to the *Rathaus*. Official policy made everything as difficult as possible for Jews. Marriage was definitely included. The Nazis wished there were no more Jews in Germany (or anywhere else, come to that). No wonder they weren't enthusiastic about anything that threatened to produce more people they hated.

"When?" the functionary echoed. "When we decide you will, that's when."

"All right." Sarah fought down a sigh. She didn't want to give the Nazis the satisfaction of knowing they'd annoyed her. They might be pretty sure, but she didn't aim to show them. She was her father's daughter—no doubt about it. She even managed a smile of sorts as she said "Thank you very much" and left the window.

"Well! About time!" said the stout gal who'd waited behind her. The woman started pouring out her tale of woe to the bureaucrats. Sarah didn't hang around to find out how she fared. Any Jew in Germany had plenty of worries of her own.

THEO HOSSBACH SUPPOSED he should have been happy that the *Wehrmacht* and its Polish, Slovakian, Hungarian, English, and French allies hadn't lost more ground to the Red Army during this brutal winter. After all, a headlong retreat would have made it more likely for something bad to have happened to the Panzer II in which he served as radioman.

But bad things could happen to the Panzer II all too easily any which way. The lightly armed, lightly armored three-man machines weren't obsolescent any more. They were obsolete, and everybody who had anything to do with them knew as much. They soldiered on regardless. A veteran crew, which his panzer certainly had, could still get good use from one. And any panzer at all made infantry very unhappy.

Besides, there were still nowhere near enough modern Panzer IIIs and IVs to go around. When the best weren't available, the rest had to do what they could.

What Theo's company was doing now was protecting a stretch of front that ran from a village to a small town closer to Smolensk than to Minsk. Just exactly where the village and town lay, Theo wasn't so sure. A good atlas might have shown him, but he didn't have one. What difference did it make, anyhow?

All he really knew was, the front had gone back and forth a good many times. Lately, it seemed to have gone back more often than it had gone forth. The Ivans were marvelous at slipping companies, sometimes even battalions or regiments, of infantry in white snowsuits behind the German lines and raising hell with them. They weren't so good at taking advantage of the trouble they caused—which was a lucky thing for everybody who had to fight them.

Theo still wore the black coveralls of a panzer crewman. They looked smart and didn't show grease stains. No doubt that was why the powers that be had chosen them. But odds were a man in black coveralls running toward a hiding place through the snow wouldn't live to get there.

"Got a cigarette, Theo?" Adalbert Stoss asked.

"Here." Theo passed the driver a tobacco pouch. He doled out the fixings for a smoke more readily than he parted with words. Adi tore off a strip from a Russian newspaper none of the panzer men could read. He sprinkled tobacco from the pouch (taken off a dead Ivan) onto the cheap pulp paper, rolled the cigarette, and lit it—he did have matches.

"Ahh," he said after the first drag, exhaling a mixture of smoke and fog—it was well below freezing. "Much obliged." He returned the pouch. Unlike a lot of soldiers Theo knew, Adi didn't steal everything that wasn't nailed down. His family must have raised him the right way . . . which didn't necessarily make him the ideal man for life in the field.

On the other hand, if anybody in a black coverall could make it to shelter running through the snow, Adi could. He was the best footballer Theo had ever seen except for a handful of professionals—and he was in their league. He was fast and strong and agile. And he was smart, which only added to his other gifts. With a sergeant's pips, or even a corporal's, he would have made a fine panzer commander.

I should be jealous, Theo thought. He'd been in the war from the very beginning. Adi hadn't. But Theo knew he would be a disaster trying to command a panzer. He was the kind of fellow other people didn't notice, which suited him fine. Give orders? Talk all the time? No thanks!

Sergeant Hermann Witt, who did command the panzer, had machine-made cigarettes of his own. Theo preferred the captured stuff. It might not be especially good, but by God it was strong. Everything that came out of Germany these days was adulterated—well, everything but the ammo, anyhow. The cigarettes that got issued along with rations tasted of hay and horseshit. The coffee was ersatz. People said the war bread had sawdust in it as a stretcher. Theo didn't know if he believed that. People also said the war bread was better than it had been in the last fight. Theo didn't know if he believed that, either. If the last generation had it worse than this, no wonder they threw the Kaiser out.

The Nazis said Germany got stabbed in the back in 1918. Well, the

Nazis said all kinds of things. Theo took them no more seriously than he had to. Since he said next to nothing himself, he wasn't likely to get in trouble on account of that.

He glanced over at Adi. Stoss smoked as intently as he did everything else. By all the signs, he didn't take the Nazis very seriously, either. And chances were he had better reasons not to than even Theo's.

No sooner there than gone. Theo didn't want to think about Stoss' reasons. He didn't want to, and so he didn't. No matter how little use he had for the Nazis, he'd learned a thing or three since the *Führer* came to power. He wasn't even consciously aware that he had, which meant nothing at all. Ideas, thoughts, went into little armored compartments. When he wasn't actively dealing with them, they might as well not have been there. No one else would ever notice them. More often than not, he didn't notice them himself.

Somebody who lived in a free country wouldn't have to think that way. Theo understood as much. But, since he couldn't do anything about it, he kept his mouth shut. Come to that, he kept it shut as much as he could.

Even though he didn't love the Nazis, he did love the *Vaterland*. And, regardless of what he thought of the current German regime, it had placed him—along with millions of other young German men—in a position where his country's enemies would kill him if he didn't fight hard.

That was underscored when mortar bombs started dropping near the panzer crewmen. Russian rifles barked. *"Urra!"* the Ivans roared. *"Urra! Urra!"* They sounded like fierce wild animals. Their officers fed them vodka before sending them into action. It dulled their fear—and their common sense.

Theo's first instinct when the mortar rounds came in was to hit the dirt. His next instinct was to get inside the panzer. That was the better notion. He'd be at a little more risk while he was upright and running, but the machine's armored sides would protect him against fragments and small-arms fire.

Sergeant Witt and Adi Stoss also sprinted for the Panzer II. Other men in black coveralls dashed toward their machines, too. A couple of them didn't make it. Those coveralls and their blood bright against the snow reproduced the German national colors. A bullet sparked off Theo's panzer just a few centimeters from his head. He dove through the hatch behind the turret and slammed it shut. A Schmeisser hung on two brackets above his radio set. If somebody started climbing up onto the panzer, he'd open a hatch and start shooting. Otherwise, the submachine gun was there more to ease his mind than for any other reason.

"Start it up!" Witt screamed at Adi. The order made sense—a panzer that was just sitting there was a panzer waiting for a Molotov cocktail. Theo didn't want to think about burning gasoline dripping into the fighting compartment and setting things ablaze in here.

But would the beast start? In a Russian winter, that was always an interesting question and often a terrifying one. The self-starter ground. Maybe Adi would have to get out and crank the engine to life—assuming he didn't get shot to death before he could. Maybe even cranking wouldn't get it going. German lubricants weren't made for this hideous weather. Sometimes crews kept a fire burning through the night under the engine compartment to keep the engine warm enough to turn over in the morning.

Adi tried it again. This time, to Theo's amazed delight, the grinding noise turned into a full-throated roar as the engine fired up after all. "Forward!" Witt said, and the driver put the Panzer II into gear. Forward it went. Back against the fireproof—he hoped—bulkhead that separated the fighting compartment from the engine, Theo started to warm up. Heat came through slowly, but it came.

Witt could traverse the turret by muscle power even if the gearing froze up. He could, and he did, spraying machine-gun fire and occasional rounds from the 20mm cannon at the oncoming Ivans. A few more bullets spanged off the panzer's steel hide, but bullets didn't bother it. Anything worse than a bullet would, but . . .

"They're running!" the panzer commander exclaimed. In the Russians' fine felt boots, Theo would have run, too. If they had no armor of their own in the neighborhood, they were helpless against panzers. A little German victory. This time. For the moment. How to turn that into something more lasting, Theo had no idea. Did anyone else, from Hitler on down?

Chapter 2

listair Walsh had spent his whole adult life in the British Army—which, unlike the Navy and the Air Force, wasn't Royal. The former sergeant sometimes wondered why not. His best guess, based on long experience, was that no King of England in his right mind wanted to lend his regal title to such a buggered-up outfit.

Almost as soon as Walsh got to France the first time, in the summer of 1918, he stopped a German bullet. The Kaiser's men had pushed as far as they could then, and soon started getting pushed instead. Walsh was back at the front before the Armistice. He saw enough action to decide he liked soldiering. He certainly liked it better than going back to Wales and grubbing out coal for the rest of his life, which was his other choice when the war ended. He managed to stay in the Army while it hemorrhaged men after peace came.

And he went to France again, this time as a staff sergeant rather than a raw private, when things heated up once more in 1938. Regardless of rank, he knew—he'd had it proved to him—he wasn't bulletproof. He'd fought in Belgium, and then in France as the Allied armies fell back under the weight of the new German assault. Once they managed to keep the Nazis from sweeping around behind Paris and winning the campaign fast—Wilhelm's old pipe dream, even if Hitler came equipped with a different mustache—he got shipped off to Norway as part of the Anglo-French expeditionary force that tried to stop the *Wehrmacht* there.

"That's when my trouble really started," he muttered under his breath. A dumpy woman coming the other way on the London sidewalk gave him a funny look. He didn't care. It wasn't as if he were wrong.

The Anglo-French force couldn't stop the Germans. Air power outdid sea power, even if the Royal Navy *was* Royal. Walsh counted himself lucky for getting out of Namsos before it fell. Plenty of soldiers hadn't. A Stuka attacked the destroyer that carried him home after sneaking into the harbor under cover of the long northern winter night, but the ship survived to make it back to Dundee.

He'd been on leave, riding a hired bicycle through the Scottish countryside, when. . . . That was when his troubles *really* started. He'd seen, and recognized, a Messerschmitt Bf-110, a long-range German fighter, buzzing along above Scotland. He'd watched somebody bail out and come down in a field not far from the narrow lane he was traveling.

Why he had to be the one to meet Rudolf Hess and take the Nazi big shot back to the authorities, he'd never worked out. It wasn't proof of God's love for him. He was too bloody sure of that. If anything, it was proof the Almighty really and truly had it in for him.

Because Hess was carrying a proposal from Hitler to Chamberlain and Daladier. The Germans were willing to withdraw from France (though not from the Low Countries or Scandinavia, and certainly not from Czechoslovakia, which was what the war was supposed to be about) in exchange for Anglo-French support of the war in the East, the war Germany and Poland were fighting against Stalin.

And Chamberlain and Daladier made the deal. Neither of them had wanted to fight the *Führer*. They'd even gone to Munich to hand him Czechoslovakia on a silver platter. But he wouldn't take it peacefully, not after a Czech nationalist took a revolver into Germany and plugged Konrad Henlein, the leader of the Germans in the Sudetenland.

It wasn't as if Stalin were a nice guy himself. As soon as he saw that Hitler wasn't sweeping all before him in the West, he demanded a chunk of northeastern Poland from Marshal Smigly-Ridz—a chunk that included the city of Wilno, which not only Poland and the Soviet Union but also Lithuania claimed.

Proud as any Pole, Smigly-Ridz said no. So Stalin invaded. He did not too well for much too long, but finally outweighed the Poles in the area by enough to be on the point of grabbing Wilno. But before he could, Marshal Smigly-Ridz asked Hitler for help. No one ever had to ask Hitler twice about whether he wanted to fight Bolsheviks. That bought him the two-front war from which the existence of Poland had shielded him up till then, but he didn't care.

Chances were Chamberlain and Daladier preferred fighting Bolsheviks to going after the Nazis. Hitler gave them the bait, and they gulped it with greedy jaws. As Hess had bailed out of the Bf-110, the *Führer* bailed out of his war in the West. With the Low Countries and Denmark and Norway firmly under his thumb, he had England and France on his side once their leaders pulled the big switch. He might be a vicious weasel, but he was a damned clever vicious weasel.

Some Englishmen couldn't stomach what their Prime Minister had done. Walsh was one of them, not that anybody cared tuppence about what a staff sergeant thought. But Winston Churchill was another. He hated Hitler and Hess and everything they stood for. He thundered about what an enormous betrayal the big switch was . . . till he walked in front of a Bentley allegedly driven by a drunk.

No one but Chamberlain and his claque *knew* whether Churchill's untimely demise was an accident or something else altogether. No one knew, but plenty of people suspected. Alistair Walsh, not surprisingly, was one of them. He couldn't stand the idea of fighting alongside the bastards in *Feldgrau* and coal-scuttle helmets who'd come so close to killing him so often. And he couldn't stand the idea of fighting for a government that might well have murdered its most vehement and most eloquent critic.

They let him resign from the service. He was far from the only man who couldn't abide the big switch. Plenty of veterans found themselves unable to make it. But, because he'd seen that parachute open up there in Scotland, he'd acquired better political connections than most of the rest. Churchill might be dead, but other, mostly younger, Conservatives still resisted the government's move. (It wasn't Chamberlain's government any more. Chamberlain was dead, of bowel cancer. But Sir Horace Wilson, his successor, was more ruthless than he had been—and even more obsequious to the Nazis.)

When Walsh casually glanced back over his shoulder, then, he really wasn't so casual as all that. A nondescript little man was following him, and not disguising it as well as he should have. Someone from Scotland Yard, probably. The police were the government's hounds. Military Intelligence was split. Some people followed orders no matter what. Others couldn't stand the notion of being on the same side as the *Gestapo*.

Walsh rounded a corner and quickly stepped into a chemist's shop. As the aproned gentleman behind the counter asked "How may I help you, sir?", the sergeant peered out through the window set into the shop's front door.

Sure enough, the shadow mooched around the corner. Sure enough, he stopped right in front of the chemist's to try to work out where Walsh had gone. He came to the proper conclusion—just as Walsh threw the door open and almost hit him in the face with it. The shadow showed admirable reflexes in jumping back. The way his right hand darted under his jacket showed he probably had a pistol in a shoulder holster.

At the moment, Walsh didn't care. He knew he would later, but he didn't now. That gave him a startling moral advantage. "Sod off," he growled. "The more grief your lot gives me, the more trouble I'll give you. Have you got that?"

"I'm sure I haven't the least idea what you mean, sir." The shadow gave a good game try at innocence.

Walsh laughed in his face. "My left one," he jeered. "You tell Sir Horace to leave me alone. Tell him to leave all of my mob alone. We can make him just as sorry as Adolf can—he'd best believe it, too. Tell him plain, do you hear me?"

He had the satisfaction of watching color drain from the other man's face. "I don't speak to the likes of the PM," the shadow gasped.

"I'll wager *that's* the truth, any road," Walsh said brutally. "But you talk to somebody who *does* talk to him, right?" Without waiting for an answer, he went on, "Tell him it's still a free country, and it'll go right on being one, too. We aren't bloody Fritzes. We don't put up with his kind of nonsense. Think you can remember that?"

"Oh, I'll remember." The shadow regained spirit. "And I'll lay you'll remember, too—only you won't be so happy about it. The cheek!" He did walk off then, which surprised Walsh. Was someone else following the follower, and Walsh as well?

If someone was, he wasn't blatant enough to give himself away. As luck or irony would have it, Walsh hadn't been going anywhere or intending to meet anyone who would have interested either the shadow or his superiors, up to and including Horace Wilson, in the slightest. He hadn't tried to tell that to the man he'd confronted. He knew it would have done him no good. England remained nominally free. But its people were starting to learn totalitarian lessons, and one of the first of those was that nobody believed you when you said you were doing something altogether innocent. And the more you insisted on it, the worse off you ended up.

HANS-ULRICH RUDEL eyed his Ju-87 like a parent looking at a child just out of surgery. The groundcrew men who'd performed the operation seemed proud of themselves. "There you go, sir," said the *Luftwaffe* corporal who'd bossed the crew. "Now you can take off and land your Stuka no matter how shitty the weather gets."

"Well . . . maybe," Hans-Ulrich answered. As far as he was concerned, that maintenance sergeant had just showed why he stayed on the ground.

Not that the fellow didn't have a point. Putting skis on the Ju-87 in place of wheels let the dive bomber take off and land in conditions it couldn't normally handle. The Ivans did that kind of thing all the time. If any flyers in the world were used to coping with vicious winters, the men of the Red Air Force were the ones. And Stukas' fixed undercarriages made the conversion easier than it would have been on planes with retractable landing gear.

Even so, anybody who tried to take off or land in the middle of one of these screaming blizzards would crash and burn. You did want to be able to see when you were getting airborne or coming down. Mistakes at the beginning or end of a flight wrote off almost as many planes as enemy fighters and flak.

Sergeant Albert Dieselhorst ambled up. The radioman and rear gunner considered the skis with enthusiasm hidden amazingly well. His gaze traveled from them to the panzer-busting 37mm gun pods mounted under the wings. "Happy day," he said. "We'll be even less aerodynamic than we were already."

Rudel winced. Those heavy, bulky gun pods did up the drag and make the Ju-87 slower and less maneuverable than it was without them. All the same, the pilot answered, "Take an even strain, Albert. She couldn't get out of her own way even before they bolted on the skis."

"Sir!" The groundcrew corporal sounded hurt. Hans-Ulrich half expected him to clap a hand to his heart like an affronted maiden in a bad melodrama.

"Hell, he's right," Dieselhorst said. "We count more on our armor than on our guns and our speed—ha! there's a laugh!—to get us through when we're in a jam."

He wore the Iron Cross First Class on his left breast pocket. Rudel wore the Knight's Cross on a ribbon around his neck. A lowly groundcrew corporal with only the ribbon for the Iron Cross Second Class—a decoration that, in this war, you had to work hard *not* to win—hooked to a tunic button couldn't very well argue with either one of them.

Two days later, the weather was good enough for flying. The Stuka's big Junkers Jumo engine fired up right away when the groundcrew men cranked it and spun the prop. They had a mechanical starter mounted on a truck chassis, but nothing they did would make the truck motor turn over. Muscle power and bad language sufficed. A minister's son, Hans-Ulrich rarely swore and almost never drank. If not for that *Ritterkreuz* and all it said about his nerve, he would have been even more a white crow to his comrades than he already was.

Snow and the skis smoothed out the dirt airstrip's bumps and potholes better than the wheels had. But Rudel quickly found Sergeant Dieselhorst had made a shrewd guess. The Ju-87 flew like a garbage truck with wings. If any Russian fighter found him, even one of the obsolete biplanes the Ivans kept flying, he and Albert were in a world of trouble.

Snowy fields, bare-branched birches with bark almost white as snow, pines and firs and spruces all snow-dappled . . . The Russian landscape in winter. The sun never climbed far above the southern horizon, not in these latitudes. Because it stayed so low, it cast long shadows. The Reds were better at camouflage than even the thorough Germans dreamt of being, but not for all their ingenuity could they hide shadows. Neither whitewashing them nor draping them with netting did Stalin's men the least bit of good.

Hans-Ulrich might not have noticed the Russian panzers moving up to the front. They *were* well whitewashed, and Soviet soldiers trotted in their wake with whisks made from branches to smooth out their tracks so those didn't show up from the air. They did a pretty good job of that, too. Rudel might not have seen the tracks. Shadows, though . . . Shadows he saw.

He gave Dieselhorst the number of panzers he observed and their approximate position. The radioman with the rear-facing machine-gun mount relayed the news to the Germans on the ground. Hans-Ulrich added, "You can tell them I'm attacking, too." He tipped the Stuka into a dive.

Acceleration pressed him against the armored back of his seat. He wondered if the skis would act as small airfoils and change the plane's performance, but they didn't seem to. The groundcrew men hadn't touched the Jericho trumpets mounted in the landing-gear struts. The screaming sirens terrorized the Russian foot soldiers, who ran every which way like ants from a disturbed nest.

Panzers couldn't scatter like that—and, inside those clattering hulls, even the wail from the Jericho trumpets took a while to register. The machines quickly swelled from specks to toys to the real thing. Rudel's finger came down on the firing button. Each 37mm gun bellowed and spat flame.

Recoil from those monsters slowed the Stuka even better than dive brakes. Hans-Ulrich yanked back hard on the stick. Things went red in front of his eyes as the Ju-87 pulled out of the dive. If you weren't paying attention, you could fly a dive bomber straight into the ground. Several Germans in the Legion Kondor had done it in Spain. Stukas got autopilots after that, but the men who flew them unanimously hated the gadgets. Hans-Ulrich had had groundcrew men disable his, and he was far from the only pilot who had.

"You got the bastard!" Sergeant Dieselhorst's voice through the speaking tube was like sounding brass. "Engine's on fire, crew's bailing out."

"Good." Rudel couldn't see behind him, so he had to rely on the radioman's reports. Experience in France and here had taught him to aim for the engine compartment. Almost any panzer's armor was thinnest on the decking there. He manhandled the Stuka into a climbing turn. "Let's see if we can kill another one, or maybe more than one."

The pillar of greasy black smoke rising from the rear of the panzer he'd struck told him it wouldn't be going anywhere any more. He nodded to himself in somber satisfaction. He'd killed a lot of enemy armor with the big guns. He must have killed a lot of enemy panzer crewmen, too, but he tried not to dwell on that.

After he'd gained enough altitude, he chose another whitewashed Russian panzer and tipped the Stuka into a new dive. Again, the Jericho trumpets howled. This time, though, they didn't take the Ivans on the ground by surprise. Hans-Ulrich had a low opinion of Russian brains, but not of Russian balls. The Reds opened up on the Stuka with their small arms. The commander of Rudel's new target vehicle fired a burst from the turret with a submachine gun.

All that might have made the Ivans happier, but did them no good. You couldn't shoot accurately at a dive bomber from the ground—it was going too fast. Even if you got lucky and hit it, the engine and the compartment that housed the two crewmen were armored against rifle-caliber bullets.

Blam! Blam! The Stuka's big guns thundered again, at almost the same instant. Hans-Ulrich pulled out of the dive. He brought his fist down on his thigh in triumph when Sergeant Dieselhorst reported that he'd nailed another one. "Aim to go after number three?" Dieselhorst asked.

"Why not?" Rudel said. "Hardly any Russian panzers carry radios. They won't call fighters after us."

"Some do, so you hope they won't," the veteran underofficer replied.

That was nothing but the truth. Hans-Ulrich didn't want to meet fighters, not in his ungainly machine. He got more ground fire in this dive than he had before. At least one lucky round clanged into the Stuka, but it did no harm. And when the 37mm guns belched fire once more, they wrecked another Soviet panzer.

Part of Rudel wanted to go after a fourth Russian machine, but common sense told him that was a bad idea. Sooner or later, fighters blazoned with the red star *would* show up around here. The best thing he could do was to be somewhere else when they did. He hauled the Stuka's nose around and flew off to the west.

IVAN KUCHKOV COUNTED HIMSELF lucky to be alive. He was a short, squat, brawny Russian peasant. The authorities had yanked him off the collective farm where he grew up and put him in the bomb bay of an SB-2 medium bomber. Short, squat, and brawny were ideal qualifications for a bombardier. Smart wasn't, and nobody, including Ivan himself, had ever claimed he was.

He hadn't tried to keep track of how many missions he'd flown, for instance. He just knew there'd been a lot of them. He also knew that, if you flew a lot of missions against the Nazis, you were waiting for the law of averages to catch up with you.

And it did. The Tupolev bomber had got hit and caught fire on the way back from a run into German-held Byelorussia. Kuchkov bailed out. He didn't think either the pilot or the copilot and bomb-aimer made it. He'd flown with Sergei Yaroslavsky ever since they "volunteered" to aid Czechoslovakia against Fascist invaders when the war was new. Unless his brain was totally fucked, he wouldn't be flying with the lieutenant any more.

He wasn't sure he'd be flying at all. Red Army men rescued him and got him away from the Germans after he landed. The first lieutenant commanding the company didn't want to give him back to the Red Air Force. Lieutenant Pavel Obolensky recognized a hard-nosed son of a bitch when he saw one. Obolensky wanted Kuchkov fighting for *him*.

"The air force? Faggots fight in the air force," the lieutenant declared. "You're a real man, right? Real men belong in the Red Army!"

That was nonsense, as Kuchkov had reason to know. "I bet my

bombs killed more Fascists than all the fuckers in your cocksucking regiment, sir," he said. He wasn't being deliberately disrespectful. He just spoke *mat*, the obscenity-laced underworld and underground dialect of Russian, as naturally as he breathed. He almost didn't know how *not* to swear.

Luckily for him, Lieutenant Obolensky, like Yaroslavsky, recognized as much and didn't come down on him on account of his foul mouth. "Maybe they did," the infantry officer said. "But fuck your mother if we don't get to watch the cunts die when we nail 'em." Like most Russians, he could use *mat*, too, even if he didn't make a habit of it the way Kuchkov did.

"You've got something there," Ivan admitted. He thought it over, then nodded. "Why the hell not?" Remembering such manners as he owned, he saluted. "Uh, sir."

For the moment, the Red Air Force probably thought he was as dead as the rest of the SB-2's crew. That made turning into a foot soldier easier. One of these days, his proper service would figure out that he'd kept breathing after all. That was likely to complicate his life. But it wasn't as if he'd deserted, and he'd never been one to borrow trouble. Plenty came along on its own, thank you very much.

Such calculations had nothing to do with his choice. Along with being short and squat and strong, he was dark and ugly and uncommonly hairy. In the Red Air Force, they called him the Chimp. He hated it. Anyone who came right out and used the nickname to his face, he did his best to deck, and his best was goddamn good. But he knew people called him Chimp behind his back. Maybe joining up with a bunch of strangers would let him escape it.

He might be rugged as a boulder, but he was curiously naïve. He could get away from the nickname he despised for about twenty minutes—half an hour, tops. As soon as anybody with even a little imagination got a look at him, he was as sure to be tagged Chimp (or maybe King Kong) as a redhead was to get stuck with Red or Rusty.

Lieutenant Obolensky was making calculations of his own. The main one was that Sergeant Kuchkov would be worth eight or ten ordinary guys in a fight. At least. And so the lieutenant grinned when Kuchkov didn't make a fuss about staying in the air force.

"*Ochen khorosho!*" Obolensky exclaimed. As far as he was concerned, it was very good indeed. "Let's get you kitted out."

Ivan's fur-lined flight suit gave him better cold-weather gear than most of his new comrades enjoyed. Thanks to Obolensky, though, he got a white snow smock to put over it. He also got a tunic with collar tabs in infantry crimson rather than air force blue. And he got a submachine gun to replace the Tokarev pistol he carried as a personal weapon. He didn't ditch the pistol, though. You never could tell when an extra weapon would come in handy.

He'd maintained the machine guns in the SB-2's dorsal and belly turrets. Next to them, the PPD-34 might have been a kiddy toy. It was plainer and uglier than the Nazis' Schmeisser, but it had a seventy-one-round drum magazine. That made it heavier than a Schmeisser, but so what? It kept firing a lot longer, too. He knew he'd have to clean the magazine even more often than the weapon itself, which boasted a chromed barrel and chamber. Dirt could foul the clockwork mechanism that fed cartridges into the PPD. A jam was more likely to prove fatal than just embarrassing. No jams, then.

Ivan shifted the three metal triangles that marked his rank from old collar tabs to new. Lieutenant Obolensky gave him a squad right away—infantry units took more than their share of casualties, and Obolensky had had a corporal who barely needed to shave running it. The junior—very junior—noncom didn't resent losing the position he hadn't held long. Lucky for him, too; if he had, Kuchkov would have whaled the piss out of him.

One advantage of air force life was sleeping out of artillery range of the enemy, sometimes even in a real cot in a heated barracks. Nothing like that here. There weren't even tents. You wore as many clothes as you could, rolled yourself in a blanket (if you had a blanket) as if you were a cigar and it the wrapper, and either you slept or you didn't.

The soldiers in Ivan's new squad eyed him warily, wondering how he'd cope with living rough. No one came out and said anything about it to him. Not all the infantrymen could read and write, but ignorance didn't make them stupid. If they pissed him off, he'd make them sorry. He had the look of somebody who wouldn't worry about regulations when he did it, either.

Three days after parachuting down into the Red Army, he led his squad out on patrol. He picked a skinny little nervous Jew called Avram as point man. Somebody like that was liable to jump at shadows, but he wouldn't happily amble into a Nazi trap.

Even with his fur-and-leather flying togs on under the snow smock, Ivan was miserably cold. In wool greatcoats, the ordinary Red Army men would be even colder. But, from everything everybody said, the Germans would be colder yet. Russians made jokes about Winter Fritz. Ivan hoped all the jokes were true.

A private trotted back to him. "There's a field up ahead, and a village out past it," the fellow reported. "Avram says the Germans are holed up in the houses."

"Oh, he does, does he?" Ivan still didn't know how far he could rely on Avram—or anyone else in the squad, come to that. "I'll fucking see for myself."

"Be careful going forward, he says," the private told him. "A sniper in the village can hit you if he sees you."

"Right." Kuchkov wasn't sure if the *Zhid* was only warning him or trying to find out if he was yellow. He didn't know all the ground-pounders' tricks yet. He did know enough to keep his head down and to stay behind trees as much as he could. He made it out to Avram without getting shot at. The point man sprawled behind a stout pine. "So? Nazi cocksuckers in the village?" Ivan asked him.

"*Da*, Comrade Sergeant." Avram nodded. "If you want to look—carefully—you'll spot them."

Only his eyes showing under the snow smock, Ivan peered out from behind the pine. The Germans in the village weren't being nearly so cautious. "They're fucking there, all right," he agreed. "Scoot back to the lieutenant. Tell him where the cunts are at. Tell him we can take 'em—bet your ass we can—if the machine gun and mortar help keep our dicks up."

After another nod, Avram silently disappeared. He made a *good* point man. Half an hour later, Lieutenant Obolensky crawled up to check things out for himself. The mortar crew and machine gunners set up not far away. Ivan smiled wolfishly. Obolensky didn't think he had the vapors or was showing off, then. Outstanding.

Other men from the company took places near the edge of the

woods. They'd be ready to go forward as soon as they got the word. The lieutenant put a hand on Kuchkov's shoulder. "You're right," he whispered. "We *can* take them. And we will."

Soldiers swigged from their hundred-gram vodka rations, borrowing bravery for the fight ahead. Kuchkov drank, too, because he liked to drink. The mortar dropped bombs on the village. The machine gun sprayed death toward it. Obolensky's brass officer's whistle squealed like a shoat losing its nuts to the knife. "Forward!" he yelled.

"*Urra!*" the Russian soldiers roared as they swarmed out of the woods. A few rifle shots answered them, but no machine gun. Either the Germans didn't have one there or the mortar'd knocked their crew out of action. Ivan pounded forward with the rest. Till he got a lot closer, the PPD was just a weight in his hands.

He never did have to fire it. The Nazis put up only a token resistance. Then they got the hell out of there. A bullet broke one Red Army man's arm. Another fellow lost the bottom half of his left ear and bled all over his snow smock. The Nazis left two dead men behind. How many casualties they took with them, Ivan couldn't guess.

The village came back into Soviet hands—not that any peasants remained in it. It had been a dreary little place even before the Germans overran it. Kuchkov didn't care. He'd proved himself in front of his men. *That,* he cared about.

VACLAV JEZEK FOUND HIMSELF even more isolated in Spain than he had been in France. The Czech hadn't imagined such a thing possible, but there you were. The Spanish Republic might have been the most isolated country, or half a country, in the world. When England and France forgot about fighting Fascism and turned on the Bolsheviks instead, they made a point of forgetting about their erstwhile Iberian ally.

Great Powers had the luxury of doing such things whenever they pleased. Jezek didn't. He'd battled the Nazis ever since the day they jumped Czechoslovakia. Instead of surrendering after the Germans overran Bohemia and Moravia and Father Tiso led Slovakia into Fascist-backed "independence," he crossed the border into Poland and let himself be interned.

The Russians hadn't jumped the Poles then, so Poland remained neutral. Czech soldiers were allowed—even unofficially encouraged—to go to Romania (likewise neutral in those days) and from there by sea to France to take service with the Czechoslovak government-in-exile. Vaclav did all that. His thinking, and the government-in-exile's, was that keeping the Nazis from conquering France was his own country's best and perhaps only hope for eventual resurrection.

That best hope looked none too good. The Czech lands (and Tiso's puppet Slovakia) remained under the *Reich*'s muscular thumb. Which was not to say Corporal Vaclav Jezek hadn't done the Germans as much harm as one man could. From a *poilu* who'd never need it any more, he'd acquired an antitank rifle: a godawful heavy weapon that kicked like a jackass but could drive a thumb-sized armor-piercing bullet right through the hardened steel plating on a German light tank or armored car.

He also discovered that the antitank rifle made a great sniper's piece. It shot far and fast and flat. After he mounted a telescopic sight on it, he could pick off a man more than two kilometers away: not always, but often enough to be useful. At half that range, he'd blow off a Nazi's head with nearly every round.

His countrymen and allies loved him—till the French suddenly turned into Hitler's allies instead. Just as suddenly, the Czechoslovak government-in-exile and its little army became embarrassments. France somehow did find the courtesy not to intern the men who'd given their blood to help keep her free. She let those of them who so desired cross the Pyrenees to Republican Spain instead.

In France, Sergeant Benjamin Halévy, a French Jew with parents from Prague, had interpreted for the refugee soldiers. Now he was a refugee himself, having no more stomach for fighting on the *Führer*'s side than did the stubborn Czechs.

Someone fluent in French like Halévy could follow a word of Spanish here and there, the same way a Czech could understand bits of Russian. Vaclav had learned just enough French to swear with. The only foreign language he really spoke was German. That was of no more use to him here than it had been in France. It was the enemy's tongue in the

Spanish Republic as it had been on the northern side of the mountains, but fewer people in these parts understood it . . . and most of the ones who did backed Marshal Sanjurjo's Fascists, not the Republic.

Most, but not all. The fighters from the International Brigades had come to Spain to lay their lives on the line to halt the advance of Hitler and Mussolini's malignant ideology. Some were from America, some from England, but more from Central and Eastern Europe. An awful lot of them could speak German or Yiddish, even if they were no more native speakers than Vaclav.

By what amounted to a miracle in this bureaucratic age, the powers that be in the Republic realized as much. Instead of sending the Czechs to some threatened border region (and all the Republic's borders except the one with France were threatened), the Spaniards grouped them with the Internationals defending Madrid.

The Internationals were Red, Red, Red. Vaclav couldn't have cared less. Just like him, they killed Fascists. They didn't seem to worry about anything else but a soldier's universals: ammo, food, tobacco, and pussy. Nobody tried to make him bow down toward Moscow five times a day.

They appreciated the antitank rifle and what he could do with it. "We have a few of those ourselves, but we never thought of using them for sniping," said a fellow who called himself Spartacus. It was a *nom de guerre;* he spoke German with a throaty Hungarian accent.

Vaclav loved Magyars hardly more than Germans. He had to remind himself he and Spartacus were on the same side. "It works," he said. He wasn't about to let anybody take the man-tall monster away from him.

But that wasn't what Spartacus had in mind. "I bet it does. That's the idea," he said. "Why don't you start thinning the herd of Fascist officers?" His thin, dark mustache made his smile even nastier than it would have been otherwise.

"I can do that. As a matter of fact, I've been doing it, in France and here," Vaclav said. No one here would have paid much attention to what he'd been up to. That was what you got for being a newcomer, especially if you had language troubles.

"All right. Good. Very good." The Hungarian International seemed on the stupid side to Vaclav, to say nothing of overbearing. Most Magyars seemed that way to most Czechs. Magyars weren't as bad as Germans, but they were a devil of a long way from good . . . if you eyed them from a Czech's perspective, anyhow.

How Czechs seemed to Magyars was another question altogether—not one Vaclav had ever thought to ask himself, and not one he was likely to ask himself, either.

His biggest complaint was one he hadn't expected to have in sunny Spain: the trenches northwest of Madrid got as cold as a German tax collector's heart. Sunny Spain was, even in wintertime. But the central plateau lay some distance above sea level, and the winds seemed to blow straight through him. He'd been warmer up near the Franco-Belgian border.

As long as he didn't shiver while he pulled the trigger, though, he could do his job. If anything, it was easier here than it had been in France. However much he despised the Germans, he couldn't deny that they made sensible soldiers. Officers didn't look much different from their men. Sometimes they'd even turn their shoulder straps upside down to make it harder for a sniper to spy their rank badges.

Marshal Sanjurjo's soldiers weren't like that. A man in those ranks who was somebody wanted to show that he was somebody. He prominently displayed the gold stars that set him off from the common, vulgar mob. And he often wore a uniform of newer, finer cloth and better cut than the ragged, faded yellowish khaki the ordinary Fascist soldiers had to put up with.

All of which made it much easier for Vaclav to spot enemy officers. An aristocrat in a neatly pressed uniform, his stars of rank glittering under the bright Spanish sun, sometimes had a moment to look absurdly amazed when he made the acquaintance of one of the antitank rifle's fat slugs.

More often, the Fascist bastard just fell over. Vaclav wasn't fussy; nobody gave out style points.

Chapter 3

Sergeant Luc Harcourt shivered as he led his squad into the Russian village. That wasn't fear; the village lay several hundred kilometers behind the line, and was unlikely to have holdouts in it. No, Luc was just cold. French greatcoats and other winter gear weren't made for weather like this.

If not for the felt boots he wore over his own clodhoppers, he would have been colder yet. He'd stripped them off a dead Russian, and they were lifesavers. The Ivans had to deal with this crap every year, poor bastards, and they knew how.

He'd noticed that German soldiers wore *valenki* whenever they could get hold of them, too. That left him obscurely amused. So the Master Race didn't know everything there was to know about winter warfare, either? Well, good!

Daladier might declare that France and Germany were allies against the Bolsheviks now. Luc might have taken a train trip through the *Reich* so he could get at the Red Army. But before that he'd spent two years shooting at the Nazis and trying like hell to hide when they shot back. Some *Boche* had shot his father during the last war. No matter what fucking Daladier declared, Luc didn't love the Germans. No, sir, not even close.

A lot of Russian villages the Germans and their allies had overrun were empty. The locals had cleared out instead of sticking around to see what occupation would be like. Luc sympathized. Plenty of Frenchmen and -women had fled when the Germans invaded, too. And there were lots of Jews in these parts. If he were a Jew, he wouldn't have stayed under German rule for anything.

Not everyone had run away from this place, though. A few men and women came out of their battered shacks to eye the soldiers trudging down the main street—an unpaved track with some of the dirty snow trampled into the frozen ground. All the Russians, regardless of sex, had *valenki*. Luc thought they were foolish to put the overboots on display. Some of his men were liable to steal them right off their feet.

A fellow with a graying, stubbly beard wore a wool scarf, a sheepskin cap and jacket, and baggy wool pants stuffed into the tops of his *valenki*. He surprised Luc by asking, "You're Frenchmen, aren't you?" in fluent French.

"That's right," the sergeant answered. "Where did you learn our language?"

The Ivan smiled a sweet, sad smile. "Once upon a time, I studied medicine. I learned French then. I learned German, too." The smile got sadder still. "I used to think I was a cultured fellow."

"Well, what the devil are you doing here?" Luc asked. This miserable village was as far from culture as anything could get.

"Tending my garden," the Russian said, as Candide might have done. He went on, "What I grow in my own plot, I get to keep and sell. The state takes what we grow on our collective lands, of course. And I still do what I can when someone gets hurt or comes down sick."

"Why aren't you a doctor in some big city?" Luc inquired.

"The council of workers and peasants was going to send me to a labor camp for being an intellectual," the Russian answered, as calmly as if he were talking about someone else. "But they decided I could work out my antiproletarian prejudices here on the *kolkhoz* instead. I've been here since 1922."

"Well, now we've come to set you free." Luc trotted out the propaganda line the Germans had fed their new allies to see what this cultured Russian would make of it.

By the way the fellow looked at him, he might have pissed in the baptismal font—except the building that had been a church before the Revolution was currently a barn. "If you'd come here in 1923, I would have welcomed you with open arms," the Russian said. "So would almost everyone else. But now? No. We've spent a generation building up and getting used to the new ways of doing things. You want to tear down everything we've managed to do and tell us to start over one more time. We would rather fight for General Secretary Stalin than go through that again."

He didn't make fighting for Stalin sound like a good choice—only like a better choice than starting from scratch. Chuckling, Luc said, "Maybe I ought to shoot you now, then, to keep you from making trouble later on."

"It could be that you should." The Russian wasn't joking. "I see that, because you are French, some shreds of civilization still cling to you. The Nazis would not talk like that. They would just start shooting and burning. It has happened here in the Soviet Union many times already. No doubt it will happen many more."

Luc wanted to tell him that was all a pack of lies: nothing but garbage served up by the propaganda cooks in Moscow. He wanted to, yes, but the words stuck in his throat. After all, the Germans had invaded his country twice since 1914. They weren't gentle occupiers either time. From all he'd heard, they were more brutal now than they had been a generation earlier. Why would he expect them to be gentle here in the East, then?

Uneasily, he said, "International law gives them the right to be hard on *francs-tireurs*." If you picked up a rifle without being a soldier, any army in the world that caught you would give you a blindfold and—if you were lucky—a cigarette and then fill you full of holes.

Of course, the Germans took hostages if *francs-tireurs* troubled them. They murdered them by dozens or scores to remind the people they were fighting not to get frisky. Here in the East, they probably executed hostages by the hundreds. Would such frightfulness intimidate the Russians or only make them hate harder?

Looking into the doctor-turned-peasant's pale eyes, Luc didn't like the answer he thought he saw. "Keep your nose clean, or you'll be sorry," he said, his voice rougher than he'd intended.

"Oh, but of course, *Monsieur,*" the Russian said, his tone so transparently false that Luc wondered whether he should plug him right there.

A Nazi would have. The Ivan understood as much. So did Luc. It was the biggest part of what stayed his hand. He didn't have his men camp inside the village, as he'd intended when they approached it. Instead, he led them on for another kilometer. They were grumbling by the time he finally let them stop.

He didn't feel like listening to them. "Put a sock in it, you clowns," he said. "We go to sleep in one of those houses, we'll wake up with our throats cut."

"We'll freeze here in the middle of nowhere," one of the *poilus* retorted. "Is that so much better?"

"We won't freeze. We'll just be cold. There's a difference," Luc said. He knew what the men would be saying about him—that he wouldn't feel it because his heart was already cold. He'd said the same kind of thing about his sergeant back in the days before he wore any hash marks on his sleeve.

Sergeant Demange was Second Lieutenant Demange now. A veteran noncom from the last war, Demange didn't want to be an officer. But the know-it-alls above him kept getting shot, and he finally won a promotion whether he liked it or not. The way he chain-smoked Gitanes said he didn't. Or maybe not—he'd smoked like a chimney as a sergeant, too.

Luc told him about the French-speaking Russian back in the village. "You *should* have scragged the asshole," said Demange, who had very little use for his fellow man. "It would've given the rest of the shitheads back there something to stew on."

"The *Gestapo* would be proud of you, sir." More than two years of serving Demange had earned Luc the right to speak his mind.

Up to a point. "Fuck you," Demange answered evenly. "Fuck the Ivans, too. You want to make sure they don't cause trouble, you've got to boot 'em in the balls. Oh, yeah—and fuck the *Gestapo*. Fuck 'em up the ass, except the ones who like it that way."

"*Merde alors!*" Admiration filled Luc's voice. "You hate everybody, don't you?"

"Close enough," Demange said. "With most of the bastards you run into, it just saves time." He was looking at—looking through—Luc right then.

If that wasn't a hint, Luc had never run into one. "Don't worry, sir. Everybody loves you, too," he said. Sketching a salute, he went back to his squad. Behind him, the reluctant officer chuckled.

In the middle of the night, the Russians dropped a swarm of mortar bombs on the village . . . and on the *poilus* who'd paused there for the night. Several soldiers got hurt. Luc's squad was far enough from the buildings that nothing came down on them.

He didn't point that out to the men he led. If he had, they would have figured he was blowing his own horn. If they figured it out for themselves, though, they'd see what a clever fellow he really was. Back in his days as a sergeant, Demange would have played it the same way. Luc had learned more from him than he would ever admit, even—maybe especially—to himself.

THE HACKED-UP BOARDS the *Landsers* fed into the fire came from a house a Russian shell had knocked flat. The gobbets of meat they toasted over the flames came from a horse that had hauled a 105mm howitzer till another shell broke its leg. Willi Dernen had shot it to put it out of its misery. He'd long since lost track of how many enemy soldiers he'd killed or wounded, but he couldn't stand to see or listen to an animal suffer.

He took a bite. The meat was half charred, half raw. It was also gluey and gamy. It was horsemeat, in other words. It wasn't the first time he'd had it, and he was sure it wouldn't be the last. He turned to his fellow *Gefreiter*—senior private—and said, "I've probably eaten enough horse to let them enter me in next year's Berlin steeplechase."

Adam Pfaff shook his head. "Not fucking likely, Willi. I've eaten plenty of pussy, but nobody's gonna put me in a goddamn cat show." While Willi was still digesting that, so to speak, his buddy added, "Besides, have you taken a look at yourself lately? You're no three-year-old, believe me, and no thoroughbred, either."

"Oh, yeah? And you are?" Willi said. They grinned at each other. Like the rest of the men in their section—like the rest of the German *Frontschweine* in Russia—they were scrawny and filthy and badly shaven. A crawly itch under Willi's whitewashed *Stahlhelm* said he was lousy again, too. One of these days, he'd get deloused. And he'd stay clean till the next time he went through a Russian village. Say, half an hour after he left the delousing station. Then he'd have company once more.

"Who's got some tobacco he can spare?" Corporal Arno Baatz asked.

Willi had a nice little sack of *makhorka*—Russian tobacco, cheap and nasty but strong—in a trouser pocket. He would have bet Adam Pfaff had a similar stash. Adam knew what was what about keeping himself supplied. Neither *Gefreiter* said a word. Willi had had to put up with Awful Arno since the war started. Adam was much newer to the regiment, but he'd rapidly learned the *Unteroffizier* made a piss-poor substitute for a human being.

"Here you go, Corporal." A private named Sigi Herzog gave Baatz a cigarette. Willi had already pegged him for a suckup. One more suspicion confirmed.

"Good." Awful Arno didn't bother thanking Sigi. He took such tribute as no less than his due. Another reason to despise him, as far as Willi was concerned: one more to add to a long list. Were Baatz a gutless wonder, everything would have been perfect—and the company would have had a perfectly good excuse for shipping him back behind the lines where he could annoy people without risking lives. But he actually made a decent combat soldier. It was everything else about him that Willi—and anyone else who got stuck serving under him—couldn't stand.

He lit the cigarette and sucked in smoke. His plump cheeks hollowed. How any German on the Eastern Front stayed plump was beyond Willi, but Awful Arno managed. He shaved more often than most *Landsers* bothered to, but he was still plenty whiskery right this minute.

After blowing out a stream of smoke and fog, he let loose with a blast of hot air, straight from the Propaganda Ministry: "As soon as the weather gets even a little better, we'll roll up the Ivans like a pair of socks."

That he believed—and, worse, parroted—such bullshit was also on the list of reasons why he'd got his nickname. Willi rolled his eyes. Adam Pfaff rounded on Sigi. "What did you put in that smoke you gave him, man? Has to be better than tobacco, that's for sure. If you've got more, give me some, too."

Baatz sent him an unfriendly look: about the only kind the corporal kept in stock. "So what are you saying, Pfaff? Are you saying we *won't* roll up the Reds?" he asked. "That sounds like defeatism to me."

Defeatism could get you tangled up with the SS, the last thing anybody in his right mind wanted. Pfaff shook his head. "Don't talk more like a jackass than you can help, Corporal. Anybody who's seen me in action knows I'm no defeatist. Is that so or isn't it?"

"If you make other soldiers not want to fight their hardest, that's defeatism, too," Baatz said stubbornly. "And you'd better remember I'm not too big a jackass to know it."

Pfaff didn't back down. "Nobody here's gonna run home to *Mutti* on account of anything I come out with. And we all know we'd better fight hard, or else the Russians'll cut off our cocks and shove 'em in our mouths."

"Do they really do that shit?" asked a kid who'd come up to the front only a few days earlier. His uniform wasn't so patched and faded as the ones the other *Landsers* wore. But for that, there wasn't much to choose between him and the rest.

"They sure do," Pfaff replied. Awful Arno nodded—they agreed on that much, anyhow.

Willi nodded, too. He'd seen it for himself, however much he wished he hadn't. "You don't want to let the Ivans take you prisoner," he said. "Save a last round for yourself. Maybe the guys they do that to are already dead, but you don't want to find out for yourself, do you?"

"So what do we do with the Russians we capture?" the new fish asked.

The veterans squatting by the fire eyed one another. Nobody said anything for a little while. At last, Willi answered, "Well, sometimes we send 'em back to a camp like good little boys, the way we would have in the West." *We would have most of the time in the West, anyway,* he thought. The French and English weren't perfect about sticking to the Geneva Convention, either. Aloud, he went on, "Sometimes, though . . ." He shrugged. "It's a rough old war. I don't know what else to tell you."

"If we catch commissars or Jews, we do for them right away," Awful Arno said. "Pigdogs like that don't deserve to live."

Not every commissar or Jewish Red Army man died right away. The *Wehrmacht* kept some alive for questioning. The ones who did live for a while probably wound up envying their comrades who perished on the spot. German interrogators weren't likely to be gentler than their Soviet opposite numbers.

The kid chewed on that for a few seconds. Then he asked, "If we treat them rough, doesn't that give them an excuse to do the same to us?"

Arno Baatz laughed at him. "You want to spout the Golden Rule, sonny, you should put on a chaplain's frock coat before you start."

He waited for the other men who'd been through the mill to laugh with him. Sigi Herzog did, but he was the only one. Awful Arno scowled at the others. Willi stonily stared back at him. The kid had a point of sorts.

But only of sorts. "Look, when this fight is over, either we'll be left standing or the damn Russians will," Willi said. "You fight a war like that, and who has room to be a gentleman?"

"Isn't that what the Geneva Convention's for?" the new fish asked. "To keep things clean on both sides, I mean?"

Awful Arno laughed some more—a mean, nasty laugh. "Didn't they tell you anything before they shipped your sorry ass up here? Yeah, that's what the Geneva Convention's all about. When we fought the Tommies and the frogs, we played by the rules, and so did they. But you know what? *The fucking Bolsheviks never signed the fucking Convention!*"

"Oh," the kid said in a small voice. And that was about the size of it. There were no formal rules in the fight between the Third *Reich* and the Soviet Union. They could go at it however they pleased. They could, and they did. The kid made one more try: "If we told Stalin we'd follow the Convention whether we have to or not, wouldn't he almost have to do the same?"

Baatz laughed one more time. However little Willi wanted to, he found himself laughing along. It was either laugh or weep, and laughing hurt—a little—less. "Stalin doesn't have to do anything he doesn't want to do," Awful Arno said. "What he wants to do now is kill all the Germans he can."

He was right about that. Of course, Hitler didn't have to do anything he didn't want to, either, and what he wanted to do was kill carload lots of Russians. Which left the soldiers in *Feldgrau* or khaki stuck in the middle between them in one hell of a rough spot.

Like I didn't know that already, Willi thought. His bayonet got most of its use as a belt knife. He hacked off another hunk of horsemeat with it. Then he skewered the meat and held it over the fire. At least his belly would be full, anyhow.

CHAIM WEINBERG LIKED having the Czech holdouts around. They might not be Marxist-Leninists the way he and most of the Internationals were, but they were good, solid men. The American Jew had nothing against Spaniards. He wouldn't have come to Spain to fight for the Republic if he had.

Spaniards—Spaniards on both sides, dammit—were extravagantly brave. They put up with shortages and fuckups with good humor he could only admire, because he sure couldn't imitate it. But they were flighty. They were temperamental. They could be cruel for the fun of it (he'd never got used to bullfighting). And they liked to talk. Jesus H. Christ, did they ever!

It wasn't as if he didn't enjoy the sound of his own voice. He did. He argued and converted and preached the Red faith with as much zeal as any friar taking on the latest jungle tribe who knew not the word of God. But when it came to passion, Chaim had to admit the Spaniards had him beat.

He'd fallen hard for La Martellita, a Party organizer in battered Madrid. He would have said (hell, he did say, to anyone who would listen) he'd fallen in love with her. The emotion involved, though, sprang from an organ south of his heart. She was tiny. She was stacked. She was gorgeous, in the blue-black-haired, high-cheekboned, flashing-eyed Spanish way. She had what he couldn't help thinking of as a blowjob mouth. And the way she painted it said she knew as much, too.

She wouldn't look at him for the longest time. It wasn't that he was no movie star himself, even if he *was* no movie star himself. He was not too tall, kind of dumpy, and looked as Jewish as he was. But what really bothered her was that he wasn't ideologically pure enough. He had the American gift, or curse, of thinking for himself, not blindly swallowing the latest twist in the Party line out of Moscow.

He got into her bed by the oldest, most time-tested method in the world: he waited till she got smashed, went back to her place with her, and had his fun while she was too loaded to care—almost too loaded to notice. She was anything but delighted to discover him next to her the next morning, and her lethal hangover had only a little to do with it. But he'd tended to the hangover and sweet-talked her till she let him back in bed fully conscious; he owned the memory forever.

Then she found out she was pregnant.

She could have got rid of it easily enough. The Republic had probably the most progressive social policies in the world. But she didn't want to. Maybe a strict Catholic upbringing still lurked in the unexamined basement of her soul. No, she wanted her little surprise to carry a proper surname.

And so Chaim found himself a married man. He felt like Brer Rabbit in the briar patch. La Martellita—her revolutionary name meant The Little Hammer, and suited her all too well—promised she'd divorce him after the baby was born. Divorce was even easier here than abortion. And, unlike abortion, it didn't trouble her tender conscience.

In the meantime . . . It could have been a white marriage, like one between a fairy and a dyke wearing masks for the sake of the world's good opinion. La Martellita, though, was as thorough in marriage as she was in everything else. And she had discovered that Chaim wasn't half bad in the sack. It surprised her, as it had quite a few other women before her.

"I may not be pretty, but by God I can screw," he said, not without pride.

"You may be able to screw, but by God you're not pretty," La Martellita answered, not without truth.

Despite such devastating candor from his more-or-less beloved, he went back into Madrid from the front as often as he could. And he returned to the front less and less worried that she hoped he would stop something up there so she could give the baby a name as a respectable widow and not have to go on worrying about the messy details that went into marriage.

Little by little, the Republicans were driving the Nationalists back from the northwestern edge of Madrid. There'd been months of bitter fighting over the corpse of the university. Now those battered buildings lay several kilometers behind the line. Pretty soon, most of Madrid would be out of artillery range for Marshal Sanjurjo's thugs.

Mike Carroll had served in the Abraham Lincoln Battalion for as long as Chaim had. Mike was tall and fair and lean and handsome. Chaim should have hated him on sight. Instead, they'd been buddies since the moment they met. Like so many buddies, they sassed each other all the time.

"You're the only Abe Lincoln who doesn't want us to advance any more," Mike said one chilly morning, a certain gleam in his eye.

"My ass!" Chaim retorted. "The fuck that supposed to mean?"

"Means the farther the front goes from the city, the tougher the time you have getting back there and getting your end wet," Carroll answered.

Chaim suggested that one way he could achieve such an objective was by having his comrade-in-arms perform an unnatural act on him. Said comrade-in-arms made reference to his mother, and also to the possibly relevant body parts of a ewe. Chaim surmised that the ewe might be diseased due to earlier intimate acquaintance with said comrade-in-arms. If they both hadn't been laughing their heads off, they would have tried to murder each other.

After the filthy jokes ran thin, Chaim said, "Seriously, man, we better push the Fascists back as far as we can. I've got the bad feeling this summer won't be a hell of a lot of fun."

"Amazing, Sherlock!" Mike said. "What leads you to this deduction?"

"Ah, cut the crap. You know as well as I do," Chaim answered.

"We aren't licked yet," Mike said, which wasn't a ringing denial.

Everybody on the Republican side knew what was wrong. As in a sickroom where the patient still seemed strong but was plainly sinking, no one wanted to talk about it. Now that England and France were backing Hitler's push against Stalin, Republican Spain was definitely the girl they'd left behind. The Republic was lucky to have got those Czechs, and the handful of French Jews who'd come with them. Not many more soldiers would make it over the Pyrenees.

Not many more supplies would, either. France and England didn't want to sell to the Republic any more. Stalin did, but he had his own war to worry about and a swarm of enemies between him and Spain. Meanwhile, nobody was stopping the *Führer* and the *Duce* from shipping Marshal Sanjurjo all kinds of goodies.

"Maybe FDR will come through," Mike said.

"And rain makes applesauce," Chaim returned. "I'll believe that when I see it."

America was at war with Japan, not with Germany. Roosevelt hadn't even tried to get a declaration of war against Germany through Congress. Had he tried, he would have failed. The USA had been selling billions in weapons to the so-called Western democracies . . . till the big switch. After that, FDR pulled the plug. The munitions makers might have found a market in Spain to take up some of the slack—if the new war against Japan hadn't got them going full speed ahead again.

Chaim paused to scratch. Why wasn't it too cold for bugs in the trenches? Because they lived on nice, warm people—that was why. "Even if we are fucked, we've lasted three years longer than anybody thought we could," he said. "The government was going to take the Internationals out of the line, remember, 'cause we'd done all we could do. Or we thought so, anyway, till Hitler jumped on the Czechs and all of a sudden England and France liked the Republic again."

"And now they don't any more, and we're fucked again," Carroll said. "Till the roulette wheel stops on a new square, we are. I wish Hitler *would've* declared war on America. That would have fried his fish for him."

"Boy, you got that straight," Chaim said. "Can you imagine all the shit that'd pour into Spain then?" He imagined it with the dreamy, half-hopeless awe a starving prospector gave to striking the mother lode.

"In the meantime . . ." Carroll poked him in the ribs. "In the meantime, you've got your little cutie back in town. If she doesn't give you something to fight for, you've got to be dead."

Chaim would no more have called La Martellita a little cutie than he would have hung the same handle on a 155mm shell. It wasn't obvious which was more dangerous, or more explosive. Still, some guys did talk about weapons that way, even if he didn't. His features softened for a reason different, if related.

"I'm gonna have a kid. A half-Spanish kid, a kid who's gonna live here in the country we end up making," he said softly, his eyes dreamy and far away. "That, now, *that* gives me somethin' to fuckin' fight for."

SOME GERMAN PROPAGANDA sheets lay next to the bubbling samovar when Anastas Mouradian walked into the Red Air Force officers' meeting room. He could tell what they were right away. For one thing, even by Soviet standards, the paper they were printed on was amazingly cheap and cruddy. For another, the font the Nazis had chosen looked like something from before the last war.

The Armenian bomber pilot wondered why they'd picked something so outdated. Maybe they didn't have any more modern type. Or maybe, since the alphabet wasn't their own, they were just style-blind. It wasn't the alphabet Stas had grown up with, either, but he saw it all the time. Couldn't Hitler's clowns have found a defector to fill them in on their own stupidity?

Most likely, they hadn't even gone looking. Germans were so convinced of their own superiority, they often didn't bother asking advice from anyone else. Sometimes they paid for their arrogance, too.

He picked up one of the sheets. A misspelled word and some bad grammar leaped out at him. The Nazis were trying to persuade non-Russians in the USSR to go over to them. *You thought the tiranny of the Tsars was bad. Stalin's is even worser!* the flier said. No, no one would take you seriously if you stuck your foot in your mouth as soon as you opened it.

A Russian pilot paused at the samovar to pour himself a glass of tea. He chuckled when he saw what Mouradian was looking at. "So, Stas, you going to fly your plane over to a Hitlerite airstrip?" he inquired.

He was joking. Stas knew that perfectly well. All the same, the Armenian set down the propaganda sheet as if it burned his fingers. "Not me!" he declared, sincerity ringing in his voice. "Only thing I'll give them is a thousand kilos of high explosive!"

The trouble with jokes was, you never could tell who was listening to the answers. Stas had no reason to think Boris there belonged to the NKVD or informed on his fellow officers. He had no reason to think that about any of the other flyers sitting down with tea and hard rolls and fatty pork sausages and *papirosi*, either.

But he couldn't afford to joke back with the Russians, because there was always the chance . . . He didn't care to see the Lubyanka, the NKVD headquarters in Moscow, from the inside. He didn't want to go to a labor camp in Turkmenistan or Siberia just on account of a misunderstood joke. He didn't want to go to a place like that at all, but especially not for such a stupid reason.

And so, remarking, "This stinking thing wouldn't even make a good asswipe," he poured himself a glass of tea, too, and walked away from the table without a backward glance at the propaganda sheet.

His copilot came in a few minutes later. Ivan Kulkaanen also picked up one of the sheets. After a quick glance, he put it down again. "Fascist bullshit!" he said loudly, and got himself some tea and a roll.

It *was* Fascist bullshit—no possible doubt about that. With better propaganda, the Nazis might have had more chance of prying people away from the Soviet regime. Not everyone in the USSR loved it; not even close. If you had to choose between Stalin and his henchmen on the one hand and people who turned out crap like that on the other, though, you turned into a Soviet patriot almost by default.

Lieutenant Colonel Tomashevsky came in. The squadron commander waved to his men, telling them not to bother to jump up and salute. Discipline in the Soviet armed forces had tightened up since the war started. Leaders had discovered that, while a revolutionary military sounded good, a hierarchical one performed better. They'd found the same thing in Spain. They'd rediscovered it after the French Revolution. No doubt Spartacus, that Soviet hero, had had to learn the lesson, too.

After snagging tea and breakfast, Tomashevsky said, "Looks like we'll fly today, Comrades." He sat down. By the way he shoveled sausage into his chowlock, action didn't leave him too nervous to eat. Anastas Mouradian felt the same way. He wanted some ballast in there when he went up. Some people worked differently. They'd puke or get the runs if they went into combat with a full stomach. They weren't cowards. They just came equipped with anxious insides.

"What's our target, Comrade Colonel?" someone asked.

"There's an enemy concentration east of Vitebsk," Tomashevsky said. "Mostly Englishmen and the French, Intelligence says." His lip curled in fine contempt. "If they want to play these games, we have to show them the price. And if we smash them up before they get to the front, that's one thing less for the Red Army to worry about."

Groundcrew men were bombing up the Pe-2s and making sure their machine guns had full belts when Mouradian and Kulkaanen went to their plane. Some of the bombs had slogans chalked on the casings: *For Stalin!* and *Death to Fascists!* and the like. The only way the enemy would find out about one of those was if the bomb proved a dud. But the groundcrews did that kind of thing all the time. It made them happy and didn't hurt anything, so why not?

Fyodor Mechnikov profanely directed bomb stowage. The blocky sergeant reminded Stas a lot of Ivan Kuchkov, with whom he'd served before getting promoted away. He wasn't quite so hairy or quite so ugly, and he didn't have quite such a foul mouth, but he came close on all three counts.

"We'll give 'em hell, right?" he said to Stas.

The Armenian nodded gravely. "That isn't borscht we're dropping on them."

"Borscht." The bombardier didn't need long to decide what he thought of that. "You're weird . . . sir."

"It could be," Mouradian agreed. "It probably is, in fact. But as long as I get the plane there and back, as long as we deliver the load, what difference does it make?"

"When you put it that way, not fucking much," Mechnikov allowed.

Flying the Pe-2 was a pleasure. It had so much speed and maneuverability, people called it the fighting bomber. Of course, they'd said the same thing about the SB-2, the plane Stas had learned on, only a few years earlier. The state of the art had passed the SB-2 by. One of these days, the Pe-2 would also grow obsolescent. But it hadn't happened yet.

"If we're gong after the English and French, we won't have to worry so much about 109s, will we?" Kulkaanen asked as they reached cruising altitude.

"I hope not," Stas said sincerely. Calling a Pe-2 a fighting bomber meant it had a chance against a Messerschmitt. A good chance? Well, no. From what he'd heard, English fighters were about as good as the 109, French machines not quite. Neither country had swarms of them in these parts, the way the Nazis did.

The squadron droned on toward the west. A few antiaircraft guns fired at them as they crossed the front. Russian? German? Both? No one got hit, so it didn't matter. Somewhere down there in the snow . . .

"Approaching the target." Tomashevsky's voice echoed in Stas' earphones. The pilot wondered how he could tell. Then he saw fairly well camouflaged tents below—and antiaircraft fire abruptly picked up.

"Let 'em go, Fedya!" he called to the bombardier through the speaking tube.

Away they went. All at once, the bomber grew nimbler. It needed to, for English Hurricanes—Mouradian thought they were Hurricanes—tore into the formation less than a minute after the Pe-2s turned for home. Tracers scored deadly, fiery lines across the sky. Two bombers spun earthward, one after the other. A Hurricane went down, too, flames licking back from the dead engine toward the cockpit.

Stas didn't see a parachute open there. He didn't look very hard, either. He was too busy throwing his plane around the sky, trying to keep any Hurricanes from getting on his tail. Mechnikov fired a burst from the belly machine gun. No answering storm of lead tore into the Pe-2, so maybe he scared off the enemy. Or maybe he was shooting at nothing. Stas didn't care. As long as he got away, he didn't care about anything else.

Chapter 4

Julius Lemp swept the horizon with his Zeiss binoculars. Ratings up on the U-30's conning tower scanned all segments of the sky. The Baltic was a damned narrow sea. You had to stay alert every second you were on the surface. Trouble would land on top of you with both feet if you didn't.

Estonia lay to the south, Finland to the north. Under Marshal Mannerheim, Finland was neutral or even friendly to the *Reich*. Estonia would have liked to be. Stalin didn't give the little country the choice. The Reds still resented losing the Baltic states when the Russian Empire fell apart. (They resented losing Finland, too, but they weren't in such a good position to do anything about that.)

When the Soviet Union sneezed, Estonia came down with the sniffles. When Stalin said *Do something!*, his little neighbor did it. Otherwise, especially in troubled times like these, the Red Army would march in.

As a matter of fact, the Red Army—and the Red Air Force and Red Navy—*had* marched in. That was why Lemp cast an especially wary eye toward the south. But things could have been worse. Estonia still remained independent in name. Stalin had promised that his forces would leave once the emergency was over. Even an idiot knew Stalin's pledges were worth their weight in gold, but at least he'd bothered to make this one.

Lithuania was as much a German sphere as Estonia was a Russian. Hitler had reannexed Memel, and the Lithuanians seemed pathetically eager to cede it to him. He might have grabbed the whole country if they hadn't. Like Stalin, he swore up and down that the *Wehrmacht* would pull out after he'd won the war. Lemp chuckled nastily. Once a guy got it in, he always promised he'd pull out.

"What's funny, Skipper?" one of the ratings asked. The field glasses never left his eyes; his steady scan of the sky never faltered. Lemp told him. He laughed.

So did the rest of the sailors up there. "You used that line, too, did you?" another one said.

"Who, me?" Lemp answered in a voice brimming with innocence. More goatish laughter erupted. Aboard the *Kriegsmarine*'s surface ships, Prussian discipline was alive and thriving. Everything was bright metal and fresh paint and sharp trouser creases and smooth shaves and *"Zu befehl, mein Herr!"*

U-boats weren't like that. By the nature of things, they couldn't be. No one wasted precious fresh water on shaving. Like his men, Lemp wore a scraggly growth of face fungus. His uniform was as grimy and smelly as theirs were. The only thing that distinguished his from theirs was the white cover on his service cap; theirs were all navy blue. He'd taken the stiffening wire out of the crown, as every U-boat skipper did: one more silent swipe at spit and polish.

The sun glinted off the sea to the south and threw dazzling reflections into his face. It stood higher in the sky than it had in the depths of winter—not that anybody who had to sail the Baltic in that season saw it very often. But the wind still blew down from the north—straight off the North Pole, by the feel of it. Despite a heavy peacoat and quilted trousers, Lemp shivered.

One of the ratings stiffened. He pointed southeast. "Smoke on the horizon!"

Lemp's binoculars swung that way. Yes, the dark smudge was there—

low and hard to make out, but there, sure as hell. And smoke, in these waters, could come only from a Russian ship. "Good job, Anton. I'll see it goes into your file," the skipper said. Then he called down the hatch to the exec, who had the helm: "Change course to 135. All ahead full. Anton spied the smoke."

"Changing course to 135, Skipper." Klaus Hammerstein's voice floated up from below. He was a good officer. He'd get promoted away from the U-30 into a boat of his own before too long. When he was the Old Man himself, he could let more of his good nature show. He'd have an exec to do the dirty work for him then, instead of his doing it for someone else. Lemp heard him call the setting change back to the engine room. The U-boat's diesels throbbed harder. The Type VIIA could make sixteen knots on the surface. That would be plenty to run down a freighter. If Anton had found an enemy warship . . .

I'll worry about that later, Lemp told himself. He did not hold the Red Navy in high regard. Yes, the Ivans were brave. But he'd spent most of the time since the war started facing off against the Royal Navy out in the North Sea and the Atlantic. Those were the best surface sailors in the world. Better than their opposite numbers in the *Kriegsmarine*? He nodded to himself. They were the men from whom the Germans—and everybody else—tried to learn their craft. Set against competition like that, the Russians didn't come close to measuring up.

He went to the big, pier-mounted binoculars on the conning tower. They had a narrow field of view, but more magnification and far more light grasp than the ones he and the ratings wore on straps around their necks. And now he wasn't scanning for things that might be there. Something was, and he knew just where to look for it.

Distant waves leaped toward him. So did that smoke smudge, not quite so low on the horizon now as the U-boat hurried toward it. Before long, he got what he was waiting for: both the U-30 and the enemy ship rose on swells at the same time. He didn't get to study that lean shark shape for very long, but he didn't need long, either.

"Destroyer," he said crisply.

He glanced at his own boat's exhaust. There wasn't that much to see. Diesels ran cleaner than turbines, and his engines were smaller than the ones powering the Soviet ship. An outstanding lookout might spot his smoke or, now, the U-boat's silhouette against the sky. But how many outstanding lookouts did the Red Navy boast? Not many. And not many German officers were better equipped to judge that than he was.

So he waited, and waited, and waited some more as the gap closed. Only when he figured any halfway-awake fellow with binoculars was liable to see the U-30 did he order the ratings below. As usual, he was the last man off the conning tower. As he dogged the hatch behind him, he ordered, "Take her down to *Schnorkel* depth and raise the periscope."

"*Schnorkel* depth. Aye aye," Hammerstein said. The snort let the diesels breathe under water. It gave the boat better performance than she had on her electric motors . . . as long as she didn't dive deep. The Dutch had invented the gadget, but more and more German U-boats used it these days.

Also, of course, the *Schnorkel's* stovepipe tube and the skinnier one that housed the periscope were a lot harder to spot than the U-30's hull would have been. Lemp peered through the 'scope and tried to work out the destroyer's speed, course, and distance.

"Have we got a shot?" the exec asked.

"I . . . think so," Lemp said slowly. "They have no idea we're around. They're strolling along at eight knots, tops." That was about a quarter of the destroyer's full speed. "We're within four kilometers now. We can close some more, too."

He fed the course and speed information to Hammerstein, who had a kind of glorified slide rule that helped him calculate the torpedo settings. Regulations said the skipper's *Zentrale* was to be closed off from the rest of the boat. Like most skippers, Lemp ignored that reg. Easier just to call orders forward than to shout through the voice tube.

They closed to just over two kilometers. That was still a longish shot, but it was as good as they were likely to get. Any closer and somebody on the Russian destroyer was liable to wake up and spoil things. A ship like that could show them her heels easy as you please . . . or make an attack run instead, which wouldn't be any fun.

Lemp ordered a spread of three torpedoes. One by one, at his shout of *"Los!"*, the eels sprang away from the U-30. Seawater gurgled into the boat's forward ballast tanks to make up for the several tonnes of weight now vanished and to keep the trim level.

The stopwatch's hand seemed to crawl around the dial with maddening slowness. Lemp looked from it to the periscope's eyepiece again and again. The destroyer made sudden smoke and started to turn . . . too late. The first eel caught her up near the bow, one of the others not far from the stern. Both explosions rumbled through the U-30. As badly broken as a dog hit by a car, the destroyer went down fast.

"They got a signal off, dammit," the radio operator said, emerging from his tiny sanctum.

"Change course to 270," Lemp said. "We'll stay at *Schnorkel* depth. Let's see their planes spot us then."

"Right you are, Skipper. I am changing course to 270." The exec swung the U-30 back toward the west, the direction from which the boat had come. A rare smile spread across his face. "The lords will be extra happy we've made a kill, eh?"

"Think so, do you?" Lemp smiled, too. The most junior crewmen—the lords, in U-boat crews' jargon—bedded down in the torpedo room. As long as it was full of eels, some of them slept on top of torpedoes. Once the reloads went into the tubes, they'd have more room to place their bedrolls and sling their hammocks. To them, that had to outweigh sinking a Soviet destroyer. It didn't for Julius Lemp, but he knew how they felt all the same.

SERGEANT HIDEKI FUJITA was busy counting logs. The count had to come out perfect for every unit at Pingfan under his command. If it didn't, somebody would catch hell. Oh, the logs would, of course, but they counted for nothing in a Japanese soldier's view of things. The person who would catch hell if the count screwed up was the man in charge—Fujita himself.

He glowered at the logs as he counted them. The *maruta* stood at stiff attention, their faces as expressionless as they could make them. They, or most of them, wanted the count to come out right, too. Until the Japanese authorities were satisfied, the prisoners of war wouldn't get fed.

That simple truth should have nipped all escape attempts in the bud. If somebody got out of one of the barbed-wire enclosures, nobody who stayed behind would get anything to eat. The *maruta* didn't get that much to eat as things were. They would have got even less if the bacteriologists of Unit 731 didn't need reasonably healthy subjects for some experiments.

In spite of themselves, the *maruta* shivered. Pingfan was a little south of Harbin, but only a little. Winters in Manchukuo were nothing to sneeze at—unless you got influenza or pneumonia or any of the other illnesses you could catch all by yourself in cold weather.

Fujita felt the chill himself, and he wore a fur cap with earflaps, a double-breasted greatcoat with a fur collar and a thick lining, heavy mittens, and *valenki* he'd taken off a dead Russian in the forests on the far side of the Ussuri. The *maruta*—Red Army men in this enclosure—had only their ordinary service uniforms.

They also had more than cold weather to worry about. To the Japanese bacteriologists, they were nothing but guinea pigs to be used up as needed. That the Japanese called them something like logs showed what they thought of them. Brave soldiers, proper soldiers, wouldn't have let themselves get captured. Proper officers wouldn't have surrendered, not when they were defending a place as vital to their country as Vladivostok.

(The other useful thing about calling a POW a log, of course, was that you didn't have to think of him as a human being once you started doing it. Japanese soldiers—and scientists, too—had trouble thinking of prisoners as human beings like themselves anyhow. By surrendering, you threw away your manhood, your self: your honor, in essence. Who could possibly care what happened to you afterwards? But tagging the POWs at Pingfan *maruta* made that dehumanizing process all but official.)

One of the privates helping Fujita with the count—doing most of the actual work, in other words—came up to him and stood at attention, waiting to be noticed. After a delay designed to remind the soldier he was only a private, Fujita deigned to nod. "Yes?"

"Please excuse me, Sergeant-*san,* but I make the count out to be a hundred and seventy-four."

"Does that include the two bodies?" Fujita pointed toward the corpses lying in front of the Russians' neat ranks. You had to show your dead. How else could the guards be sure they hadn't run off to join the Chinese bandits bedeviling Manchukuo and to spread wild, lying rumors about what went on at Pingfan?

"*Hai,* Sergeant-*san.*" The private nodded eagerly. The other new conscript with Fujita hustled up a moment later and reported the same figure. They'd gone down opposite sides of the prisoners' ranks, so they couldn't have put their heads together to come up with it.

It also matched the number of men this compound should hold, taking the deaths yesterday into account. Fujita knew that—he kept track of such things—but he checked the figure on the paper stuck in his clipboard even so. He couldn't afford to be wrong, not on something this important. Yes, 174. Nobody'd run off in the night, not here.

He raked the Red Army men in the front row with his eyes. They were only prisoners, after all. They deserved no better. "*Khorosho!*" he shouted. His accent was terrible, but he didn't care. It was up to the round-eyed barbarians to be grateful that he'd wasted any time to learn a few words of their stupid, ugly language.

"*Arigato gozaimasu,* Sergeant-*san!*" the Russians chorused. Naturally, they had to thank him for finding their numbers acceptable. They reached as one for the mess tins on their belts—if they had belts—and trooped off to the kitchen for their meager morning meal.

Fujita pointed to the scrawny dead bodies. "Have these disposed of when the *maruta* come back," he told the privates.

"Yes, Sergeant-*san!*" one of them said, while the other went, "Of course, Sergeant-*san!*" Fujita had taken his lumps while he was a private. Now he could hand them out. These fellows had to keep him sweet, as he'd had to suck up to his sergeant before. That was how the system worked.

Later that day, a microbiologist came up to him. "Sir!" Fujita said, stiffening to rigor mortis–like attention. "What do you need, sir?" Whatever it was, Fujita would get it for him or die trying. His orders were that a scientist's white lab coat was as good as an officer's collar tabs. If somebody wearing one gave him orders, he had to follow them.

An officer would knock you around at the slightest suspicion of reluctance. The scientists were friendlier than that, or maybe just more naïve. Dr. Tsuruo Yamamura was a nice guy. Sometimes he even said please when he told people what to do, a courtesy no officer would ever show. He did it now: "We have a new shipment of *maruta* coming in by train this afternoon. Please take a squad of guards and meet them at half past three, then take them to the new compound—is it number twenty-seven?"

"Yes, sir. Compound twenty-seven." Fujita tore off a parade-ground salute.

"Be gentle with them unless they try to escape," Yamamura said. "They are important to the war effort."

"Yes, sir!" the sergeant repeated. But then he risked a questioning "Sir?" He wasn't used to orders like the ones he'd just got.

Dr. Yamamura was willing, even eager, to explain, where an officer would have either snarled or hauled off and belted Fujita for his gall. "These are American Marines captured in Peking and Shanghai," the bacteriologist said. "Their reactions to our experiments will help show how Americans and Englishmen differ from Chinese and Japanese, and will let us make more effective weapons to use against them."

"I see," Fujita said slowly. He'd talked to more than a few soldiers who'd served in one or another of the major Chinese cities. From what they said, American Marines were very bad news: big, tough, clever fighters who backed away from nobody. If they were as tough as all that, though, why did they let themselves be taken prisoner instead of killing themselves or making their foes finish them?

That wasn't a sergeant's worry. Being at the railroad siding with a squad well before 3:30 was. Fujita made sure he and his men were in place. The train down from Harbin, naturally, ran late. That also wasn't his worry—or anything close to a surprise.

More than a hundred Americans stumbled off the train when it finally showed up. They'd been packed in like rice grains jammed into a sack. Close to half of them wore dirty bandages that showed they'd been wounded. They jabbered in incomprehensible English.

Shouts and gestures with bayoneted rifles got them moving in the right direction. Most of the time, the Japanese soldiers would have clouted some of them with rifle butts to speed things along. But Fujita had spelled out Dr. Yamamura's orders, so his men took it easy.

Compound 27 had a barracks hall with a central stove inside the barbed wire. The prisoners wouldn't be too crowded. They could recover from whatever they'd gone through on the train. Fujita thought they were almost living in a hotel. By the way his men rolled their eyes, they also figured the Americans had it soft. But they were only soldiers. The officers and scientists set over them didn't care a sen's worth what they thought.

SOMEWHERE OR OTHER, Adam Pfaff had got his hands on a pair of field glasses. They were such an obviously useful thing for an infantryman to have, not even Awful Arno complained about them. And Baatz complained about everything. He'd sure pissed and moaned about the gray paint Pfaff had slapped on his rifle's woodwork. Somehow, though, the nonregulation Mauser hadn't made the world come to an end or handed the war to the Ivans on a silver platter. Baatz was used to the piece by now. Willi Dernen wouldn't have been surprised if he'd started ordering other people to paint theirs the same way.

Had Willi owned binoculars, he would have used them for something practical, like ogling girls getting into or out of clothes from ranges where they couldn't catch him at it. His buddy didn't do that—or, if Pfaff did, he didn't brag about it or share the field glasses when he spotted something juicy the way most guys would have. Instead, when he wasn't using them to search out male Ivans with rifles, he pointed them up into the sky. He tended to mumble to himself when he did that.

"What do you see up there? Bombers?" Willi asked one evening at sunset when he caught Pfaff doing it. He didn't hear aircraft engines, but that might not signify. Sometimes the Ivans flew so high, you couldn't hear them. And spotting planes against the darkening sky was a bitch. Again, binoculars would clearly come in handy.

But the other *Gefreiter* shook his head without lowering the field glasses. "Heavenly bodies," he answered.

That made Willi think of naked women again. He wasn't as big a cockhound as some of the guys, but he wasn't a priest, either. Nowhere close. He looked up into the sky himself. He didn't see any naked girls up there, only the first-quarter moon and a growing number of stars. He said so.

This time, Pfaff did lower the binoculars. He shook his head again in some annoyance. "Not *that* kind of heavenly bodies," he said. It wasn't that he had anything against women, either.

"Well, what, then?" Willi inquired. He was getting annoyed himself.

"If you really want to know, I was looking at the moon."

Willi eyed it himself. There it was, up in the sky. It looked like half a coin. The straight line that ran from top to bottom wasn't *quite* straight. It seemed ever so slightly chewed, which made it different from the rest of the moon's outline. It still wasn't very exciting, or even interesting. Again, Willi didn't hesitate to say so.

Pfaff handed him the field glasses. "Have a look through these. You know how to adjust them for your eyes?"

"Oh, sure. I've used 'em before." Willi aimed at the moon. It wasn't very far out of focus even before he carefully twisted each eyepiece in turn to sharpen things up. His buddy's vision couldn't have been too different from his own. But once he got the image as clear as he could . . . "Wow," he breathed, hardly even realizing he was making a noise.

"It's something, isn't it?" Pfaff spoke with quiet pride, as if, instead of Galileo, he were the first one ever to see the heavens close up.

That pride was wasted on Willi, who didn't even hear him. The moon hung there, seeming close enough to reach out and touch if he took one hand away from the field glasses. It wasn't just a light in the sky any more. It was a *world*, a world out there in space. The faint gray patches you could make out with the naked eye (and Willi didn't so much as think of naked women, the truest proof of how fascinated he was) swelled into plains that had to be hundreds of kilometers across. Craters pocked them and filled the brighter, whiter areas of the moon.

Shadows stretched across the craters closest to the straight line. The others, under higher sunlight, showed less contrast. "What made them?" Willi asked. "Volcanoes?"

Adam Pfaff understood what he was talking about right away. "Nobody knows for sure. We've never been there, after all," he answered. "But that's one of the best guesses."

"Wow," Willi said again, staring and staring.

"You see the three craters, one above the next, near the sunrise line—the terminator, they call it?" Pfaff said.

Willi peered again, then nodded. "I see 'em."

"They're called Ptolemaeus, Alphonsus, and Azrachel."

"All the shit on the moon has *names*?" That had never occurred to Willi before. You could make maps of what was up there, the same as you could down here. It really *was* another world.

"You think they look impressive through these, you should see 'em through a telescope," Pfaff said. "Back home, I've got an eight-centimeter refractor. It's little and pretty cheap, but it'll let you magnify a hundred times, not just seven. Then you can really start to get an idea of how much there is to see."

Willi tried to imagine the moon appearing that much bigger and closer than it did even through binoculars. He felt himself failing. After you'd started playing with yourself, you could try to imagine what a girl would be like, but you wouldn't know what counted till one let you get lucky.

"What else can you show me here?" he asked.

"Well, you see those two bright stars close together, a little west of the moon?" Pfaff asked. Willi nodded once more. One of them was the brightest star in the sky; the other, the more easterly one, was fainter and more yellow. His friend went on, "You can take a look at them if you want. The bright one is Jupiter. Maybe you'll see a couple of its moons if you hold the binoculars real steady. The other one's Saturn."

"Rings!" Willi exclaimed, remembering from school.

"Rings," Adam agreed, "only the binoculars won't show them. Through a telescope, they've got to be the most beautiful thing in the sky. You think they can't possibly be real."

If they were more beautiful than the magnified moon, Willi wished he had a telescope. Through the field glasses . . . The stars stayed stars. They looked brighter and you could see more of them, but they didn't get bigger. Jupiter and Saturn did. Jupiter especially showed a tiny disk. It probably wasn't even a quarter as wide as the moon through the naked eye, but it was there.

And, sure as hell, it had two little stars dancing attendance on it.

That was interesting—not so glorious as the moon, but interesting all the same. "What else is there?" Willi'd ignored the heavens as long as he'd been alive. Now he wanted to look at everything at once.

Adam Pfaff pointed to the left of the moon this time. "See those faint stars in what looks like mist? You can't make 'em out real well because the moon's so close, but they're there." Following his finger, Willi spied what he was talking about. Pfaff said, "That's the Pleiades. They look different through the field glasses."

"Different how?" Willi asked. Pfaff didn't enlighten him, so he turned the binoculars that way. He whistled softly. Had someone taken a bag of diamonds—along with the odd sapphire and ruby—and spilled them on velvet of the deepest blue imaginable, a blue only a whisper from black, he might have made an inferior copy of what Willi saw. Jewels don't shine by their own light. The stars of the Pleiades did. Even more than with the moon, the naked eye gave no hint of what hid in plain sight.

"Hey, what are you clowns up to?" Arno Baatz's grating voice made Willi yank down the binoculars, as if the corporal had caught him with dirty pictures. Baatz brayed on: "Trying to freeze your stupid dicks off? You don't have to try real hard, not here you don't."

Willi had forgotten he was cold. Out in the open in the middle of a Russian winter, that would do for a miracle till a real one came along. "We're just looking at the moon and stuff through my field glasses," Pfaff said. "Want to see?"

"Nahh." Awful Arno laughed at the idea. That saddened Willi without surprising him. "I got better things to do with my time, I do," the corporal added. Willi almost asked him what they were, but held his tongue instead. If Baatz didn't want to know, Willi didn't want to tell him.

IN THE RED AIR FORCE, political officers were like epaulets on a uniform: they were decorative, but you didn't need them. Most of them had sense enough to know it, too. If a *politruk* tried to countermand a squadron commander's orders, the arrogant fool would be ignored if he was lucky. If he wasn't so lucky, he might leave a bomber without a parachute from several thousand meters up. Any half-clever officer could cook up paperwork explaining the unfortunate accident. It wasn't as if the jerk it happened to would be there to give him the lie.

Ivan Kuchkov soon found out things in the Red Army were different. Political officers here took the job of indoctrinating the men seriously. They preached Communism the way priests preached religion. And, like priests, they thought what they were doing was important.

They also expected everybody else to think it was important. When a *politruk* started gabbing, he expected all the soldiers within range of his yappy voice to pay close attention. Ivan soon mastered the art of seeming to listen while his mind roamed free. He didn't take long to realize he wasn't the only one.

Lieutenant Vasiliev went on and on about the benefits of Party membership. The most important one for most Red Army men was that their families were sure to get word if they fell on the field. Unlike the Nazis, Soviet soldiers wore no identity disks. The government kept only loose track of them; they were interchangeable, expendable parts. But Communist Party members were part of the elite. They mattered to the state, so it monitored them more closely than ordinary fighters.

That might have been a selling point for most soldiers, but not for Ivan. His mother was dead. He couldn't stand his brother or sister. And if he ever saw his old man again, he'd smack him in the snoot to pay him back for all the beatings he'd dished out when Ivan was a kid. Or he'd try, anyhow. His father was a sneaky weasel, and might get in the first lick himself.

So all that recruiting crap went in one ear and out the other. But sometimes Vasiliev went on about other stuff, too. One morning after breakfast—black bread, sausage, and tea, plus whatever the soldiers could scrounge from the countryside—he gathered the company together in the woods and spoke in portentous tones: "Romania has declared war against the *Rodina*."

Back when the war was new, Kuchkov's SB-2 had flown across Romanian airspace so Soviet "volunteers" could reach Czechoslovakia to fight the Fascists. That aid wasn't enough. They'd had to get the hell out of there again a month later. But they'd tried, which was more than anybody else could say. Now . . .

Now the *politruk* went on, "Marshal Antonescu shows he always was a Fascist at heart. He thinks the Nazis and their lackeys are a better bet than the USSR. But our heroic soldiers, our brave workers and peasants, will show him what a big mistake he has made. This widens the war. Now it stretches from the Baltic to the Black Sea. Have the Nazis got enough men for such an enormous fight? No! Can Romania hope to fight the Red Army by herself? No again! We will push forward through her and tear into the Hitlerites' soft underbelly!"

He waited for applause. He got some. The men had learned he shut up sooner if they cheered. "Fuck the Romanians!" Ivan called. "Bugger 'em with a pine cone!" He took the Germans seriously. They were too good at their trade for anything less. But the Romanians? They had to be worse humpties than the Poles. The Poles, at least, were brave. Nobody'd ever said that about the Romanians.

Lieutenant Vasiliev beamed at him. "There's the Soviet fighting spirit! Are you a Party member, Sergeant?"

"No, Comrade Lieutenant." Kuchkov wished he'd kept his big mouth shut. You didn't want to draw their notice. They'd dump garbage on your head if you did.

"Would you like me to begin your paperwork for you? It's easy enough to arrange."

"However you please, Comrade Lieutenant." Ivan wanted to become a Communist almost as much as he wanted to shit through his ears. But you couldn't just tell the sons of bitches no. Then you'd go on a list. People who landed on those lists had bad things happen to them.

"You're Kuchkov, right? Yes, of course you are." Vasiliev had the politician's knack for matching names and faces. Well, most of the time; with a self-deprecating chuckle, he added, "Please remind me of your name and patronymic."

"Ivan Ivanovich, sir."

"Can't get much plainer than that, can you?" The *politruk* smiled as he wrote it down. "Me, I'm Arsen Feofanovich, so I'm at the other end of things." Kuchkov nodded. Both Vasiliev and his father had uncommon first names, all right. But the lieutenant made a mistake if he thought Kuchkov might care.

The Germans started shelling the forest where the company sheltered. Digging proper foxholes in ground frozen stone hard was a bitch. And the Nazis had come up with an evil trick (one the Red Army also used, though Ivan didn't worry about that): they set their fuses to maximum sensitivity, so most shells went off as soon as they touched branches overhead. Then the bursts sprayed sharp fragments of hot metal down on the men huddled below.

It was Ivan's first real time under shellfire. He couldn't shoot back, any more than he could when his bomber drew the unwelcome attention of antiaircraft guns. All he could do was stay low and try to dig himself in, though his entrenching tool took only pathetic little bites of dirt.

Something hissed in the snow a few centimeters from his hand: a shard of brass that could have skewered him as easily as not. "Fuck your mothers!" he yelled, though of course the Nazis serving those distant 105s couldn't hear him. "I hope your dicks rot off!"

He also hoped one of those nasty fragments would wound Lieutenant Vasiliev. He didn't want Vasiliev dead, just hurt enough to forget about putting him up for Party membership. If the *politruk* spent a few weeks in the hospital and then got sent to a different unit, that would do fine.

Other soldiers swore, too, to let out their fear. And wounded men shrieked and wailed. The unhurt soldiers closest to them did what they could to relieve their comrades' agony. Too often, that wasn't much. Slapping a wound dressing on a leg ripped from knee to crotch was sending a baby boy to do a man's job.

Ivan wondered whether the Germans would follow up the shelling with an infantry attack. Russians laughed at Winter Fritz, yeah. Propaganda posters showed scrawny, shivering Nazi soldiers with icicles dangling from the ends of their long, pointed noses. That didn't match what Kuchkov had seen. Yes, wide-tracked Russian tanks had the edge on German machines in the snow. The German foot soldiers around here seemed to know what they were doing, though. Some of their gear was improvised or stolen from the locals, but it wasn't bad.

And yes, sentries shouted in alarm. Submachine guns stuttered out death. Far more Red Army soldiers carried them than any other nation's troops. They didn't have a rifle's range, true, or a rifle's stopping power.

But they were cheap and easy to make, and they spat a lot of lead. Inside a couple of hundred meters, a company of men with submachine guns would massacre a company of riflemen.

The Germans, by contrast, made sure almost every squad included a light machine gun. That was another way to get firepower in carload lots. German MG-34s were far more portable than their Soviet equivalents. Ivan hadn't been a foot soldier long, but he already hated them.

Snatching up his own PPD, he ran for the edge of the woods. Shells kept falling, but you did what you had to do. The artillery might get him. If the Nazis made it in among the trees, he was a dead man for sure.

As soon as he saw figures in whitewashed coal-scuttle helmets running toward him, he threw himself down behind a tree and started shooting. The Nazis were pros. They flattened out. Most of them had snow smocks or bedsheets for camouflage, though a few wore only their field-gray greatcoats and stood out like lumps of coal.

Two Germans served an MG-34. Ivan burned through most of his big drum magazine before he took them out, but he made damn sure he did. Without that monster supporting them, the Fritzes lost enthusiasm for the attack across open ground. Sullenly, in good order, they drew back. Ivan's sigh of relief filled the air in front of him with fog. His number wasn't up . . . this time.

Chapter 5

Benjamin Halévy had all the answers. He was a Frenchman and a Jew, so he sure thought he did, anyhow. "Marshal Sanjurjo inspects the Madrid front every so often," he said. "The Nationalists still don't realize everything your elephant gun can do. Put a round through his giblets at a kilometer and a half and watch the assholes on the other side thrash like a chicken after it gets one in the neck from the farmer's wife."

"You make it sound so easy." Vaclav Jezek eyed his cigarette with distaste. Spanish tobacco was even harsher than French. Every drag sandpapered his throat. The only thing worse would be no tobacco at all. This was a misfortune. That would be a catastrophe.

"You've done it before," Halévy said. "You just have to be in the right place at the right time, that's all."

"You make it sound so easy," Jezek repeated, even more dryly than before. Like so many things, sniping had to look simple to people who didn't do it. The positioning, the concealment, the waiting, the shot . . . Everything had to go perfectly, or you wasted a bullet. More likely, you never got your shot off. Or else some canny bastard on the other side, somebody who was better or luckier than you were at that particular moment, blew out the side of your head.

"Well, think about it," the Jew told him. "I'm starting to get connections, and sometimes they hear things from the other side. If you punch Sanjurjo's ticket, the Republic will pin so many medals on you, you'll look like a Fascist general."

"I think I'd rather get laid," Vaclav said. Halévy laughed. Vaclav sent him a sour stare. "And how are you getting connections? You don't speak Spanish."

"No, but if people here speak any foreign language, they speak French." Halévy made it sound natural and easy.

It probably was, for him. Vaclav grunted, pinched out the cigarette's coal, and stowed the little butt in a tobacco pouch. Waste not, want not. A Jew would land on his feet anywhere—even in Spain, evidently.

Somebody on the other side fired a rifle. The bullet whined high over the Republican line. It would come down somewhere, but long odds it would hurt anybody when it did. A lot of shots fired in war were like that. You wanted to get the other guys, but you didn't want them to get you. So you fired without sticking your head up to see what you were doing. You made them keep their heads down, anyway.

More often than not, the Czechs and Internationals holding this stretch of the line would have ignored such a wild round. But guys here must have been jumpy, because two rifles in quick succession answered the Fascist shot.

That spooked Sanjurjo's men. Vaclav couldn't imagine what they were thinking. That the veterans on the other side would swarm out of the trenches and charge them? They had to be nuts to believe anything like that.

Nuts or not, more of them fired back. Bullets started snapping past, much closer to the trenches. You didn't want to stick your head up over the parapet, or you'd stop one with your nose. Halévy chambered a round in his rifle. "I didn't much want a firefight, but . . ." He shrugged. War wasn't about what you wanted. It was about what you got stuck with.

Along with the antitank rifle, Vaclav carried a pistol to defend himself at close range. The big piece was no good for work like that. Neither weapon was much use in a fight like this. Machine guns on both sides started yammering. Vaclav realized what a long way from home he was. But he didn't want to be back in Prague, not with the Nazis' swastika flying over it.

Mortar bombs whispered when they came down. The first couple burst a few bays over from the sniper and the Jewish sergeant. Vaclav had dug a bombproof into the forward edge of the trench, with some help from Halévy. They'd reinforced it with bits and pieces of wood scavenged here, there, and everywhere. Both men dove into it now.

If a mortar round burst right behind them, even the bombproof wouldn't help. Vaclav wished such thoughts wouldn't cross his mind. They just made this business even more horrible than it would be otherwise.

"What if they try to rush us?" Halévy yelled through the din.

"What if they do?" Vaclav returned. "The machine guns will slaughter them, that's what." The machine guns had heavily protected nests. Even a direct hit from a mortar bomb might not take one out. An ordinary soldier who got up on the firing step, though, was asking to get murdered.

Before the war started, Jezek had figured Jews for cowards. He'd got over that. The ones in the Czechoslovakian army hated Hitler even more than Czechs did, which was saying something. They made up a disproportionate number of the men who served under the government-in-exile. And Benjamin Halévy held up his end of the bargain as well as anyone could want.

Vaclav still didn't like Jews. He saw no reason why he should. But he wasn't dumb enough to disbelieve what he saw with his own eyes. Jews weren't yellow, or no more yellow than anybody else.

Little by little, the firefight ebbed. There was no particular reason for that, any more than there had been for its start. Combat wasn't always rational. Not even a goddamn German General Staff officer with a volume of Clausewitz under his arm could deny that.

Wounded men moaned or shrieked, depending on how badly they were hurt. Off in the distance, the same sounds rose from the Nationalists' positions. Suffering had a universal language.

Stretcher-bearers hustled wounded Republican fighters to aid stations behind the lines. If the men got there alive, they had a pretty good chance to stay that way. To his surprise, Vaclav had discovered that they knew far more about giving blood transfusions in the field here than they had in either Czechoslovakia or France.

He crawled out of the bombproof and dusted himself off. The stink of shit hung in the air. Maybe it came from men killed on the spot, maybe from men scared past endurance. He'd fouled himself a time or two. He wasn't proud of it—who would be? But he wasn't anywhere near so ashamed as he had been when it happened. He wasn't the only one it had happened to—nowhere near, in fact. It was just one of those things.

Sergeant Halévy came out, too. "Such fun," he said.

"Fun," Vaclav echoed in a hollow voice. "Right."

"If Sanjurjo were watching the football game right now—" Halévy said.

"Then what?" Vaclav broke in. "I'd have to spot him. I'd have to know he was there to spot in the first place. He'd have to be somewhere the rifle could reach. I'd have to be somewhere I could shoot from. And I'd have to hit him when I did. Snipers never talk about all the times they miss, you know. So why don't you give it a rest, huh?"

"All right," Halévy said. "But Sanjurjo does come right up to the front line to see what's going on. Whatever else you can say about the miserable fat turd, he's no coward."

"Oh, joy," Jezek answered. Men who hadn't seen action always figured the miserable turds on the other side wouldn't show courage. But he'd seen that the Nazis were as brave as Czechs or Frenchmen or Tommies. No one here in Spain had ever accused the Nationalists of lacking balls. Brains, yes, but brains weren't the same thing. Not even close.

"I'm just telling you it's not impossible you'll get a shot at him, that's all." Halévy wouldn't leave it alone.

"And I'm just telling you it's not impossible monkeys'll fly out my ass next time I fart, but I'm not gonna wait around till they do," Jezek retorted irritably.

He couldn't faze the Jew. "With all the *singe* we've both eaten, it wouldn't surprise me one damn bit," Halévy said. *Singe* was what the French called the tinned beef they got from Argentina. It meant monkey meat. Vaclav had never eaten real monkey, so he couldn't say how much *singe* tasted like it. He was sure nobody in his right mind would eat the stuff if he didn't have to.

He did say, "That Spam the Americans ship over is a hell of a lot better."

"You're right." Halévy grinned and made as if to lick his chops. "It sure is."

"It's pork," Vaclav reminded him, not without malice.

"You're right," Halévy agreed once more. "It sure is." Vaclav thought that over, then shrugged. He wasn't a perfect Christian. Why should he expect the French sergeant to make a perfect Jew?

SURABAYA, on the north coast of Java, was even hotter and muggier than Manila. Pete McGill hadn't dreamt any place could be, hell included, but there you were. And here he was, with the *Boise*, thanking the Lord the Japs hadn't sunk the light cruiser before she got here.

Joe Orsatti had an answer for the weather. Joe Orsatti, Pete was discovering, had an answer for everything. Sometimes he had a good one; sometimes he was full of crap. But the other Marine always liked to hear himself talk.

"We're on the other side of the Equator now," he said. "So it's summer here, not winter. No wonder it's so fucking sticky."

"We aren't more than a long piss on the other side of the Equator," Pete pointed out. "Looks to me like it'd be this way all the fuckin' time here."

"Maybe that's what makes the local wogs so jumpy," Orsatti said. "Shit, if I had to live in a steam bath the goddamn year around, you can bet your sorry ass I'd be mean, too."

"Who says you aren't?" Pete thought that was one of Joe's crappy answers.

The Javanese didn't look a whole lot different from Filipinos, at least to American eyes. They were small and slight and brown. When they talked among themselves, their jibber-jabber sounded pretty much the same as the Filipinos', too.

But a lot of Filipinos knew English, and some of the ones who didn't knew Spanish instead. If a Javanese spoke any European language, he spoke Dutch. And, to Pete's way of thinking, that was a big part of the problem right there.

When the United States took the Philippines from Spain, it was with the notion that eventually the islands would turn into a country of their own. (That was how Pete had heard it, anyway. Americans tended to forget they'd fought a nasty little war against Filipinos who wanted a country of their own right away.)

Holland, by contrast, didn't want to turn the Dutch East Indies loose. As long as Dutch forces in the Indies were strong enough to squash revolts, the locals put up with being ruled by a little country halfway around the world. They might not like it, but they put up with it.

Now, suddenly, all that was tottering. The Japs were on the way. They weren't white men. They were little and kind of brown themselves. They'd made the *Boise* bail out of Manila Bay like a cat running from a big, mean dog. They had troops on the ground in the Philippines now. And they were heading this way, because they were desperately hungry for the oil and tin and rubber the Dutch East Indies and British Malaya had in such abundance.

And it didn't look as if the Dutch—or the Americans, or the British, or the Australians—would be able to stop them. Against what Japan could throw into the fight, the white powers didn't have enough troops or ships or planes, and what they did have wasn't good enough.

Pete could see that. He wouldn't have been in Surabaya if the Americans could have hung on in Manila. If he could see it, didn't it stand to reason the Javanese could, too? If they figured the Japs were going to set them free or take them over, why did they have to kowtow to white men any more?

How many of them listened to Japanese propaganda on the radio every chance they got? How many were quietly helping the invaders? Pete had no way to know stuff like that. He did know the *Boise*'s skipper had put even the harborside dives off limits for the ship's crew. They were officially judged unsafe, and not just because the local joy girls would give you the clap. The Dutch, who were supposed to run this town, wouldn't go through the streets in groups smaller than squad-sized. If they did, they were much too likely to get their heads smashed with a brick or their throats slit.

A plane buzzed over the *Boise*: a Dutch fighter with fixed landing gear. Everybody said the Japs built junk. Everybody said that, yeah, but they'd sure done a number on the U.S. Army Air Force in the Philippines. The Dutch plane looked hotter than an Army Peashooter, but not by one whole hell of a lot.

Joe Orsatti eyed the Dutch plane, too, and the orange triangles under the wings. "A Fokker," he remarked.

"A mother-Fokker," Pete agreed.

Orsatti sent him a pained look. "Har-de-har-har. Y'oughta take it on the road."

"I did," McGill answered. "What do you think I'm doing here?"

"Funny again—like a truss."

"I know," Pete said. "But I'd sure rather see those triangles than the big old Jap meatballs."

"Better get used to it," Orsatti said. "Five wins you ten we ain't gonna stick around here real long. We're useless here. We gotta get up farther north if we're gonna keep the Japs from landing, y'know what I'm saying?"

"Uh-huh," Pete replied, not altogether happily. "Talk about sticking your head in the tiger's mouth . . ."

"Gonna be a shitass excuse for a fleet, all right," the other Marine said. "Us, a coupla our destroyers, some Dutch tin cans, that limey light cruiser . . . Should be fun, getting all of us dancing to the same tune."

Pete hadn't thought about that. He'd been away from ships too long before he found himself back aboard the *Boise*. Trying to get skippers from three countries to act in concert? "Fun. Right." One thing for sure: the Japs wouldn't have that problem.

They might have others. Pete could hope so. If they didn't, the allies here were in a lot of trouble. Pete had seen enough of the Japanese in China to have more respect for them than a lot of higher-ranking Americans did. They might not be white men, but they were sturdy and tough. And they were proud of not being white, the same way a lot of Americans and Englishmen—and, evidently, Dutchmen—were proud because they were.

Perhaps because Orsatti had had a lot of shipboard duty, his feel for what the fleet at Surabaya would do next was pretty good. They headed north two days later. Pete wondered if word had come in that Japanese landing forces were on the way. No one said so—but then, nobody ever told the guys who would do the fighting and dying any more than they absolutely had to know. Sometimes not even that.

Then the destroyers steamed away and left the light cruisers behind. "Something's goin' on," Orsatti opined.

"You oughta be a detective—a private dick, like," Pete told him, which won another dirty look. They were practicing at the five-inch gun, uneasily aware that the practice could turn real any second. Look-outs constantly eyed the skies. Planes that appeared out in the middle of the ocean would be Japanese. Did the enemy fleet have carriers along? They'd struck at Hawaii, but that hadn't gone so well as they would have liked. Manila, unfortunately, proved a different story.

Night fell. The gun crews were on watch and watch, so Pete's sleep got ruined. He gulped hot coffee to keep his eyes open. He wasn't the only one. Drinking java near Java was . . . almost funny.

The *Boise* sliced through the Java Sea, kicking up a phosphorescent bow wave and wake. If any Japanese subs were in the neighborhood . . . *With any luck at all, we're going too fast for 'em,* Pete thought, yawning. He wasn't used to sack time chopped into little bits. Yeah, it had been too long.

"Our destroyers are in contact with enemy warships and transports off Borneo," the intercom blared in harsh, metallic tones. "They are making torpedo runs at the transports."

Pete waited to hear reports of Jap freighters blown to smithereens, and he wasn't the only one. But the intercom stayed quiet after that. Little by little, he realized the silence wasn't a good sign. So did the other leathernecks on the gun crew. Their high spirits faded.

The sun came up within a few minutes of 0600, as it always did in these waters. A plane buzzed down out of the north to look over the al-lied fleet. Orders came to fire at it. All the antiaircraft guns on the *Boise* roared together. The bursts didn't come close to reaching the plane. It saw what it wanted to see and flew away. And nobody said another word about the destroyers and what they might be doing—or what might have been done to them. Pete kept his mouth shut along with everyone else. But he knew damn well that wasn't a good sign.

A HORSE SLOGGED up a road pulling a *panje* wagon after it. The wagon had tall wheels and an almost boat-shaped bottom. Russian peasants had—and needed—plenty of experience building wagons that could plow through even the thickest mud.

Thaw's early this year, Ivan Kuchkov thought. More freezes would probably come, but little by little the winter snowfall would melt and soak into the ground. For the next four to six weeks, nobody would go anywhere very fast. No one in his right mind would order any major actions during the *rasputitsa,* because action just bogged down in the mud.

The Poles knew as much about the *rasputitsa,* the mud time, as their Russian neighbors. The Germans had fought in the East last year and during the last war, so they knew something. Ivan had heard they knew enough to steal as many *panje* wagons as they could, anyhow. Their trucks got stuck in the muck just like everybody else's.

What the Germans' French and English lackeys knew . . . Kuchkov's lips skinned back from his teeth in a nasty grin. He suspected the Red Army would teach them a few lessons. He also suspected they wouldn't enjoy the instruction. The few schoolmasters Kuchkov had known used a switch to make sure their teaching sank in. The Red Army had a bigger switch than even the meanest, most brutal village schoolmaster, and could swing it harder.

Lieutenant Obolensky squelched up. Kuchkov pretended not to see him. It was at least possible that Obolensky needed to talk to somebody else in the squad. Avram, maybe; the nervous little Jew had his fingers in a million different pies. Ivan wouldn't have been surprised if he was NKVD.

But no. Obolensky looked around till he spotted Kuchkov. "Come here a moment, Sergeant," he said.

"I serve the Soviet Union, Comrade Lieutenant!" That was never the wrong answer. Kuchkov added a salute. The mud tried to suck off his boots as he made his way over to the junior officer. When he got there, he stood and waited. Let Obolensky show his cards.

The lieutenant also waited, but he was the one who spoke first: "What shape is your squad in, Sergeant?" Ivan smiled to himself. Obolensky was an educated guy, a city guy—his attitude, his accent, his very way of standing all said as much. No way in hell he could outstubborn or outwait a man from a village where the creek was the only running water . . . when it wasn't frozen, anyhow.

"Well, sir, we're kinda fucked. We lost three guys taking that last village from those Nazi dicks." No, Ivan neither knew nor cared what was regular Russian and what was *mat*. "We got one back—cocksucking bullet only grazed the bitch, y'know? And we got a replacement, but the pussy's so green we'd be better off without him. So yeah, we're fucked."

To his surprise, Lieutenant Obolensky smiled. "You sound just like every other sergeant in charge of a squad. Maybe the Red Air Force isn't so different from the Red Army after all."

Kuchkov was convinced the Red Air Force was a damn sight better than the Red Army. No one would ever have accused him of being bright, but he had enough animal cunning to know saying so would only get him in deeper. Deeper in what? He didn't know that, either, and he wasn't interested in finding out. He waited some more. Maybe Obolensky would go away and pick some other squad for whatever shitty job he had in mind.

Maybe pigs had wings. Not around here, though. The lieutenant pointed west, toward—no past—the birch and pine woods over there. "You know the Fascists are set up in the fields beyond the trees."

"Uh-huh." Kuchkov only nodded. The Germans had dug in as well as they could while the ground was frozen. Now they had to be shoring up their trenches with boards and sticks and twigs and straw and anything else they could grab. The mud would ooze through anyway. It sure did here.

"Our battalion has orders to shift them," Obolensky said.

"Happy fucking day, sir!" Kuchkov said. "The whoremongers'll have machine guns set up and waiting for us." German machine guns scared the piss out of him, and he wasn't ashamed to admit it.

"We have orders," Obolensky repeated in a voice like doom. "This company is on the right wing. I am going to place your squad as the last feather on the wing. You will try to outflank the Nazi position and roll it up."

"What? With one little piss-dribble of a squad?" Ivan burst out. Obolensky just looked at him. He made himself nod and salute. Sometimes you got stuck with it. And things could have been worse. He'd feared the lieutenant would send his squad in ahead of everybody else. If that wasn't suicide . . . then this might be.

He gave his men the news. "Oh, boy," Avram said, and then, *"Gevalt."* Talking like a German was liable to get him killed, but sometimes he did it anyway. He took off his submachine gun's drum magazine and started cleaning the works. Anything he could keep from going wrong, he would. The trouble was, you couldn't keep everything from going wrong.

They sneaked through the woods during the night. As black began to yield to gray, Ivan and everybody else gulped a hundred grams of vodka. It made him fierce. It also made him even more what-the-fuck than he had been before.

There was supposed to be an artillery barrage before the attack went in. Red Army artillery was usually reliable. Not today. A few mortar rounds woke up the Fritzes without hurting them much. They started yelling. A machine gun and a few rifles fired at nothing.

"Gevalt," Avram said again. Kuchkov's mouth was dry. The Nazis would be waiting now. No chance in hell to catch them by surprise. Kilometers back of the line, some fat Russian colonel was probably eating out his secretary's twat instead of telling the 105s to get busy.

No help for it. Yelling *"Urra!"*, the battalion burst out of the woods and rushed the German trenches. Some men wore snow smocks; some didn't. Some smocks were clean and white; some weren't. With slushy snow dappling the mud, the mixture camouflaged the Russians as well as any more rigid scheme would have.

The Germans opened up on them, of course. Facing machine-gun fire, camouflage hardly mattered. Either a bullet got you or it didn't. All luck, either way. Something tugged at Kuchkov's left sleeve. When he looked down, he found the leather of his flying suit had a new rip. But he didn't hurt and he wasn't bleeding, so he ran on.

A potato-masher grenade flew out of the forwardmost German trench, and then another one. Ivan dove for the mud. His tunic would never camouflage him against snow again, but all the fragments went over him and none into him. He yanked the pin from his own egg grenade and chucked it at the Germans from his knees. Then he scrambled up and dashed forward again.

Despite the grenade, a German in a whitewashed helmet popped up and fired a Mauser at him from point-blank range. As often happened in the rage and terror of combat, the Fritz missed. Kuchkov gave him a burst from the PPD before he could work the bolt for his next shot. It was like spraying a hose—you didn't have to be a sniper to get two or three hits. The German toppled with a groan, his tunic front all over blood.

"Come on!" Ivan yelled to his men still on their feet. "Let's clean out these motherfucking cunts!" He jumped down into the zigzagging Nazi trench. Grenades and submachine guns were the right tools for the job.

A German dropped his rifle and threw up his hands. "*Kamerad!*" he squealed, terror on his face. Kuchkov gave him a burst, too. Considering what happened to prisoners, he might have done the fellow a favor. Chances were he would have shot him anyway, though.

The Fritzes had been thinner on the ground than he expected. They pulled back in good order. What was left of the Red Army battalion began looting the corpses left behind in their trenches. The Russians had taken a devil of a lot of casualties themselves to win this hectare of blood and mud. Was it worth them? Kuchkov had no idea. He was busy spreading meat paste from a dead German's tinfoil tube onto a chunk of black bread. *If the bastards eat like this all the time, no wonder they're so fucking tough,* he thought, and squeezed the tube for more.

WHEN SAMUEL GOLDMAN came home from his laborer's job, unusual excitement lit his gray-stubbled face. (No one in Germany had enough soap, and Jews' rations were smaller than Aryans'. He didn't shave very often.) "What's up, Father?" Sarah asked. "Something is—I can see it in your eyes."

"You're right," he said. "They've finally gone and arrested the Bishop of Münster. The *Gestapo* took him away in an armored car."

"Oh. Oh, my," Sarah said. "He's been asking for it, hasn't he?"

"Just a little bit," Father answered. "I knew him—not well, but I knew him—back in the days when knowing a Jew didn't destroy someone's reputation. Clemens August von Galen is a proud, stiff-necked man."

"With a name like that, he's an aristocrat, too," Sarah said.

"Right again," her father agreed. "He's not the kind to be happy when a jumped-up shoe salesman or whatever tells him what to do. You can hear that in every sermon he preaches—well, every sermon that doesn't have to do with foreign policy, I mean."

Sarah nodded. Hardly a German had ever had a good word to say for the vengeful Treaty of Versailles. She hadn't herself, back when she was a kid before the Nazis took over. Yes, she'd partly been parroting her parents, but even so. . . .

Maybe Bishop von Galen could forgive the war, which was designed not least to give Germany her proper place once more. But he couldn't forgive the Nazis for confiscating church buildings, for expelling members of religious orders from the *Reich,* or for their program of what they called mercy killings. He said so, loudly, from the pulpit. After RAF planes bombed Münster, he delivered a sermon on loving one's enemies.

Not a word of that, of course, got into the local newspapers. Radio broadcasts kept quiet about it, too. The regime controlled every official news source. It got around all the same. People who heard Bishop von Galen speak spread word of what he said. People who heard them spread it wider. Everyone in town knew the bishop and the Nazis were on a collision course.

"What will happen now?" Sarah asked.

"They'll keep him in jail, or else they'll kill him," Father said. "I don't think they'll kill him right away. They have other ways to put the screws to him. He has a brother—Franz, I think his name is. The *Gestapo*'s already grabbed other priests from the diocese."

"Did they hope Bishop von Galen would take a hint?" Sarah inquired.

Samuel Goldman beamed at her. He might be tired, but he was also proud. "How did you get so grown-up when I wasn't looking?" he said.

Sarah made a rude noise. Her father laughed but went on, "Yes, I'm sure they did hope he'd do that. But if he were the kind of man who took those hints, he wouldn't be the kind of man who preached those sermons."

That made sense to Sarah. Father usually made sense to her, except for his hopeless, unrequited love affair with being a real German. She found the only question she could think of that really mattered: "What happens next? Do people let the Nazis get away with it?"

"I don't know. I don't think anyone else does, either," he said slowly. "But I'll tell you this: we heard they'd arrested von Galen about an hour before quitting time, and the whole labor gang was furious. Not just Catholics. Everyone. The men were cussing out the *Gestapo* like you wouldn't believe. When I was walking home"—Jews couldn't use buses or trams—"I heard more people up in arms about it, too."

"What will they do? Rally in front of the *Rathaus*?" Sarah laughed at the idea. "That would just give the blackshirts the chance to arrest all of them at once."

"You might be surprised," her father said. "The Catholic Church still has some clout, and it's always been more leery of the Nazis than most Protestant churches were. No 'German Christians' among the Catholics, or not many, anyhow." He screwed up his face.

So did Sarah. So-called German Christians believed Nazi ideals were compatible with those of Jesus. As far as she could see, that was well on the way toward being like the Red Queen in *Alice in Wonderland,* who made a habit of believing two impossible things every day before breakfast. But German Christians dominated most Protestant denominations these days. Didn't you also believe in impossibilities if you thought you could tell the Nazis no and get away with it?

"Where's your mother?" Samuel Goldman asked. "Now I'll have to tell the story twice."

"She's out shopping." Sarah's voice was sour. Jews could only do it at the very end of the day, when everyone else had already had the chance to pick over the little in the stores. Sarah added, "I was peeling potatoes when I heard you come in."

Her father sighed. "Bad food, and not enough of it." He flipped his hand up and down. "It's not your fault. I know it's not. You and mother do everything anyone could with what the *Reich* lets us have."

"That's not enough, either."

"If it were, the *Reich* wouldn't let us have it," Father said.

He paused then. Sarah could read his mind. He was looking for the best—or worst—way to make a pun about how the *Reich* really wanted to let them have it. He did things like that. But before he could this time, the front door opened behind him. He looked absurdly affronted as he half turned on his good leg, as if Mother had squashed his line on purpose.

Hanna Goldman hadn't, of course. Her little two-wheeled collapsible wire shopping cart was almost as empty as it had been when she set out. Some sorry turnips, some insect-nibbled greens . . . That kind of stuff might have done for fattening hogs. People just got thinner on it, as Sarah had sad reason to know.

But Mother's jade-green eyes snapped with excitement. "They've arrested Bishop von Galen!" she exclaimed.

"We knew that." By the deflationary way Father said it, he *was* miffed he hadn't got to make his horrible pun.

Mother refused to be deflated. "Did you know there's a great big crowd out in front of the cathedral? Did you know they're yelling at the police and the blackshirts, and throwing things at them, too?"

"*Der Herr Gott im Himmel!*" Father burst out. Sarah felt the same way. Germans mostly didn't do such things. She'd heard that, when machine guns opened up on demonstrators in the mad Berlin of 1919, the crowd fled across a park to escape the deadly fire—but people obeyed the KEEP OFF THE GRASS! signs while they ran for their lives.

"It's true. I saw the edges of it. I got away from there as fast as I could afterward," Mother said. "I didn't want to wait till the blackshirts started shooting—and I didn't want to give them any reason to arrest a Jew, either."

"If each of us would have tried to take one of those pigdogs with him when they came for him . . ." For a moment, Father looked and sounded young and ferocious, the way he would have in the trenches in the last war. But then he sighed and shook his head and went back to his familiar self. "The Nazis wouldn't care. They'd thank us for handing them an excuse to murder us all."

"They can't murder everyone out by the cathedral," Mother said.

Distant gunfire seemed to give her the lie. Even more faintly, Sarah heard screams and shrieks and shouts. She supposed they'd been going on before, but she hadn't been able to make them out. She could now. People made more noise when bullets snarled past—or when they struck home.

"They'll blame the Communists for this," Father predicted.

"There aren't many Catholic Communists," Sarah pointed out.

"They won't care," Samuel Goldman said. "Outside agitators, they'll call them, and they'll say von Galen was working with them." He spread his callused hands. "I mean, otherwise they'd have to blame themselves, and what are the odds of that?"

Chapter 6

oming back into port should have been a relief for Julius Lemp and
the rest of the U-30's crew. Most of the time, it was. Coming back
meant they'd made it through another patrol. RAF bombs wouldn't
sink them. Russian shells wouldn't tear through the U-boat's thin steel
hide and send it to the bottom. Slow-crawling crabs wouldn't pick out
Lemp's bulging dead eyes with their claws . . . this time.

The men could shave their beards. They could take proper showers.
They could eat food that didn't come out of tins. They could go into
town and drink and pick up barmaids and brawl. They could walk off
by themselves, without someone else always at their elbow. Or they
could lie on real mattresses and sleep and sleep.

It was wonderful. Most of the time.

Every once in a while, politics got in the way. And politics, in the
Reich, turned bloody in a hurry. They'd just come back in to Wilhelmshaven when the generals tried to topple the *Führer.* You didn't want to
hear machine-gun fire at the edge of the base, especially when you
weren't sure who was shooting at whom or why.

Now they were in Kiel—at the edge of the Baltic rather than the

North Sea—and politics was rearing its ugly head again. Everyone should have been proud of them for sinking the destroyer and two Soviet freighters on their latest patrol. If Lemp's superiors were, they had a gift for hiding their enthusiasm.

"*Ja, ja.* Well done, I am sure," said the graying *Kapitän zur See* who heard Lemp's first report. The bare bulb above the senior officer's desk gleamed off the four gold stripes on his cuffs. He scribbled a note or two, but only a note or two. "No doubt your log gives the full details."

If he wasn't a distracted man, Lemp had never seen one. "Yes, sir," he said.

The captain looked up and seemed surprised to find him still there. "Do you require something else, uh, Lemp?" He had to remind himself who the squirt in front of him was. Considering some of the things that had happened to Lemp, he didn't know whether to be relieved or alarmed—for better and for worse, he hadn't had the kind of career that lent itself to obscurity.

"Require? No, sir. Of course not, sir." Lemp lied with great sincerity, as a junior sometimes had to do with a superior. "But if it's not too much trouble, sir, I would like to have some idea of what's going on."

He might have stuck the *Kapitän zur See* with a pin. "What makes you think anything out of the ordinary is going on?" the older man demanded. Lemp didn't answer; he didn't think that needed an answer. The four-striper's sigh said he really didn't, either. He lit a cigarette. It was only stalling, and he and Lemp both knew it. His sigh sent a stream of smoke up toward the lightbulb. "Tell me, Lemp—what is your religion?"

"My religion, sir?" The U-boat skipper would have been more surprised had the captain asked him which position he most fancied in bed, but not much more surprised. "I'm a Lutheran, sir, but I haven't been to church in a while."

The senior officer blew out more smoke, this time in obvious relief. "Well, I could say the same thing. As a matter of fact, I did say the same thing to my own superiors the other day."

Lemp had to remind himself that even an exalted *Kapitän zur See* had men to whom he needed to answer. "Why on earth did they ask you, sir?" he said, in lieu of *Why on earth are you asking me?*

A brief spark in the captain's gray eyes said he also heard the question behind the question. "There are certain . . . advantages to being away at sea, tending to the *Reich*'s business," he replied. "You won't have heard that the Catholics are, mm, well, some of them are, mm, unhappy about the way things are going."

"Sir?" Lemp said, this time in lieu of *What the devil are you talking about?*

"It's the Bishop of Münster's fault," the four-striper said. He sounded like a man trying to convince himself. Or that could have been Lemp's imagination, but he didn't think so. The answer also explained next to nothing. The *Kapitän zur See* must have realized as much. He stubbed out the cigarette with a quick, savage motion. "He spoke out against the *Führer*'s policy. From the pulpit. Repeatedly. And so the security services decided they had no choice but to take him into custody."

"I . . . see," Lemp said slowly. You needed nerve to do something like that. You needed to have your head examined, was what you really needed.

"There are . . . demonstrations of unhappiness about this here and there in the *Vaterland*," the *Kapitän zur See* said. "This is why I asked you, you understand."

"*Aber natürlich,*" Lemp said, which seemed safe enough. Demonstrations of unhappiness? What was going on in Germany? Was the whole country bubbling like a pot of stew forgotten on the stove? He wouldn't have been surprised. You couldn't just go arresting bishops. These weren't the Middle Ages, after all. But the blackshirts didn't seem to care. They were Hitler's hounds. Do something they didn't like and they'd bite.

"So that's where we are. That's why passes into town are limited," the *Kapitän zur See* said. Schleswig-Holstein had been Danish till a lifetime before, and was solidly Lutheran. Even so . . . "The less trouble we stir up, the better for everyone."

"The men won't like being restricted to base, sir," Lemp said. As the other officer had to know, that was an understatement.

"Yes? And so?" The *Kapitän zur See* sent him a hooded look. "They aren't the only crew here, you know."

"*Jawohl, mein Herr.*" Lemp knew a losing fight when he saw one. "I'll tell them what they need to understand." He rose, saluted, and got out of the four-striper's office as fast as he could.

By the time he returned to the barracks, the U-30's crew had already found that next to none of them would be able to go into town. They weren't happy about it, which was putting things mildly. "What, the shitheads don't think we deserve to blow off steam? They can blow it out their assholes, is what they can do." That was Paul, the helmsman—a chief petty officer, and as steady a man as Lemp had ever known. If he was within shouting distance of mutiny, the rest of the submariners had to be even closer.

Lemp spread his hands in what looked like apology, even though U-boat skippers weren't in the habit of apologizing to their men. "There's nothing I can do about it, friends," he said. "It's politics, is what it is." He summarized what the *Kapitän zur See* had told him. He wouldn't have been surprised if the senior officer didn't want ratings to know such things. Well, too damn bad for him if he didn't.

Some of the sailors, naturally, were Catholics. Some were convinced Nazis. The largest number cared little for religion or politics. "So this bullshit is what's keeping us confined to base?" one of them said. "That's nothing but *Quatsch*. If we want to get into fights, we've got better things to brawl about than some stupid, loudmouthed bishop."

"Do we?" another sailor said. "The government shouldn't tell us how to be religious. They fought wars about that back in the old days."

"A bishop's got no business telling government what to do, either," the first man retorted. "They fought wars about that in the old days, too." By the way the two ratings glared at each other, they were both ready to square off on the spot. By the way their friends shifted toward one or the other, everybody knew which side of the fence he stood on.

"That will be enough of that," Lemp said sternly. "As you were, all of you." For a bad couple of seconds, he didn't think they'd listen to him. That was the worst feeling an officer could get. Obedience sprang from consent, no matter how much the military tried to conceal that. When men stopped listening to their leaders . . . You got the end of 1918 all over again. No German in his right mind wanted to repeat that long fall into chaos.

But then one of the ratings said, "Ah, fuck it. It's got nothing to do with crewmates." After a moment, the other man nodded. Tension left the barracks hall like water leaving a dive chamber when a U-boat surfaced. The rating went on, "If we can't go into town, the least they could do would be to bring some broads onto the base and set up a brothel here." All the sailors nodded in unison to that.

It seemed like a good idea to Julius Lemp, too. "I'll see what I can do," he promised, and headed back toward the *Kapitän zur See*'s office. A few girls, even homely ones who smelled of onions, would go a long way toward making sure the men remembered what they were supposed to be doing and why. They'd also go a long way toward making sure the men remembered their superiors cared about them. And that would help them remember what they should be doing and why, too.

SOME OF THE STREETS in Bialystok had trees growing alongside them. The locals bragged about their tree-lined boulevards, and said they made Bialystok just like Paris. Only a bunch of provincial Poles and Jews could imagine that a Polish provincial town was anything like Paris, but try and tell them that.

Hans-Ulrich Rudel didn't. For one thing, life was too short. For another, he'd never been to Paris himself. He'd bombed the place when the *Wehrmacht* fought its way to the suburbs, but that wasn't the same thing. He'd promised himself leave in the French capital after it fell, but it didn't.

So here he was two years later, on leave in Bialystok instead. At the moment, the trees were bare-branched, even skeletal. But the leaf buds were starting to swell. Spring was on the way. Before long, Bialystok would be green again, even if not Parisian.

Signs on shops and eateries were in incomprehensible Polish and just as incomprehensible Yiddish. The one had the right alphabet but alien words, the other pretty much familiar words in an alien script. Both added up to gibberish for him.

But he'd come here before, often enough to know where he was going from the train station. If he had got lost, spoken Yiddish made far more sense to him than the written kind, and Bialystok was full of Jews. He could have asked one of them. These days, the town also had its share of chain dogs—German *Feldgendarmerie,* their gorgets of office hung around their necks from chains. He was glad he didn't need to talk to them. The less he had to do with them, the better.

A drunk Pole reeled out of a tavern. That would have been a cliché, except the Pole, in a uniform of dark, greenish khaki, was arm in arm with an equally plastered German in *Feldgrau.* They were both murdering the same tune, each in his own language. Drunken Germans weren't such a cliché, which didn't mean Hans-Ulrich hadn't seen his share of them and then some.

As a matter of fact, he was heading for a tavern himself, though not this one. Another block up from the station, half a block over . . . He nodded to himself. He recognized the Polish sign out front, even if it made no sense to him. He walked in. The place smelled of tobacco and sweat and beer and fried food—and stale piss from the jakes out back.

Poles and Germans drank together here, too. So did Jews and Germans, which would have been unimaginable back in the *Reich.* The Poles didn't like their Jews, but they didn't hit them with the same legal restrictions the Germans did. Maybe they couldn't; one person in ten in Poland was a Jew, only one in a hundred in Germany. *Wehrmacht* personnel here had orders to conform to local customs and laws.

A short, swarthy barmaid sidled up to Hans-Ulrich. She spoke in throaty Yiddish: "You may as well sit down, not that the boss'll make a zloty off you if you keep on drinking tea."

"Hello, Sofia. Won't you at least tell me you're glad to see me?" Rudel didn't grab her or kiss her in public. She didn't like that. Did she go with other men while he was in the East fighting the war? If she did, he'd never heard about it. The way things were these days, that would do.

"I'm at least glad to see you," she answered, deadpan. She wasn't exactly a Jew; she had a Polish father, which in the *Reich*'s classification scheme made her a *Mischling* first class. But she thought of herself as Jewish, and she was snippy like a Jew. Back in Germany, Hans-Ulrich would have endangered his career by having anything to do with her. He could get away with it here—could, and did.

She took him to a corner and brought him a glass of tea. She found his teetotaling as funny as most of his service comrades did. She was also as nervous about seeing a German—and a Nazi Party member at that—as he was about going with a Jewess. In bed, everything was fine. The rest of the time . . . Hans-Ulrich sometimes thought they came from different planets, not just different countries.

Sofia was well informed about his planet, though. Along with the sweet, milkless tea, she gave him a mocking grin. "So even the Catholics in Germany say Hitler can't get away with some of the stuff he's trying to pull?" she said.

As a Lutheran minister's son, his opinion of Catholics had never been high. "A lot of that is just enemy propaganda," he said. None of it had come over the German radio or appeared in any army or *Luftwaffe* newspaper. That didn't mean he hadn't heard a few things, or more than a few. It did mean he wasn't obliged to believe them—not officially, and not when Sofia tried to rub his nose in them.

She quirked a dark eyebrow. "Well, if you say so," she answered, which meant she wasn't obliged to believe him, either. She went on, "The big switch was good for something, anyhow. I got a card from my mother the other day, from Palestine."

While England and Germany were at war, mail from Palestine—a British League of Nations mandate—didn't travel to Poland because it was friendly to Germany. Now that England had joined the crusade against Bolshevism, things moved more freely. "There's rather more to it than that, you know," he said stiffly. He often was more literal-minded than might have been good for him. Sofia enjoyed getting under his skin. As if having a mother who felt strongly enough about being Jewish to go to Palestine after the Pole she'd married (a drunkard, if you listened to Sofia) walked out weren't enough!

"If you say so," Sofia repeated. Big things—like who would win the war—meant little to her. Or, if they did, she wouldn't let on. A small thing—like getting a card from her mother after a long silence—counted for more.

"I think you're trying to drive me crazy," Hans-Ulrich said.

"It would be a short drive," she retorted, which made him regret—not for the first time—getting into a battle of words with her. He was a good flyer, not such a great talker. But everybody knew Jews were born talking, and in that Sofia took after her mother. Rudel assumed as much, anyhow, without even thinking about it.

He tried to change the subject: "What time do you get off today?"

"Why? What have you got in mind?" She didn't just answer a question with another question. She answered one with two.

"Whatever you want, of course," Hans-Ulrich said. Bialystok's nightlife consisted of a few movie houses, a dance hall or two, and a Yiddish theater. Even with trees lining the streets, Paris it was not.

Sofia laughed raucously. "Whatever *you* want, you mean. And what else does a man ever want?"

Rudel's ears heated. "Well, what if I do? If I didn't, you'd think I was sleeping with somebody else, and you'd give me trouble on account of that."

"I wouldn't give you trouble. I'd drop you like a grenade. No—I'd throw you like a grenade." She cocked her head to one side. "You mean you don't visit the officers' whorehouse? I'm sure they've set one up somewhere not far from you. They always do things like that, don't they?"

As a matter of fact, they did. An officers' brothel—and one for other ranks—operated in a village a couple of kilometers from the airstrip. Hans-Ulrich knew Sergeant Dieselhorst had visited the one for enlisted men. He hadn't called at the officers' establishment. That gave his fellow flyers one more reason to think he was strange, though they knew about Sofia and didn't think he was a fairy.

"The girls there would just be doing it because they were doing it," he said slowly, trying to put what he thought into words. "They wouldn't be doing it because they wanted to do it with me."

And I do? He waited for the barmaid's jeers. Rather to his surprise, it didn't come. She eyed him as if she were seeing him for the first time. "That matters to you?"

"Yes, it matters to me." He was in his midtwenties. He often risked his life several times a day. He gave Sofia a crooked grin. "Well, most of the time, anyhow."

He wondered if she'd get mad. Instead, he startled a laugh out of her. "You'd better watch yourself. If you aren't careful, you'll make me think you're honest."

Hans-Ulrich prided himself on his honesty—he *was* a pastor's son.

He started to get angry, then realized she was teasing him. "You . . ." he said, more or less fondly.

She grinned at him, altogether unrepentant. "Did you expect anything different?" Before he could answer, the soldiers at another table yelled for her to fetch them another round of drinks. She fluttered her fingers at him and hurried away. Hans-Ulrich realized she never had told him when she got off. How much tea would he soak up before she finally did? He wasn't even that fond of tea. But he was fond of Sofia, and so he waited and ordered glass after glass.

ALISTAIR WALSH'S PRINCIPAL USE to the Conservative conspirators against Sir Horace Wilson's alliance with the *Reich* was that he knew soldiers. Some of them had put on the uniform after the Nazis invaded Czechoslovakia, but he'd worn it for more than twenty years—for his whole adult life, till his political unreliability led him to resign from the service and led the army to accept his resignation.

So he knew soldiers in ways the toffs didn't. And he also knew soldiers—literally. At one time or another between the wars, he'd served under most of England's prominent and high-ranking officers. Senior officers tended to remember senior noncoms. Those long-serving veterans were the army's backbone. They counted for more in the scheme of things than lieutenants and captains and sometimes even majors because they knew all the things the junior officers were just learning—and more besides, especially if you listened to them.

And Walsh could do things in an unofficial capacity that would have raised eyebrows—to say nothing of hackles—had an MP gone about them. If the conspirators talked to a general, for instance, Sir Horace and his none too merry men would naturally suspect them of skullduggery. The Prime Minister and his henchmen would be right, too.

But if Alistair Walsh called on General Archibald Wavell—well, so what? He was only an out-to-pasture underofficer. For all Scotland Yard could prove, he was asking for a job, or maybe a loan.

That was also true for all General Wavell knew. He might not have had any idea of the company Walsh was keeping these days. He did know who Walsh was, though, and did agree to meet him at General Staff headquarters. In baggy civilian tweeds, Walsh felt dreadfully out of place in that sanctum of creased khaki, gleaming brass tunic buttons, shoulder straps, and swarms of the red collar tabs that showed officers of colonel's rank and above. In uniform himself, he would have had to salute till his shoulder ached. As things were, his arm kept twitching as he fought down the conditioned reflex again and again.

Wavell was an erect, thin-faced man in his early fifties. "I can give you fifteen minutes, Walsh," he said as he closed his office door to let them talk privately. Scotland Yard might be able to plant microphones in many different places, Walsh judged, but not here.

"Thank you, sir," the ex-serviceman said. "I appreciate it, and so do my friends."

One of Wavell's bushy eyebrows rose an eighth of an inch. "Your . . . friends?" He let the word hang in the air. By the look on his face, he might have taken a bite of fish that was slightly off.

"Yes, sir," Walsh said stolidly. "You may or may not have heard I was the bloke who had the bad luck to bring in Rudolf Hess after he parachuted from his Messerschmitt 110."

"Were you, now?" The general's gaze sharpened. "Yes, that's right. You were. I remember seeing the report, now you remind me of it. And so?"

"And so I wish I'd had a pistol with me and plugged him instead," Walsh answered. "Then maybe we wouldn't be in bed with Hitler now. My friends"—he deliberately reused the word—"still wish we weren't."

Wavell snorted. "They aren't the only ones, I'm sure." But he checked himself. "It's up to the politicians to set policy, of course. The military's here to back their play when the usual peacetime methods fail."

"Invading Russia, sir?" Walsh said. "Isn't that going a bit far?"

"If your friends are of the pink persuasion, Walsh, I don't think we have much more to say to each other." Twenty degrees of frost crisped up Wavell's voice.

"They're Tories almost to a man. Churchill was one of them, till he met that Bentley," Walsh replied. Winston Churchill hated the idea of helping Hitler, not that Neville Chamberlain cared a farthing what Churchill thought. People still wondered whether the rich young man behind the wheel of the auto that ran Churchill down was truly as drunk as the bobbies claimed.

"That was a bad business," Wavell said quietly, so he might have been one of those wondering people. He studied Walsh. "So you're in with that lot, are you? No, they're not pinks, no doubt of that."

"I am, sir. It seems the best way to honor Churchill's memory—and, to my mind, he was dead right about the Nazis." Walsh hadn't used the phrase with malice aforethought. But he quite fancied it once it was out of his mouth. "Dead right," he repeated.

"I can't imagine what you or your friends expect me to do about it, though," Wavell said. "This isn't Argentina or Brazil or one of those places. The army doesn't interfere in politics here. It would be unthinkable."

Walsh just sat there and waited. If General Wavell was talking about it, he was thinking about it. What he was thinking about it . . . Walsh would discover in due course.

The general glanced at his wristwatch. "Well," he said with forced briskness, "I'm afraid I've given you all the time I can spare at present. There *is* a war on, you know, and someone does have to run it, or at any rate to try."

"Certainly, sir." Walsh got to his feet. "Is there anything you'd particularly like me to tell my friends?"

"Tell them . . . Tell them they don't know what they're playing at, dammit."

"I think they do, sir. I think it's the Prime Minister and his lot who've gone off the rails, not these other fellows."

"You can say that. You've taken off the uniform. No, I don't hold it against you—no denying you had your reasons," Wavell said. "But I still wear it. If I were to speak in the same fashion, or to act in addition to speaking, it would be treason, nothing less."

"General, I don't know anything about that," said Walsh, who knew far more about it than he'd dreamt he would before he watched that lone parachutist descend on the Scottish field. Taking a deep breath, he continued, "I do know we can't go on the way we're going. It would ruin the country forever. Anything would be better, anything at all. Or do you think I'm wrong?"

"I think—" Wavell broke off, shaking his head like a horse pestered by gnats. "I think you'd best go, Walsh, is what I think. And deliver my message to your associates."

Walsh did, at a pub not far from Parliament. They kept no favorite table: that would have made it too easy for Scotland Yard, or perhaps the PM's less savory associates, to arrange to listen in. Walsh didn't think they could bug every table in the place. The noise from the rest of the crowd—more politicos, solicitors, newspapermen, and other such riffraff—drowned out the conspirators' conversations. He hoped like blazes it did, anyhow.

Ronald Cartland slammed his pint mug down on the tabletop in disgust when Walsh finished. It wasn't empty; some best bitter slashed out. "Good Lord!" the MP exclaimed. "The man has no more spine than an eclair! One of you, Walsh, is worth a thousand of him."

Cartland had volunteered for service when the war broke out, and fought in France as a subaltern. That, to Walsh's mind, gave his opinions weight and made his praise doubly warming. But Walsh thought his dismissal of General Wavell was premature. "I don't know about that, sir," he said. "He didn't have the military police arrest me for treason, the way he might have done. He didn't even chuck me out of his office. He listened to me. He may not be ready to move yet, but he doesn't half fancy the way things are heading."

"Who in his right mind would?" said Bobbity Cranford, another leader of the anti-alliance crowd. "But if he listened to you, old man, he'd better watch out for Bentleys the next time he crosses the road."

That produced a considerable silence around the table. Walsh broke it by loudly calling to a barmaid to fill up his pint again. He needed the fresh mug. Cranford had reminded him they weren't playing a game here, nor was the government. If it felt itself seriously threatened, it would lash out. Anyone who didn't believe that had only to remember Winston Churchill.

LUC HARCOURT UNSLUNG his rifle and carried it instead of leaving it on his shoulder. His regiment was heading up to the front again, and he wanted to be ready if they ran into any Russians. Besides, fronts here were far more porous than they'd been in France. Some enemy soldiers were bound to have leaked through what was supposed to be the line.

His boots squelched as he tramped up the road, but only a little. The mud didn't try to pull off his footgear, as it would have a couple of weeks earlier. Pretty soon, both sides would be able to start moving again. There were prospects Luc relished more.

Up ahead, Lieutenant Demange was singing obscene lyrics to the tune of a peasant song about spring. Luc had known Demange since before the shooting started. Not many others from the old company survived, and even fewer in one piece. Knowing Demange as he did, Luc also knew those foul verses were a way for the reluctantly promoted officer to hide his own nerves about what lay ahead.

Anyone who didn't know Demange so well would assume he owned no nerves. Luc had, for a long time. But underneath the chrome-steel *salaud* lay a human being. *A nasty human being, but even so,* Luc thought.

One thing Demange didn't believe in was taking needless chances; a soldier had to take too many that were necessary. He carried a rifle instead of the more usual and less useful officer's pistol. And he *carried* it, like Luc. He was ready for anything. And things needed to be ready for him.

"Halt! Who goes there?" a sentry called in nervous, German-accented French. "Give the countersign!"

"Your mother on a pogo stick," Demange snarled. He might be here, but he still despised the *Boches.*

"*Qu'est-ce-que vous dites?*" the sentry said: a reasonable enough question. He added, "Give the countersign, or I fire!"

Demange did, which confirmed Luc's thought about not taking chances he didn't have to. The German passed him and the men he led. Well, why not? They were doing some of Hitler's work so the rest of the Fritzes wouldn't have to.

The trench system was well enough organized and shored up to show the lines hadn't moved much for a while. What with the way Russia turned to mud soup as the snow melted, the lines couldn't very well move.

Which didn't mean the Reds were asleep behind their rusting barbed wire. The regiment hadn't been in place for half an hour before an Ivan with a megaphone shouted at them in much better French than the German sentry spoke: "Here they are again—Colonel Eluard's little darlings."

How did the bastard know? Luc wouldn't have thought any of the handful of Russian peasants he'd seen had paid the least attention to the Frenchmen tramping up to the front. He really wouldn't have thought they could tell one regiment from another. And he *really* wouldn't have thought that, even if they could, they'd be able to pass the word on to their countrymen so fast.

That only went to show how much he knew. With noxious good cheer, the French-speaking Russian went on, "Now that you're back, we should welcome you the way you deserve!"

"Jump for the bombproofs, boys!" Demange shouted, a good twenty seconds before mortar bombs started raining down on the trenches.

His instincts saved lives. Luc had already curled up in a place where fragments couldn't get him when the shooting started. But not everybody was so lucky. Machine guns and German artillery kept the Russians at bay. Stretcher-bearers hauled off the wounded Frenchmen.

"Those fucking stovepipes are bad news," Demange said, lighting one more in his endless chain of Gitanes.

"How did the Russians know who we were?" Luc asked.

"How doesn't matter. But they knew, all right. That jeering prick . . . He sounded just like a captain I served under in the last war. That asshole stopped a 77—or maybe it was a 105—with his face. Hardly enough left of him to bury. I hope the same thing happens to this son of a bitch, too."

"He was just the mouthpiece," Luc said. "It's the ones who told him what to say who need killing."

"They all need killing," Demange said. "And they think we all need killing. And if everybody gets his way, nobody'll be left when this stupid war's done, and you know what? The world'll be a better place after that. For a little while, till the cats or the rats learn how to lie."

"Heh," Luc said uneasily, not at all sure the older man was kidding. He decided to change the subject: "What are we going to do now?"

"I don't know about you, but I'm going to shore up these works the best way I know how." Demange stopped, an evil smile lighting up his face. He shook his head. "No. Fuck that. I'm an officer now, right? I'm going to have a bunch of sorry-ass privates shore this shit up for me."

"Sounds good, Lieutenant." Luc grinned. With a sergeant's hash marks on his sleeve, he wouldn't have to thicken up the calluses on his palm with an entrenching tool so much, either.

"And then," Demange went on, "and then, what I'm going to do is sit right here on my ass and not move a centimeter forward till some cocksucker in a fancy kepi makes me do it."

"That sounds good, too," Luc agreed. "But what about the crusade against Bolshevism?"

"What afuckingbout it?" Demange retorted. "I'm here, aren't I? You're here, aren't you? As much as you're ever anywhere, I mean."

"I love you, too, sir," Luc put in.

Demange ignored him, not for the first time and no doubt not for the last. The veteran went on, "We've both shot Russians. If they come at us again—no, when they do—we'll shoot some more of them so they don't shoot us. I'll do whatever I've got to do to stay alive. But if you think I'm enough of a jackass to give a fart about any of that political horseshit, you're even dumber than I give you credit for."

"Mmp." Luc left that right there. He looked up and down the trenches. No one was paying special attention to him and Demange, except perhaps to see what kind of nasty orders the lieutenant and sergeant doled out next and who'd get stuck with them. Lowering his voice, Luc continued, "Some of the guys in the ranks are still Reds, you know. They didn't come close to weeding all of 'em out before they sent us east."

"Oh, sure." Lieutenant Demange nodded. "But so what? Most of 'em'll shoot Ivans to keep from getting killed themselves, and that's all they've really got to do. A few of 'em'll desert."

"A few of them have already deserted," Luc pointed out.

"Uh-huh." Demange nodded again. "And you know what? I bet the fucking Russians ate 'em without salt. We're only here because Daladier's got his head up his ass. Those miserable Russkis, they're here on account of the Nazis and Poles and us, we're in their country. It makes all the fucking difference in the world. Even a sorry turd like you didn't fight too bad when the Fritzes invaded France."

"That's the nicest thing you ever said about me." Luc tried to sound sarcastic. He did less well than he would have liked, mostly because he meant it. That *was* about the nicest thing Demange had ever said about him.

"Yeah, well, you didn't know your ass from your elbow when you started out. But you were luckier than most of the other poor stupid new fish: the Nazis didn't nail you or blow you up right away, so you got the chance to learn," Demange said. "By now, you know what you're doing. One more time, you'd be even dumber than I figure you for if you didn't."

"Thanks a bunch," Luc said, deflated. He'd been cut and scratched and bruised, but he never did get badly hurt. Was that all it took to make a good soldier? Staying in one piece long enough to learn the ropes? The more he thought about it, the likelier it seemed.

Even a good soldier, though, had to stay lucky all the time. Things had to keep missing him. Superiors had to steer clear of idiotic orders that put him in a place where things couldn't help hitting. Otherwise, he'd go down and thrash and scream just as loud as any clodhopper fresh out of training. He knew that, too.

Chapter 7

olonel Otto Griehl commanded the panzer regiment of which Theo
Hossbach was a small and none too vital part. Theo didn't think the
regimental commander was such a bad guy. Had the colonel known as
much, that doubtless would have warmed the cockles of his heart, whatever the hell those were. But even if Griehl wasn't such a bad guy, he did
like to hear himself talk.

"Men, we've been stuck in the mud too damn long," he declared to
the troopers in black coveralls with the silver panzer *Totenkopf* on their
collar patches. "Now we can move around again, so we're going to go
out and give the Ivans what-for."

Some of the assembled panzer troopers clapped their hands. Adi
Stoss leaned close to Theo and muttered, "Who's this *we* he keeps going
on about? Him and his tapeworm?"

Theo snickered. He might not think Griehl was a bad guy, but that
didn't mean he took authority any more seriously than he had to. Con-
templating the exalted colonel's equally exalted tapeworm was as good
a cure for that as he could imagine, and better than most.

Hermann Witt clucked in reproof—mild reproof, but reproof even so. "Griehl comes forward with the rest of us," he said.

"*Ja, ja,*" Adi said. Theo nodded. It was true enough. In a panzer regiment, company commanders and the regimental CO did lead machines of their own, and did advance with—sometimes ahead of—everybody else. They didn't inflict their wisdom on the troops from kilometers behind the line, the way high-ranking officers had in the last war.

Well, Witt was a sergeant himself, and a panzer commander. Being a small-scale leader had to give him more sympathy for the worries of a large-scale one. Theo had no urge to tell anybody else what to do. He also had no desire whatsoever to have other people tell him what to do.

He wasn't an ideal fit for the *Wehrmacht,* then. Ideal fit or not, here he was. He glanced over at Adalbert Stoss. Adi wasn't such a great fit, either. He might not mind giving other people orders, but he was even less thrilled about taking them than Theo. To Theo, other people were equals, and equals had no business telling other equals what to do. As far as Adi was concerned, other people were idiots until they proved otherwise.

He wouldn't have deferred to Sergeant Witt if Witt hadn't shown he knew what he was doing. That was part of the trouble he'd had with the previous panzer commander. The rest of that trouble, though, had been more on the order of two rams banging heads in the springtime. Heinz Naumann wouldn't do any more head-banging. He lay somewhere to the west, under a cross unless the Russians had desecrated his grave.

Woolgathering meant Theo'd missed some of the colonel's harangue. He wouldn't lose any sleep over that. As he started paying attention again, Griehl was saying, "—will surround Smolensk in a ring of steel and fire. Along with our brave allies, we'll smash the Russians inside that ring."

He got some more applause. Theo marveled that he could talk like that with a straight face. The English and French were here, but didn't want to be. The Poles were more enthusiastic, but short of everything bigger than a machine gun. The less said about the Magyars and the Slovaks, the better. Anyway, they were farther south. Theo didn't know what to think of the Romanians, but the way they'd gone belly-up in the last war didn't make him figure Stalin's teeth were chattering.

"I know you'll serve the *Reich* well. I know you'll serve the *Volk* well. And I know you'll serve the *Führer* well." Colonel Griehl's arm shot up and out in the Party salute. "*Heil* Hitler!"

"*Heil* Hitler!" The panzer men echoed the shout and the salute. Since the failed *Putsch* against the *Führer,* it was supposed to have replaced the traditional military salute. And so it had—where anyone you didn't trust could see you saluting. Theo muttered something wordless to himself. What was one more mask among the many he already wore?

He scrambled up into his familiar place behind the Panzer II's turret, away from the world and its cares—except, of course, when it started screaming at him through the radio earphones. The fighting compartment smelled of metal and leather and sweat and exhaust and smokeless powder. It smelled like home to Theo, even if home was thinly armored, too lightly armed, and rapidly becoming obsolete.

From the turret, Witt said, "One of these days before too long, we'll get ourselves a Panzer III instead."

"God, I hope so!" Adi Stoss exclaimed as he started the engine. Theo wasn't so sure he did. Yes, a Panzer III had thicker armor, a better cannon, and a bow machine gun to go with the one in the turret. But it also had a loader and a gunner in the turret along with the commander (the radioman handled that bow gun). Was getting to know two new people scarier than attacking the Ivans in this old crate? To Theo, that seemed too close to call.

They didn't have the new panzer yet. No matter what Sergeant Witt said, reports that they'd get one soon were only scuttlebutt. With a good crew—which this machine did have—a Panzer II could still do the job. Stoss put the beast in gear. They not only could do the job, they damn well had to.

Witt rode with his head and shoulders out of the turret. Any panzer commander would do that when he wasn't in combat. You could see a lot more that way; unlike the III and some French and English machines, the Panzer II had only a hatch, not a cupola. There was talk that new IIs would come with them, but that didn't do this one any good.

A good panzer commander would stay head-and-shoulders out of the machine even in action. The vision ports in the turret just weren't an adequate substitute. Witt did. Heinz Naumann had, too. That was how he'd stopped something. No one could fault Naumann's guts: not even Adi, who'd hated them.

"There are some Frenchmen," Adi said over the Maybach engine's rattling growl and the squeak and clank of the caterpillar treads. "They're by the side of the road, trying to get their trucks going again."

"Surprise!" Sour amusement filled Hermann Witt's voice. Russian roads went from bad to worse. Road maps showed as paved were either rutted dirt tracks or, more often, not there at all. Theo didn't know who'd made the maps. Some fool who believed Soviet propaganda, probably. He did know that Western European soft-skinned vehicles made to run on asphalt or concrete fell to pieces trying to deal with Russian potholes and mud and engine-abrading dust. German trucks broke down as fast as their French and English counterparts.

In spite of his earphones, Theo started hearing gunfire. The Ivans knew when things could get rolling. They did what they could to stop their foes from pushing deeper into Russia. Witt ducked into the turret, but only to grab his Schmeisser. Then he popped up again like a jack-in-the-box.

"Infantry reporting enemy panzers in the woods ahead," someone said on the radio. Theo relayed the message to Sergeant Witt.

"Oh, they are, are they?" Now Witt sounded almost gay. "Well, that's what we're here for, right?" Theo didn't answer. He had no idea why he was here. He only knew he was, and that he wanted to go on being here. Philosophy in the back of a panzer? Witt would never understand.

Then half a dozen people started screeching in Theo's earphones at the same time. "Oh, my God!" Hermann Witt exclaimed, while Adi Stoss yelled, "What a fucking monster!" One of the people on the radio said something about the biggest panzer he'd ever seen, so Theo decided it wasn't King Kong coming out of the woods after all.

Which didn't mean it wasn't dangerous. Witt fired several 20mm rounds at the Russian machine. He slapped in another ten-round clip and fired some more.

"They just bounce off!" he said in horror. Beauty wouldn't kill the Red beast, and maybe nothing else would, either. Witt came out with something even more horrified—and horrifying: "Dodge like hell, Adi! He's aiming at us!"

Adi did his best to comply. Russian panzer gunners were often lousy, especially against moving targets. Often, but not always. *Wham! Clanng!* The hit almost threw Theo out of his seat. The round didn't get through into the fighting compartment, but the Panzer II slewed sideways and stopped.

"Out! Out fast!" Adi shouted. "He knocked a track off! If he hits us again—"

He didn't go on, or need to. Theo grabbed his Schmeisser and bailed out. The other two panzer crewmen left through his hatch, which exposed them to less enemy fire than their own. They huddled in the lee of the disabled panzer.

"I don't know about you guys, but I feel like a deshelled snail," Adi said.

Theo nodded. He did, too. He peered around the damaged Panzer II. He wanted a glimpse of the machine that did the dirty work. It *was* a monster. It seemed twice the size of the light German panzer, and mounted a gun that looked like a piece of field artillery. The cannon belched flame. *Wham! Clanng!* Another Panzer II exploded into fire. That crew had no prayer of getting away. Theo shuddered. Roasting inside your shell was even worse than coming out of it.

"MOSCOW SPEAKING." By the self-important way the words came out of the radio, the whole city might have been talking through the speaker, not just an announcer holed up in a studio somewhere. Or so it seemed to Anastas Mouradian, anyhow. He didn't share the conceit with his fellow flyers. They already thought he was strange. He didn't want to give them any more reasons.

"Red Army forces have struck more and more heavy blows against the Fascist and reactionary invaders west and south of Smolensk," the newsreader went on. "The enemy's tanks continue to show themselves unable to face in the field the latest products of Soviet engineering."

Radio Moscow gave forth with great steaming piles of propaganda. Anyone with an ear to hear—which Mouradian certainly owned— knew that. Here, though, as best he could tell, the announcer meant every word. The new heavy tanks named for General Kliment Voroshilov were bigger and tougher than anything the Nazis or their friends built. Facing Panzer IIs—even Panzer IIIs—a KV-1 was like a bear against a pack of yapping dogs. But the KV-1s came in ever-growing packs, too.

"Farther south," the radio newsman went on, "the soldiers of the glorious Red Army are being welcomed as liberators in Bessarabia, which the Romanians stole while reactionary forces attempted to strangle the infant Soviet Union in its cradle."

That sounded impressive. Mouradian wasn't old enough to remember much about the Russian Revolution and its aftermath. He remembered that Armenia had been independent for a little while, and then part of a bigger Trans-Caucasian Soviet Socialist Republic. Then, after the Whites and their foreign allies were beaten, Moscow reasserted its authority over the region. No, he didn't remember all the political details. What he mostly remembered was going hungry all the time.

Anyone who'd lived through the Revolution had memories like that. If you were a Ukrainian, you had several sets of them, and you were probably lucky to be alive. Rumors said lots of Ukrainians welcomed German and Polish soldiers the way the radio reported the Bessarabians were welcoming the Red Army. The louder and more stridently Radio Moscow denied those rumors, the more Stas believed them.

"Unrest in England against the government's unnatural alliance with the Hitlerite barbarians continues to grow," the newsreader said. "Police have been uncommonly brutal in suppressing demonstrations against Prime Minister Wilson."

He went on to talk about ever-swelling Soviet war production. Plan after plan was overfulfilled, quota after quota exceeded. Stas wondered if he was the only flyer listening who thought about what would happen if people demonstrated against Stalin in Red Square. The NKVD, which was commonly brutal, would be uncommonly so for something like that. Would captured protesters be killed out of hand or sent to the gulags so they had more time to think about what reckless fools they'd been? An interesting question. Either way, the poor devils wouldn't like the answer.

There was war news in the Pacific, too. Mouradian couldn't make much of it, not least because the announcer kept stumbling over unfamiliar place names. He gathered that Japan was advancing and everyone else falling back. Having served for a while in the Far East, Mouradian knew only too well that the Japanese were no bargain. Now the rest of the world was discovering the same thing.

Germany and her friends were no bargain, either. Japan could annoy and gnaw at the Soviet Union, and had done exactly that. But thousands of kilometers separated her from the USSR's vitals. If Hitler paraded through Moscow in a Mercedes, could Stalin keep up the fight from Sverdlovsk or Kuibishev or some other town on the far side of the Urals? Mouradian had his doubts. He suspected Stalin did, too.

Which meant the General Secretary of the Communist Party of the Soviet Union would move heaven and earth to keep the Nazis out of Moscow and as far from the USSR's capital as he could. It also meant Mouradian moved through the heavens toward Mogilev, which had recently fallen to the invaders. Along with him in the Pe-2 moved a thousand kilos' worth of bombs. Stalin wouldn't care that a stubborn Armenian was flying. The explosives, though, the explosives would matter to the director of the Soviet state.

The squadron's target was the railroad yard. Maybe withdrawing Soviet troops hadn't torn it up well enough. Maybe enemy railroad men had got it back in operation faster than the Russians figured they could. Keeping trains from going through Mogilev would help defend Smolensk, and Smolensk was Moscow's most important shield.

Fires and plumes of greasy black smoke from burning tanks marked the front between Mogilev and Smolensk. Not all the burning armor came out of enemy factories. Soviet light tanks were still depressingly easy to kill. And even the KV-1s could go up in flames. Maybe some German Panzer III got lucky, or maybe the foe had a field gun in a good place.

In the Pe-2's cockpit, Ivan Kulkaanen turned to Mouradian and said, "The stinking Fascists aren't having it all their own way, anyhow."

"No, they aren't," Stas agreed. Yes, that was true. But he would have felt obliged to agree even if the Nazis were driving the Red Army back headlong. Disagreeing with something like that would have been defeatism. England might tolerate such disagreement in wartime—or, if the morning news held any truth, might not. The Soviet Union never had and never would.

A few antiaircraft shells burst near the formation of Pe-2s. Stas didn't see any planes catch fire or go down. That was good news. They flew on. Once they got past the front, things quieted down. It often worked out that way. If the Germans didn't also have plenty of antiaircraft guns in and around Mogilev, though, Stas would be happily surprised.

After a while, he didn't just hear the engines' drone. It became a part of him, so that his toenails, his muscles, his spine, and his spleen all vibrated to the same rhythm. The oxygen-enriched air tasted of rubber and leather.

Kulkaanen pointed through the armor-glass windshield. A city lay ahead. Unless the squadron had really buggered up its navigation, that had to be Mogilev. They'd dive to make the attack more accurate. Pe-2s weren't Stukas; they didn't stand on their noses to deliver ordnance. (They could also fly rings around the clumsy German bombers.) But they did have dive brakes, and used them on attack runs.

That also brought them down closer to the flak gunners on the ground. Stas tried not to dwell on such things as the slotted flaps lowered and grabbed air. "Be ready," he called to Fyodor Mechnikov back in the narrow bomb bay.

"What the hell else am I gonna be—sir?" the bombardier answered through the speaking tube. Behind goggles and oxygen mask, Mouradian grinned. Sure as the devil, it was almost like flying with Ivan Kuchkov again.

The Germans did have guns waiting for the Soviet bombers. Stas wished he were more astonished. Yes, they'd protect the railroad yards. And yes, they'd probably got a few minutes' warning. Unlike Russians, Germans knew what to do with a few minutes' warning, too.

Had he flown through heavier flak? He supposed he must have, but he couldn't remember offhand just when. Something tore half the left wing off the Pe-2 diving next to his. The stricken bomber spun out of control. The crew had no chance to bail out.

"Now!" Stas yelled through the speaking tube. As soon as the bombs fell free, he leveled out and scooted away at full throttle and low altitude. Any Messerschmitt pilot who wanted to run him down was welcome to try. He turned back toward Soviet-held territory. The railroad yard, or something in its neighborhood, had taken one mighty thorough pounding.

Of course, the bombs also came down on the heads of the people who still lived in Mogilev. Stas' superiors thought they'd do more harm to the enemy than to Soviet citizens. He had to hope they were right.

SPRING WAS IN THE AIR outside Madrid . . . spring and the stink of shit and garbage and unburied bodies, and the occasional bullet or shell fragment. But when things started turning green, when the birds came back from the south, Chaim Weinberg was less inclined to be critical.

Mike Carroll gave him a peculiar look when he started going on about birdsong. "Chirp, chirp," the other Abe Lincoln said. "Hot diggety dog."

"It's pretty," Chaim insisted. "And it doesn't sound the same here as it does in the States."

"What? The fuckin' birdth thpeak Thpanish?" Mike put on a sarcastic Castilian lisp.

"No, but there's different ones here," Chaim said. He was going to get pissed off if his buddy couldn't see what he saw, couldn't hear what he heard. He could feel it coming like a rash.

"Sparrows. Pigeons. Starlings. Crows. Stop the fucking presses. Call Walter fucking Winchell." Mike was tall and slim and blond and handsome, none of which adjectives applied to Chaim. At the moment, the other American was also a royal pain in the ass.

"Only reason there's pigeons and sparrows—these kindsa sparrows—and cocksucking starlings in the USA is that they're imports," Chaim said. "And the crows here aren't the same as crows on the other side of the ocean. They've got bigger beaks, and they make different noises."

"*You'd* notice the stupid beaks," Mike said.

"Your mother," Chaim said without heat. Had somebody who wasn't his friend made even an indirect crack about his own very Jewish beak, he would have rearranged the guy's face for him. From Mike, though, he'd take it.

"How's your wife?" the other Yank asked with a leer.

Chaim shrugged. "She's back in the city, doing what she's doing. And I'm here, doing what I'm doing." That he'd made it with La Martellita struck him as a marvel. That she'd been willing to tie the knot for the sake of giving their accidental kid a last name was whatever came one step up from a marvel.

Mike tried to pinch off a hangnail with the other hand's thumb and forefinger. "Doesn't sound like the recipe for living happily ever after, y'know?"

"Yeah, yeah." Chaim would rather have talked about birds. He hadn't even started in on the hoopoe's aerial ballet.

"What'll you do when she dumps you after Junior comes out?" Mike found the sixty-four dollar question, all right.

All Chaim could do was shrug again. "Get drunk, I guess. Shoot some Fascists. What else is there to do?" Like Mike, he assumed she'd dump him once the baby was born. He also assumed the war in Spain would still be going on this fall. The way things looked right now, the war in Spain was liable to go on forever.

"Aren't you tired of going hungry over there?" The enormous voice came from a microphone and speaker in Marshal Sanjurjo's lines. "Come over to our side. We'll give you a big bowl of mutton stew!"

Before, the Fascists had tempted Republican soldiers with chicken stew. Maybe they'd hired a new chef. More likely, they'd just put a new liar on the payroll. Chaim had captured Nationalist troops. They were every bit as skinny and miserable as the guys on his own side.

"Baa!" he bleated at the propaganda message. "Baa!"

Mike Carroll joined in. "Baa!" he yelled, even louder than Chaim. "Baa! Baa!"

"Mutton stew! Delicious mutton stew!" blared from the speaker.

"Baa!" This time, half a dozen Abe Lincolns bleated back. Before long, the whole stretch of Republican line northwest of Madrid was going "Baa! Baa! Baa!" in ragged chorus.

"Now look what you went and started," Mike said. Chaim grinned. He was proud of himself.

Marshal Sanjurjo's men didn't think it was funny. Fascists, in Chaim's experience, had all had their sense of humor surgically removed when they were very small. They had nasty ways of making their unhappiness known, too. Machine guns rattled. Mortar bombs whispered down. Even a battery of old German 77s well behind the line started up.

Naturally, the Internationals and the Czechs and the Spanish Republican soldiers in that stretch of the line fired back. "*Now* look what you went and started," Mike Carroll repeated, this time in an altogether different tone of voice.

A bullet cracked not far enough above Chaim's head. He ducked automatically. "The fucking Battle of the Mutton Stew," he said.

It was a joke, and then again it wasn't. Bleating at the silly propaganda set off the shooting, sure. No matter what set it off, though, men on both sides were getting killed and maimed. He could hear wounded men screaming, all because he'd decided to make a noise like a sheep.

He didn't want anything like that on his conscience. He told himself they would have got hit anyway. Himself told him he was full of it. Himself had a point, too. He'd been in Spain a long time. He'd seen how random war was. This guy bought a plot the day after he came into the line. That guy went without a scratch for years. Why? If it was anything more than God's crapshoot, Chaim couldn't imagine what. And, when he remembered not to, he didn't even believe in God.

After both sides hauled their wounded away for whatever help the docs could give them, the Fascist announcer started going on about mutton stew again. He had a script, and he had his orders. This stretch of line was going to get so many repetitions. Then he'd go inflict himself somewhere else.

"Fuck you!" Chaim screamed, almost as loud without the loudspeaker as the announcer was with it. If he heard about mutton stew one more time, he'd snap. Or maybe he already had. "Fuck you up the ass! Fuck your mother! And fuck the sheep your fucking mutton stew comes from, too!"

That produced scattered cheers from the Internationals. He thought the only reason it just produced scattered cheers was that they didn't want to risk starting up the firefight again. And, to his amazement and delight, it also produced a few scattered cheers from the Nationalist trenches. Those had to come from men sure they were off by themselves so nobody could rat on them.

Mike heard the cheers from Sanjurjo's side, too. "Wow, man," he said. "You really struck a nerve there."

"Bet your ass I did," Chaim replied. "When's the last time you figure one of those poor sorry dingleberries even smelled mutton stew, let alone tasted any? That clown with the mike probably drives them even crazier than he drives me."

Carroll sent him a speculative stare. "Oh, I wouldn't say that."

The next day, Brigadier Kossuth summoned Chaim to his head-quarters behind the lines. Like La Martellita, the Internationals' CO used a *nom de guerre,* though he was a Magyar like his namesake. "I hear you've been running your mouth again," he said in German. He was old enough to have learned it in the dead Austro-Hungarian Empire.

Thanks to Yiddish, Chaim could follow German. "Afraid so," he admitted cheerfully.

Yiddish didn't faze the brigadier. "Why?" he asked with a glower that would have turned a basilisk to stone.

But nobody's glower was going to make Chaim quake in his drafty boots. He'd been through way too much for that. "Because I got sick and tired of all that crap about mutton stew," he said.

Kossuth eyed him the way a chameleon eyes a fly just before its tongue flicks out. "Are all Americans as deranged as you?" he asked with what sounded like clinical detachment and probably masked fury.

"Some of us are even worse," Chaim said: he wouldn't let the country down.

"Oh, I doubt that." Kossuth knew what he was up against, all right. "And you managed to knock up that human hand grenade, too. . . . Tell me, if you would: how does one man find so much trouble?"

"I volunteered for it," Chaim answered. "I could have stayed back in the States."

"Everyone might have been better off if you had. Including you," Kossuth said.

"Spain wouldn't." Pride rang in Chaim's voice.

That basilisk-petrifying glower again. When Chaim refused to wilt under it, the Magyar brigadier sighed. "Anything is possible—but nothing is likely." He jerked a thumb toward the tent flap. "Now get out." Whistling, Chaim got.

PEGGY DRUCE WAS getting the urge to travel again. After her adventures and misadventures in war-torn Europe, she would have bet she'd be content—hell, be overjoyed—to stay in Philadelphia the rest of her days. But things didn't work out like that. After so long living by her wits and by what she could browbeat out of unhappy officials, ordinary life seemed Boring with a capital B.

She didn't put it that way to her husband. It would have hurt Herb's feelings, which was the last thing she wanted to do. Then again, she didn't need to say much to him. It wasn't as if he didn't know how she ticked. One morning at breakfast, he set down his coffee cup and said, "You ought to do something for the war effort, you know?"

"Like what?" she said. It wasn't as if the suggestion came out of the blue. She'd been thinking along those lines herself.

Herb was a jump ahead of her, though. "Well, you've seen a lot of stuff other people haven't," he answered. "You ought to go around and tell them what a mess Europe is. Some of these chowderheads are still mad 'cause FDR won't let 'em sell stuff over there any more."

"Too bad for them," she said. She'd been all for sending England and France everything but the kitchen sink when they were fighting the Nazis. Now that they were fighting on the Nazis' side, she was as ready to say to hell with them as FDR seemed to be. But swarms of people who'd made big stacks of cash by shipping them this, that, and the other thing were jumping up and down and bawling like a three-year-old throwing a tantrum.

Herb chuckled. "You know how to win friends and influence people, you do."

"I looked at that stupid book when it was new," Peggy said. "I wouldn't waste my money on it. It was a bunch of hooey, nothing else but."

"Maybe so, but the guy who wrote it's laughing all the way to the bank," her husband answered. "I'd like to have a quarter of what he raked in from the son of a gun."

That was bound to be true, no matter how unfortunate Peggy thought it was. She'd never been one to stay gloomy long, though. If she were, her time in Europe would have driven her nuts. She brightened as a new thought came. "A lot of the big shots who want to go on doing business with Europe will be making even more money pretty soon by selling the government what it needs to fight the Japs."

"There you go." Herb made silent clapping motions. "Now you've got your text. You can go and preach it all over the place, like St. Paul."

"I don't want to preach in St. Paul," Peggy said with malice afore-thought. "If there's a duller town anywhere in the world, I don't know where."

Herb eyed her through a veil of cigarette smoke. "When you start making cracks like that, you need to get out of the house, all right, and PDQ, too."

But getting out of the house wasn't so simple. The government had clamped down on travel. Tires and gasoline were rationed. That made sense, since you couldn't win a modern war without rubber and petro-leum. It was still a pain. And, if she was going to head out on what amounted to the campaign trail, she was damned if she wanted to spend her own money—or even Herb's—to do it. It wasn't that she couldn't afford to; it was the principle of the thing. So she told herself, anyhow.

She rapidly discovered she didn't have to. To most Philadelphia Main Line families, Roosevelt was and always would be That Man in the White House. Philadelphia Democrats fell all over themselves to get help from someone in that group who didn't see him that way. Train fare? Yes, ma'am! Hotel bills? Expenses? Yes, ma'am!

They asked her if she wanted a speech writer. She looked at them as if they'd asked if she wanted a positive Wassermann. "I can talk for my-self, thanks," she said coolly. "If you don't believe me, ask my husband. Or ask Hitler. I got him to do what I wanted, and I was speaking Ger-man then. I'm better in English."

She'd never heard so many stammered apologies in her life. They were just suggesting . . . They didn't mean to hurt her feelings. . . . To show they didn't, they upped her expenses.

When she told Herb that, he guffawed. "Squeeze 'em for all they're worth," he said. "They've got more moolah than they know what to do with, and most of it doesn't exactly belong to anybody, so they can throw it around."

No matter how much money the Philadelphia Democrats had, they didn't send her very far on her first run—only to York, on the west side of the Susquehanna. She didn't blame them for that. If she turned out to be a dud, they'd want to know at minimum expense.

York sat in the valley formed by Codorus Creek. It was a medium-sized town: 50,000 people, or maybe a few more. It had been a brick-making center, and many of the older neighborhoods were one brick home or apartment house after another. The public buildings and the many Gothic churches were of red brick with white trim, as if they'd come from early nineteenth-century England.

The local women's club had arranged for her to speak at the First Presbyterian Church, a few blocks east of Continental Square. It was another Gothic brick building, built in 1789 and rebuilt in 1860. For variety's sake, perhaps, its brickwork was painted gray; the renovation added brownstone and wood trim. Loretta Conway, the woman who picked her up at the station, told her the graveyard next to the church held the remains of James Smith, a signer of the Declaration of Independence.

"That's nice," Peggy said.

Her nonchalance flustered the woman from York, but only for a moment. Then Mrs. Conway turned pink. "I forgot you're from Philly," she said. "You've got more Revolutionary War stuff there than you know what to do with, don't you?"

"Pretty much," Peggy answered. She knew York had some, too, and she was ready to be a good sport if Loretta wanted to show it off, but the other woman didn't. Instead, she talked—very sensibly (which meant her views matched Peggy's)—about the need to knock the snot out of the Japs and to keep Hitler from getting too big for his britches. She had a twenty-year-old son who'd just volunteered for the Marines. That brought the war home for her in a way Peggy hadn't felt since Herb got back from Over There in 1919.

"Maybe you should give the speech," Peggy said.

"Forget it," Loretta answered. "I go up in front of more than four or five people, I freeze up like a block of ice."

Peggy laughed. "Okay. You aren't the only one, heaven knows. But whatever else they say about me, I'm not shy."

She got her chance to prove it a little later. The church wasn't packed, but it came close. The minister, a white-haired man named Ruppelt, introduced her. "Here is a lady who can talk about the world situation because she's seen more of it than most people, Mrs. Peggy Druce."

She got polite applause as she stepped up to the lectern. "Thank you, Reverend Ruppelt," she said. "A lot of what I saw, I wish I never did. But that's the point about war, isn't it? That's what's happening to our boys in the Philippines right now. If the Japs had been a little luckier, it might be happening in Hawaii, too. So we've got some work we need to take care of. If Hirohito thinks Japan can do whatever it wants in the Pacific, FDR's going to show him things don't work that way."

More applause, and more enthusiastic. Peggy warmed to her task: "When I finally did get to England, a customs man there said, 'Welcome to freedom.' I was glad to hear it, too. But what's freedom worth if you use yours to take away somebody else's? Isn't that what England's doing in Russia right now? Didn't she learn better right here in Pennsylvania in 1776? And how can you expect to stay friends with us if you're friends with Hitler, too?"

If she'd been talking with Herb, she would have said *in bed with Hitler*. She almost did here. She thought her husband would have been proud of her because she showed restraint. You didn't talk about sex in church.

And she didn't need to. The raucous clapping that followed showed people got the message even when she kept it clean. The ones with minds that ran in the same gutter as hers could gloss *in bed with Hitler* for themselves. The others . . . were dull, but they were here, too.

They cheered—some of them stood up—when Peggy got done. They bought bonds. They contributed to the Democrats. And they made sure she'd be on the road a lot from now on.

Chapter 8

Before coming to Pingfan, Hideki Fujita had never had anything to do with Americans. The only white men he'd dealt with were the Russians who'd tried to kill him in Mongolia and Siberia, and the Russian prisoners on whom the Japanese microbiologists and biochemists experimented here.

You had to watch yourself with Russians. They were tough, and they were sneaky. If they saw an opening, they would grab it in a heartbeat. But as long as you made sure they recognized they couldn't get away with anything, they grew docile enough.

Pingfan held tens of thousands of Russians. Most of the men who'd surrendered around Vladivostok were marched here afterwards. Not all of them made it here—nowhere close. Fujita had been one of the soldiers herding them along. He knew how many fell by the wayside. He also knew how fast the Japanese scientists were using them up. Still, the experimental station had plenty left.

Americans . . . Americans were different. They were different all kinds of ways. There weren't very many of them. The U.S. Marines had had only small garrisons in Peking and Shanghai. A lot of the Marines in both places had made the Japanese kill them after war broke out between the two countries. Despite being insanely outnumbered, they'd killed a lot of Japanese, too. You had to respect men like that.

In the end, though, some of the Marines did surrender. Perhaps to pay them back for the fight their comrades put up, they got shipped straight to Pingfan. The Japanese scientists were excited to have them. American POWs let them try to tailor germ-warfare weapons against Anglo-Saxons in particular.

Which was fine—for the scientists. Fujita and his soldiers had to ride herd on the Americans in the meantime. They had to keep them from making trouble, and they had to keep them from escaping. And Fujita didn't need long to figure out that Americans were born troublemakers.

Russians would escape if you gave them half a chance, too. And Chinese! No one in his right mind would trust Chinese to stay where they belonged unless you kept your eye on them every second—and they knew you were keeping your eye on them every second. Then they couldn't behave better.

But the Americans played games with the system that Fujita wouldn't have believed if they hadn't been messing around with him. The essential feature in controlling them was the count. They stood in ranks of ten, which made it easy for the guards to know exactly how many of them there were on any given morning or evening.

Or it should have made things easy. Somehow the Marines managed to convince the Japanese that there were three more of them than there were supposed to be. How? Fujita didn't know. Obviously, they were moving around in the ranks, but not where anybody could catch them at it.

He'd already worked out that one of the chief nuisances was a big, burly fellow named Szulc. The American didn't understand Japanese, of course. He didn't understand Chinese, either—Senior Private Hayashi was a smart fellow, and knew quite a bit.

"I am very sorry, Sergeant-*san*, but I think he really is ignorant and not faking," Hayashi reported to Fujita.

"How could he be?" Fujita asked irritably—everything about Szulc irritated him. "These Marines serve in China for years. They must learn some of the language while they're there."

"It seems not, Sergeant-*san*. Please excuse me, but it does." Hayashi didn't want Fujita working off that irritation on him.

Fujita growled like an angry tiger. A sergeant could do pretty much as he pleased with—and to—the men under him. But thumping Hayashi wouldn't tell him how the Americans were pulling off their stupid stunt. Neither would thumping Szulc, if nobody could understand him when he yelled as he got thumped.

Sudden inspiration struck. Fujita snapped his fingers in delight. "Some of our scientists went to the university in America, *neh?* They'll know English, and they'll be able to talk to this Szulc." He couldn't even pronounce the round-eyed devil's name. In his mouth, it came out something like *Shurutzu*.

"That's right! They will!" Hayashi said. When a sergeant came up with a halfway decent idea, of course a senior private sounded enthusiastic.

"Good. Glad you think so, too." Fujita pointed to Hayashi. "So you get one of the scientists to find out how the Americans are doing whatever they're doing. It's gone on for four days now. That's too stinking long."

"Me? Why me?" Shinjiro Hayashi yipped, but his heart wasn't in it.

"You're the educated fellow," Fujita answered remorselessly, as Hayashi must have known he would. "So go use some of your education for a change." Fujita himself felt like an idiot whenever he had to talk to one of the microbiologists. That, no doubt, was a feeling they did nothing to discourage.

Sighing as if to say he didn't think life was fair, Hayashi went off to do as he was told—a definite good point in a subordinate. Fujita already knew life wasn't fair. He'd had his nose rubbed in it again and again before he made sergeant. Life wasn't fair now, either, but most of the time he found himself on the other end of the stick for a change.

Hayashi eventually came back with a man who wore spectacles and a white lab coat as if they were extensions of his skin—the way, say, Fujita wore a uniform. "Here is Dr. Doi, Sergeant-*san*," Hayashi said. "He will ask Szulc the questions you need."

"Good." Fujita bowed deeply to Doi, inferior to superior. "Thank you very much for your help, sir."

"You are welcome. I am glad to assist. I am also glad for the chance to practice my English. When you do not speak a language for a while, it gets rusty."

Armed guards brought Szulc over to the compound. He towered over them. He'd be a rough customer in a fight. But who wanted to fight a man who'd thrown away his honor by surrendering? To Dr. Doi, Fujita said, "Please ask him how the Americans are making the count come out wrong."

Doi spoke English. Fujita could hear that he sounded slow and uncertain. Szulc's reply was a quick bass rumble that couldn't have sounded more different from the Japanese scientist's reedy tenor if it had burst from the throat of a buffalo. Dr. Doi frowned. "He says he does not understand what I say."

Fujita frowned, too, ominously. "Is that likely?"

"No one will ever think I am an American, but he should be able to follow me," Doi answered.

That was about what Fujita had expected. "All right, then," he said, and nodded to one of Szulc's guards. The man gave Szulc one in the side of the head with his rifle butt. Szulc yelled and staggered, but he didn't fall over. He didn't dab at the blood running down his cheek and chin, either. He did give Fujita a hate-filled glare. Fujita cared nothing for that. "Please ask your question again, Doi-*san*. Please also tell him he'll get worse if he keeps playing the fool."

More English from the bacteriologist. Whatever Szulc said this time, it was different from before. It seemed less scornful. A rifle butt to the side of the head would do that, as Fujita had reason to know. "He says he understands now, but he knows nothing about how the count is disarranged," Doi reported.

"That's funny, but not funny enough to laugh about," Fujita said. "Tell him this, very plainly—the next time the count is out of order, we'll kill enough Americans to set it right."

"That would waste an important resource," Dr. Doi protested in Japanese.

"Please tell him anyhow, sir. Let him and the others think we will do it. That will make them behave themselves. I can hope so, anyhow."

"Ah. All right. I understand." Doi returned to English. Szulc studied

Fujita, as if sniffing for a bluff. Fujita gave back his stoniest stare. On his own, he certainly would kill POWs who complicated his life. Why not? It wasn't as if prisoners of war were human beings any more. They were just . . . *maruta*. Szulc muttered something. Doi said, "He will take word of this back to camp, even though—he claims—he knows nothing of the scheme."

"He claims, *hai*." Fujita gestured to the guards. "Take him back."

As usual, Fujita had two different men run the count that evening before supper. One reported the proper number of Americans, the other one Marine too few. Fujita lost his temper. He had all the Americans lie down so they couldn't move without being instantly noticed. He used gestures to explain to them that they'd get shot if they were noticed. This time, the count came out three men light.

"*Zakennayo!*" Fujita shouted. "How long ago did they get away, and how big a start on us do they have?"

Those were both good questions. He had an answer for neither. Big, strong white men should have been conspicuous around Pingfan. Were the locals sheltering them from the Japanese? Another good question. Fujita wasn't sure he had an answer for that one, either, but he could make a pretty good guess.

"We need to report this," Senior Private Hayashi said regretfully.

"I know," Fujita answered, more regretfully still. They'd catch it for allowing an escape, and catch it again for not noticing right away. But they couldn't cover it up. Somebody'd blab. Even the American Marines might, to get their guards in trouble. "*Zakennayo!*" he yelled again, even louder this time.

OUT OF THE FRYING PAN, into the fire. That was how Peggy Druce thought of it, anyway. As soon as the people in Philadelphia discovered she really could stir folks up about the war, they sent her out to do it again and again.

After York, Lancaster. Red Roses instead of White. When she made that crack in Lancaster, somebody told her the two towns' bush-league baseball teams actually did refight the War of the Roses every time they took the field against each other. She laughed, but later she wondered why. That showed more of a sense of history than was common in the United States.

Not in Europe. They had a sense of history there, all right. Everybody could give you all the reasons for the past 900—or sometimes 1,900—years that showed why he deserved to kick his neighbor in the teeth with a steel-toed jackboot. And his neighbor had reasons just as numerous and just as ancient for kicking *him.*

And the Japanese were responding to something ancient, too. For hundreds of years, Europeans and Americans had lorded it over the proud, ancient, weak empires in Asia. They'd had the warships and the guns and the military doctrine that let them do it. They'd had the arrogance that let them do it, too. What was that sign in the Shanghai park supposed to say? NO DOGS OR CHINESE, that was it. Maybe the sign really was, or had been, there. Maybe it was just a story. Either way, it showed an attitude that was definitely there.

Now the Japs had licked the Russians twice. So they thought they were strong enough to swing the bat against the white men's first team. The United States was going to have to throw a high hard one right at Hirohito's head to convince them they weren't ready for the big leagues yet.

Or maybe they were. The war news coming out of the Pacific was uniformly lousy. The Philippines were falling. A bomb from a Japanese plane was said to have blown General MacArthur into dog food. The Japs claimed that at the tops of their lungs. The USA said nothing one way or the other. Peggy's time in Europe had made her sensitive to the nuances of propaganda. You didn't talk about what you didn't like.

By the same token, the American papers weren't saying much about the way Japan was overrunning Malaya and the Dutch East Indies. You heard occasional stories about how heroic the handful of American ships in the area were. If you paid close attention and checked a map, you notice that fewer and fewer U.S. Navy vessels got mentioned by name. Even the survivors were reported as being heroic farther and farther south.

But how many people checked that closely? How many Americans knew off the tops of their heads whether Borneo was south of Java or the other way around? Peggy hadn't, not till she looked, and she'd traveled a lot more than most folks. Timor? Sumbawa? Cerami? They sounded like the noises your stomach made after you ate bratwurst and sauerkraut. (At least it wasn't Liberty Cabbage in this war. Then again, Germany still remained officially neutral toward the USA.)

Peggy didn't blame the administration for minimizing failures and playing up whatever small successes it could find. If she had, she wouldn't have gone to Reading, to Easton, to Scranton, to Altoona, to Williamsport. . . . You did what you needed to do, and you tried not to tell too many lies while you were doing it. If you couldn't help telling a lie, you tried not to make it a whopper.

She stuck to the principles she hoped the administration was also using. It worked. She got big hands everywhere she went. War bond sales at her rallies were bigger yet. So were contributions to the Democratic Party. An election was coming next year, after all. It seemed as if an election was always coming next year. If it wasn't, it was coming this year instead.

The one place she didn't go was Pittsburgh. The world had a North Pole and a South Pole. Pennsylvania, by contrast, had an East Pole and a West Pole. Philadelphia was bigger and older and richer and snootier than Pittsburgh. Pittsburgh was tougher and grittier—and if you didn't believe it, all you had to do was ask anybody who came from there. Pittsburgh prided itself on coal and steel the way Philadelphia bragged about the Main Line. If Chicago hadn't called itself the City of the Big Shoulders, Pittsburgh would have.

And so, even though Pittsburgh was a more reliably Democratic town than Philadelphia, Peggy wasn't welcome there. She got an invitation from Wheeling, West Virginia, so she traveled through Pittsburgh going and coming back, but she didn't get off the train there.

She also went to Erie. Pennsylvania's only Great Lakes port, Erie cared nothing for either Philadelphia or Pittsburgh. It might have turned its back on both of them. It was a low, spacious city, with only one fourteen-story skyscraper projecting above the three- and four-story business buildings in the center of town.

She made her speech. It went over as well in Erie as it had anywhere else. It might even have gone better there than most places. A plump, prosperous fellow who sold real estate came up to her after she was done and spoke in tones of wonder: "I don't recollect the last time Philadelphia remembered we were alive, much less did anything about it."

"We're all one state. We're all one country. If a war doesn't remind us of that, what will?" Peggy said.

"Well, I don't know. My guess was that nothing would," the real-estate man answered.

After he went away, a weather-beaten woman in her late sixties came up to Peggy and introduced herself as Matilda Jenkins. The name was as ordinary as she was. "You spoke very well," she said, her voice almost painfully genteel. "No wonder you impressed my son so much."

"Your son?" Peggy didn't remember meeting anybody named Jenkins at one of her earlier rallies. But that might not prove anything; she didn't have a pol's photographic memory for names and faces.

"Yes, of course," Mrs. Jenkins said—she wore a thin, plain gold band on the ring finger of her left hand. "My son Constantine, at the American embassy in Berlin. He thought you were the cat's pajamas, he did."

"Oh!" Peggy blurted. She felt herself blushing. She had no idea when she'd last done that. Now that she looked, she saw the resemblance. But the suave embassy undersecretary—so suave, she'd guessed he was queer—seemed more than an ocean removed from this mousy woman clinging so hard to lower-middle-class respectability. Something more than *Oh!* seemed called for. Peggy tried again: "How about that? He helped me a lot." The second part was true, the first usually safe.

Matilda Jenkins beamed. "He said you knew what you wanted and how to go about getting it. Just listening to you, I can see that. He said you were mighty sweet, too. Constantine usually knows what he's talking about, all right."

"How about that?" Peggy repeated, this time through clenched teeth. Exactly how much about her had Constantine Jenkins told his mother? He wouldn't have bragged about . . . that, would he? Not to his mother!

"He said you had such a good time at the opera and afterwards," Mrs. Jenkins went on, oblivious—Peggy sure hoped she was oblivious, anyhow. After the opera in Berlin . . . What Herb didn't know wouldn't hurt him—she hoped. Matilda Jenkins kept burbling: "Such a pleasure to get the chance to meet you. I never dreamt I would."

"How about that?" Peggy said one more time, wondering how soon she could get the hell out of Erie.

COLONEL STEINBRENNER LOOKED at the Stuka pilots in his squadron. Hans-Ulrich Rudel looked around at them, too. Not many faces were left from the ones he'd seen when the balloon went up in Czechoslovakia. He'd been shot down once himself, and thanked heaven he'd been able to bail out. Too many of his former comrades hadn't been so lucky.

"Things are heating up again," Steinbrenner said. "Our infantry and armor can move forward now that the roads are drying. They need air support." He grinned wryly. "We have a chance to give it to them, too, because the runways are drying."

Rudel chuckled, though it wasn't as if the squadron CO were kidding. Planes flying off forward airstrips had to deal with mud just like panzers and trucks and foot soldiers. There were times when nobody could deal with it. At times like those, the Ju-87s stayed on the ground.

At times like those, he always wished he could hop on a train and go back to Sofia in Bialystok. If he couldn't do the *Reich* any good at the moment, why shouldn't he enjoy himself instead? Unfortunately, *Luftwaffe* higher-ups disapproved of such little jaunts. As far as they were concerned, it would always turn thirty Celsius tomorrow—day after at the latest—and the deep Russian mud would magically dry up so the flyers could get back to walloping the snot out of the Reds.

Well, it had finally happened, or enough of it had. It wasn't thirty Celsius—it probably wasn't even twenty—and the mud hadn't cleared up by magic. But it wasn't twenty below any more, and neither was it pouring rain. The Stukas *could* get back to walloping the Ivans.

After lighting a *papiros*—German quartermasters weren't too proud to dole out captured stocks of smokes—Steinbrenner went on, "The Russians tried to knock us back from our bridgehead in the direction of Smolensk during the winter, but they couldn't bring it off. So we—and our allies—are going to keep pushing that way. Once Smolensk falls, I suspect it will be time to start thinking about Moscow."

Moscow! Driving Stalin out of his lair, taking the lair away from him? No wonder an excited hum rose from the flyers. Napoleon had taken Moscow away from Tsar Alexander, but he hadn't had much joy afterwards. He couldn't fight a winter campaign, not in weather like what they got here he couldn't. The *Wehrmacht* had already proved it could.

"Questions?" Steinbrenner asked. He pointed toward a pilot who raised his hand. "What's on your mind, Helmut?"

Helmut Bauer was big and blond and broad-shouldered; he seemed almost too wide to fit inside a Stuka cockpit. But fit he did, and he flew with nearly as much reckless enthusiasm as Hans-Ulrich himself. Now he asked, "Colonel, with Romania in the war, what happens when things down south get screwed up?"

"You're assuming they will," the squadron commander said, his voice dry.

"Damn straight I am . . . sir," Bauer agreed. "I know what the Romanians've got. It isn't much, and they aren't what you'd call eager to use it, either."

Heads bobbed up and down, Rudel's among them. He didn't care for having Polish allies. You couldn't say the Poles lacked guts, but most of their equipment was junk. The Romanians mostly used junk, too, and precious few Germans had ever figured them for heroes. Hans-Ulrich sure didn't.

Even more dryly than before, Steinbrenner answered, "There may just be a few German soldiers along with the Romanians, to help remind them how to play the game and why they're playing it."

The flyers chuckled. Hans-Ulrich knew why the Romanians were playing the game: the *Führer* had promised them the Black Sea port of Odessa and the adjoining lands on the far bank of the Dniester. If nothing else could get somebody moving, good old greed would often turn the trick.

"I do understand that, sir," Bauer said. "But still . . . The Ukraine's a hell of a big place, if you know what I mean. I hope we'll have enough men and equipment in place to bite off the chunks we need—and to keep the Ivans from bunching up down there and biting our flank."

"Helmut, if they decide to move the squadron down to the Ukraine to support our men and the Romanians, you can't do anything about it, and neither can I," Colonel Steinbrenner said. "I'm sure you'll be able to find yourself another lady friend, though."

More chuckles from the pilots, and a snicker or two to go with them. "Oh, so am I," Bauer said, unmistakable complacency filling his voice. Hans-Ulrich wasn't nearly so sure he could find another girl he liked as much as Sofia.

You'll be safer if you find one who isn't half a Jew, he told himself. The SD didn't like such liaisons. Neither did the National Socialist Leadership Officer standing at Steinbrenner's elbow. Building a case against someone who wore the Knight's Cross and who wasn't shy about saying he backed the *Führer* wouldn't be easy, but it wouldn't necessarily be impossible, either. Nothing was impossible if somebody important enough decided to build a case.

"Can we get on with the war we *are* fighting, not the one we may be fighting some day?" Steinbrenner asked. Nobody told him no, so he did: "The Ivans have a concentration in front of Studenets, southwest of Smolensk. Our forces are in the neighborhood, and so are the French. If we bomb the enemy's infantry and shoot up his panzers, word will get back to Paris that the froggies would be smart not to think about changing horses again. So we'll do that, gentlemen, if it's all right with you." Again, nobody told him no. He nodded briskly. "We take off in forty-five minutes."

And they did, the first Ju-87 kicking up dust from the unpaved strip and climbing into the air right on time. Hans-Ulrich pushed back his leather flying glove and the sleeve to his fur-lined flight suit to check his watch and make sure. "Ready, Albert?" he called through the speaking tube.

"Not me," Sergeant Dieselhorst answered. "I'm still soaking in the bathtub, and after I get out I'll go pick flowers so I keep on smelling nice and sweet."

Hans-Ulrich snorted. Dieselhorst did deadpan even better than Colonel Steinbrenner. When his Stuka's turn came, he goosed the throttle. The Ju-87 rattled down the runway, then sedately got airborne. The weight and drag from the underwing gun pods made the ungainly plane even more so.

"Studenets," Rudel repeated to the rear gunner, as if they hadn't gone over it before takeoff.

"*Gesundheit*," Dieselhorst said, so it was going to be one of *those* missions.

Messerschmitt Bf-109s clustered around the Stukas. The 109s had plenty of other things to do; dive bombers got escorts only when the *Luftwaffe* feared the Red Air Force had fighters of its own in the neighborhood. And the Reds did: blunt-nosed, stumpy Polikarpov Po-16 monoplanes. They were a long step slower than the Messerschmitts, but they could have made mincemeat out of the lumbering Ju-87s had the bombers had no friends. As things were, one of them tumbled to the ground, trailing smoke. Two more made halfhearted runs at the Stukas and then peeled off. The rest decided to go somewhere else, to some place where misfortunes like 109s never happened.

After that, the Stukas worked over the Ivans' positions in front of Studenets with only ground fire to worry about. That wasn't negligible, however much Hans-Ulrich wished it were. One Ju-87 took a direct hit from a flak shell and never pulled out of its dive, exploding in a fireball when it hit the ground. You had to ignore such things and do your job.

Rudel did. He shot up four panzers. A couple of rounds of small-arms fire clanged into the plane, but none of the instruments showed any damage. The panzers were all ordinary Soviet models. He didn't see any of the KV-1 mastodons that made German panzer men break out in a cold sweat. What you didn't find, you couldn't kill.

Which, given Russian camouflage methods, might or might not mean something. But he'd done what he could. Having done it, he flew off to the west again. Studenets looked as if it would fall soon.

SULLENLY, THE RED ARMY pulled out of Studenets. The *Wehrmacht* moved into the town from straight out of the west, the French expeditionary force from the southwest. Luc Harcourt saw a couple of men in khaki uniforms trotting away in the distance. He raised his rifle to his shoulder and fired at them. One of the men ran faster. The other, a smarter fellow, dove behind a battered wall and thus out of sight.

He wished he still commanded a machine-gun team, as he had when he was still a corporal. But that was beneath a sergeant's dignity. Dignity or no, a burst from the Hotchkiss and those Ivans wouldn't have got away.

If they were Ivans. The range had been long. He might have seen *Feldgrau* through the sights, not faded Soviet khaki. He wasn't the only French soldier who thought of the same thing at the same time. With a sly chuckle, one of his men said, "Wouldn't it have been a shame if those *cochons* were really *Boches* instead of Russians?"

"Oh, but of course, Jacques. That would have been a real pity." Luc could only have sounded more sardonic had he been Lieutenant Demange. Demange was somewhere not far away; Luc could hear him swearing at somebody in the company.

Jacques laughed out loud. "A pity you didn't hit 'em, you mean?"

"I didn't say that. You did." Now Luc did his best to seem severe, though Jacques was right—scragging a couple of Fritzes "by accident" wouldn't have broken his heart. But he also had his reasons for sounding the way he did: "And watch what falls out of your big, fat gob, all right? The Germans are in town, too, remember, and more of those cocksuckers know French than you'd figure."

"I'm not afraid of them." Jacques was all nineteen-year-old bluster.

"Then you're an even bigger *con* than I give you credit for, and that's saying something. I sure am," Luc answered. Jacques' eyes widened. Luc didn't care. He'd been through enough to admit fear without fearing to seem a coward. And it wasn't as if he were lying. Anybody who didn't fear Germans with weapons in their hands hadn't seen enough to know which end was up.

The *Boches* were in town, too. Like the French, they were cleaning out the last few Red Army holdouts. Mausers banged off to the north. Their reports sounded harsher than those of French MAS-36s. Luc thought so, anyhow. There definitely was a difference, whether it lay in harshness or what.

And then an MG-34 opened up. That fierce snarl still gave him the willies, even if his country and the Nazis had the same enemy nowadays. The German machine gun fired so much faster than a Hotchkiss—and faster than anything the English or the Russians made—that you couldn't possibly mistake its malignant roar for anything else. The noise went hand in hand with agony and maiming and limb-sprawled death.

Jacques was a new conscript. He'd never had to glue himself to the ground like a slug while MG-34 bullets kicked up dry leaves and slammed into tree trunks and spanged off stones, all the while trying to let the air out of his precious, irreplaceable self. He didn't get how very deadly that German toy was. *You dumb, lucky fuck,* Luc thought scornfully.

As the firing around here eased off, Russian civilians started coming up from their cellars and showing themselves. A plump, apple-cheeked *babushka* in a head scarf smiled, showing a mouthful of startling gold teeth. *"Amis!"* she said, which startled Luc again. He didn't care about making friends with her. Her granddaughter, now, if she had one . . .

Not all the people emerging from cellars and from under the bed and from wherever the hell else in Studenets were Russians. Some were Jews, the men dark and bearded and hook-nosed in long black coats, the women just as swarthy in scarves of their own and in even longer black dresses.

The Russians looked relieved to be alive. The Jews looked relieved to be alive and even more relieved to be in a part of town the French had overrun. Like the *babushka,* they said, *"Amis!"* And they said *"Kameraden!"* and much else in Yiddish and in more standard German. Luc understood little of that, but some of the French soldiers here would follow more. As he'd told Luc, many Germans could *parler français*— and probably just as many Frenchmen could *Deutsch sprechen.*

An old Jew with a beard down to the second button of his shirtfront handed Luc a bottle that sloshed. "Here. You take. You like," he said in broken French. "Me, I have nephew in Paris. He drive taxi." He mimed steering motions.

Luc did take the bottle. He did like it, too. He'd expected vodka, potent but next to flavorless. But no. He got plum brandy, fiery and sweet at the same time. He gave Jacques a quick nip, then went looking for Demange. The lieutenant would make him sorry if he didn't share a prize like this.

Lieutenant Demange had men going through a warren of little shops for holdouts. They seemed to be flushing out nothing but unarmed Jews. Demange cradled a Soviet PPD submachine gun. It was ugly, but good for killing lots of people in a hurry—quite a bit like the veteran himself. The inevitable Gitane in the corner of his mouth twitched when he saw Luc's offering. "What have you got there?"

"Jew with a white beard gave it to me." Luc held out the bottle.

Demange took it and drank. A slow smile spread across his skinny, ratlike face. "Heyyy! That's the straight shit, all right. Let's hear it for the kike."

"Yeah. Let's hear it," Luc said, not quite comfortably. He thought there were a couple of Jews among the men Demange commanded. But Demange wasn't an anti-Semite, or not particularly. The race he despised was the human race.

He passed the bottle back to Luc, who killed it and tossed it in the rubble. Two stiff knocks of brandy didn't get him drunk. They did mean he eyed the wreckage that was Studenets with a slightly less jaundiced eye.

Demange pointed toward where the center of town ought to be. "Bring a few guys with you. We'd better make contact with the Nazis. Long as everything stays nice and official, the chance for some dumb fucking accident goes down."

"Happy day," Luc said, his enthusiasm distinctly tempered. It wasn't that Demange was wrong, because he wasn't. But Luc wanted to pretend France was at war with the Russians, and there weren't any Germans around for hundreds of kilometers. They'd come closer to killing him than the Ivans ever had, and he'd sure done for his share of them . . . Muttering, he shambled off to obey.

He muttered even more when he saw that the Germans in the town square didn't belong to the *Wehrmacht*. They came from the *Waffen*-SS: they wore the SS runes on the right side of their helmets and on the right collar patch of each man's tunic. They looked like tough assholes; the few times he'd faced *Waffen*-SS troops, they'd fought like tough assholes, too. He still would rather have shot at them than at the Ivans.

A few more SS men herded some Jews into the square. One of the Jews might have been brother to the guy who'd given Luc plum brandy. Laughing, an SS sergeant drew his Luger and raised it to the back of the Jew's head.

Maybe he just meant to scare the graybeard. Maybe. Luc didn't wait to find out. He had his rifle pointed at the SS noncom's belly button in nothing flat. *"Halt!"* he yelled. He didn't speak much German, but he had that one down solid.

Slowly, his mouth dropping open in disbelief, the SS man lowered the pistol. An SS officer spoke in badly accented French: "But this foolishness is. We are allies, *n'est-ce pas?* And these are only Jews."

Other SS men looked as ready to fight their "allies" as Luc was to plug that sergeant. Lieutenant Demange dove behind some shattered masonry. He shouted in German probably as lousy as the SS officer's French. Then he translated for Luc: "I told 'em I'd give 'em the whole fucking drum of ammo if they didn't leave the damn Hebes alone."

The *Waffen*-SS officer quivered with outrage. "Tell me your name," he snarled at Demange. "I shall to your superiors report you."

"Fuck off and die," the lieutenant replied *auf Deutsch,* not breaking cover. Luc got that fine. Demange said something else in German, then repeated it in French: "You want to report us for stopping a murder, you'll be at war with every Frenchman in Russia by this time tomorrow."

Luc nodded. So did the *poilus* he'd brought along. The SS man swore in his own language, but he let the Jews go. And nobody reported the confrontation to anybody's superiors.

Chapter 9

The major standing by Alistair Walsh murmured to himself: "'If it were done when 'tis done, then 'twere well it were done quickly.'"

"What's that, sir?" Walsh kept looking across the street toward what had to be England's most famous address.

"That"—the major's handsome face set in disapproving lines at Walsh's ignorance, and very likely at his accent, too—"*that* is Shakespeare. *Macbeth,* to be precise." He was the sort who'd set great stock in precision. Yes, the Army needed that kind of man . . . which didn't mean the bloke would have a great pack of friends.

"We ought to move a bit, not let ourselves be seen staring at the place," Walsh said. He didn't think he himself was important in the grand scheme of things: not in the other side's calculations, at any rate. He didn't know what kind of reports they had about the major. He didn't even know the man's name. What you didn't know, you couldn't tell, no matter how clever—or cruel—the questioner.

Absently, the major nodded. "Quite," he said, and started mooching down the street. Sighing, Walsh went along. The major was bound to be very good at . . . well, at whatever he was good at. Whatever that might be, it wasn't acting. He might have drawn more notice with a battery-powered signboard featuring flashing electric lamps. On the other hand, he also might not have.

Walsh didn't notice anything out of the ordinary about the guards in front of the famous address. Of course, if the other side was on the job, he wouldn't. But if the other side were on the job, he wouldn't have been strolling along with the officer.

He did some murmuring of his own: "Gunpowder."

"Oh, we've got better toys than that these days," the major said.

"I meant the Gunpowder Plot, sir. Guy Fawkes' Day."

"Well, don't equivocate, then," the major snapped. "Say what you mean."

"Yes, sir," Walsh replied with dour precision. Since he was nominally a civilian, he couldn't salute, even sarcastically, but he had to remind his twitchy arm of that. "What I mean, *sir,* is that if we bugger this up little tykes a hundred years from now will take lessons about the Second World War Traitors and get browned off because they've got to memorize our names."

"Little tykes a hundred years from now will take lessons about the Second World War Traitors regardless." The major spoke with gloomy certainty. "The only question left is which list of names they'll have to memorize."

Walsh grunted. That was much too likely to be true. A nice-looking blonde came up the street past him. Of itself, his head swiveled so he could check her hip action, too. The little things in life went on no matter how grandiose the big things were. A blackbird on a rooftop opened its yellow beak and poured out springtime song. It hopped into the air and flew off, right over Walsh and the major.

The officer ducked away. Walsh eyed him sympathetically. He must have had a rugged war if a thrush could remind him of a grenade or a shell fragment. The ribbon for the Military Medal on his chest did nothing to argue against that. But then the major said, "Ought to be a bounty on those bloody things. Did you ever try to clean bird shit off your cap visor?"

"Er—no." Walsh's sympathy evaporated.

"Stinking nuisance," the major said, before returning to the business at hand: "I'm told you know something of this business. What do you think of our chances for success?"

Do I know something of this business? Walsh wondered. He'd planned and led attacks on strongpoints in urban settings—no doubt of that. It made him more of an expert than most people, even probably more of an expert than most soldiers. He pursed his lips, weighing what he'd seen. "So long as we do keep the advantage of surprise, chances look tolerably good to me. If they're waiting for us when we make the attempt . . ."

"We're ruined for fair, then," the major finished for him, which wasn't how Walsh would have gone on. Again, though, that didn't make him wrong.

A boy on a street corner was waving the *Times of London* and bawling out the latest war headlines. The British Expeditionary Force and the rest of the Nazis' allies were advancing deeper into Russia. In Malaya and Burma, the Japanese kept pushing imperial troops back. Even Singapore, said to be the strongest fortress in the world, might come under attack soon.

"Strange business," the major said, walking past without buying a paper.

"How's that, sir?"

"Well, the bleeding Japs are supposed to be Hitler's chums. But we're supposed to be Hitler's chums, too, and we're at war with Japan. And the Russians are Hitler's deadly enemies, but they've already had their war with Japan, so they're neutral now. And the USA and Japan are fighting, but Russian ships can cross the Pacific free as so many fish, load up on guns in American ports, and haul all that stuff back to Russia to fire it off against the Nazis—and us."

When you thought of it like that, it was enough to make your head swim. Walsh found one problem: "How many ships in the Pacific have the Russians got left now that Vladivostok's fallen?"

"They have some yet. And there's a road connection—not a good one, but it's there—between Magadan and what the Russians still hold of the Trans-Siberian Railway. No, the real question is, how much can they bring in whilst the harbor at Magadan's not iced up?"

Walsh had never heard of Magadan. He had no idea where in Siberia it lay, or, for that matter, whether the major was simply inventing it to bolster his argument. The officer ducked into a pub. Walsh followed. A pint of bitter made him stop caring whether Magadan was real.

Beer, steak-and-kidney pie, more beer . . . A French *estaminet* couldn't hold a candle to a proper pub. Two wars' worth of experience on the other side of the Channel and years of diligent experimenting in his own country left Walsh as sure of that as made no difference. The major wasn't the best drinking companion he'd ever had, but also wasn't the worst.

It was dark by the time Walsh went back to his little furnished room. London's lights were on again. With Germany friendly, the need for a blackout disappeared. Sometimes conveniences came at too high a price. Walsh thought so, anyhow. The Prime Minister would have disagreed. Walsh reckoned disagreeing with Sir Horace Wilson sure to put him in the right.

Because of the beer he'd taken on board, the knock at the door took longer to rouse him than it might have. He lurched off the bed—which doubled as a sofa in daylight hours—ready to give whoever was out there a piece of his mind. But the two somber men in trenchcoats hadn't the slightest interest in listening to him.

"You're Alistair Walsh—is that right?" one of them said.

"What if I am?" Walsh answered indignantly. "Who wants to know?"

Both men produced Scotland Yard identity cards. "You're under arrest," said the one who did the talking. "Come along with us—quietly, if you please."

Ice and fire chased each other along Walsh's spine. "The devil I will," he blustered. "Show me your warrant."

With startling speed, the copper or detective or whatever he was produced a pistol: a .455 Webley and Scott Mark VI, a great man-killing brute of a revolver, the same weapon British officers carried into battle. "Here's all the warrant we need, mate. Let out a peep and I'll blow a hole in you they could throw a cat through."

The other Scotland Yard man spoke up for the first time: "Don't tempt us, either. Shooting's better than a damned traitor deserves."

"I'm no traitor!" Walsh said, wondering how many MPs and Army officers were being scooped up in the same net.

Both men in the hallway laughed—two of the nastiest laughs he'd ever heard. "Now tell us another one," said the fellow with the Webley and Scott. "No—tell your stories at headquarters. Get moving, right now. This is your first, last, and only chance." He gestured toward the stairway with the pistol.

Numbly, Walsh got moving. The Fritzes had almost captured him a couple of times. He'd counted himself lucky to escape that fate. Now his own countrymen had him by the ballocks. Better if the Nazis had got him. At least they were enemies, and honest enough about that at the time. These bastards imagined they were patriots. It only went to show how crazy and useless a thing an imagination could be.

PETE MCGILL HADN'T thought of Australia as a tropical country. When he was on shipboard duty, before he got posted to China, he'd put in at Sydney and Melbourne and Perth. They weren't half bad—they kind of reminded him of Southern California. He'd never been to Darwin before.

Here he was in Darwin now. It wasn't the Dutch East Indies—it wasn't right on the Equator. No, it lay all of twelve degrees south. That made a difference. As far as Pete was concerned, it didn't make nearly enough.

He was just glad he'd got here in one piece, and that the *Boise* had got here under her own power. Most of the ships and sailors who'd fought the Japs with the American light cruiser farther north weren't so lucky. The Dutch East Indies were falling, if they hadn't already fallen. All that oil, all that rubber, all that tin . . . They lay in Japanese hands now.

How long the *Boise* would be able to keep running under her own power—and how long she'd stay in one piece herself—he had no idea. Japanese bombers called on Darwin night after night. They were, not to put too fine a point on it, knocking the crap out of the place. Darwin was just a little town at the edge of nowhere. The Japs seemed intent on knocking it over the edge.

And so Pete wasn't astonished when the *Boise* steamed out of the harbor one evening just when the sun was going down. If one of those bombers with the meatballs on the wings got lucky, the light cruiser wouldn't go anywhere again, except to the bottom. So she was getting out while the getting was good.

It seemed that way to him, anyhow. Joe Orsatti was much less happy about it. "I'm sick of running from those shitass little yellow monkeys," he groused as the Marines manned the five-inch guns in case an enemy plane or a sub or even an arrogantly aggressive destroyer spotted the *Boise*.

"Who isn't?" Pete agreed. They hurried east. Scuttlebutt said they were bound for New Zealand, and ultimately for Hawaii. Pete hoped the scuttlebutt was true. He wouldn't be sure till they made it through the Torres Strait. If they kept heading east after that, New Zealand it would be. If they swung more to the south, paralleling Australia's coast, they were liable to be bound for Melbourne or Sydney. He understood that the Aussies needed to keep up the fight. But so did America, and he wanted to help. He figured he owed the Japs more than Orsatti did.

The other leatherneck warmed to his theme: "I'm a white man, God damn it to hell. Those lousy slant-eyed cocksuckers got no business pushing me around."

Plenty of Marines in Peking and Shanghai had felt the same way. Pete wondered how his buddies were doing these days. He wondered how many of them were still alive. Not for the first time, guilt stabbed at him because he wasn't up there sharing their fate, whatever it turned out to be. He couldn't do anything about that, of course, but his impotence made him feel worse, not better.

He'd had some of that white man's arrogance himself, but only some. "I saw a lot of the Japs in China," he said slowly. "They're just as sure they're hot shit in a gold goblet as we are."

"Yeah, but they're really nothin' but cold diarrhea in a Dixie cup," Orsatti replied, which got a laugh from everybody in the gun crew, including Pete. He went on, "You wait and see. We'll make 'em wish they never took us on. We get the whole fleet together at Pearl, then we sail west and bash 'em." His voice went all dreamy. "The Big Fuckin' Pacific Battle. It'll make Jutland look like a couple of kids playin' with toy boats in the bathtub."

"There you go," Pete said. There weren't many sailors or Marines who didn't daydream about the Big Fuckin' Pacific Battle. Anybody with a brain in his head had seen that the USA would tangle with Japan one of these days. Why else had both sides built all those battlewagons and carriers and cruisers and destroyers and subs, if not to get ready for the day? So we'd put all of ours together, they'd put all of theirs together, and then both sides would bash heads. And the winner would go forward, while the loser . . . What about the loser?

He'd get what losers always got. T.S., Eliot.

Without warning, the *Boise* heeled to port, as hard as she could. A split second later, klaxons hooted. "Torpedo attack!" The shout burst from the loudspeakers' iron throats. "We are under torpedo attack!"

They'd gone to battle stations as soon as the ship left port. Pete stood by the open ammunition locker, ready to pass shells to the loader. He couldn't do anything else except wait and worry and hope like hell he wouldn't get his ankles broken when the Jap fish slammed into the cruiser.

"There's the wake!" Orsatti said hoarsely.

Sure as hell, a phosphorescent line arrowed through the tropical sea, seeming to run straight for the *Boise*'s vitals. Now—how many fish had the Japanese sub launched? Holy crap! Here came another one, much too soon after the first. It sped along on a track almost identical to the other.

Could the *Boise* dodge them? She was sure as hell trying. Smoke spurted from her stacks as the engines roared up to emergency full. Machine gunners opened fire on the torpedoes, trying to detonate them before they could hit . . . if they were going to hit.

"Hail, Mary, full of grace . . ." Orsatti rattled off the prayer. The hand in his pocket was probably working a rosary. Pete wished he could pray that way. He'd seen how it made people feel better. But he'd never got the habit when he was a kid, and talking to God now only made him feel like a phony.

He tried the next best thing, saying, "I think the bastards are gonna slide on by us." The *Boise* had turned into the torpedoes' paths, and was running along them in the opposite direction—straight toward the sub that had turned them loose. If that sub was still surfaced, it would be mighty sorry mighty fast. Pete peered forward. He saw nothing that looked like a periscope or a conning tower, but how much did that say?

Bow on, the *Boise* also offered torpedoes the smallest possible target. They did slide past, both to port. One seemed close enough for Pete to spit on. He refrained. No grinding, rending crash told of a cruiser-submarine collision. The *Boise* threw a few depth charges into the warm, dark water. The deck shook under Pete's feet as they burst one by one. The ocean boiled above the bursts.

"I wish I thought we were really after those assholes," Joe Orsatti said. "Way it feels, though, is we're just makin' 'em keep their heads down."

"Fine by me." Pete profanely embellished that. "All we're doing now is getting out of town any which way. So we'll go, and they can give somebody else a hard time next week."

The other Marine grunted. "Yeah, you got somethin' there. I didn't look at it from that angle. Maybe you're smarter'n you act most of the time."

"Ahh, up yours," Pete said without heat. "Besides, if I'm so goddamn smart, what am I doing here?"

That drew another laugh from everybody at the gun. "Well, if I remember straight, your other choice was staying in Manila," Orsatti answered. "Like I said a minute ago, maybe you ain't so dumb after all."

Pete wondered what he would have done if he hadn't come aboard the *Boise*. He didn't need to wonder long. He would have picked up a Springfield, found a tin hat that came close to fitting, and joined the Americans and Filipinos trying to hold off the Japanese invaders. From the reports trickling out of the Philippines, the defenders were losing ground day by day.

Well, the *Boise* and the handful of other American ships in the western Pacific hadn't done much to slow down the Japanese attacks on Malaya or the Dutch East Indies, either. Here on the cruiser, though, he wasn't shivering with malaria. He had plenty of chow. It might not be great, but it wasn't terrible, either. He wouldn't come down with amoebic dysentery if he ate it or drank water that wasn't heavily chlorinated. If you wanted to fight a war in comfort, a ship was the place to do it—unless you got hit, of course. Getting hit was bad news no matter where or how it happened.

It wouldn't happen right this minute. That sub lurked somewhere deep in the sea, with luck damaged by the ash cans the *Boise* threw at it. Any which way, the cruiser would be long gone before the sub surfaced again. And then . . . ? New Zealand and Hawaii? Sydney or Melbourne? In a way, which choice hardly mattered. They both meant that, sooner or later, the Japs would get another chance at the *Boise* and everybody she carried.

TO SAY THAT the Spanish Republic wasn't rich only proved what a poor, inadequate thing language could be sometimes. Vaclav Jezek had heard that the Republic had sent all its gold to Russia for safekeeping (and, incidentally, to buy weapons). Giving Stalin your gold reserves struck him as the exact equivalent of handing a fox the keys to your chicken coop. He might be here fighting for the Republic, but he had scant use for Stalin.

Because the Republic was chronically broke, soldiers' pay chronically ran late. He didn't much care about that; he had little to spend money on but cigarettes and booze, and he usually found enough in his pockets for those. Before long, the Spaniards doled out rank insignia so their people would know who was who and what was what among the Czechs. Vaclav got two gold cloth stripes with red borders.

"Is the mark of a *brigada*," the fellow who gave it to him said in German with a Spanish accent strong enough to make it almost incomprehensible to Jezek. "A sergeant, they say in this language."

"But I'm only a corporal," Vaclav answered, also in German.

"People from European armies, we promote one grade," the Spaniard said. "You have combat experience soldiers from Spain do not." His face clouded. "The Fascists, they also this do with the men of the Legion Kondor."

"Oh, terrific," Vaclav said, fortunately in Czech. Gaining a privilege because a pack of Nazis also enjoyed it was the last thing he wanted. But he damn well *did* have combat experience the locals lacked. And, if his pay went up to match the Spanish rank, he'd get more money even if they stiffed him now and then. So he managed to compose himself when he returned to German: *"Danke schön."*

"Bitte," the Spaniard answered, and showed himself a true student

of *Kultur* by clicking his heels German-style. Vaclav didn't tell him any Czech despised that nonsense as a reminder of the not-quite-dead-enough Austro-Hungarian past. The fellow doubtless meant well. Then again, when you thought about which road was paved with good intentions ...

Because Benjamin Halévy was already a sergeant, the Spaniards made him into a second lieutenant. He took it for a joke, which made Vaclav think better of him. "I sure as hell never would have turned into an officer if I'd stayed in France!" the Jew exclaimed.

"Maybe if you'd gone to Russia and done something brave, the Germans would have given you a battlefield promotion," Vaclav suggested with a sly grin.

Halévy told him what he could do with any battlefield promotion won from the Nazis. It sounded uncomfortable, especially if Vaclav tried to do it sideways, as the other man urged. When the Czech said so, he found Halévy remarkably unsympathetic.

By the time the Spaniards got through, none of the Czechs had a grade lower than PFC, and most of them were at least corporals. It might matter when they dealt with the locals. Their relative ranks remained unchanged, so for their own purposes the promotions gave some merriment but otherwise might as well not have happened.

More serious business for Vaclav was picking off any of Marshal Sanjurjo's officers who came within range of his elephant gun. The Nationalists made his murderous work easier by prominently displaying their rank badges and medals. "Stupid," he said, after potting a fellow he thought was a colonel. "They'd be a lot safer if they showed off less."

"But they'd be less *macho*," Halévy told him.

"Less what?" Vaclav hadn't run into the Spanish word before.

"*Macho*. It means being tough for the sake of being tough. It means, if you've got a big cock, you wear a codpiece so it looks even bigger. It's like elk growing antlers every spring so they can bang heads with other elk."

"Elk can't help growing antlers every spring," Vaclav protested.

"Spaniards, or a lot of Spaniards, can't help showing how *macho* they are," Halévy said with a shrug.

"If they had any brains, they could," Jezek said. "That colonel would still be breathing if he'd worn a private's tunic and kept his medals in the boxes they came in. The way he was strutting around with all those gold stars and ribbons, he might as well have written SHOOT ME! across his chest in big red letters."

"If they had any brains, Vaclav, how many of them would be officers in a Fascist army?" Benjamin Halévy asked.

Vaclav pondered that. "Well, you've got something there," he admitted.

The next day, the Spanish papers that came out from Madrid had big headlines. The only problem was, Vaclav had no idea what those headlines said. Spanish was even more a closed book to him than French had been.

Halévy, who read French like the native he was, could make a stab at written Spanish, just as a native Czech speaker would recognize some written Polish words and might be able to extract sense from a Polish newspaper story. "Something's going on in England," the Jew reported. "Somebody—the army, I think—doesn't like the way the government's jumped into bed with the Nazis, and they're trying to do something about it."

"And?" Vaclav said. "Don't cocktease, goddammit! Are they winning? Are they losing? Will England tell Hitler where to head in? That'd be something, wouldn't it?" He imagined the Royal Navy and the RAF pounding the hell out of German-held Europe again.

"I don't know 'and,'" Halévy replied in an unwontedly small voice. "Either the paper doesn't say or my Spanish is too crappy for me to figure it out. Maybe they're hanging traitors from lampposts. Or maybe the traitors are still running things and they're translating 'Deutschland über Alles' into English right now."

"Give me that goddamn thing." Jezek snatched the newspaper out of Halévy's hand. As usual, the Czechs and the men from the International Brigade held adjoining stretches of the Republican line. The Republic naturally grouped its best fighters together. And the Czech didn't take long to find somebody who could read Spanish and speak German.

"It just says there's unrest in England," the International told him. By the way the man pronounced his r's, Vaclav guessed he was a Magyar. Had they met anywhere but in Spain, they probably would have quarreled—Hungary had sat on Slovakia for centuries, and mistrusted Czechs for wanting to help Slovaks. Here, they both had bigger things to worry about.

"Who's winning?" Vaclav asked, as he had with Halévy.

The Magyar spread his hands. "We'll have to wait and see," he said. "The guy who wrote this doesn't know. He's trying to hide that so he won't look dumb, but he doesn't."

Vaclav made a disgusted noise down deep in his throat. "Sounds like a newspaperman, all right."

"It sure does." The Magyar studied him. The fellow had green eyes, high cheekbones, and an arrogant blade of a nose. He looked the way Vaclav would have expected a Magyar to look, in other words. And he sounded faintly surprised when he added, "You're not such a fool, are you?"

For a Czech, he might have meant. To Magyars, Slovaks were nothing but bumpkins, and Czechs were a lot like Slovaks, so . . . Vaclav thought Slovaks were bumpkins, too, and Fascist-loving bumpkins at that, but he knew Magyars were dead wrong about Czechs. How did he know? By being a Czech himself, of course.

"Well, I try," he said dryly.

"Heh," the Magyar said. He tapped the paper with his left hand. The little finger was missing its last joint. "Thanks for bringing this. I hadn't seen it yet. If England really is having second thoughts, that could be big."

"What do you think the odds are?"

"Either she'll change her mind or she won't. Right now, you can toss a coin," the Magyar answered. Grimacing, Vaclav nodded. If you tried to guess when you didn't know enough, you were bound to end up looking like an idiot. The Magyar declined that dubious honor. Declining made sense. Vaclav still knew what he hoped.

THEO HOSSBACH DIDN'T LIKE any SS men, as a general working rule. He disliked the *Waffen*-SS less than the other branches, though. Men who joined the SS intending to fight foreign foes took more risks than the ones who joined to hit prisoners who couldn't fight back.

These bastards were still bastards. Unlike their comrades in the Black Corps, they were brave bastards. He'd seen that in France. *Waffen-SS* units there went straight at obstacles the *Wehrmacht* would have tried to outflank or would have ignored altogether. Sometimes taking a position was more expensive than it was worth.

So it seemed to the *Wehrmacht,* anyhow. So it certainly seemed to Theo. The SS men looked at things differently. Sometimes they bulled through where the *Wehrmacht* would have hesitated, perhaps not least because the enemy often thought they wouldn't be crazy enough to attack *here.* Sometimes they got slaughtered for their trouble.

Not that Theo necessarily thought slaughtering SS men a bad idea . . . He did disapprove of waste, though. Even when the SS broke through, its butcher's bill was higher than the *Wehrmacht's* would have been.

Right now, Theo and Adi Stoss and Hermann Witt were messing with their Panzer III's transmission, trying to figure out which gear in the train didn't want to mesh and whether they had or could get their hands on a replacement. "The Ivans don't worry about shit like this," Adi said. "Their drivers have a mallet next to their seat. When a gear doesn't want to engage, they give the stick a good whack. That makes the son of a bitch behave."

"You're making that up," Sergeant Witt said. "I know the Russians can be rude and crude with their equipment, but that's over the line even for them."

Lothar Eckhardt, the panzer's gunner, and Kurt Poske, the loader, watched without saying much. They were both new men, much less experienced than the three veterans. Theo wished it were a new Panzer III, but no. Somebody else got the new machines. This one was a hand-me-down, not so old and beat-up as the Panzer II that was now being cannibalized for spare parts if its carcass had been brought in and quietly rusting if it hadn't.

Adi raised his right hand with the first two fingers raised and crooked, as if he were swearing an oath in court. "Honest to God, Sergeant. I've seen the damn things with my own eyes."

"Me, too." Theo rarely contributed to the conversation, but a fact was a fact—and this one cost him only a couple of words.

"Well, fuck me," Witt said mildly. Heinz Naumann wouldn't have let his juniors get away with disagreeing with him, even when they were right—maybe especially when they were. Theo missed Naumann not a bit, and suspected Adi missed him even less than that. Seeing that a fact was a fact even when it wasn't *his* fact was one of the many things that made Witt a better panzer commander than Naumann had ever dreamt of being.

Adi pounced with a wrench. Three minutes later, he held the culprit in the palm of his hand. "Will you look at that?" he said. "One tooth gone, and another one going. No wonder things were getting sticky."

"No wonder at all," Witt agreed. "Have we got a new one we can swap in?"

"I'm pretty sure we don't," Adi said.

Witt nodded unhappily. "I'm pretty sure you're right." He tossed the toothed steel disk to Eckhardt. "Go on back to the maintenance section and get a replacement. Check it out before you take it, too. Don't let 'em give you one that's had new teeth welded on. They'll tell you it's just as good, but that's a bunch of crap."

The kid looked shocked. He was very fair, and couldn't have been above nineteen—he hardly needed to shave. "They'd try to dump defective stuff on us?"

"Listen to me." Witt spoke with great conviction. "You know the Russians are the enemy, right? But your own side will screw you just as hard if you give 'em half a chance. Go on, now. Scoot."

Theo wondered if Witt would ask Adi or him to go along with Eckhardt. But the sergeant didn't. The new guys had to learn the ropes. Whenever you had the chance, you broke them in a little at a time. Trouble was, a fast-moving campaign—which this one had become, now that the mud was dry—didn't always give you chances like that.

Witt pulled out a pack of Junos and offered everybody else a smoke. "We may as well take ten," he said. "We sure aren't going anywhere till he comes back with that gear."

New green grass was pushing up through the dirt and through the gray-yellow dead growth from the year before. Theo sat down and sucked in smoke. Not far away, a skylark sang sweetly. The clear trilled notes couldn't drown out the distant rumble of artillery, though. Theo cocked his head to one side, listening to the guns. *Ours,* he decided, and relaxed fractionally.

Another panzer crew was working on their machine at the far edge of the field. Resting infantrymen sprawled in clumps between the two panzers. They all wore SS runes on helmets and collar patches. They were eating or smoking or passing around water bottles that probably didn't hold water. Some of them lay with their eyes closed, grabbing a little sleep while they could.

They were doing all the things *Wehrmacht* foot soldiers would have done, in other words. Theo still looked at them differently. Anybody could end up in the Army. He had, for instance. So had Adi Stoss. You had to volunteer for the *Waffen*-SS, and you wouldn't do that unless you were a convinced Nazi. They wouldn't take you unless they were sure you were a convinced Nazi, either, so that worked both ways.

One of the guys propped up on an elbow maybe ten meters away bummed a chunk of black bread from his buddy and squeezed butter onto it from a tinfoil tube. Theo's stomach rumbled. He told it to shut up. It didn't want to listen.

"Can you believe those stupid goddamn Frenchmen?" the trooper asked after he swallowed a heroic bite of bread.

"Jesus Christ, but that was chickenshit! For twenty pfennigs, I would've blown the fuckin' froggies a new asshole with my Schmeisser," answered the other man from the *Waffen*-SS. Theo's stomach rumbled again. Once more, he told it to keep quiet. It might not want to listen, but all of a sudden he did.

The first fellow who wore the runes couldn't have looked more disgusted had he tried for a week. "Once we finish with the Ivans, we're gonna have to do for the froggies, all right," he said. "It's a hell of a note when we can't give the Hebes what they deserve on account of our so-called friends don't like it." He spat in the dirt.

"Damn straight," his friend agreed. "*Damn* straight. This whole stupid, stinking war, it's about Reds and kikes. If the Frenchmen can't see that, tough shit for them, that's all I've got to say."

"Amen!" the first trooper said, as if in church. "The *Führer's* gonna bring things around to the way they're supposed to be, even if he's got to wipe out all the goddamn Jews to do it." The other fellow with the SS collar tab nodded, then started cleaning his submachine gun.

Ever so casually, Theo's gaze swung toward Adi Stoss. He wouldn't have been surprised to find Adi hopping mad, or else sizzling inside and trying to pretend he wasn't. But the panzer driver lay on his back, his hands clasped behind his head, staring up at the clouds drifting across the watery blue sky. If he'd paid any attention to what the infantrymen were saying, he gave no sign.

Lothar Eckhardt came back with the gear. He anxiously showed it to Sergeant Witt. "Is it all right?" he quavered. No doubt he was imagining bread and water, if not a blindfold and a last cigarette at dawn, if the answer was no.

The panzer commander carefully inspected the part. If it wasn't all right, he would go back to the maintenance section and give those clowns a piece of his mind. But he nodded. "Looks good. They knew they couldn't pull a fast one on you, so they didn't even try."

"Wow!" Eckhardt breathed.

"Now you and Kurt are going to install the son of a bitch," Witt said. "The more you know about keeping your panzer running on your own, the better off you'll be. One of these days, you'll run into trouble where you can't go off to the mechanics."

Eckhardt and Poske both gulped. "I'm not sure we know how to do that, Sergeant," the loader said, which could only mean *We have no idea how to do that.*

Witt chuckled; he understood at least as well as Theo. "Adi and I will coach you," he said. "It isn't black magic. It isn't even real hard, as long as you don't mind getting your hands dirty. And you'd damn well better not. Now come on, both of you." He led them back to the waiting Panzer III.

Chapter 10

oing back to Madrid was nothing new for Chaim Weinberg. Going back to Madrid with money in his pocket was. He was carrying the proverbial elephant-choking roll. He'd played a lot of poker since coming to Spain. (He'd played a lot of poker before he came to Spain, too, which didn't hurt.) When luck and skill came together . . . He shook his head in wonder. He'd never known a night when luck and skill came together like the night before.

Fins, sawbucks, pound notes, fivers . . . It was just about all good money, not asswipes like pesetas and francs. Poker, after all, was serious business. It brought out the hard currency.

On rattled the ancient, beat-up French truck. Chaim tried to listen for aircraft noises over the engine's farting and the rattle of stones off the undercarriage. Of *course* a Nationalist bomber or a Legion Kondor Messerschmitt would pick this exact moment to target this ratty truck. . . .

But none did. Brakes squealing—hell, brakes shrieking—the truck shuddered to a stop. *"Raus!"* the driver yelled. He wasn't a German. He was an Estonian, or something like that. But he knew *Raus!* was something everybody in the back of the truck would get. And everybody did. Out scrambled the soldiers. The Spanish kid who hopped down just in front of Chaim mimed rubbing at his abused kidneys. Chaim chuckled and nodded.

He looked around. As always, Madrid saddened and awed him at the same time. You could kill tens of thousands of people if you bombed the crap out of a big city. Everyone between the wars had seen that clearly. The heavy-duty thinkers hadn't understood just how big a big city was, though. With the worst will in the world, bombers couldn't smash all of one.

And bombing a city didn't cow the people it failed to kill. Instead, it really pissed them off. The heavy-duty thinkers missed that one, too—missed it by a mile. They underestimated the proletariat's resilience (and the bourgeoisie's, though Chaim had no great use for the bourgeoisie, either).

So Madrid looked like hell. Streets were cratered. Buildings had chunks bitten out of them. There were mounds of rubble that had been buildings in happier times. Window glass was a prodigy; whenever Chaim caught a glimpse of some, his head started to whip around, as if toward a pretty girl.

Communist Party headquarters, where his own particular pretty girl worked, had taken a pounding. Naturally, the Nationalists wanted to knock it flat. But you couldn't hit one building in particular with high-altitude bombing—one more place where the theorists had it wrong. And enough antiaircraft guns surrounded the place to make even the most fanatical Stuka pilot think twice before tipping his plane into a dive.

Men from one of the gun crews waved to Chaim as he walked into the building. They recognized him by now. "You lucky so-and-so!" one of them called—they knew who La Martellita was, too. Chaim laughed and waved back.

If his Spanish ladylove was glad to see him, she hid it very well. "What are you doing here?" she snapped when she looked up from the report she was working on. Chaim couldn't read Spanish upside down. He wondered what the report was about, and how many people would wind up in trouble because of it. Party reports always landed people in trouble—that was what they were for. He counted himself lucky that none of La Martellita's reports had had his name in them.

"What am I here for? I'll show you, babe." Chaim reached into one of his front pockets and extracted the roll. (He wasn't dumb enough to carry it in a hip pocket, where it practically begged to get stolen.) He started peeling off greenbacks and British banknotes and laying them on the desk one after another. "Here you go. These are for you—and for the kid, *claro*."

He startled her, enough so she couldn't keep from showing it. "Where did you get all this?" she asked, as if sure he couldn't have come by it honestly.

I earned it by oppressing the working class. Communist or not, Chaim made that kind of joke without even thinking about it. But he did have to think about it to translate it into Spanish. And thinking about it, this time, made him decide *not* to translate it. La Martellita wouldn't appreciate it.

That should have warned that they weren't destined for many long and happy years together. But she was stunning, she tasted good, and she felt even better. Infatuation had blinded plenty before him. It wasn't likely to stop after he ran aground, either.

Instead of joking, he said, "Cards," and let it go at that.

She was counting the money and, he supposed, turning the count into pesetas. "You don't win like this all the time," she said accurately.

"*Querida,* nobody wins like this all the time. Nobody who doesn't cheat, anyhow," Chaim answered, also accurately. "But at least I have the sense to use the money. I'm not going to waste it, and I didn't lose it all again as fast as I won it."

"You didn't gamble the sun away before morning," La Martellita said.

It sounded like a proverb, but it wasn't one Chaim had heard before. "The sun?" he echoed.

"One of the *conquistadores* in Peru got a big golden sun disk as his share of the loot from the Incas. He lost it at dice before the real sun came up," La Martellita explained.

"Gotcha." Chaim knew plenty of guys like that. Spaniards weren't the only ones who came down with gambling fever. Oh, no—not even close.

She looked from the cash on the desk in front of her to him and back again. "You *didn't* waste it or lose it again," she agreed slowly. "You brought it to me. Why?"

"Why do you think?" He knew he sounded irritable, but he couldn't help it. "Because I want to take care of the baby the best way I can. And because I love you." Speaking Spanish imperfectly meant he had to say what was on his mind: he couldn't beat around the bush, as he might have in English.

Saying what was on his mind didn't necessarily help him, though. By the look on La Martellita's face, she was on the point of laughing in his. She didn't—quite—do that. She did say, "The more fool you. The people's cause matters more than any personal attachments."

"Really?" he said. "What is the people's cause, if it isn't to make people happy with other people?"

"It has nothing to do with love," La Martellita insisted.

"What a pity!" Chaim answered. *¡Qué lástima!* sounded much more pitiful to him than its English equivalent did.

A slow flush heated her olive-skinned face. She tossed her head in annoyance, as if that could make the blush go away. She might have wanted to tell him where to head in, but she didn't quite do that, either, not with all the money he'd given her still sitting on top of her desk. Her elegant nostrils flared. "You enjoy being as difficult as you can," she accused.

"I'm sure Marshal Sanjurjo's soldiers agree with you," he said. "They probably talk about it a lot down in hell."

"None of this would have happened if I hadn't got drunk that one night." Was she reminding him or herself?

"You can't pretend it didn't happen, though." With a certain sardonic relish, Chaim added, "It's part of the historical dialectic now, after all."

Those gull-winged nostrils flared again, wider this time. "And I suppose you'll tell me it's part of the historical dialectic that I should sleep with you some more because you thought to bring me this money. Well, I'll tell you right now that the historical dialectic hasn't made me your *puta.*"

Chaim had been thinking about saying something like that if he could find a way to do it that wasn't quite so blunt. Since she'd fore-stalled him, all he said was, "The historical dialectic did turn you into my wife."

"*Sí*," La Martellita answered. That wasn't delight filling her voice, no matter how much Chaim wished it would have been.

"I am trying to take care of you, and take care of our child, the way a husband ought to," he said. "I'm doing my best."

"*Sí*," she said again, a little more warmly this time. "Maybe—*maybe*—I'll do the things a wife ought to do, as long as you don't try to make me do them."

That kind of reply should have made him bang his head against the wall. Coming from La Martellita, who was mercury fulminate in a sweetly curved wrapper, it made a weird kind of sense. "Whatever you say," Chaim told her, which only proved him a born optimist.

ALISTAIR WALSH HAD spent some time in the stockade, and in civilian jails as well. Boys will be boys, and soldier boys will be soldier boys. Sometimes the police, military or otherwise, showed up before the tavern brawl finished. He'd never hurt anybody badly in those little dust-ups, and he'd never spent long behind bars.

Things were different this time. And he liked none of the differ-ences. If they jugged you for rearranging a bloke's face after he tried to smash a pint mug over your head, you knew what you'd done and you knew how long you'd stay jugged on account of it.

If they jugged you for treason, though . . . In that case, they were making up the rules as they went along. He'd asked for a solicitor. They didn't laugh in his face, but they didn't give him one, either. They might as well not have heard him.

But when they asked him questions, they expected answers. Oh, yes! No one asked you questions after a barroom brawl, except maybe *Why were you such a bloody idiot?* Here, they wanted to know everybody he'd ever met, what all those people had said in the past six months, and what he'd said to them. They weren't just building a case against him. He was a minnow. They were trying to use him to hook the big fish.

They weren't fussy about how they went at it, either. Bright lights, lack of sleep . . . "No wonder you back the buggers who threw in with the Nazis," he told one of them. "The SS must have taught you all its tricks."

That won him a slap in the face. They didn't bring out the thumb-screws and the hot skewers. He wondered why not. Some lingering memory of the days when they were decent coppers? It seemed too much to hope for.

They told him all the other traitors were in cells, too. They told him the others were singing like canaries. They told him half a dozen people had named him as one of the earliest and most deeply involved plotters. "Then you don't need me to tell you anything more, do you?" he said.

He got another wallop in the chops for that. When his ears stopped ringing, one of the detectives—if that was what they were—said, "You can make it easier on yourself if you give us what you know."

"If you think I'm a traitor, you won't go easy on me any road," Walsh said. He might be sore. He might be half drunk with sleepiness. No matter what he was, that seemed obvious to him.

The interrogators muttered amongst themselves. Things didn't seem to be going the way they wanted. One of them gave him another whack. "Talk, damn you!" the bastard bellowed. Blood salty on his tongue, Walsh rattled off his name, former rank, and pay number. The Scotland Yard man glowered. "You aren't in the Army any more, and you aren't a prisoner of war, either."

"Then give me a solicitor," Walsh said yet again. He got another slap for his trouble. He also got frogmarched back to his cell. He counted that a victory of sorts. He'd made them change plans.

Which was worth . . . what? Anything? They didn't let him see news-papers, of course. They also didn't let him listen to the BBC. That they still held him and went on knocking him around argued that Sir Horace Wilson remained Prime Minister, and that England remained allied to Hitler.

If they decided he was too big a nuisance—or if they decided he didn't know anything they had to learn—they might just knock him over the head and get rid of his body. They went on and on about trai-tors, but they were at least as far outside the law as any traitors could be.

They fed him slop, and precious little of it. He'd eaten more and better in the trenches. He couldn't think of anything worse to say about prison rations.

Then one day they opened his cell at an unexpected time. Alarm ran through him even before one of them pointed a service revolver at his head. Any jailbird quickly learns that breaks in routine aren't intended for his benefit. "Come on, you," the pistol packer snarled.

"Where? Why?" Walsh asked.

"Shut up. Get moving. You waste my time, it's the last dumb thing you'll ever do." The fellow from Scotland Yard seemed to be trying to sound like an American tough guy in the movies. Only his accent spoiled the effect.

Something rattled outside. If that wasn't a machine gun, Walsh had never heard one. And if that *was* a machine gun . . . Walsh held out his hand. "Here, you'd better give me that," he said, as if to a little boy. "You don't want the soldiers to catch you carrying it."

"Soldiers? What soldiers? I'm not afraid of no bleeding soldiers." The copper kept talking tough. The wobble in his voice gave him away. Outside, the machine gun brayed again.

"You'll be doing the bleeding any minute now," Walsh said. "Come on, hand over your toy. What do you think it can do against the kind of firepower the Army's got, anyway?" Something blew up, a lot closer than the stuttering machine gun. Helpfully, Walsh explained: "That's a Mills bomb—a hand grenade, if you like. They're going to get in here. They won't like it if they catch you with a weapon in your hand."

Glumly, the copper handed him the Webley and Scott. Two other Scotland Yard men, moving with slow caution, laid their pistols on the ground. Walsh was tempted to plug each of them in turn after he scooped up the weapons. Not without regret, he refrained.

Pounding feet announced the arrival of soldiers. No one not in the military stomped with that percussive rhythm. "Over here!" Walsh called. "I've got 'em!"

Some of the men carried rifles with fixed bayonets. One of the bayonets dripped blood. A police official must have made a fatal mistake. At the soldiers' head was the major with whom Walsh had examined 10 Downing Street. He cradled a Tommy gun as gently as if it were a baby. "Hullo, old man," he said. "We're in the driving seat now. First job of this sort in upwards of two hundred and fifty years, but we've brought it off."

"That's—" one of the Scotland Yard men began. The Tommy gun's muzzle swung in his direction. He went pale as skimmed milk. Whatever his detailed opinion was, he kept it to himself. He wasn't a complete fool, then. Walsh had had his doubts.

"Elections soon," the major went on. "We'll let the people have their say about what we've done. If they're daft enough to *want* to go along with the Nazis . . ." He rolled his eyes to show what he thought of that. "But in the meanwhile, our troops in Russia are ordered to hold in place against anyone—anyone at all—who attacks them. We'll get them out of there quick as we can."

"But what if old Adolf goes after them hammer and tongs?" Walsh knew he sounded worried, and well he might—he had more than a few friends fighting in Russia. "They're hostages to the Fritzes, you might say."

"It's possible, but I don't believe it's likely. Hitler would have to be raving mad to do anything like that. He'd be handing Stalin four prime divisions on a silver platter, eh?" the major replied.

That made perfect sense. Walsh wondered why hearing it didn't reassure him more. Probably because, when dealing with Hitler, the most perfectly sensible things turned out to be nonsense after all as often as not. Changing the subject looked like a good idea: "Where are Sir Horace and the Cabinet?"

"They're safe. None of them tried anything foolish." The major answered without giving details, which didn't surprise Walsh.

The Scotland Yard man who'd handed over his pistol worked up the nerve to ask, "What does the King think of all this?"

"One of the reasons Edward's off in Bermuda is, he was too pally by half with Adolf and Musso," the major said. "As soon as General Wavell brought his Majesty word the government had, ah, changed, King George knighted him on the spot. And Queen Elizabeth, God bless her, kissed him."

All the captured coppers seemed to shrink in on themselves. They'd been following orders, and they'd been just as sure they were following the path of righteousness. Almost everyone was. Walsh supposed even

Hitler didn't face the mirror when he shaved each morning and think *Today I'll go out and do something really evil.* But if enough others thought that was what he was doing . . . Well, in that case England got the most abrupt change of government since James II bailed out one jump ahead of the incoming William and Mary. *And a good thing, too,* he thought, *or else they would have hanged me.*

LIEUTENANT COLONEL TOMASHEVSKY looked out at the assembled Soviet flyers in his squadron. "Today we bomb west of Chernigov," he said. "Our targets are the German and Hungarian troops in the area, not—I repeat, not—the English expeditionary force. The English have seen reason. They are no longer hostile to the workers and peasants of the Soviet Union . . . which means Hitler's Fascist hyenas and the jackals who follow them are now hostile to the English."

If a quarter of what the Soviet radio and newspapers were saying was true—always an interesting question, as Anastas Mouradian had reason to know—the Nazis were doing their level best to smash the English expeditionary force for presuming to change sides. And, as any Soviet citizen had reason to know, the Nazis' level best was liable to be entirely too good.

"Do not—I repeat, do not—bomb English positions," Tomashevsky went on. "English soldiers are crossing the Soviet lines. They will be repatriated so they can rejoin the struggle against Fascism. English troops will mark their positions with Union Jacks spread out on the ground."

All sorts of interesting questions occurred to Stas on account of that. The Union Jacks might ward off Soviet bombers, but they'd surely attract the *Luftwaffe.* Which worried the English more? And how would those soldiers get back to their homeland? By sea from Murmansk or Arkhangelsk, running the U-boat gantlet? Or would they go down through Persia and take ship there . . . again, running the U-boat gantlet?

"Questions?" Tomashevsky asked.

Stas' hand went up. Tomashevsky pointed to him. The Armenian didn't ask any of *those* questions. He knew he wouldn't get an answer for them. No, the one he did ask was purely practical: "Excuse me, comrade Colonel, but what do we do if we suspect the Germans are setting out Union Jacks to keep us from bombing *them*?"

"Bomb those positions," the squadron commander answered. "But you'd better be right if you do. Our superiors will not be happy if they hear reports from the English that the Red Air Force attacked them."

You'll end up in the gulag *if you bomb Englishmen.* Mouradian had no trouble working out the underlying meaning there. By the looks on the faces of the men around him, neither did they.

When he and his bomb-aimer went out to their Pe-2, the young Karelian said, "We'll have to be careful about what we hit." He wanted to make sure Stas got it.

"Yes, I figured that out, thanks," Mouradian answered dryly. Ivan Kulkaanen nodded back. His expression remained serious, and he seemed not the least bit embarrassed. Staying out of the *gulag* was important business, at least as important as fighting the foreign invaders.

Sergeant Mechnikov greeted his superiors with, "So it's back to bombing the Nazis, is it? Well, the bombs don't care whose heads they fall on." Plainly, he didn't care whose heads he dropped them on. And why should he? His work stayed the same no matter who the enemy was.

One of the crews had FOR STALIN! painted on its Pe-2's fuselage in big red letters, right behind the Soviet star. Did that make them more likely to be reckoned politically reliable? Or did it just make them more likely to get shot down? If it made both more likely, did the one protect more than the other endangered?

Soviet life was *full* of interesting questions.

The Pe-2 jounced down the unpaved runway and climbed into the air. "A lot more power than the old SB-2," Stas remarked as he leveled off.

"Well, I should hope so!" Kulkaanen exclaimed.

"It was a hot plane once upon a time," Mouradian said. "One of these days, this beast will be just as obsolete."

"Oh, sure," the bomb-aimer said. "That's the way things work." He took it for granted. If his narrow, New Soviet Man–style soul held any room for nostalgia, he wouldn't be so weak as to show it.

I'm supposed to be a New Soviet Man, too, Stas thought. For some reason, the indoctrination hadn't taken with him, the way a smallpox vaccination sometimes didn't. He wondered what had gone wrong in his case. Maybe it was just that he was an Armenian. He wasn't so good at swallowing things whole as most Russians were . . . although plenty of his countrymen were, or at least seemed to be, ideal New Soviet Men and Women.

A few badly aimed rounds of antiaircraft fire came up at them as they droned southwest. They were still over terrain the Red Army held. Some New Soviet Men down below feared they belonged to the *Luftwaffe.* That made those nervous gunners New Soviet Idiots, but it happened on almost every mission.

Sergeant Mechnikov expressed his opinion of the antiaircraft crews through the speaking tube. The Chimp couldn't have put it better. Mouradian wondered how—and whether—Kuchkov was doing these days.

What should have been the front was mostly confusion. English troops were crossing the Soviet line. Red Army men were rushing in to take their places and tear a hole in the enemy position. The Germans were doing their damnedest not to let any of that happen.

Bombs burst among the English positions. Stas looked around, wondering whether some of his squadronmates were dropping too soon. But those bombs didn't come from Soviet planes. The *Luftwaffe* had bombers in the neighborhood, too: Mouradian spotted two stacked V's of Do-17s.

The Flying Pencils were unmistakable, and not just because of the yellow band the Nazis painted on the fuselages of their *Ostfront* aircraft. No one else built bombers with such skinny bodies. Even the Germans used that Flying Pencil nickname for their Dorniers.

No matter how slim the Do-17s were, they didn't perform much better than the USSR's obsolescent SB-2s. Stas' current mount could fly rings around them. The Pe-2 was pretty skinny, too, since it was originally intended as a heavy fighter. And so . . . Stas swung the Pe-2 into a sharp right turn.

"What the—?" Kulkaanen exclaimed.

"I'm going to get after those Germans," Stas answered.

A moment later, another startled question came from his radio earphones. He gave the squadron CO the same answer. Several silent seconds followed as Lieutenant Colonel Tomashevsky considered it. At last, he said, "Our mission is to keep the Fascists from harassing the English now that they've come to their senses. You're doing that. Good luck."

"*Spasibo*," Stas said dryly. He noticed that none of the other pilots was peeling off to attack the Dorniers. That made his own job harder. It also made his Russian comrades as imaginative as so many oysters. He chuckled sourly. *Tell me something I didn't already know,* he thought.

One of the things he did already know was which Flying Pencil he wanted: the last and highest in the second V. That was the fellow least able to protect himself, and also the one whose buddies could help him least.

The Do-17's pilot and crew didn't notice him till he was almost close enough to open up. Only one machine gun at the back of the cockpit would bear on him. He had two forward-firing machine guns, and two 20mm cannon to go with them. As tracers whipped past the Pe-2, he watched chunks fly off the German bomber's wing. Flame licked, caught, spread. The Dornier went into a spin the pilot hadn't a prayer of controlling.

Kulkaanen whooped. "Good shooting!" he yelled.

"Thanks." Stas wanted more German planes. But the Flying Pencil he'd attacked must have radioed a warning to its friends before it went down. The rest of the Do-17s dove for the deck as fast as they would go. He might have caught them had he chased them. Then again, 109s might be on the way to give them a hand. A Pe-2 could give a good account of itself against a Messerschmitt, but it wasn't something you wanted to try unless you had no choice.

He did have a choice, and made it—he flew back toward the rest of the Soviet bombers. He also had a mission to fulfill. Even though he'd shot down the German plane, he still needed to do that. Orders were, and always would be, orders.

TO SAY HIDEKI FUJITA was not a happy man was to prove the power of understatement. He'd got demoted to corporal for letting the three

Americans escape from Pingfan, and he'd got a hell of a beating besides. Then, when neither Japanese nor Manchukuan patrols managed to stumble across the white men on the loose, he got another beating, this one worse than the first.

Adding insult to injury—literally—he remained on watch at the Americans' compound. His superiors left him in no doubt about what would happen to him if any more Yankees got away. That would be the last mistake he was ever allowed to make.

Self-preservation made him tighten things up even more than was usual at Pingfan. The Americans' compound ran by the clock, as if it were a factory cranking out Fords. Any prisoner in there who was late for a roll call or a lineup or even slow in bowing to a Japanese guard got pounded on with fists and boots and rifle butts.

Fujita would have done worse than that to them had the scientist-officers who ran Pingfan not made it plain they needed the Americans in relatively good shape. That disgusted him. He couldn't even wallop the Yankees as hard as his own people had walloped him—some of his bruises were a long time fading. Where was the fairness in that?

On the other hand, those scientist-officers didn't take him inside the enormous walled-off facility that was Pingfan's beating heart. He didn't know what happened to the *maruta* who went in there, not in any detail. He wasn't interested in finding out, either. And, unless you were a scientist yourself, once you went behind those high walls, you didn't come out again: not alive, anyhow.

For a little while, he'd feared he'd infuriated the authorities enough to make them decide to turn him into a *maruta*. Next to that fate, a couple of beatings didn't seem so bad.

The sergeant soon set over him, a bruiser named Toshiyaki Wakamatsu, made him remember all the reasons he'd despised sergeants before becoming one himself. Wakamatsu was loudmouthed and brutal. He fawned on officers but wouldn't listen to anyone of rank lower than his own.

Was I like that? Fujita wondered. He hoped not, but feared he might have been. He couldn't ask the enlisted men from his squad. They'd never give him a straight answer, any more than he would give one to Wakamatsu. Giving straight answers was a most un-Japanese thing to do. You told your superiors what you thought they wanted to hear. If they had any sense, they knew how to interpret what you said. If they didn't, their heads swelled up with all the praise you lavished on them.

Sergeant Wakamatsu had his own way of dealing with the Americans. He couldn't talk to them, any more than Fujita had been able to. Fujita had learned that some of the Americans knew scraps of Chinese. Senior Private Hayashi spoke Chinese fluently. Fujita said not a word of that to the man now holding down his place. Neither did Hayashi. His silence made the demoted noncom feel good. The clever senior private still felt loyal to him—or at least didn't want to do the blowhard who'd taken his slot any favors.

Instead of talking to the Americans, Wakamatsu gestured to show what he wanted. When the prisoners didn't catch on fast enough to suit him, he clouted them. That helped him less than he'd seemed to think it would.

"*Bakatare! Bakayaro!*" he roared at the Yanks. Had he really expected them to cooperate? If he had, he was an idiot himself, even if he called them by that name. Prisoners might have lost their honor simply by letting themselves be captured, but they didn't go out of their way to help their captors. Anyone with a gram of sense should have been able to see that.

Since Sergeant Wakamatsu couldn't . . . Fujita did his best to stay out of the sergeant's way. His new superior was setting himself up to crash and burn. Fujita didn't want to catch fire when Wakamatsu did. He hardly cared if the authorities gave him back his old collar tabs.

He kept an eye on the American named Herman Szulc. Wakamatsu still hadn't figured out that Szulc was a leading troublemaker. And Szulc had a buddy, a smaller fellow called Max Weinstein. One look at that fellow and anyone with a suspicious mind would hear alarm bells.

Weinstein knew some Chinese. Fujita had heard him jabbering with the laborers who did the work around Pingfan that the Japanese didn't care to do for themselves. Sergeant Wakamatsu must have heard him, too. Did Wakamatsu take any special notice? Fujita was convinced Wakamatsu wouldn't have noticed his own cock if he didn't need to piss through it now and then.

"What is the American saying?" Fujita asked Senior Private Hayashi.

"When I've heard him, he's been trying to get extra food from the Chinese," the conscripted student answered.

"What do you suppose he's talking about with them when you're not around to hear?" Fujita persisted.

"Please excuse me, Sergeant-*san*—I mean, Corporal-*san*—but how am I supposed to know that?" Hayashi sounded and looked as exasperated as an inferior could afford to do when responding to a superior's stupid question.

But Fujita still didn't think it was so very stupid. "Come on. Use your fancy brains," he snapped. "Is the American a Red? Have the Chinese Reds infiltrated our labor force?"

The Japanese often worried more about Communists in China than they did about the forces that followed Chiang Kai-shek's government. The Communists were sneakier than the regular Chinese forces, and they made more trouble. They were committed to what they did in ways the regular Chinese forces couldn't approach.

All the same, Senior Private Hayashi replied, "How can an American be a Red? The Yankees hate Communists almost as much as we do."

"Maybe," Fujita replied, in tones that declared he didn't believe it for a minute. And he had his reasons, too: "In that case, how come they're cheering when England stops helping Germany and starts helping the miserable, stinking Russians again?" He knew exactly how he felt about the Russians. How else could he feel, considering the too many times they'd come too close to killing him?

To his surprise, Senior Private Hayashi had a comeback. "I think it's because Hitler scares Roosevelt, Corporal-*san*," he said. "Hitler scares just about everybody. He would scare us, too, if he weren't on the far side of the world."

"Nothing scares Japan," Fujita declared.

"Of course, Corporal-*san*." Hayashi might have been humoring a boy who was too little to know he'd come out with something silly.

"Nothing does, dammit," the nettled Fujita said. "If anything scared us, would we have beaten the Red Army? If anything scared us, would we go to war against America and England at the same time as we're fighting in China?"

Hayashi pursed his lips, as if wondering how much he might safely say. He and Fujita had served side by side in Mongolia and Siberia before coming to Pingfan. Even so, he chose his words with obvious care: "I hope it doesn't happen that we bit off more than we can chew."

"Don't be silly! The Navy is kicking the crap out of the American fleet," Fujita said. "The Yanks are on the run. The Philippines are falling. If the Americans want a war with us, they'll have to fight their way through islands that belong to us. *Honto?*"

"*Honto,*" Hayashi said, because it *was* true. Somehow, though, even his agreement sounded dubious.

Fujita didn't push it. He'd lost face as well as rank; he didn't want to antagonize someone who still seemed to respect him. He went back to what they'd been talking about before: "Do pay attention to that Weinstein. If he starts talking to the Chinamen about anything *but* food—"

"Shall I tell Sergeant Wakamatsu?" Hayashi broke in.

"Oh, yes. Of course. That's just what you should do." No one could claim Fujita hadn't given the proper response. If his tone didn't match his words . . . well, how could you report something like that? He and Hayashi both smiled. Yes, they understood each other, all right.

Chapter 11

Bam! Bam! Bam! A battery of German 88mm antiaircraft guns thundered away at the Russian bombers high overhead. Willi Dernen watched puffs of black smoke appear among the planes. None of them caught fire and fell out of the sky, though. How many thousands of meters up there were they? However many it was, they didn't make easy targets.

Even though the gunners kept missing, Willi waved to them as he trudged past their position. He liked having 88s around. They might have been designed as flak guns, but the high mucky-mucks had made sure they could do other tricks, too. They had armor-piercing rounds in their inventory, for instance. And a high-velocity AP round from an 88 could make even a KV-1 say uncle, when the huge Soviet panzers laughed at almost every other weapon in the German inventory.

"Come on, Dernen! Get it in gear!" Arno Baatz barked.

"*Jawohl, Herr Unteroffizier!*" Willi answered, as abjectly as if Awful Arno were a field marshal, not a lousy corporal. He did get it in gear, too—for half a dozen paces. As soon as Baatz started yapping at someone else, Willi slowed down again. He hadn't figured it would take long, and it didn't.

"Naughty, naughty," Adam Pfaff said in a prison-yard whisper Awful Arno would never hear.

"Ahh, your mother." Willi's reply was no louder. They both chuckled as they marched on. Hating the noncoms set over you was as old and as universal as soldiering. Willi was sure the Ivans' privates couldn't stand their corporals and sergeants, either. He would have bet the Japanese and the Amis felt the same way. Caesar's legionaries must have felt the same way, too. So did King David's warriors, chances were.

When Willi told that to Pfaff, his buddy snorted. "Who cares what David's guys thought?" said the *Landser* with the gray Mauser. "They were nothing but a bunch of kikes."

Willi laughed, but nervously. He eyed Pfaff from under the beetling brim of his *Stahlhelm*. Was Pfaff joking, or did he mean that? Willi had no enormous use for Jews, but he didn't get all hot and bothered about them. He figured the Nazis' hot air was just that and no more. Most of the soldiers in his outfit seemed to feel the same way.

Most, but not all. Some *Landsers* took all the hot air as seriously as SS men would. And some of these Russian villages and towns were chock full of Jews. He'd watched some bad things happen. He hadn't joined in, but he also hadn't tried to stop anything or report anybody. Reporting, he knew instinctively, was a waste of time at best, and might land *him* in trouble. Better to look the other way.

So far as he knew, Pfaff hadn't killed kikes for the fun of it or soaked a Jew's beard in oil and set it on fire or done anything else along those lines. So far as he knew, his buddy hadn't gang-raped any Jewish—or Russian—women, either. But that was only so far as he knew. One of the things he knew for sure was that he didn't know very far.

Artillery shells howled past overhead. Those weren't from the 88s: they were 105s, searching for the Russians on the ground. And it didn't sound as if any of them would fall dangerously short. You were just as maimed if your own side's shell blew off your leg as you were when the enemy did it to you.

MG-34s rattled, off to the northeast. Slower-firing Russian machine guns answered. Willi's stomach knotted, the way it always did when he got close to places where he could get hurt. He unslung his rifle and made sure he had a cartridge in the chamber. "Ready to have some fun?" he asked.

"*Aber natürlich!*" Adam Pfaff said, as gaily as if he were a girl Willi had invited to dance. But this was the *Totentanz,* and not everyone would get up after the drumbeat of death stopped.

"Let's go! Forward! We'll give the *Untermenschen* the hiding they've got coming to them!" Awful Arno shouted. He was a true believer in all the stuff Dr. Goebbels cranked out, sure as hell. But then he said the magic words: "Follow me!"

He might be—as far as Willi was concerned, he had to be—the biggest unwiped asshole in the history of the world. If only he were yellow, that would have made the perfect finish for his personality, such as it was: a maraschino cherry on a bowl of ice cream, so to speak. But, whatever else you could say about Arno Baatz, you couldn't call him a coward. He was as brave as anyone could want a soldier to be, and then a little more besides.

And anyone who yelled "Follow me!" commonly found men who *would* follow. A noncom or officer laying his own life on the line got *Landsers* to do the same. Even colonels and generals led from the front in this war. People who'd gone through the mill the last time talked about how their superiors stayed kilometers behind the line and ordered them to their doom. No more.

Those MG-34s were firing from hastily dug foxholes, not from a regular trench line. With the front so fluid, there was no regular trench line. Soldiers in *Feldgrau* crouched in other foxholes and sprawled behind scrapes that might or might not stop a bullet. Some of them got up and advanced with the newly arrived units. Others stayed right where they were. They did lay down supporting fire for the troops moving forward. Willi gave them . . . some . . . credit for that.

A bullet cracked past his head. He threw himself flat and wriggled forward on his belly through grass tall enough to hide him from the Russians—as long as he didn't do anything stupid like sticking his butt in the air, anyhow. Every so often, he'd go up on one knee, fire, and then flatten out again. Nobody was tracking his movements, anyhow: the proof of which was, he didn't get killed when he popped up.

He wondered how the Russians used this stretch of ground when no one was fighting over it. Did they graze sheep or cattle or horses on it? Or did it just lie here not doing anything? Germany didn't have much land like that, but Russia seemed full of it. The country was so goddamn big that, even though it had a lot of people, it didn't have nearly enough to use all these vast sweeps of ground. This one might have been forgotten—or, for all Willi knew, maybe no one had ever paid enough heed to it to begin with for anybody to forget it now.

The direction from which enemy fire came told him which way to crawl. The grass smelled all green and growing. A rich scent rose from the black earth, too. Willi might be a city boy, but his nose said the Ivans were missing a bet by not raising wheat or beets or *something* right here.

Then that nose of his almost ran into the snub nose of a Red Army soldier crawling through the grass toward the German positions. Both men yelped in horror. Neither had had the slightest idea the other was there till the sea of grass parted and they nearly banged heads.

Willi tried to aim his Mauser at the Russian. The Ivan had a rifle, too, but jerked his hand away from it as if it were red-hot. *"Kamerad!"* he bleated, and *"Freund!"* After that, he gabbled out a stream of Russian, of which Willi understood not a word.

He could have murdered the Red Army man in cold blood. He had no doubt Awful Arno would have plugged the Ivan without a second thought, or even a first one. But the guy was trying to surrender. Willi supposed he was, anyhow. The Russian didn't say boo when Willi grabbed his rifle. Then Willi frisked him—he didn't want to send the guy on his way and end up catching a grenade. Like the English, the Russians used round bombs. They held less explosive than a German potato-masher, but you could throw them farther. Willi confiscated the three on the Ivan's belt, and his sheathed bayonet, too.

He found the soldier's identity book. It had a photograph of the guy and a bunch of writing in an alphabet that was just squiggles to Willi. He handed it back to the Ivan. Why not? It wasn't any use to *him*. He jerked his thumb toward the southwest, the direction from which the German advance was coming.

The Russian gave forth with what Willi guessed were thanks. He was pretty sure *spasibo* meant *danke*, anyhow. "Go on," Willi said roughly, hoping he hadn't missed any lethal hardware—or that, if he had, the dirty, scared-looking, sorry son of a bitch in khaki wasn't inclined to use it.

Off Ivan went. What happened to him afterwards, Willi never knew. He cared very little. The guy didn't double back on him or have a spare grenade Willi'd missed. That, Willi cared about. He crawled on. The *Landsers* behind the line could send the Russian to a POW camp. Or they could shoot him, if they decided they'd sooner do that. It wasn't Willi's worry. The Red Army men still ahead were.

OUT THROUGH the Kiel Canal. The abrupt change in the U-30's motion would have told Julius Lemp when they got out into open water even if he'd been below. But he was up on the U-boat's conning tower. As soon as the North Sea waves started slapping the boat, she began rolling in the way he'd found so familiar for so long.

One of the ratings up there with him didn't take the new motion for granted like the skipper. "Fuck me," the sailor said, gulping. "I'd forgotten how rough it gets out on the open sea."

"If you've got to puke, Hans, don't puke into the wind," Lemp advised. "The idea is to get rid of what ails you, not to wear it."

"Right." Hans gulped again.

"If you can't keep scanning, I'll send you below with a bucket and call up somebody who can," Lemp said. "Now that England's turned her coat, we've got to worry about the Royal Navy and the RAF again. They aren't half-assed like the Russians. Give them even a piece of a chance and they'll sink us."

"I'll stay, Skipper," Hans said quickly. Lemp would have said the same thing in his unhappy place. Up here, the fresh air fought seasickness. Down inside the reeking pressure hull, the boat's rolling would have a potent, pungent ally.

All the same, Lemp knew he would have to watch Hans as well as the horizon. He hadn't been joking. Anyone inefficient up here would have to go. You might get away with taking chances against the sloppy Slavs. Against the English? A good thing everyone had a will on file.

Diesels thrumming through the soles of Lemp's shoes, the U-30 made fifteen knots on a course a little west of due north. The boat would round Norway's southwestern bulge and then follow the country's coastline farther north and east. Too many Tommies on the *Ostfront* had made their way through Soviet lines. The easiest, fastest way to bring them back to England would be to ship them out of Arkhangelsk or Murmansk.

The *Führer* didn't want them to come home—and who could blame him? Sooner or later, probably sooner, they'd get back into the war against the *Reich*. Better to send the freighters or liners carrying them to the bottom. Then Germany wouldn't need to worry about them any more.

"Perfidious Albion," Lemp muttered. His breath smoked. Spring might be here, but the North Sea was damned if it wanted to admit it.

"What's that, Skipper?" Hans asked.

"Nothing. Just swearing at the damned limeys."

"They're a pain, all right," the rating agreed.

"How's your insides?"

"Not *too* bad, as long as I don't think about 'em. Maybe I'll cuss England out, too."

Somebody—whether it was Hans or not, Lemp didn't know—gave back a meal inside the hull before they put in at Namsos on their way north. That made the stink in there worse, but not by so much as an outsider might have expected. It wasn't the first time somebody'd heaved in the boat, and an overturned bucket meant the nasty stuff had got into the bilgewater. Once that happened, a stench would stay with the U-30 as long as the boat lasted.

The *Kriegsmarine* had started to fit Namsos out as a U-boat base after the town fell. Then, with the war against England and France suddenly forgotten, the work was forgotten, too. Now the war—or part of it, anyway—was on again, and so was the work.

Namsos probably hadn't been an exciting place before the *Wehrmacht* took it away from its defenders. It was a real mess now. German crews with torches went about carving up the English warships and freighters that had gone down in shallow water trying to resupply and evacuate the town. The steel would be useful; whatever could be salvaged intact, even more so.

Namsos itself could have used cutting up and salvaging, too. Bombing and artillery meant hardly a building didn't have a chunk or two bitten out of it. Lemp saw only a few Norwegians. Most of them looked sullen. If they were delighted to have come under German occupation, they hid it very well.

Two or three men wore the uniform of the *Nasjonal Samling*, the Norwegian equivalent of the German NSDAP. The head of the NS, a former officer named Vidkun Quisling, helped the Germans govern Norway. The only problem was that his party, unlike the Nazis, enjoyed next to no popular support. German bodyguards accompanied the NS men walking through the harbor.

The head of the base, a *Kapitän zur See* named Waldemar Böhme, was blunt when he discussed the issue with Lemp as fresh food went into the U-30. "Anybody who doesn't belong to the NS figures anybody who does is a traitor," Böhme said gloomily. "And nobody belongs to the NS."

Lemp glanced toward one of the uniformed Norwegians. It wasn't quite a German uniform, but it was in the same general style. "He does," the U-boat skipper remarked.

"There are a handful of them," Böhme agreed. "It would almost be easier if there weren't any. Then we wouldn't have to waste our own men keeping the rest of the Norwegians from murdering these . . . people." Had he known Lemp better, he might have called the NS officials worse. But you never could tell who might report you. Staying innocuous was safer.

"Quisling must have *some* support," Lemp said.

"Some, *ja*." Böhme still sounded glum. "The *Nasjonal Samling* got less than two percent of the vote in 1936, down from a hair over two percent in 1933. And as soon as the fighting started here, half their members—more than half—bailed out and picked up rifles and tried to shoot us."

Shrewdly, Lemp said, "But now that the fighting's over and we won, going along with us will look like a good idea to some people."

"That has happened—a little," Böhme admitted. "Most of the squareheads would still sooner spit on us, though."

"As long as we can get on with the war, what difference does it make?" Lemp said.

HARRY TURTLEDOVE

"With England back in it, who knows?" Captain Böhme seemed determined to look at the cloud, not the silver lining. "Now the Norwegians won't have to be Reds to have somebody who'll help give us trouble."

"I'm sure you'll manage, sir," Lemp said, by which he meant *I'm damn glad it's your worry and none of mine.* The wry quirk of one of Böhme's bushy gray eyebrows meant he understood that all too well.

Narvik, north of the Arctic Circle, was a smaller, even more battered base than Namsos. Because it was so inaccessible except by sea, it had stayed in Allied hands longer than the country farther south. Without the warm waters of the Gulf Stream, the place would have been uninhabitable. And without the last gasps of the current from the far southwest, Murmansk and Arkhangelsk would have stayed frozen up the year around, and Lemp's mission would have had no point.

But up toward the Barents Sea the U-30 went. It wasn't summer yet, but daylight stretched and stretched in these latitudes. Lemp had heard about the white nights of St. Petersburg—Leningrad, these days. He was ten degrees of latitude north of St. Petersburg now. The sun set in the far, far northwest and soon rose again in the far, far northeast. While it ducked below the horizon, twilight never got dark enough to show any but the brightest stars.

That meant the U-30's crew had to stay alert around the clock. A rating might spot a troopship at any hour of the day or suppositious night. On the other hand, an English plane, or a Russian one, might come across the U-boat at any time.

Or nothing might happen. No matter how long it stayed light, the ocean was vast. Troopships full of Tommies might slip past unseen. For all Lemp knew, there *were* no troopships full of Tommies. The *Kriegsmarine* brass had plenty of bright ideas that didn't pan out.

A whale spouted a couple of hundred meters to port. The great beast wasn't that much smaller than the U-boat. Lemp watched it with awe from the conning tower. It paid the U-30 no heed. That suited Lemp fine. A collision with a whale would be like a truck hitting an elephant on the *Autobahn*—except the truck wouldn't sink afterwards.

He cruised his assigned area, awaiting new orders from Berlin—or even from Namsos. In due course, new orders came. Once decoded, they read, *Continue current assignment.* Lemp was anything but thrilled—as if his superiors cared. Continue he did.

LUC HARCOURT HAD JUST got a fire going on the floor of a half-wrecked peasant hut when a private stuck his head through a hole in the wall and said, "Excuse me, Sergeant, but could I please talk to you for a little while?"

Sighing, Luc asked, "What d'you want, Charles?" Whatever it was, it would be trouble. Whenever a private asked that question in that tone of voice, it had to be trouble. Maybe Charles' father was desperately ill, and he wanted compassionate leave. Right now, of course. Maybe his girlfriend was two-timing him, and he needed a shoulder to cry on or permission to go back to France and whale the stuffing out of the loose, stupid bitch. Or maybe . . .

"What are we doing here, Sergeant?" Charles couldn't have been more than nineteen. His voice still cracked sometimes. He was trying to grow a mustache, but only looked as if he had dirt on his upper lip.

After hacking the top off a ration tin with his bayonet, Luc heated monkey meat over the flames. "What do you mean, what are we doing here? Do I look like a priest, to answer a question like that?"

He sounded even more like Sergeant—now Lieutenant—Demange than he realized. Almost everything he knew about soldiering, and about dealing with inferiors in the army, he'd learned from the veteran. Demange's sarcasm had rubbed off on him, too.

Charles flushed. "I don't mean it like that, Sergeant. I mean, what are we doing here in Russia? The Englishmen packed it in. Why can't we?"

As far as Luc was concerned, that was a damn good question. He gave the only reply he could: "When Daladier wants us to quit, we will. Till then, you'd better fight. You think the Ivans won't cut your dick off, you'd better think again."

"It isn't fair," Charles whined.

"Since when is life fair?" Yes, Luc sounded like Demange.

"You can joke all you want," Charles said, which, since Luc was a sergeant, was true enough. "But we're liable to get killed for no reason at all, and that isn't funny." His nostrils twitched as if he were an angry rabbit.

As a matter of fact, he was wrong. Luc had seen both enemies and friends die in ways idiotically ridiculous enough to make him laugh like a jackass. Anyone who'd been up at the front for a while could say the same thing. Most of the laughter sprang from relief that you were still alive to giggle.

But that wasn't the point. The savory aroma—if you got hungry enough—of sizzling bully beef distracted Luc, but he answered, "I don't know what you want me to do about it. If you think I'm going to cross over to the Russians' lines, you're even crazier than I give you credit for."

"They put out all those safe-conducts." Charles displayed one. Sure as hell, it promised that the bearer would be treated well if he deserted.

"It's written in good French—better than the ones the *Boches* used to throw around," Luc said. "But so what?"

"See? You call them *Boches,* too! And now they're on our side—I mean, we're on theirs—even though we still hate them and even though we almost started shooting at them on account of what they did to those Jews." Charles' nostrils quivered some more. "Wouldn't you rather fight against them than for them? Five gets you ten they're still doing that horrible shit to Jews, only in places where we can't catch 'em at it."

He was no Jew himself; Luc was sure of that. And Luc hadn't thought he was a Red, either. As a matter of fact, Luc still didn't think so. But the question was a lot harder to deal with when Charles put it that way. Slowly, Luc said, "The Russians aren't nice people, either. Don't forget that for a minute. So many Russians and Ukrainians and whatnot wouldn't fall all over themselves to help the fucking Nazis if they liked Stalin. Right?"

Most reluctantly, Charles nodded. "I guess so."

"Other thing to remember is, the Russians never signed the Geneva Convention. Even the Germans did that," Luc went on. "So who gives a rat's ass what that safe-conduct says? Once the Reds have you, they can do whatever they damn well please. Nobody's gonna stop 'em. The Red Cross never gets a look inside their POW camps—if they bother keeping POWs alive long enough to put 'em in camps. You understand what I'm saying?"

"You're saying you like Hitler better than Stalin." Charles might have been accusing him of picking his nose and eating the boogers.

"No! No, God damn it to hell! I'm saying I can't stand either one of those shitheads, and you can't trust either one of them." Luc paused to take the tin off the fire. The monkey meat was as ready as it ever would be. His stomach growled gratefully when he stuffed a mouthful into his chowlock. After a gulp an anaconda might have used to engulf a half-grown tapir, he resumed: "It's like I told you before. I don't set our foreign policy, and neither do you. We go where they tell us and we do what they tell us to do there. And if we don't, our own side'll make it rougher on us than the Nazis and Reds put together."

Artillery rumbled, not far enough away. Charles gestured in that direction, asking, "How?"

"They can jail you. They can shoot you, too. And they can make life hell on earth for your kinfolk. If your brother keeps getting fired; if your son, when you have a son, ends up in a crappy school and blames you for it . . . They remember. It's how they stay on top—remembering. And paying back."

His words made the youngster—three or four years younger than he was now—recoil in horror. "They wouldn't do anything like that! They couldn't get away with it!"

"My ass they couldn't." Luc scooped more hot bully beef out of the tin.

"You're no help at all, dammit." Charles stomped away from the hut in dudgeon as high as a corpse four days gone.

Luc finished the tin of monkey meat. Then he hunted up Lieutenant Demange. He recounted the conversation with Charles, adding, "You'd better tighten up the sentries, sir. He's liable not to be the only one who'll try and go over to the other side."

"Yeah, chances are you're right." Demange shifted his Gitane to one side of his mouth and spat in disgust out of the other. "That stupid fucking Russian asswipe of a safe-conduct! Jesus God, the clowns like Charles are smart enough to see that their own government lies to them every chance it gets, so how come they aren't smart enough to see all the other governments're full of bullshit, too?"

"Beats me." It seemed as obvious as an axiom of geometry to Luc. Had he thought that way before the war broke out? He had trouble remembering. He didn't believe he had—he hadn't worried much about politics at all then. So what, though? Lies and incompetence hadn't come close to sinking France then. Things looked different these days.

Charles didn't try to desert. Luc dared hope he'd put the fear of God into him. A couple of nights later, though, two other *poilus* did slip away. Lieutenant Demange swore in furious disgust.

Supplies came up in horse-drawn wagons. Both French and German trucks literally fell to bits when they had to deal with what were alleged to be Soviet roads. Horses didn't break down, and wagons were easier to repair than motor vehicles. As long as Luc kept getting ammo and food, he didn't care how.

With the Germans on their left flank and Hungarians to their right, the French pushed forward. Fighting well was the best way to improve your chances of staying alive. Luc didn't have anything in particular against the Russians, the way he'd had against the *Wehrmacht* men when they tried to overrun his country. He shot at them anyhow, to keep them from shooting at him.

And, before long, the advancing French troops came upon a fresh grave in the woods with an Adrian helmet for a tombstone. They dug it up. In it lay one of the deserters. He hadn't stopped a mistaken bullet. The Ivans had sported with him for a long time before they let him die. The French soldiers quickly buried him again.

"Where's your safe-conduct?" Luc asked Charles. "Feel like using it now?"

"No, Sergeant," the kid answered in a very small voice.

As if on the training ground, Luc snapped, "What was that? I can't hear you!"

"No, Sergeant," Charles said again, rather louder this time.

"All right, then." Luc let it go. He didn't need to worry that Charles would skedaddle, not after the youngster saw what was left of that other damn fool. The Russians would have drawn more deserters had they treated people who went over to them well. But if they wanted to play the game the other way, they'd soon discover the French could, too.

IVAN KUCHKOV PATTED the round drum that held his PPD's ammunition with almost the same delight he would have used to pat a barmaid's round backside. He never wanted to have anything to do with an infantry rifle again. You didn't need to aim a PPD. You just pointed it and fired. If one bullet didn't do for a Fascist, the next would, or the one after that.

A Nazi with a Mauser could hit him from much farther away than he could hit the Fritz with his submachine gun. In the kind of fighting they were doing, in woods and villages and towns, that seldom mattered. You mostly didn't see your enemy till he was right on top of you. Then you needed to kill him in a hurry. The PPD was made with just that in mind.

His outfit kept falling back toward Smolensk. It infuriated him. He wanted to drive the Germans west, not to dance to their tune. The Red Army counterattacked whenever officers thought they saw a chance— or whenever orders came down from above. Sometimes the Russians gained a little ground. Even when they did, they rarely held it long.

He wasn't sure about the name of the village where they were fighting now. It might have been called Old Pigshit, a handle it would have kept for centuries. Or it might have been rechristened something like Leninsk after the glorious Soviet Revolution. Either way, it was a stench in the nostrils—and a lot like the miserable hole in the ground where Ivan had grown up.

One way in which it differed from that particular hole in the ground was the broad expanse of grainfields and meadows to the north, south, and west. "Couldn't be better country for panzers," said Lieutenant Vasiliev. Ivan was convinced the political officer fucked pigs, but even a pigfucker got it right every once in a while.

About half the villagers had been rash enough to stick around instead of hightailing it to the east. Maybe they thought the Red Army would push the Nazis back, in which case they were optimists. Or maybe they thought things would get better once the Nazis took over, in which case they were *really* optimists.

Any which way, the *politruk* took charge of them. He set them digging deep, wide ditches across their fields and meadows, not so much to stop tanks as to channel their movements toward antitank guns.

A peasant with a gray mustache had the nerve to complain: "How the devil can we farm after we tear up the land like this?"

Lieutenant Vasiliev drew his Tokarev automatic from the leather holster on his belt. He held it up to the peasant's head and pulled the trigger. The report was harsh, flat, undramatic. The peasant fell over. He kicked a few times and lay still. Blood puddled under him. A wrinkled woman in a headscarf shrieked.

"Any other questions?" the *politruk* asked pleasantly, reholstering the pistol. Vast silence, but for the woman's sobs. The *politruk* nodded. "All right, then. Get back to work."

And they did—all of them, including the *babushka* who'd just lost her husband. Sometimes life could be very simple.

Some of the soldiers dug alongside them. Others turned the village into a strongpoint. Field fortification was a Russian art. *Maskirovka*—camouflage—was another. Making buildings into places that were much stronger than they looked combined the two.

They got less done than Ivan wished they would have. German artillery started probing early in the afternoon. Not even the *politruk*'s pistol could keep the *muzhiks* working after that. They ran for the trees, more afraid of the big shells bursting—and with reason. Artillery was the great butcher. Everything else was an afterthought beside it.

The soldiers stolidly labored on. Every so often, they flattened out in the antitank ditches when incoming shells sounded close. After the shelling moved on for a while, they stood up again, brushed themselves off, and went back to digging. A few shells hit in the ditches. A man or two walking around above ground got wounded by fragments.

Scouts fell back toward Old Pigshit or whatever it was, skirmishing as they came. "Stupid Germans aren't far behind us," one of them said as he jumped into a trench close to Ivan. *Nemtsi*, the Russian word for *Germans*, meant *tongue-tied ones* or *mumblers;* it went well with the notion of stupidity. The scout lit a *papiros.*

"Let me have one of those fuckers, will you?" Ivan said. The scout glanced his way, saw he was a sergeant, and gave him a smoke. Kuchkov had expected no less. After a couple of drags, he asked, "Have they got tanks along?"

"I saw some," the scout answered. He carried a PPD, too. A Red Army soldier was more inclined to believe in firepower than in God.

"They would, the clapped-out cunts," Ivan muttered. One of the scout's eyebrows twitched. All soldiers swore, but Ivan was in a class by himself. He found another question: "Are their peckers up?"

"Why not? They're advancing," the scout said bleakly.

Ivan glanced over his shoulder. Maybe a company of KV-1s would clank forward and save the day like the warriors who whipped the Teutonic Knights in *Alexander Nevsky.* Now there was a flick for you! *And maybe green monkeys will fly out of my ass, too,* Ivan thought, mocking himself. Life wasn't like a movie. Tanks didn't show up from nowhere just because you needed them like anything. And wasn't that a goddamn shame?

German soldiers appeared in the distance. Field-gray blended in about as well as khaki, but the Nazis' black helmets stood out on the horizon. The *Germans* had tanks along: three Czech machines, either captured or newly built in conquered factories. They were better than Panzer Is and IIs, not so good as IIIs: about like any Soviet tanks this side of the KV-1.

Cautiously, the tanks with the white-edged black crosses on them advanced. Foot soldiers loped between them. A Soviet mortar started thumping. Earth fountained up as the bombs hit. The Nazi infantrymen dove for cover. One of them was blasted off his feet. Ivan didn't think he'd get up again.

A tank crew thought about crossing a ditch, but the obstruction proved too wide and too deep. The machine came straight toward the village, then, as the defenders had planned. A hidden antitank gun opened up on it. The gunners needed several shots before they scored a hit, but the tank stopped and began to burn when they did.

That told the other enemy tanks where the gun was, though. They shelled it into silence, then rolled forward with greater confidence. Another antitank gun knocked one of them out in nothing flat. The last tank scuttled back out of range.

Red Army men with rifles fired at their German counterparts. A machine gun in a tavern opened up on the Fritzes, too. The Germans hit the dirt and started digging foxholes. They were veteran troops. They weren't about to make things easy for their foes.

"Well, we've stopped 'em," the scout said. Neither he nor Ivan had fired a shot. The Fascists hadn't drawn close enough to turn their submachine guns deadly.

"For now, yeah. Right here, yeah," Ivan said. The Red Army could usually stop the Germans right here, and for now. Then, somehow, they'd break through a little later somewhere else, and stopping them right here for now wouldn't matter any more. You'd have to retreat, or else they'd close the ring behind you and grind you to pieces at their leisure.

Lieutenant Obolensky and the *politruk* wanted to make the Germans fight a regular battle for Old Pigshit. Unfortunately, the officers in charge of the advancing Nazis had too much sense to bang their heads into a stone wall. They were like water; they slid around obstructions. Before long, their 105s started pounding the Red Army men who held the woods a few kilometers south of the village. Ivan could follow the fighting to the south by ear. The Russians in the woods gave way. The Germans pushed through. That meant Old Pigshit would start flying the swastika pretty soon.

Maybe the place would have held if troops from here had helped the handful of Russians in those woods. Maybe not, but maybe. No one thought to weaken the strongpoint, though. And so, instead of weakening it, the company had to abandon it.

They retreated in good order. They'd be ready to fight again somewhere else before long. The Soviet Union was vast. It could afford to trade space for time. But you couldn't win a war with endless retreats . . . could you?

Chapter 12

Something in the mail for you, dear." Sarah Goldman's mother handed her an envelope.

"For me?" Sarah couldn't remember the last time she'd got a letter. It wasn't as if Saul could write, after all. Not having any idea where her brother was, she had to hope he was all right.

This was no letter. The envelope bore an appallingly official eagle holding a circled swastika in its claws. The eagle's tiny printed eye caught and held hers, as if commanding her to obedience. One of the things that made the Nazis so scary was the attention they gave even such pic-ayune details: German thoroughness run mad and in power.

"You'd better open it," Mother said.

"I suppose so," Sarah agreed insincerely. Attention from the *Reich* was the last thing she or any Jew wanted. The best you could hope for, most times, was to be overlooked.

But the envelope in her hand wouldn't go away if she didn't open it. Whatever the Nazis were telling her they would do, they would do whether she read about it first or not. Better to know ahead of time. Well, it might be, anyhow.

A reluctant fingernail slid under the flap. The envelope opened easily—almost too easily. Even mucilage was of an inferior grade these days. She unfolded the notice inside and read it.

"*Nu?*" Hanna Goldman asked. "If you open your mouth any wider, a bug will fly in, or maybe a bird."

Sarah hadn't noticed her jaw drop. She wasn't surprised it had, though. She couldn't remember the last time she'd been so astonished. She held up the document as if it were a bream she'd just hauled out of a creek. "It's—" She had to try twice to get the words out: "It's my permission to get married. They've—they've approved it."

She'd shivered in line more than once, waiting to duel with the Nazi bureaucrats at the Münster *Rathaus*. Back then, her breath had smoked. She'd worn her shabby old coat, which didn't do nearly enough to hold out winter. Nevertheless, she'd wear it again when frost came back. A Jew's meager clothing ration wouldn't stretch to getting her another one.

No need for a coat now. Spring burgeoned outside. Birdsong sweetened the air. Grass was green. Flowers bloomed in perfumed rainbow profusion. Butterflies flitted from one to another to another. Bees buzzed. The sun blazed down from a blue, blue sky dotted with friendly little white clouds.

Mother rushed up and hugged her. "Oh, sweetheart, that's wonderful! You see? Even they couldn't say no in the end." If she didn't want to name the Nazis, who could blame her?

"Took them long enough to say yes," Sarah answered tartly.

"They're . . . what they are," her mother said. Sarah couldn't imagine a worse thing to say about Germany's masters. Mother went on, "It doesn't matter any more, though. You have their permission. They can't take it away again."

Of course they could, if they decided they wanted to. But even Sarah saw no reason that they should. She smiled a secret smile. It was a good thing permission had come when it did. She wasn't in a family way, but not because of lack of effort. She and Isidor spun the roulette wheel every time they lay down together—rubber was a war material, too important for much to be allotted to prophylactics. They also made some of sheep's gut, but so few that Jews had no chance of getting their hands on any.

You could do other things in bed besides *that*. You could, and they did. But the other things, however good they felt, also felt like substitutes. *Ersatz* filled life in Germany. How could anybody not want the original here? If you took a chance—well, fine, you took a chance.

Her mother's smile, seen from a few centimeters away, seemed uncommonly soft and tender. "Grandchildren," Hanna Goldman murmured. Did she know she might have had one sooner than she would have wished? If she did, she'd never said anything about it. That was as much discretion as a daughter could hope for.

Sarah wasn't sure she wanted babies, not in this day and age. Hostages to fortune . . . Were truer words ever spoken? Was this world, and this particular part of the world, a fit place for bringing up little Jews? Not likely! But that coin had two sides. If you didn't want children, if you decided to let things end with you, the Nazis won by default. They wouldn't hate Jews any more if they had no Jews left to hate.

She hadn't talked about any of that with Isidor. They'd worried about her getting pregnant before they could marry, not afterwards. All the same, she had a good notion of how she'd feel. He was more down-to-earth about such things than she was. Like her father, she pondered and worried before she acted. Isidor just went ahead. Chances were he'd go ahead with a family, too, and then see if he could get it through the war in one piece.

"We'll have to see if we can knock a doorway between your room and the one that used to be Saul's," Mother said. "The two of you could almost have your own little flat then."

Almost was the word, all right. They'd still have to share the kitchen and the bathroom with her parents. Even so, she quickly said, "We'll manage, whether we can knock the door through or not." Isidor already lived in a flat with his folks. There'd be no room for Sarah—which didn't stop new in-laws from moving in when they had no other choice. Here, for once, they did.

Like any choice, this one had its downside, too. Mother said, "It's a shame he'll have to go across town every day to get to work."

"He's got a bicycle," Sarah said. With all private cars vanished from the streets except those belonging to doctors, and with Jews banned from buses and trams, a bike was the best way to get around. Aside from shank's mare and possibly roller skates, a bike was about the only way to get around.

Hanna Goldman rolled her eyes nonetheless. "If you want to call it that," she said. Isidor's bicycle had to be older than he was. It had been a cheap rattletrap when it was new, and neither he nor any of the people who'd used it before him had kept it up very well. In happier times, anyone in his right mind would have been ashamed to be seen riding such a rickety contraption.

Permission to wed still in her hand, Sarah made herself look on the bright side. "No one will want to steal it."

Mother laughed, but answered, "You never can tell these days." And that, sadly, was also true. Because so many people had so little, and because they could legitimately buy even less, a lot of them took what they needed or what they wanted—or whatever caught their eye—when they saw the chance. Anything not nailed down was liable to disappear . . . and anybody with a claw hammer was liable to draw out the nails and steal them, too.

Sarah knew all that perfectly well. She couldn't even say she'd never pilfered; what else were Jews going to do when they got even less than Aryans? She could say, "I still think that bicycle's pretty safe," and mean it. Her mother didn't try to tell her she was wrong, either.

Her father kissed her when he got home. Then he fell asleep in his chair before supper. He woke up enough to eat another meager, unexciting meal. After that, he fell asleep in the chair again. When Mother and Sarah went upstairs to bed, he staggered along with them like a man coming out from under the ether cone.

Sarah sank deeply into sleep herself. When you were hungry all the time, it was easy. And sleep's anesthetic meant you didn't feel how hungry you were. If only she could have slept all the time . . . till the wedding, anyhow.

She didn't get to sleep all night tonight. Some time after midnight, Münster's air-raid sirens began to wail. Sarah thought it was—thought it had to be—a drill, one more example of Nazi thoroughness run amok. Since Jews weren't allowed to use public shelters, anyway, she stayed under the blankets till flat, harsh thuds outside and windows rattling in their frames told her the RAF had come back to Germany and was playing for keeps again.

Calling to one another, she and her parents (who'd also stayed in bed as long as they could) stumbled down the stairs and huddled under the dining-room table: the best protection they had. Engines droned overhead. Flak guns barked.

After an hour or so, the raiders went away. Nothing came down too close to the house. Sarah hoped the Brucks had come through all right, too. She'd have to get over there and see, if Isidor didn't—maybe couldn't—get over here first.

As Father creakily crawled out from under the table, he said, "Well, I won't go short of work for a while. Happy day!" Filling in bomb craters was a long way from lecturing about the coming of the barbarians at the end of ancient history. Or maybe it wasn't. Who but barbarians would set things up so a university professor could live only as a road-gang laborer? Sarah chewed on that while she went upstairs. Along with the raid, it kept her from getting any more rest till dawn.

PEARL HARBOR. Honolulu. When Pete McGill got back to Hawaii—got back on American soil for the first time in much too long—he found he had a third stripe waiting for him. Making corporal wasn't that hard. Sergeant . . . Sergeant meant you'd been a leatherneck for a while. Well, he damn well had.

Repair crews swarmed over Pearl like ants on sandwiches forgotten after a picnic. The Japs' attack had done more damage than U.S. authorities were letting on to the folks back home. He was amazed their carriers could have got near the place, but they damn well had.

Two carriers and a couple of battlewagons had been badly damaged. And a heavy cruiser charging out of the channel to go after the enemy fleet had taken a torpedo amidships from a lurking Japanese submarine and gone down with almost all hands. That sure hadn't made the evening news.

A couple of bombs had started fires in the vast fuel dumps alongside the harbor. One of those still sent greasy black smoke up into the sky. How many gazillions of barrels or gallons or whatever of fuel oil had burned? How badly would that screw up American operations in the Pacific? God surely knew, and maybe the brass here and back in D.C. Even as a newly minted sergeant, Pete McGill hadn't the faintest idea.

He took the streetcar into Honolulu when he got a seventy-two-hour pass. Promotions didn't happen every day. He'd blow a lot of the pay bump he hadn't seen yet buying drinks for the other Marines from the *Boise* and getting his ashes hauled. He mourned Vera. He missed her, too, more than he'd ever missed anybody. He really had loved her, as well as an American Marine could love a White Russian taxi dancer. But she was dead, dammit, and he was here in Hawaii without having even seen a woman since Manila. It wouldn't be the same as it had been with her; he wondered if anything would ever be that good again. But it was still pretty fine when you bought it from a hooker who would rather have been doing her nails than you.

Honolulu felt funny. It always did, whether you were coming from the U.S. mainland or the Orient. It was neither the one nor the other, and seemed pulled both ways at once. It was crawling with soldiers and sailors and Marines. Most of the signs were in English, and most of the English you heard on the street had one familiar American accent or another.

But most of the faces that didn't belong to military personnel had narrow eyes, high cheekbones, low noses, and golden skin. Japs, Chinamen, Filipinos, Koreans . . . More Japs than any other group, white people included. A leatherneck on leave didn't go into the neighborhoods where they lived. Japanese restaurants, Japanese movie houses, Buddhist temples, even Japanese Christian churches for converts and the children of converts . . .

Pete saw none of that, though he knew it was there. On the mainland, they were shoving Japs into internment camps in case they felt more loyalty to Tojo than to FDR. They couldn't do that here, even if the authorities might want to. Too goddamn many Japs in Hawaii; the place would grind to a halt without them. And nobody'd actually *proved* they were giving Tokyo a hand.

So a Jap bartender poured Pete a scotch on the rocks and congratulated him on his promotion. It was crappy scotch, but hey, there was a war on. And it could still get you smashed. Next to that, everything else ran a distant second.

Before long, they headed off to another joint, one Joe Orsatti knew. The Hibiscus Blossom was closer to Hotel Street, Honolulu's main drag for joy bought and sold. It was a rowdier place than the one they'd just left. Barmaids in short, tight skirts and halter tops fetched drinks. The one who took care of Pete and his pals was also a Jap. If only her eyes were blue, she would have looked like a Siamese cat.

Orsatti patted her on the ass after she brought the second round of drinks. She glared at him. "Don't handle the merchandise, Mac," she snapped in tones not far removed from Hoboken or Long Island.

The Marine leered back. "If it's merchandise, sweetheart, how much are you peddling it for?"

"More moolah than *you've* got, Charlie, however much that is," she retorted. Somebody at another table waved to her. Off she went. The way she moved, a football referee would have flagged her for backfield in motion.

Orsatti sighed as he watched. "If she's playing Mata Hari for old Hirohito, I bet she hears all kinds of good shit."

"Listen to her talk without looking at her and you'd bet she's never even heard of fuckin' Hirohito," Pete answered. "For all we know, she hasn't."

"Fat chance," Orsatti said. Pete didn't argue with him; he was bound to be right. The other Marine went on, "'Sides, I like looking at her. For a slanty-eyed gal, she's pretty goddamn cute."

Pete wouldn't have bothered with the qualifier. But then, he'd had his long tour in China. Even though he'd ended up falling for a blue-eyed blonde, it wasn't because he didn't like the way Asian women looked. They took a little getting used to, but so did beer and scotch and cigarettes and other good stuff. Orsatti had never drawn duty in Peking or Shanghai. Oriental girls still seemed exotic to him.

When the barmaid came back with another round, he tried to pick her up again, this time a little more smoothly. He still wouldn't have given Gregory Peck or Cary Grant anything to worry about. And he struck out like a high-school kid flailing against Bob Feller.

"Well, hell. Let's get outa here," he said after she wiggled off once more, as if it were the Hibiscus Blossom's fault he had bad luck and worse technique.

They wound up on Hotel Street, as Pete had known they would. Bars, strip joints, whorehouses masquerading as hotels—anything the horny heart could desire was there for the taking—if you had the jack.

Naturally, military men packed the street. So did MPs and Shore Patrolmen. Pete had his pass checked three times inside of fifteen minutes. Since it was legit, he didn't mind showing it. Somebody who was there without proper authorization swung on the Shore Patrolman who asked for his papers. That wasn't exactly Phi Beta Kappa. The SP and his buddies drastically revised the jerk's phrenology with their billy clubs. Then they slung him into a paddy wagon. It hauled him off to the brig.

"Man, if you want to fight, don't fight those assholes," Pete said. "More expensive than it's worth."

"That sorry SOB was screwed any which way," one of his friends said. "Soon as they found out he was AWOL, he was gonna catch it."

"Yeah, but he didn't have to bleed, too." Pete was a practical man.

"Sometimes you just feel like brawling and you don't care who," the friend said.

"Well, sure." It wasn't that Pete had never walked into a bar looking for a fight. It wasn't that he'd never found one, either. "But even so . . ." When you took on the SPs, your movie wouldn't have a happy ending.

His night did, at one of the joyhouses along Hotel Street. If the blonde he chose looked a little like Vera, he didn't consciously think about that till later on. Polly wasn't from Russia by way of Harbin; she told him she came from Fargo, North Dakota.

"So why'd you end up in Hawaii, then?" Pete asked. They had time for a Chesterfield afterwards; having been away from women for so long, he'd come in a hurry. Maybe he'd rise again fast enough for another go. He hoped so. In the meantime . . .

She laughed. "You go where the customers are at, Jack. In my line of work, this here is the Promised Land. And besides, if you was ever in Fargo through the winter, you'd get the hell outa there like your pants was on fire."

"That makes sense," he agreed. Honolulu was bound to have better weather than some pissant burg in North Dakota. Honolulu had better weather than anywhere, possibly including heaven. He stubbed out his cigarette. "How's about you go down on me for a little while? Then I think I can do it again."

"How's about you give me another fin first?" For somebody from Fargo, she imitated his Bronx accent pretty well. Of course, he wouldn't be da foist guy she evah hoid who talked liked dat.

He pulled an engraved portrait of Abe Lincoln out of his billfold. She stashed it in the nightstand next to the bed in the bare little room. They went on from there.

ALISTAIR WALSH FELT LIKE a new man with the uniform back on. He shook his head when that thought crossed his mind. It wasn't quite right. He felt like his old self again, was what he felt like. He'd felt like a new man in civvies, and he hadn't fancied the way the new man felt—not a farthing's worth, he hadn't.

But he'd left the army out of shame at Neville Chamberlain's bargain with Hitler, and out of suspicion that the Bentley that ran down Winston Churchill after Churchill loudly and eloquently denounced the deal wasn't driven by a drunk, but by someone who knew just what he was about.

England's new government was still looking into that, as it was looking into a great many things its predecessor had done under Chamberlain's lead, and then under Sir Horace Wilson's. But one thing that didn't need looking into was the bargain with Hitler. That went straight into the dustbin. The war was on again.

The former government had put a lot of soldiers out to pasture: men who, like Walsh, couldn't stomach the big switch, and whom the civilians who'd made the switch couldn't trust to stay loyal. That was funny, if you liked.

George VI had gone on the BBC, saying the change in government and the change in policy had his blessing. In a separate address of her own, his wife had done the same. Walsh had read somewhere that Hitler called Queen Elizabeth the most dangerous woman in Europe. Considering the source, there was a compliment to be proud of.

No matter what the King and Queen said, the *putsch* had horrified many, many Britons. The Army hadn't shot Sir Horace, the way Walsh was convinced the collaborating polecat deserved. Instead, it put him into what some higher up with an unfortunately bureaucratic turn of phrase called "preventive detention."

If only Walsh knew what the detention was supposed to prevent. It didn't prevent Horace Wilson from getting endless complaints out and seeing them printed in the *Times* and the other papers that had fawned on him while he was PM. The Army didn't come down on the papers for printing that self-serving drivel, either. The generals running the country bent over backward to show they didn't intend to abridge free speech or any other fundamental rights.

"Meaning no disrespect to you, sir, but it's bloody ridiculous," Walsh complained to Ronald Cartland. "The buggers we ousted were more tyrannical than we dare be."

Cartland nodded and waved to a barmaid for another whiskey: they sat in the pub near the Houses of Parliament where they'd done so much conspiring. "No great surprise there," the MP said—no, the captain, because he was back in uniform, too. "No matter how odious Sir Horace's government was, it was constitutionally legitimate. That meant it could do all sorts of outrageous things and get away with them. Because we are extraconstitutional, we have to be much more scrupulous or everyone will start wailing that we're worse than Hitler. Ironic, what?"

"Oh, perhaps a trifle," Walsh allowed. He smiled at the barmaid. "Let me have another pint, too, would you, dear?" She was young enough to be his daughter, but he was old enough that a girl young enough to be his daughter could look delicious to him.

Which, sadly, wasn't the same as saying he was likely to look delicious to her. "Another pint. Okey-doke," she said in a pseudo-American accent she must have picked up at the cinema. For all the warmth in her voice, he might have been a post—a thirsty post, but a post nonetheless.

He sighed. He was getting to the age where, if he wanted a young, pretty girl to make him happy, he had to lay silver on the dresser beforehand. That was an even bigger shame than any of the troubles related to the change of government.

She brought the pint of bitter and went off without a second glance—

at him, anyhow. Ronald Cartland, she noticed. Well, he was younger and of higher rank and therefore probably richer—and better-looking. If you were going to complain about every little thing . . .

"The real danger of our position is that we've damaged all the principles this country's run on the past two hundred years and more," Cartland said. "Anyone who tries to overthrow us will have as much right to do so as we did to throw out Sir Horace—which is to say, none."

"We may not have had the right, but we had justice, by God," Walsh said. "If we didn't, what was I doing in a cell when I'd committed no crime?"

"You'd plotted treason, old man. And the people with whom you'd plotted it brought it off, too," Cartland answered with justifiable pride, since he was one of those people.

"Next interesting question is, what does old Adolf do now that the RAF's in the air again?" Walsh said.

"No. The question is, what *can* he do?" the officer replied. "He's got the *Luftwaffe* heavily committed against the Russians. How much can he take away and turn against us?"

"He could have the Frenchmen do his dirty work for him. They've got plenty of planes left at home." Alistair Walsh had crossed the Channel in two wars to help pull French chestnuts out of the fire. Familiarity with England's nearest neighbor did not warm to liking or trust.

Cartland looked horrified. "Daladier would never do that! . . . I don't think. We aren't at war with France. God willing, we never shall be."

"We're at war with the Fritzes. France is on their side in Russia. The froggies don't look like giving up the fight there. If we're at war with them and France is on their side . . ."

"We aren't speaking about axioms of geometry. I hope like blazes we aren't, any road." Cartland still sounded worried. Maybe the nasty possibility hadn't crossed his mind. Walsh hoped it had occurred to someone in charge of running England these days.

He thought of something else. "Is anybody listening to us? We were certain the PM's people were before we threw out the rascals. Are they still?"

"No." This time, Cartland sounded sure. He also sounded more than a little relieved he could sound sure. "We were certain—and we were damned well right. Some changes have been made at Scotland Yard. Yes, indeed, they have. In case it makes you feel any better, the blokes who jugged you and grilled you afterwards have got their walking papers."

Draining his pint, Walsh considered that. "As a matter of fact, sir, it does make me feel better. I'd sooner see the buggers behind bars them-selves, because they were playing fast and loose with the law, but we were, too, so what the deuce? If they're scrounging dog-ends from the gutter and cadging pennies off their betters, I'm happy enough, by God."

He knew he was stretching things. Bastards like that didn't have to fall back on begging, no matter how much you wished they would. Not all of their friends in high places had fallen foul of the new regime. The ones who'd kept their noses clean would give the sacked coppers a hand. You never could tell—they might need their services again one day.

If the new military government looked like losing the war it had restarted, those quiet, powerful men might need the ex-coppers' ser-vices again quite soon.

That thought came back to Alistair Walsh with painful force two nights later. London's air-raid sirens began to scream. The blackout had been reimposed, but it was still spotty. Too many folks didn't care to believe the war had picked up again. The *Luftwaffe* bombers wouldn't have had much trouble finding the English capital.

Walsh stumbled to a Tube station in the more-or-less dark. It was packed with frightened people, and smelled as bad as some trenches he'd known. Up above ground, antiaircraft guns thundered. Search-lights would try to pin enemy planes in their beams for the guns. Teth-ered barrage balloons would make the Nazis fly high and, with luck, drop inaccurately.

Drop they did. Big explosions mingled with the guns' shorter, sharper reports. Once or twice, the ground shook under Walsh as he lay on a straw pallet and tried without much luck to sleep. People around him—not all of them women—squealed. Those hits weren't close, but he didn't blame the Londoners for panic and inexperience.

He went back to his room after the all-clear sounded. Fire engines clanged toward blazes that scarred chunks of the horizon with orange and gold. None of the fires was close, or likely to trouble him. His room had no damage. He promptly fell asleep once more.

In the morning, the BBC claimed thirty-one German bombers shot down by guns and night fighters. That seemed like a lot to Walsh. But then, his own side wasn't immune to the attractions of propaganda. Or maybe they were telling the truth. Stranger things had happened . . . hadn't they?

VACLAV JEZEK WAS gloomily certain he would never learn any Spanish. If a man had grown up speaking Czech, the sounds and vocabulary of this new language were too strange to stick on his tongue or in his memory. And finding a Spaniard who knew any Czech made the loaves and fishes seem a minor miracle.

When he got leave and went into Madrid, he did find some Spaniards who knew a bit of German. His own accent wasn't perfect—nowhere close. The locals wanted to impose the staccato rhythms of their own speech on the alien tongue. They weren't used to making noises in the back of the throat, either. Comprehension was always an adventure.

He could get drinks. The word for wine didn't change much from one language to another. The Spaniards used some horrible lisping word for *beer*, though most barkeeps understood *Bier*. But Spanish beer wasn't worth drinking, not if you had a Czech's standards. So he mostly stuck to wine or hard stuff.

He could get laid, too. Brothels were easy to find and not too expensive. Unlike Czech whores, a lot of girls in the Republic seemed proud of what they did. They even had a union. So another soldier on leave told Vaclav, anyway. He thought that was the funniest thing he'd ever heard, but the International swore up and down it was true. So maybe it was and maybe it wasn't.

"They going to strike for a raise in pay?" he asked the other guy.

"Better working hours, too. And maybe softer mattresses," the International said. His German was better than Jezek's. He was a Dutchman named Jan, though, and got pissed off if anybody took him for a German.

They went on to invent other demands striking prostitutes might make. Those got sillier and lewder the longer they went on. Of course, they drank more and more while they were at it, too. Vaclav wondered if he'd remember any of it when he sobered up.

The way his head felt the next morning, he wished he didn't remember his name, let alone last night's foolishness. Strong coffee—the Spaniards didn't fool around when they brewed the stuff—and the hair of the dog that bit him helped bring him back to life. Aspirins were hard to come by here, but a bit of brandy took the edge off his headache.

Jan looked more bedraggled yet. He bore down harder on the brandy and went easy on coffee. After a while, he started reviving, too. "I hurt myself," he said mournfully.

"Red wine will do it to you, all right," Vaclav agreed.

"Isn't that the sad and sorry truth?" Jan said.

Of course, bullets and bombs and shell fragments would also do it to you, and they wouldn't give you any fun while they did. No wonder Vaclav and so many other soldiers drank and screwed as if there were no tomorrow whenever they got the chance. For too many of them, there *would* be no tomorrow, and they knew it, whether in the head or, more often, in the belly and the balls.

Vaclav was anything but thrilled about going back into the line when his leave ended. He was even less thrilled when he got there. Spanish spring packed the punch of Central European summer. The sun blazed down out of a sky a brighter, less washed-out blue than you ever saw in Prague. Dust was everywhere. It even smelled baked. And the stink of dead flesh seemed nastier than he'd ever known before. Meat spoiled in nothing flat in weather like this.

When Vaclav complained about the reek, Benjamin Halévy said, "You notice it more because you got away from it for a while, you lucky son of a bitch."

"Ahh, your mother," Jezek replied without rancor. "That's part of it, but I don't think that's all. The heat really does make everything smell worse. And how much hotter will it get in the summertime?"

"We'll find out," the Jew said. "The Internationals talk about salt tablets and heatstroke."

"Some of that's probably just bullshit to make us turn green." Vaclav wished he'd phrased it differently. The way he made it sound, some of what the Internationals said probably wasn't bullshit. Well, they'd been here longer than he had. Chances were they knew what they were talking about, dammit.

Shouldering his antitank rifle convinced him the monster had got heavier while he was on leave. He couldn't blame that on the warm Spanish spring. Pretty soon, though, he got used to listing to the right whenever he slung the rifle on his shoulder.

He started looking for targets well behind the Nationalists' lines. He blew the head off some bigwig just getting out of a Mercedes. Remembering what Halévy had said a while earlier, he hoped it was Marshal Sanjurjo, but evidently not. The Republic didn't claim Sanjurjo's scalp, and the Nationalists didn't go into mourning—or hysterics—because they'd lost him.

They did try to pay back the Czechs and the Internationals. Artillery and mortar fire rained down on their positions. The bastards might have been saying *You want to play that way, we'll make you sorry.* In fact, that had to be exactly what they were saying.

A lot of the artillery rounds were duds, which saved some lives. Vaclav had noticed that a lot of the rounds the Republicans fired were duds, too. Which meant . . . what? That Spanish munitions factories weren't everything they might have been? Evidently.

Vaclav was a careful, thorough sniper. He didn't let himself fall into routines. He didn't keep coming back to the same hideouts day after day. Snipers who made stupid mistakes like that didn't last long. When deciding to go right or left along the line, he'd toss a coin and do what it told him. If he didn't know what he'd do till he did it, the shitheads trying to slaughter him couldn't outguess him.

He potted another Nationalist officer a few days later. It was a hell of a long shot, going on two kilometers. He was proud as hell when he watched the fellow grab at himself and slowly crumple. The Nationalist seemed much closer through the telescopic sight, but not *that* close.

Everybody on his own side congratulated him when he reported the kill. Only later, when he drank some Spanish peach brandy with Benjamin Halévy, did he think about what he'd actually done. "Mother of God!" he said. "Everyone thinks I'm the best thing since sausage because I can murder people farther away than the other guys can."

The Jew looked at him. His eyes were bottle-green. "You just figured this out?"

"Nooo." Vaclav let the word stretch. "But it kind of hit me more than it usually does."

"Well, if it makes you feel any better, maybe that was the son of a bitch who ordered the artillery barrage after you nailed the last big shot," Halévy said. "Even if he wasn't, he was no friend of ours. You think he'd worry if he'd just shot you?"

"Who knows? Who knows anything these days?" Vaclav said. Maybe the brandy was hitting him harder than he'd thought it would. Or maybe he was looking at what he really did in the war, something few front-line soldiers could ever be comfortable trying. "This is a fuck of a way to decide who gets to do what."

"What would you rather do? Roll the dice?" Halévy said. "Suppose the other guy doesn't go along with losing? Then what? You bash the asshole over the head with a rock, that's what."

That *was* what, all right. Force had a brute simplicity nothing else could match. If the other guy was dead, he couldn't stop you. If he feared you'd kill him, he wouldn't have the nerve to try to stop you. "How does that make us any better than wildcats and wolverines?" Vaclav asked.

Halévy reached out and tapped the antitank rifle's long barrel with the first two fingers of his right hand. "Wildcats and wolverines have to get close to do their dirty work," he said. "We're civilized. We can kill from a long way off."

"Lucky us." Vaclav's voice sounded hollow, even to himself. He picked up the brandy bottle and tilted it back. Sometimes *not* thinking was better. Nice, civilized brandy took care of that, all right.

Chapter 13

Once upon a time, Hans-Ulrich Rudel counted every mission he flew. That didn't last long. As soon as the German wheel behind Paris failed—as it had in 1914—it became obvious the war would be long. In a long war, you'd keep going till you got killed or till your side finally won, whichever came first. Why keep track of how often you went up, then?

He and Sergeant Dieselhorst were up again now, hunting Red panzers somewhere west of Smolensk. Down below, shellbursts and fires marked the front and the region west of it, the region through which the *Wehrmacht* had just advanced. The Russians were brave and determined; that much had been obvious from the start of the campaign against them. What had also been obvious was that neither Soviet soldiers nor—especially—their officers were skilled fighting men.

The trouble with that was, the Ivans could learn. The longer they stayed in the ring, the more likely they would. And Russia was a big place. Hans-Ulrich had known as much going in—known in his head, anyhow. One glance at a map told you how enormous Russia was. But you had to fly over it, you had to come hundreds of kilometers through it and realize how many more hundreds you still needed to go, you had to see the swarms of foot soldiers and panzers and, well, everything the commissars could throw at you, before you began to *feel* the enormousness of the place.

You also had to wonder whether Germany was taking on more than she could handle. The Kaiser's armies had smashed the Ivans again and again. They'd knocked the Reds out of the war. But they hadn't conquered Russia, beaten her and occupied her and held her down. Could the *Führer*'s forces manage that now?

If we can't, what are we doing here? What am I *doing here?* Rudel wondered. But he knew what he was doing: looking for panzers, KV-1s by choice. The *Landsers* had a devil of a time knocking out those monsters. A strike from the air could do it.

Hans-Ulrich saw Russian panzers down below. A heartbeat later, he saw a biplane fighter pop out of a cloud and buzz straight at him. If it was a biplane, it just about had to be Russian. Had he entertained any lingering doubts, the muzzle flashes from its twin machine guns would have given him a hint.

"We're under attack!" he shouted to Sergeant Dieselhorst, who of course faced the other way. "It's a *Chato!*" The name came from the war in Spain, and meant *flat-nosed. Chatos* were officially obsolescent, which didn't make this one any less dangerous to him. It was faster than his Stuka, tough, and far more maneuverable. Which meant . . . It meant he was in trouble, dammit.

"What are you going to do?" Dieselhorst asked.

Instead of answering, Hans-Ulrich did it: his right index finger came down hard on the firing button that worked the 37mm guns under the Ju-87's wings. He'd shot down a French fighter with them, and a Russian job more modern than this one. The *Chato* was almost on top of him by then. Maybe he'd get lucky one more time.

And damned if he didn't. As recoil staggered the Stuka in the sky, one of the armor-piercing rounds smashed into the enemy fighter's flat nose—the front of the engine cowling. It probably plowed all the way through the engine, and maybe through the pilot, too. Instantly a mass of flame, the *Chato* tumbled toward the ground.

"I got him!" If Hans-Ulrich sounded surprised, it was only because he was. As he had in France and earlier here, he'd mostly been trying to scare off the enemy with the 37mms' ferocious muzzle flashes. Hitting him was an unexpected bonus.

"Way to go! You're more than halfway to making ace," Sergeant Dieselhorst said. They both laughed. And well they might have. A Stuka, especially a Stuka burdened with the heavy panzer-busting guns, was a most unlikely candidate for an ace's mount.

That Russian was stupid, Rudel thought. If he'd attacked from behind, especially from below, the Stuka would have been as near defenseless as made no difference. But he'd decided to rush straight in, and he'd walked into a haymaker. War seldom forgave mistakes. The Ivan would never make another one. That was for sure. Hans-Ulrich hoped the AP round had killed him. Going down trapped in a flaming crate was a fate he didn't wish even on his enemies.

His own heart still hammered in his chest. Combat grabbed you by the throat in an instant. It was much slower letting go.

It wasn't as if he and Dieselhorst were out of danger for this mission, either. Those panzers down below hadn't gone away. If he didn't do for them, they'd do for some of his countrymen. He swung the Stuka's wing over and tipped the plane into a dive.

He thought a small sigh came through the speaking tube. Did Dieselhorst think they'd done their duty for the day by shooting down the fighter? Hans-Ulrich didn't ask him. *He* was the pilot; responsibility for what they did lay with him. Besides, he might have been wrong.

Those were KV-1s, all right. Even from a good height, they were noticeably bigger than the other Russian panzers—and noticeably bigger than even the biggest German machines. Embarrassing that the Slavic *Untermenschen* could come up with such formidable monsters.

As he had when the *Chato* filled his windscreen, he hit the firing button. A split second later, he pulled back hard on the stick, yanking the Stuka out of its dive.

"You got him!" Sergeant Dieselhorst yelled jubilantly. "He's burning like a crazy son of a bitch!"

How many men inside the panzer? Five, if it was crewed like the larger German models. They were probably burning inside the chassis. Hans-Ulrich felt less sympathy for them than he had for the *Chato*'s luckless pilot. The flyer had been a member of his guild, even if he was on the wrong side. These guys? Maybe somebody down on the ground would waste time feeling sorry for them. Rudel didn't. He climbed again to attack another KV-1.

As he dove this time, big muzzle flashes greeted him from the ground. Black puffs of smoke appeared around the Stuka. "Jesus fucking Christ!" Dieselhorst said. "They brought their flak up toward the front with them."

The blasphemy made Hans-Ulrich frown, but all he said was, "I noticed, thanks." Some Soviet officer had had a rush of brains to the head. If the Germans were going to attack your armor from the air, why *not* try your best to shoot them down while they were doing it?

Blam! Blam! The 37mm guns thundered again. He mashed the throttle down, clawing for altitude as hard as he could. Sergeant Dieselhorst's whoops told him he'd hit another panzer. That didn't make him as happy as it might have. He felt as if the Stuka were just hanging in the air, waiting for the Ivans to bite chunks off it.

And they did. Fragments tore into the back of the fuselage. "You all right, Albert?" he called.

"*Ja*," Dieselhorst answered. "We've lost some of the tail assembly, though. Does she still answer?"

Rudel cautiously tried the controls. The plane responded—more slowly than he would have wanted, but it did. The airflow felt rougher than it should have, too. He made up his mind—he wasn't going to take on any more Russian panzers today. He wasn't going to take on any more Russian flak guns, either, not if he could help it. He turned southwest: the shortest way back to his own side's lines.

"Good thing this beast can take it," Dieselhorst said fondly.

"It sure is," Hans-Ulrich agreed, but then he added, "Don't jinx it, Albert. We aren't back yet." If another *Chato* dove on them, he didn't know what he'd do. No, as a matter of fact, he did know. He'd crash, that was what.

He drew small-arms fire crossing the line, nothing worse. Some of the small-arms fire came from the *Landsers* down there. He took the Lord's name in vain himself, something he did only when badly provoked.

The controls got mushier. Dieselhorst said, "I'm looking back at it, and it won't hold together much longer." He didn't sound so fond any more.

"Right." Hans-Ulrich had been afraid of that. Time to set her down, then. No airstrips in the neighborhood, but there was a reasonably straight dirt road, one luckily without a column of German panzers or trucks rumbling along it. The landing was rough, but it *was* a landing, not a crash. He brought the Stuka to a halt and shoved back his section of the canopy. They always said any landing you could walk away from was a good one. By God, they were right!

"WELL, WELL," Willi Dernen said. "What have we here?" But he knew what they had there: a scope-sighted sniping Mauser with a bolt that bent down so a man could work it without interfering with the sight.

"If you want it, it's yours," the quartermaster sergeant said. "I remember you used one in France for a while."

"Uh-huh." Willi nodded. Unfortunately, that hadn't lasted long. The *Oberfeldwebel* who was teaching him how to pot enemies at long range got his own head blown off by a sniper from the other side. Awful Arno was only too eager to reel Willi back to ordinary duty.

"So I figured, since I got my hands on it, I'd give it to somebody who knew what to do with it." The quartermaster sergeant didn't say how he'd got his hands on it. Maybe he'd won it at skat. Maybe it had fallen off a truck—or maybe he'd swiped it from one that stopped at his depot. Any which way, he held it out to Willi now.

And Willi took it. "Thanks." He raised it to his shoulder and peered through the sight. Yes, his hand still remembered where to go to find the bent bolt. Might be embarrassing—could be fatally embarrassing—if he reached out and missed. He asked, "Have you got any of the fancy ammo that's supposed to go with a piece like this?"

"A couple of boxes." The middle-aged supply sergeant handed those over, too. "God knows if I'll be able to get hold of more, though. Save this shit for when you really need it. Use the regular rounds most of the time."

"Gotcha. Will do," Willi said. Snipers' rifles weren't just ordinary

Mausers with a funny bolt and a sight slapped on. They were generally better made, better finished, and more accurate. Firing rounds of equally special manufacture, they gave a marksman a decent chance to kill a man at a kilometer and a half. At ordinary ranges in ordinary fighting, though, ordinary ammunition would do.

The sergeant eyed Willi. "You and the guy who runs your squad don't exactly get along, do you? Will he let you use that rifle the way you're supposed to?"

He did have a good memory, all right. Willi shrugged. "Who knows what Awful Arno will do next? Half the time, I don't think he does."

"Yeah, he isn't long on brains, is he?" the quartermaster sergeant said. That made Willi laugh out loud, the way unexpectedly finding someone else who thinks like you often will.

Predictably, Corporal Baatz gave him the fishy stare when he ambled back up to the front. "Where'd you get that?" he demanded, as if he suspected Willi had stolen the rifle. He probably did.

But Willi answered with the truth, the whole truth, and nothing but the truth: "Quartermaster sergeant issued it to me."

"Sure he did. Now tell me another one," Awful Arno said.

"So help me." Willi raised his right hand in the German oath-taking gesture. "You think I'm a liar, go ask him yourself."

Baatz paused, his little piggy eyes narrowing further. "You think you can bluff me into believing your bullshit," he said at last. "Well, I'm here to tell you I didn't fall off the turnip truck yesterday. I *will* ask him, and then I'll pin your ears back for bullshitting me. You can kiss that chickenshit pip on your sleeve good-bye! The likes of you a *Gefreiter*? Ha!" He stomped away.

Adam Pfaff looked up from cleaning his own gray-painted Mauser. "Where *did* you get the fancy piece?" he inquired.

Willi grinned at him. "You'll find out."

Fifteen minutes later, Awful Arno came back, his face a thundercloud. It wasn't the first time he'd made somebody under his command out to be a liar and wound up with egg on his face. Knowing him, it wouldn't be the last, either.

He said not another word about the scope-sighted rifle. Instead, he reamed out a new replacement who hadn't done a single thing that Willi could see. That was Arno Baatz, through and through. He wouldn't blame himself for picking the wrong time to call a bluff. Oh, no. He'd take it out on somebody else, somebody who couldn't hit back. School-yards were full of bullies just like him. Unfortunately, so was the army.

"Be damned," Pfaff said as he stowed his cleaning kit. "The supply sergeant really did issue it to you?"

"He really did. And if Awful Arno doesn't like it, too bad." Willi kept his voice down. Baatz had rabbit ears, damn him. Even as things were, his head whipped around. Yes, he knew when his name was taken in vain. That was perhaps his lone resemblance to God. But he couldn't pick out the soldier who'd used the nickname he hated. It wasn't as if Willi were the only candidate.

After 105s pounded the Russian positions in front of them, the Germans moved forward again. The artillery fire hadn't squashed the Ivans. It never did. They dug like animals, and popped out of their holes as soon as the shelling stopped. Rifles and machine pistols, machine guns and mortars, greeted the *Wehrmacht*.

Willi soon got the chance to try out the new Mauser. He knocked over a Russian at about 800 meters. It wouldn't have been an impossible shot for an ordinary rifle, but it would have been a damn good one. With the sight and the silky-smooth action on this baby, it felt routine.

That Ivan must have been an officer, and one the Reds didn't want to lose. They tried to avenge themselves by smashing the Germans with artillery. The Russians were brave, but they made crappy tacticians. A lot of the time, they used guns to do what brains couldn't.

Huddling in a scrape he kept deepening every time he got the chance, Willi wished the Russians were smarter. Then they wouldn't use so much brute force. He hung on to the rifle in case the Reds followed up their barrage with a counterattack. Right now, that didn't feel likely. They were just trying to murder as many *Landsers* as they could.

When the shelling let up, Willi heard wounded men screaming and wailing. He winced and bit his lip. Under pressure like this, what kind of soldier he was hardly mattered. If a shell came down on his hole, he was a dead or wounded soldier. He couldn't do anything about it one way or the other. A kid just out of basic training cowering in another foxhole might live where he died. Fool luck, nothing else but. It hardly seemed fair.

He'd had thoughts like that ever since the war started. He was still here. Of course, so was Awful Arno. If that didn't prove how basically unfair the world was . . .

Willi might not have been able to do anything about the Russian artillery on his own, but the *Wehrmacht* could. A Fieseler *Storch* buzzed over the battleground, scouting out the Ivans' positions. The German army co-op plane could take off and land on next to no ground at all. It was ridiculously maneuverable. It could even hover like a kestrel in a strong headwind.

And it could let an observer see what he needed to see. Not long after the *Storch* flew off—by all signs undamaged despite the storm of small-arms fire the Ivans threw at it—a squadron of Stukas worked over the Russian batteries. One of the Stukas got hit during its dive and didn't pull out. A column of black, greasy smoke marked the end of the plane and its crewmen.

The others did what dive-bombers were supposed to do. A 500kg bomb would knock any artillery piece ass over teakettle. And what it did to the poor sorry bastards serving the gun . . .

Had they not been doing their damnedest to blow him into cat's-meat, Willi might have spent more sympathy on the Ivans. Then again, he might not. He hated all artillerymen, no matter where they came from. They murdered honest foot soldiers without needing to worry about getting shot themselves. Dive-bombers were just what they deserved. The only reason he put up with German artillerymen at all was that they sometimes helped the Stukas keep the other side's gunners anxious.

Whistles squealed. Officers shouted, "Follow me!" Willi and the rest of the ground-pounders did. For once, everything was easy. The Russians who didn't surrender ran away. He cherished the feeling. He knew too well he wasn't likely to meet it again any time soon.

OUT BETWEEN the Nationalist trenches and the ones the Republicans held, somebody had lain dead for too long. Or maybe it was a donkey or a horse, but Chaim Weinberg didn't think so. Their stink was different from a dead man's. He couldn't have said exactly how it was different, but it was.

The wind blew from the northwest, so there was no escaping the horrible reek. He wished he could turn off his nose. Weren't you supposed to start ignoring bad smells after a while? Everybody said so, but old Everybody'd never had to contend with a stench from hell like this one.

All the Abe Lincolns in the trench bitched about it. They all said someone ought to go out into no-man's-land, find the dead soldier or donkey or whatever it was, and shovel some dirt over it. Nobody volunteered for the job, though, not even at night. Odds were the Nationalists knew exactly where the heap of corruption lay and had a sniper just waiting to pot any enterprising International who tried to clean up the mess.

"It ain't fair," Chaim groused. "They don't even have to smell it most of the time. Cocksuckers just sit around and let us suffer."

"And so?" Mike Carroll said.

"So fuck it." Chaim lit a Gitane. That was fighting one stench with another, but harsh tobacco improved on dead meat. He supposed it did, anyhow. Mike looked wistful. Chaim doled out a cigarette. He wouldn't have if the other American had suggested that he go out there and scoop dirt over the corpse. Mike hadn't—quite. So he earned a smoke for himself.

Cigarettes were too soon gone. The death stench endured. Where were vultures when you really needed them? People talked about smells so bad they would gag a vulture. Chaim had always believed that was nothing but talk—if vultures weren't made for rotten meat, what were they made for? But they didn't seem to want anything to do with whatever that was out there.

"You know what's crazy?" Mike said.

"Besides you, you mean?" Chaim returned. "*Nu?* What?"

"Funny man. Ha, ha," Mike said patiently. Then he went back to what had been on his mind before: "What's funny is, we're only like forty-five minutes by car away from Madrid. And we've got to put up with this shit all the time."

"Front was a lot closer than forty-five minutes from Madrid when we got here. Hell, the front then was fuckin' *in* Madrid. We're the ones who pushed it back," Chaim said, not without pride. He looked up and down the trench. Too many long-familiar faces he didn't see. "Those of us who're left, anyway."

"Ain't it the truth?" Mike Carroll took a flask off his belt, raised it— not high enough to let a sniper see him—and said, "Absent friends," before drinking. He handed it to Chaim.

"Absent friends," Chaim echoed, adding, "Thanks," before he drank, too. It was Spanish brandy, snarly-strong. The Spaniards called it co-gnac, but that was a libel on the genuine good stuff. Chaim coughed as he gave back the flask. "Shit'll put hair on your chest."

"Like you don't have enough already," Mike said. Chaim knew he had more than the other American; they'd bathed in creeks side by side often enough. He wondered if not having so much bothered Mike. If it did, he picked dumb-ass things to worry about. He was tall and slim and blond and handsome. Not being any of those things sure as hell got under Chaim's skin.

But I'm the one who's laying La Martellita, dammit, Chaim thought. *When she feels like it. When she can stand me.* Even with the qualifications, that came as close to heaven as a good secular Marxist-Leninist expected to get. As far as Chaim was concerned, laying La Martellita was as close to heaven as Pius XII was likely to get. And, if Pius XII got a look at La Martellita, Chaim figured the Pope would agree with him. Unless his Holiness liked chorus boys, he would, and maybe even then. La Martellita was plenty to make any fag ever born want to try switch-hitting.

The front was only forty-five minutes from Madrid, and Madrid was only forty-five minutes from the front. Supplies came up with ease—when there were supplies, anyway. The Republican forces had been hungry for foreign munitions since France and England jumped into bed with Hitler and jumped on Stalin's back. Spanish factories did what they could, but the ammo they made was junk. Cartridges misfired or jammed. Shells too often didn't burst. If you had Mexican or French or German rounds (those, these days, came only from National-ist corpses), you saved them for when you really needed them.

And so Chaim was surprised and delighted when trucks brought case after case of French cartridges up from the capital. "Where'd these come from?" he asked a driver. "They find 'em in a warehouse they forgot about or something?"

"*No sé, Señor.*" A Spanish shrug was a much more dignified production than its French equivalent. "They loaded them into my truck. They told me to take them to the fighting men. This I have done." Anything beyond what he'd done, he plainly considered none of his business.

Mike said, "The crates don't look weathered, like they would if they'd been sitting in a warehouse or something. And the brass on the rounds is shiny, too. Stuff seems new."

"It does, doesn't it?" Chaim scratched his head with almost the determination he would have given to pursuing a louse. "But that's crazy. Why would the froggies send us fresh ammo when they've gone Fascist, or close enough?"

"Beats me," Mike answered cheerfully. "You know what, though? I don't care. I'm gonna shoot it at Sanjurjo's boys, and I'll hit more of 'em with it than I would with the Spanish crap we've been using."

"You got that right," Chaim said. But he was someone who cared about why. He always had been. He wouldn't have been a Marxist-Leninist—and he wouldn't have been in Spain—if he weren't.

He hunted up a French International he knew. Denis was older than he was: a Great War veteran. The Frenchman drank too much, but he was a good fellow to have around when things got tough. He also shared Chaim's relentless itch to know. And, since he was a Frenchman, Chaim hoped he'd got word of which way the wind blew in his native land.

Chaim spoke no French. Denis knew no English; his German was limited to obscenities and the kinds of commands you might give to prisoners. He and Chaim stumbled along in Spanish. Neither was perfectly fluent, and each had an accent that sometimes puzzled the other, but they managed.

"How much do you want to bet even the War Ministry doesn't know what's going on with the ammo?" Denis said. "Maybe the Spaniards spread some money around and loosened things up—unofficially, of course."

"Oh, of course." Chaim fought dry with dry. "But the Republic is always broke. Where did it get the money?"

Denis spread his hands. They looked a lot like Chaim's: the nails were short and ragged, and the callused palms had dirt ground into them. "I don't know *mierda* like that. Maybe they got their gold back from the Russians."

"Sure. Maybe they did." Chaim exchanged a knowing look with Denis. Now that Stalin had the Republic's gold reserves—to protect them and to pay for war supplies—how likely was he to send them back? No matter how good a Marxist-Leninist Chaim was, he didn't believe it for a minute.

The cynical glint in Denis' eye said he didn't, either. But he didn't come out with anything like that, not out loud. Talking too much could land you in more trouble than you ever wanted to see.

In musing tones, Denis said, "I wonder how happy the fucking Nazis would be if they knew France was juicing their little friends' worst enemies here."

"They'd be enchanted," Chaim answered with a sly grin. "Just enchanted." *Encantar*—the verb *to enchant*—bore an obvious resemblance in Spanish to *cantar, to sing*. After a beat, Chaim realized the relationship to a singing word was there in English, too, but it wasn't so plain in his native tongue.

"Fuck 'em all, enchanted or not," Denis said. "If Daladier'd ever spit Hitler's cock out of his mouth . . ." He shook his head. "Too much to hope for."

"Any which way, we've still got these cartridges," Chaim said. No matter who, at whatever level in the French chain of command, had turned a blind eye, the crates were here. They wouldn't go to waste, either.

AS PEGGY DRUCE CRISSCROSSED Pennsylvania and made forays into other states to promote the war effort, she found herself facing an odd fact: the fight might be on, but it didn't seem to make much difference.

For one thing, it was so far away. Two thousand miles from Pennsylvania to the Pacific. Another two thousand from the Pacific to Hawaii. And *another* two or three thousand miles after that to where the guns were actually going off. Hitler's fight against Stalin was closer than FDR's battle with Tojo and Hirohito.

And, for another, it hadn't affected the country much. Grocery stores were still full of unrationed food. Most gasoline went to the military, and you couldn't get new tires for love or money. That turned the Sunday-afternoon drive into a thing of the past, but it was about as far as restrictions went. It was more than enough to make people piss and moan as if complaining were going out of style.

Peggy thought they were nuts. Of course, she'd seen Germany. One look at what went on there would have been plenty to make the grumblers turn up their toes. No gas at all for any civilians but doctors. No tires, either—in fact, the Germans took tires and batteries from civilian vehicles so the *Wehrmacht* could use them. Rationed clothing. All the new stuff was shoddy, or else made of cheap synthetic fibers. And the food . . . Next to no fruit. Precious little meat. Milk for kids and expectant mothers only. Lots of potatoes and turnips and cabbage and black bread. Awful cigarettes, and even worse *ersatz* coffee.

The Germans bitched about it. Not even the SS could stop that. But bitching was all they did. They let off steam, and then they went back to the serious business of conquering their neighbors.

By the way a lot of Americans carried on, they wanted to string Roosevelt up from the nearest lamppost. "He said he wouldn't get us into a war, and then he went and did!" If Peggy'd heard that once, she'd heard it a thousand times. It was commonly followed by, "Who the devil cares what goes on way the devil over there across the ocean?"

"You'd be singing a different tune if the Japs had hit Pearl Harbor as hard as they wanted to," she would answer.

"If, if, if," the naysayers said. "Who gives a darn about might-have-beens? It didn't happen, so what are you jumping up and down about it for?"

What would really have got Pennsylvania's attention was a war closer to home. Had Hitler declared war on the USA . . . But he hadn't. He had warned that German U-boats would go after American ships in the Atlantic now that England was fighting him again, but that was as far as he'd gone. He seemed to be telling Roosevelt, *If you want to declare war on me, go right ahead. Be my guest.*

Peggy had a picture of FDR doing that. Right next to it, she had a picture of Congress refusing to ratify the declaration. The Japs had started shooting at the same time as they declared war on America. That didn't leave anybody much choice. Hitler, for once, seemed content to let his opponents make the first move.

And, because he did, he confused American politics. (That plenty of people wanted to see Stalin, roasted, on a platter with an apple in his mouth sure didn't hurt.) "Why are folks so blind?" Peggy asked when she got back to Philadelphia after one of her politicking swings.

Herb looked at her. "'No one in this world, so far as I know, has ever lost money by underestimating the intelligence of the great masses of the plain people,'" he quoted with obvious relish.

"Is that Barnum?" Peggy asked.

"Nope." Herb paused to light a cigarette. "Old Phineas Taylor said 'There's a sucker born every minute.' Same sentiment, different words. The other one's from Henry Louis instead."

"Oh. Mencken," Peggy said with faint—or maybe not so faint—distaste. "Back in the day, I used to think he was the cleverest man alive."

"That's okay, sweetie. So did he," her husband said.

Peggy snorted and went on, "But he started wearing thin when he went after Roosevelt like a stray dog chasing a car. And he's one of the jerks who stand up and whinny when they play *Deutschland über Alles.*" She shuddered. Whenever the Nazis announced a victory on the radio, they preceded it with the German national anthem and the *Horst Wessel Lied,* the Party's song.

"He always has been. He left the *Baltimore Sun* for a while during the last war because he liked the Kaiser too well," Herb said.

"Did he? I didn't remember that," Peggy confessed. "The other funny thing is, how come two of the snottiest so-and-sos the country's ever seen both went by initials instead of their names?"

"Well, I kind of sympathize with Barnum," Herb said. "If I got stuck with Phineas, I wouldn't want the world to know about it, either. But there's nothing wrong with Mencken's monicker. Maybe he just needed a short waddayacallit."

"Byline," Peggy said.

"Yeah. One of them." Herb nodded. "You're right, though. It's funny."

"Looking back at things, the Kaiser wasn't such a bad guy," Peggy said. She watched Herb bristle, as she'd known he would. After all, he'd put on khaki and gone Over There to settle Wilhelm's hash a generation earlier. All the same, she stuck out her chin and went on, "Well, he wasn't, darn it. Compared to Hitler, he was a regular Rotarian, honest to God."

"Compared to Hitler, Stalin's a Rotarian, for crying out loud," Herb said. "Unless you're a Rotarian yourself, I mean."

"Or unless you're Mencken," Peggy put in.

"Or unless you're Mencken," her husband agreed. "Of course, he doesn't like Jews much, either. One more reason for him to root for the Nazis against the Reds."

"I know Mencken doesn't like Jews, but I don't think he has any idea how much Hitler hates them," Peggy said slowly. "You know who the luckiest people in the world are? All the Jews in Poland."

Herb blinked. "How do you figure that?"

"Poland's on Hitler's side. If it weren't, he'd be murdering the Jews there. I mean murdering, no two ways about it. The Poles don't love Jews, either, but they don't want to see them dead. Not like that, anyhow."

Herb took a last drag on the cigarette, stubbed it out in a brass ashtray on the end table by his chair, and lit another one. A thin, straight whisper of smoke rose from the ashtray till he noticed and did a proper job of killing the butt. In a low, troubled voice, he said, "You see stories buried at the bottom of page nine in the paper: pieces where the Russians claim the Germans are massacring Jews."

"Uh-huh. You do. You don't see a heck of a lot of stories where the Germans deny it, either," Peggy said.

"I know." Herb smoked the new cigarette in quick, fierce puffs. "I'd always thought it was because claims like that weren't even worth denying, know what I mean? Now I wonder."

"I've wondered all along," said Peggy, who'd seen the fun the Nazis had with Jews ever since the day they invaded Czechoslovakia. She'd done more than wonder, in fact. She'd believed every word.

"We should do something about that," Herb said.

"Toss me your cigarettes, will you?" Peggy said, liking him very much. He was the best kind of American. Show him something wrong and he wanted to set it right. The only trouble was, Europe didn't work that way. So much history piled up on the hatreds there that sometimes pinning the blame was impossible after all this time. Which didn't stop people from slaughtering one another in carload lots to try to drown an ancient slight in blood.

Good American tobacco helped her not think about any of that for a little while. Maybe, if all the Europeans and the Japs were this prosperous, they wouldn't want to smash in their neighbors' skulls with pickaxes any more.

Or maybe they would, but they'd choose a fancier grade of pickaxe to do their dirty work. That struck Peggy as much too likely. She shook her head. The more you looked at this old world, the more fouled up it seemed to be. And she hadn't even started drinking yet.

Chapter 14

Theo Hossbach knew the way to Smolensk. Whenever his Panzer III and the other machines in the regiment turned toward the Soviet stronghold, the Ivans fought twice as hard as they did the rest of the time. And, considering how much trouble they made any time at all . . .

He didn't think the old Panzer II in which he'd gone through so much with Hermann Witt and Adi Stoss would have survived this campaign. No sooner had that gone through his head than he laughed at himself. Of course the old panzer wouldn't have survived the campaign. It damn well hadn't.

So now he'd had to get used to two new crewmen. All things considered, he would have been happier charging a Red Army machine gun with a Luger. The Russians could only kill him. They wouldn't want to try to get to know him. ·

He had new duties, too, but that wasn't so bad. Now he sat up front in the panzer, next to Adi, with the radio set between them. He could see out. He needed to see out, because he was in charge of the bow machine gun as well as the radio. He could use them both at once if he had to, controlling the gun with a padded mount that accommodated his fore-head.

Getting used to two new people's habits seemed much harder. Kurt Poske liked to sing and whistle to himself. Sometimes the loader didn't even realize he was doing it. Theo wanted to reach back and smash his kneecap with a wrench. It might have been better had Poske managed to stay on key. On the other hand, it might not. He still would have been there.

Lothar Eckhardt, by contrast, cracked his knuckles. Everybody prob-ably did that once in a while, but the gunner did it all the time. It sounded like gunfire coming from behind Theo. He could have come up with a million noises he would rather have heard.

A Panzer II's turret had room for only one man. Sergeant Witt had had to command the panzer and load and fire the cannon and the co-axial machine gun. That left him as busy as a one-armed paper hanger with the hives, but he did it for a long time. He didn't need to any more, not with this bigger, more modern machine. But everything seemed to come with a price.

Driver and bow gunner/radioman could talk to each other without their crewmates' hearing. They could, but mostly they didn't. Theo didn't talk much no matter what. Adi made more noise, but he respected his comrade's peculiarities. That was one of the things that made sol-diering beside him a pleasure.

As they rattled along one morning, Theo found a question escaping him: "You all right with the new guys?"

Adi glanced over in surprise. A sentence from Theo was like a couple of chapters from anybody else. "Ja," he answered, pitching his voice so it wouldn't carry back to the turret. "Pretty much. We'd all be dead by now if they didn't shoot straight."

He had that right, no two ways about it. Eckhardt had been a pretty good gunner before he got this slot. The *Reich*'s training centers took care of that. And Sergeant Witt, with his own wealth of experience, made the kid better than he had been. Except for singing and whistling, Poske did all right in action, too. Loader was the most junior position in the five-man crew.

None of that had much to do with what Theo meant, though. He tried again: "They give you a hard time?"

"Nah." Stoss shook his head. "No worse than usual. Nothing a guy can't handle, know what I mean?"

Theo nodded. Even the usual kind of ragging could rub a man raw. If Heinz Naumann, the guy who commanded the old Panzer II before Sergeant Witt, hadn't got killed, he and Adi would have fought it out. Theo was sure of that. He was also pretty sure Adi would have done for the late sergeant. Lucky it didn't happen—lucky for everybody but Naumann.

One more question formed in Theo's head. He didn't ask it. Like a cat, he had a very clear sense of limits.

An authoritative voice spoke into his earphones: "Look for Ivans ahead, map square Red-6."

"Red-6. I hear you," Theo responded, and relayed the news to Witt.

A brief pause followed. No doubt the panzer commander was checking his maps. German maps of Russia weren't nearly so good as the people who printed them thought, but you did the best you could with what you had. Profanity followed the pause. "Now they tell us," Witt said. "We're already *in* square Red-fucking-6."

As if on cue, machine-gun bullets clattered off the right side of the Panzer III's hull. If not for the hardened steel, some of them would have punctured Theo. They sounded like pebbles tossed onto a corrugated-iron roof—but not enough like that. Pebbles on an iron roof might startle, but they wouldn't scare the piss out of you.

Though he had a vision port over there, he didn't want to open it. That might have let in a bullet or two, and he would rather have dealt with angry wasps. Wasps only made you wish you were dead. The Russians used old-fashioned, heavy, water-cooled machine guns, like the German Maxim from the last war. They weren't very portable, which didn't mean they wouldn't chew holes in you once they did get set up.

"Panzer halt!" Sergeant Witt ordered, and Adi Stoss hit the brakes. The turret slewed sideways. Witt gave crisp commands. Eckhardt fired—once, twice. Shell casings clattered at the bottom of the fighting compartment. The stink of cordite filled the panzer. Witt grunted in satisfaction. "Forward again, Adi," he said, and traversed the turret so it faced the front once more.

That machine gun wouldn't bother anyone else. Theo still wondered how many other Ivans lurked over to the right. German foot soldiers would find out—probably the hard way. No trees off in that direction, so there probably weren't any Red Army panzers lurking there. He could hope not, anyhow. He could—and he did.

He peered out through his forward vision port. That one boasted thick armor glass, like the stuff in a Stuka's windshield. It also had a steel shutter to keep the glass from getting nicked when bullets started flying. Scars and divots on the armor glass said the shutter didn't always get used. You needed to know what was going on . . . didn't you?

Back in the Panzer II, Theo had never known what was going on, or no more than the radio and his crewmates told him. Now he could see out. Monkey curiosity made him keep doing it, too, though as often as not he couldn't change anything. He could, and did, tell himself it was line of duty. He had the machine gun, after all. But a lot of the time he was just nosy.

He stiffened in dismay at the same time as Adi let out a horrified yip: "Fucking Ivans!" Where the devil did they come from? One second nothing, the next a swarm of riflemen springing from the ground like the warriors old what's-his-name, the Greek, got when he sowed the dragon's teeth.

Well, Theo had some dragon's teeth of his own. The bow machine gun chattered, spitting brass out of the side of its mouth. The turret machine gun hammered away, too. The Russian infantrymen went down in waves like threshed barley. But the ones who didn't get shot kept coming. They were brave, too, damn them.

And they wouldn't just have rifles. Some of them would carry Molotov cocktails. Theo didn't want to think about blazing gasoline dripping into the panzer—no, not even a little bit. So many things that would catch fire, from paint to explosives to precious flesh. They'd have grenades. One of those through a hatch could ruin your day. Or bigger charges would blow off a track. A stuck panzer was like a hamstrung bull waiting to be slaughtered.

Firing short, steady bursts wasn't easy. He wanted to burn out the

MG-34's barrel so he could kill as many Russians as fast as he could. Discipline held, though. In its own harsh way, *Wehrmacht* training was a marvel.

So was whatever the Ivans did to their men. Theo was sure he would have run away. The Russians stolidly kept coming . . . till two Stukas screamed down out of the sky and landed big bombs on them, close enough to the Panzer III to make it try to rear. That did the trick. Not even the Reds could take a dive-bombing in stride. The handful still on their feet—none near the panzer—skedaddled.

Adi laughed shakily. "All in a day's work," he said.

"*Aber natürlich,*" Theo answered.

AFTER REFUELING and resupplying at Narvik, which the *Kriegsmarine* had quickly fitted out as a bare-bones U-boat base, Julius Lemp took the U-30 back up to the Barents Sea. He understood why the navy wanted to use the little town; it lay pretty close to the Barents Sea itself.

As far as he was concerned, that ended its advantages. The U-boat had got what it needed at Narvik. His men hadn't. They couldn't drink and screw and blow off steam there. A U-boat base without a brothel! What was the world coming to? There was a club for sailors, but it seemed a halfhearted affair, with bad, watery beer and not enough of it. No wonder the ratings grumbled when they put to sea again. In their shoes, Lemp would have grumbled, too. He would have grumbled in his own shoes, except a skipper had no one aboard to grumble to.

He intended to take care of that when he got back to the *Reich*. He didn't want to put anything in writing, but some of his superiors would get an earful.

The one good thing was, his men were too busy to complain as much as they would have with more time on their hands. Here up past 70° north latitude, the sun stayed above the horizon most of the summer. Perpetual daylight kept everybody hopping all the time. You never knew when you might spot a British convoy bound for Murmansk or Arkhangelsk—or when it might spot you. Prowling Russian seaplanes were another danger. Lemp had met one of those in the Baltic. He didn't care to repeat the experience.

Topside watches took all the concentration a man had. You couldn't stretch people out past two hours. With unending daylight to face, ratings who'd never stood a topside watch before got the chance to try it. Lemp got the chance to worry that they might miss something an old hand wouldn't have. He gulped bicarbonate of soda to soothe an acid stomach, wondering why he'd ever wanted to become a naval officer.

Navigation also got . . . interesting. The compass deflection was enormous. Accurate sun shoots became vitally important. With no stars in the sky, the sun was the only clue to direction they had. None of the manuals talked about times like this—U-boat men hadn't needed to worry about them in the last war. That was another discussion Lemp wanted to have with his superiors.

And, even in summer, the ocean was bitterly cold. Without the Gulf Stream, it would have been colder yet. Without the Gulf Stream, Murmansk and Arkhangelsk—and likely Narvik as well—would have been as icebound as Antarctica. *Then I wouldn't have to come up here,* Lemp thought. *That wouldn't be so bad.*

Black-and-white auks and puffins and murres bobbed on the sea, now and then diving after fish or taking off with small, hard-working wings. They weren't quite penguins, but they came close enough to satisfy anybody this side of a relentless nitpicker.

The *Kriegsmarine* sent out a coded message that a convoy had sailed from Aberdeen, bound for one Russian port or the other. Lemp admired the British sailors' courage and decided his own superiors weren't the only ones with problems. That convoy would have to face not only U-boats but also land-based planes from Norway. Talk about running the gantlet . . .

Sure enough, the planes soon found the convoy. Not only did they raid—they also shadowed, relaying its position, its course, its speed. Diesels thrumming through the soles of his shoes, Lemp brought the U-30 southwest to block its path.

He had to be careful. Destroyers or corvettes would be escorting the convoy. On the surface, they could sink him. And he wouldn't be able to submerge, then come back up later and escape under cover of darkness. Here there was no darkness.

So he made sure he had men who knew what they were doing up on the conning tower when the U-30 neared the advancing convoy. That convoy had already taken damage—he didn't know how much. U-boats transmitted only when they had to, to keep the enemy from using their signals to work out where they were.

One thing he was sure of: the freighters in the convoy would make more smoke than the U-30 did. He'd find the British ships before they knew he was around. After that was when things would get interesting.

The sun skimmed low above the northern horizon when one of the ratings spotted the smoke from the enemy. Lemp changed course so he could attack with the sun at his back. The harder he could make things for the English, the happier he would be—and the better his chances of doing it again soon.

Up went the *Schnorkel*'s stovepipe. By now, Lemp took the gadget for granted. More and more of the *Kriegsmarine*'s U-boats used it these days. It wasn't a punishment any more. It was a tool of war, one he'd come to rely on.

But the Royal Navy had its own tools of war. Sharp, almost musical pings echoed through the U-30's hull after the boat went to *Schnorkel* depth. "What the fuck is that?" Gunter Beilharz asked, reaching under his *Stahlhelm* to scratch his head.

"They have an echo locater," Lemp answered. "It's mentioned in my latest briefing reports. It isn't perfect, but it's better than anything they used before."

Beilharz eyed him in something approaching horror. "They can get range and bearing from the echoes?"

"That's the idea," Lemp allowed. "Their toy isn't everything it ought to be, though."

"It had better not be," the *Schnorkel* officer said. "If they can find us whenever they please, they'll sit on top of us and drop ash cans till we either cave in or have to come up and fight it out on the surface."

A U-boat that got into a surface engagement with a warship designed to fight up there was dead meat. Everybody knew it. Lemp would have been happier not to get the reminder. And he would have been much happier if the periscope hadn't shown him a Royal Navy corvette speeding his way with a bone in her teeth. That damned echo locater *did* work.

He didn't want to take on a warship. He could sink her with an eel before she got close enough to hurt him. He could . . . if he was good enough, and if he was lucky enough, and if he felt like telling the other English warships where he was. *Ping! Ping!* With that miserable gadget, they already had a pretty good notion.

But then other noises came through the U-30's steel hull: the unmistakable heavy *crump!* of a torpedo exploding, and after that the sound of a ship breaking up. That dreadful creaking and crackling made any man who went to sea flinch.

It also made the Royal Navy corvette spin through as tight a turn as she could make and dash back toward the vessels she was shepherding. Half a dozen men inside the U-30 gave forth with various profane variations on *What's going on?*

"Well, I don't know for sure," Lemp answered, "but unless they're sinking their own ships I'd say we aren't the only U-boat in the neighborhood." An elk struggling through deep snow would draw a pack of wolves. A convoy crossing dangerous waters might draw a pack of submarines.

Another torpedo slammed into a freighter. This ship, by the sound of it, didn't break up right away. Maybe the sailors would have a chance to make the boats and get picked up. For their sake, Lemp hoped so. The poor devils wouldn't last long bobbing in the Barents Sea.

Those two hits made the enemy forget all about Lemp's boat. The escorting warships were hellbent on hunting down the wolf that had already bitten them. With the *Schnorkel,* getting into range of a fat freighter belching coal smoke was almost unfairly easy. She even obligingly zigzagged to present her flank.

"Torpedo one—*los*! . . . Torpedo two—*los*!" Lemp commanded as soon as he had the shot lined up. Twin wet whooshes meant the eels were on their way. Both hit. One was a dud; it thunked off the coal-burner's flank. But the other eel tore a hole in her stern before Lemp really started swearing. She soon began to settle in the water.

By then, Lemp and the helmsman had swung the U-30 toward another target, this one a bit more than a kilometer off. A longish shot, but he launched only one torpedo: he saved the last one in the forward tubes for self-defense. Reloading was a slow, sweaty job, and his boat wouldn't stay forgotten now that he'd announced himself.

Cheers echoed through the U-boat when the eel struck home. As soon as it did, Lemp pulled away from the convoy. The snort let him go twice as fast underwater as he could have without it. And you had to sense when you shouldn't get greedy. There would be plenty of other chances—provided he didn't throw himself away on this one.

HAD CORPORAL HIDEKI FUJITA stood any straighter and stiffer, anyone seeing him would have thought he'd been carved from wood. But would a sculptor have included a saluting mechanism of such mechanical perfection?

"Requesting permission to speak to you, Captain-*san!*" Fujita said, his voice an emotionless rasp.

Captain Masanori Ikejiri returned the salute. "*Hai? Nan desu-ka?*" He could have just told Fujita to dry up and blow away. That he asked him what it was instead showed he didn't despise the very ground on which the demoted noncom walked. That was something, anyway. It was more than most of Fujita's superiors seemed willing to admit.

"Please excuse me, sir, but I am not useful here now that my bungling has made me lose face." If Fujita was going to grovel, he'd grovel as hard as he could. No sense to half measures, not here, not now. And he was sure groveling was his only chance to escape this humiliating situation—unless he killed himself, of course. That was always a possibility, but he didn't want to die, not yet. "Let me serve the Empire somewhere else in some different way. Please, sir, let me go forth with my rifle and kill the Empire's enemies."

Ikejiri eyed him. If the captain wasn't from a noble family, Fujita would have been amazed. He had the air of effortless ease and style plenty of people tried to imitate, but rarely with much luck. You needed to be born to it, to take it for granted, to bring it off as you should.

He also had any Japanese officer's uncompromising attitude. "If you fail, you must take the consequences," he said coolly.

"Yes, sir. But here at this place I don't have much chance to make up for failing," Fujita replied. "Put me in front of the enemy, Captain-*san*, and I'll show the Emperor what I can do."

"There are more kinds of courage, Corporal, than the one it takes to charge a machine-gun position," Ikejiri said.

"Captain-*san*?" All Fujita really heard was his new, reduced rank. Corporal was a grade a man should hold on the way up to something better. Holding it again, on the way down from something better, burned like lye.

"You have to be brave, don't you, to do your job in spite of any trouble you had?" the captain said. "Yes, other people will know what happened. But your duties here at Pingfan are still important."

"Sir, I want to kill something!" Fujita blurted desperately. "Even the *maruta* laugh at me."

"Hard to be laughed at by a log," Ikejiri said in musing tones. "Can't you make them afraid to open their mouths while you're close enough to hear them?"

"Oh, yes, sir. And I do." Fujita's hands folded into reminiscent fists. "But the sons of assfucked whores go on laughing at me behind my back. I know they do." You couldn't pound a man into the ground for an amused glint in his eye, even if the man was also a log. American *maruta* were too scarce and too valuable to let guards smash them around for the fun of it. Some of the bacteriologists' experiments required subjects in good condition. Prisoners at Pingfan often got plenty to eat because of that, not the starvation rations men base enough to surrender deserved.

"Hmm." Captain Ikejiri rubbed his chin. "We don't usually give men back to the ordinary military once they get stationed here. They know too many things that are nobody else's business."

"I wouldn't blab, sir! By the Emperor, I'd never say a word! Not a peep!" Fujita had been proud of knowing things about Japan's war effort that not many people knew—even if, as a noncom off a farm, he didn't understand much about the scientific details. Now he would gladly have forgotten everything.

In another army, Ikejiri might have mentioned the risk of his getting captured. To do so here would have been an unbearable insult. The captain knew Fujita would rather die.

Again, he could have just told Fujita to shut up and do as he was told. Fujita had been more than half expecting that. Maybe he would have obeyed. Maybe he would have obeyed for a while and then blown his brains out. Even he wasn't sure. And if he wasn't, how could Captain Ikejiri be?

Rubbing his chin again, the officer said, "How would you like to get away from this encampment for a while, Corporal?"

"Doing what, sir?"

"You know we are making weapons here—weapons to use against the Chinese and the Americans and anyone else who stands in the way of the Co-Prosperity Sphere."

"Oh, yes, sir." Fujita nodded, remembering the ride deep into the country to test the germ bomb on the Russian *maruta*. Relief filled him. He'd feared Ikejiri would give him something worthless, something useless, to do. But finding out how to kill Chinese in carload lots sounded important.

"All right, then." Captain Ikejiri spoke quickly now, with the air of a man who'd come to a decision. "You may do that. We have air bases that deliver special weapons where they are needed. I will transfer you to one of those."

"Thank you, sir! Oh, thank you!" Fujita said, all but jumping for joy. With any luck at all, the people who served on that air base wouldn't know what kind of *bakayaro* he'd been here. One thing sure: he wouldn't have prisoners laughing at him any more.

"Maybe you shouldn't thank me just yet." Masanori Ikejiri's voice was dry. "You will be going into more danger than you're likely to face here. Make sure your rifle is clean and well oiled."

"It is, sir!" Fujita assured him. "All I have to do is throw a few things in my duffel and I'm ready to leave." He'd been eager to come to Ping-fan. Now he was even more eager to get away.

"Don't get too excited—it won't happen quite so fast." The captain's voice stayed dry. "We have to go through the proper channels, and the paperwork will take a while. But I'll put in the transfer right away."

Something in his tone said *right away* meant *as soon as you quit bothering me*. For a wonder, Fujita realized as much. He wanted to grab the officer's hand and kiss it. For another wonder, he had sense enough to see that wouldn't do him any good. He saluted again—a salute extravagant enough to come out of a movie and to make a drill sergeant snarl curses at him. He figured Captain Ikejiri had earned this one.

The only person he told about the upcoming transfer was Senior Private Hayashi. They'd served together for a long time, and Hayashi had, or at least showed, more sympathy than most soldiers. "Good luck," he said. "I hope the fellow who takes your slot isn't too big a chucklehead."

"Why should you worry?" Fujita said with a wry grin. "After all, you've had enough practice putting up with me."

"You aren't bad. You've never been bad," Hayashi said. "You beat us when we'd earned it, but not just for the sake of showing us what a big cock you've got. What more could a private want from a noncom?" By the way he said it, wanting even that much—or that little—was an exercise in optimism.

And so it was. Back before Fujita got promoted, plenty of brutal corporals and sergeants thumped him for no better reason than that their rank gave them the right. That was how things worked in the Japanese army. Fujita couldn't imagine things working any other way.

Getting the transfer took longer than he thought it should. Only fear that Captain Ikejiri would rescind it if Fujita bothered him kept the corporal from asking what had gone wrong. He made himself wait. He couldn't think of many tougher things he'd done as a soldier.

At last, the precious form came through. With it came a note that said a truck would take him to Harbin. Once there, he would ride the train and then . . . well, it got complicated then. He'd end up in Yunnan Province, or maybe in Burma, depending on how things went before he arrived. He couldn't have found Yunnan on a map to save his life. He wasn't so sure about Burma, either.

He didn't care. He could go to the other end of the world for all the difference that made to him. More than half of him hoped he would. If nobody knew him when he finally arrived, wherever that was, wonderful. What more than a fresh start could a man down on his luck hope for?

THEY PINNED the Order of the Red Star on Anastas Mouradian for shooting down a Flying Pencil. He wished winning the medal would have meant more to him. What it did mean boiled down to two things. First, he'd taken a chance and lived through it. And, second, the authorities might cut him a little more slack with the medal than they would have if he hadn't won it.

Sadly, he understood he couldn't count on the second one to hold true. If the NKVD decided he was a nuisance, he'd end up in a gulag or dead as fast as the *Chekists* could arrange it. If they only wondered, the medal might make them give him the benefit of the doubt.

Well, it might.

With the war not going so well, he needed any good-luck charm he could grab. The powers that be in the Soviet Union were like bad-tempered children. When they didn't get their way, they threw tantrums. Bad-tempered children smashed toys, or maybe dishes. Bad-tempered Soviet commissars and their flunkies smashed people instead.

Mouradian didn't worry about his own side more than he did about the Germans. Hitler's minions were actively trying to kill him. The NKVD wasn't. He didn't think it was, anyhow.

Still, he couldn't help noting that, in a perfect world, he wouldn't have had to worry about his own side at all. What? This world was imperfect? What a surprise! What a disappointment!

If this were the perfect world, or even a better world, the Nazis and their parasites wouldn't be closing in on Smolensk. But they were, despite the Soviet armed forces' best—certainly most fervent—efforts to stop them. Radio Moscow tried its hardest to deny that. These days, though, *Luftwaffe* bombers could reach the USSR's capital. Once, they'd knocked Radio Moscow off the air for several hours. Only once, but Stas didn't take it for a good sign.

And, if this were the perfect world, or even a better one, the Soviet move against Romania would have bothered the Fascists more. A blow against their soft underbelly . . . Only the underbelly turned out not to be so soft. These days, the fighting wasn't in eastern Romania. It was in the western Ukraine. No doubt because it was, Radio Moscow mentioned it as seldom as possible.

So Stas relied on things he heard unofficially. You couldn't always rely on such things. Then again, you couldn't always rely on Radio Moscow, either, though saying so, or even lifting an eyebrow at the wrong time, could cost you your life. Unofficially, some Ukrainians were greeting the Nazis as liberators, giving them bread and salt and strewing flowers in the path of their armored personnel carriers.

Unofficially, things in the Ukraine had been very bad before the war. Soviet authorities were bound and determined to liquidate the kulak class. And well they might have been—the richer peasants hadn't cared to give up their land and flocks and tools and join collective farms. The authorities broke them. Nobody knew how many Ukrainians died— starved or shot—in the collectivization process. Or, if anyone did know, he wasn't talking.

If some of the survivors didn't act like good Soviet citizens now, whose fault was that? Theirs, of course, or it would be if the USSR won. Then they'd look down the barrel of another round of retribution. In the meantime, maybe they were getting some of their own back.

Stas did wonder how much. He also heard unofficial things about how the Germans behaved in Soviet territory. Some of those things were hard to believe. If the Nazis acted that way in the Ukraine, they'd wear out their welcome in a hurry. Maybe they wouldn't be so stupid down there.

Or maybe they would. Stas wouldn't have been surprised. It wasn't as if Stalin hadn't acted like a bloodthirsty monster enforcing his will there.

The Armenian flyer sighed after he got back to his tent. He was alone there—it was safe enough. As safe as anything could be these days, anyhow. No, when Stalin behaved like a bloodthirsty monster, he wasn't acting. He was showing what he really was. And so was Hitler.

Which one made the worse bloodthirsty monster? Stas was damned if he knew. The English had had an affair with Hitler and decided they would rather dance with Stalin. The French, by contrast, stayed in bed with the Nazis. So did the Poles . . . but they would have slept with Stalin had Hitler jumped them first.

Stas almost welcomed the next mission. Wasn't a clean chance of getting killed better than the muddy ocean of doubts that had filled his thoughts lately? He could make himself believe it . . . right up till the moment when shell fragments slammed into the Pe-2. As soon as that happened, he discovered how much he wanted to live.

The engines still sounded all right. There was no fire. He gave the instrument panel a quick, frightened once-over. The fuel gauge stayed steady. So did oil pressure. He cautiously tried the controls. All seemed in working order. "*Bozhemoi!*" he said—with feeling. "I didn't think we'd be that lucky."

Another German antiaircraft shell burst close to the bomber. The Pe-2 staggered in the air, but no more clangs or rattles warned of another hit.

Ivan Kulkaanen frowned. He fiddled with his earphones. His frown deepened. "Radio's out," he reported.

No one was talking in Stas' earphones at the moment, either. Was that because no one was talking or because nobody could get through? Mouradian did some fiddling of his own. Then he eyed the set's dials. He hadn't done that before—he'd had more urgent things to worry about. Sure enough, every needle lay dead against its peg.

"Well, it could be worse," he said. "We can get back without a radio, and they'll slap in another one or splice the cut wires or do whatever else needs doing."

"Sure." Kulkaanen nodded. "Nobody can order us to do anything stupid now, either."

"No one would ever do anything like that." Virtue overflowing filled Mouradian's voice. He and the young blond Karelian in the other seat exchanged amused looks. Of course their superiors were always wise and careful. Of course.

No one would warn them if Messerschmitts attacked the squadron, either. Stas spent the rest of the flight wishing for eyes in the back of his head. Wishing failed to produce them. He got back to the airstrip anyhow, and put the Pe-2 in the hands of the repair crews.

He hadn't been down long before the squadron commander summoned him. Saluting, he said, "I serve the Soviet Union!"

"Do you?" Lieutenant Colonel Tomashevsky growled. "Then why didn't you move up in the formation when I ordered you to, dammit?"

"Sir, I never heard that order." Mouradian explained what had happened, finishing, "You can check with the groundcrew men. They'll tell you I'm not making any of this up."

Tomashevsky eyed him. "I won't check. But if I ever find out you were lying, you're dead. No demotions. No camps. No punishment details. Dead." He spoke without melodrama. Stas might have wished to hear some. That would have left him less than sure the squadron commander meant it. As things were, he had no room for doubt.

Tomashevsky kept looking at him, waiting for him to say something, willing him to say something. So he did: "Sir, if I ever lie, it won't be about anything where you can catch me."

"I should hope not," the senior officer said. "You'd have to be stupid to do something like that. Dark-haired men aren't stupid. They have other things wrong with them, but they aren't stupid."

Russians often lumped Armenians and Georgians and Jews together that way. Stas mildly resented it. So did most Armenians and Georgians and, he supposed, even Jews. With a crooked smile, he answered, "Sir, I didn't come here to pick your pocket. I came here to blow up Germans."

"Always a worthy cause," Tomashevsky agreed dryly. "But if a pocket walks by begging to be picked, will you hold back?"

"Maybe not," Stas admitted. "But then, would you?" For a moment, he feared he'd cut too close to the bone. But the squadron commander laughed and waved him away. Away he went, before Tomashevsky could change his mind.

Chapter 15

This was the biggest damn fleet Pete McGill had ever seen. If it wasn't the biggest damn fleet in the history of the world, that sure wasn't from lack of effort on the U.S. Navy's part.

It stretched from horizon to horizon. Pete was sure it stretched over the horizon. The destroyers and cruisers and battlewagons and carriers stayed well separated from one another to make sure the Japs couldn't do too much in any one spot.

That didn't worry Pete. "If I was that cocksucker Tojo, I'd be shaking in my boots right now," he declared.

"Got that right, Ace," Joe Orsatti agreed. The gun chief waved expansively. "All the firepower we're bringing to the dance, we won't just lick the fucking Jap navy. We'll sink their lousy islands, too."

"There you go!" Pete liked the sound of that.

Planes from the combat air patrol droned overhead. The American fleet hadn't come far from Oahu yet, but the brass already knew the Japs liked playing with naval air power. The fighters up there were F-4 Wildcats. The Japanese Zero was supposed to be hot shit. It *was* hot shit; Pete had seen as much in the Philippines. But he had confidence in good old

American know-how. If the Wildcat couldn't mop the floor with the Jap fighter, something was badly wrong somewhere.

And if the American fleet couldn't mop the floor with the Japanese navy, something was badly wrong somewhere, too. Pete didn't know the details of the attack plan. Such things were not for Marine sergeants to worry about. Like most of the tens of thousands of other men in the fleet, he did grasp the basic idea. They'd steam west till they ran into the slant-eyed sons of bitches steaming east. Then they'd knock the living snot out of them and clear their garrisons off all the Pacific islands they infested. What could be simpler?

A pair of albatrosses scudded past the *Boise.* Their wingspan didn't seem much smaller than a Wildcat's. Pointing to them, Orsatti asked, "Ever shoot the shit with a guy who was stationed on Midway?"

"I don't think so," Pete answered. "How come?"

"That's where the gooney birds lay their eggs, like. When it's mating season or whatever the hell they call it, there's thousands of 'em."

"Must be something. They're amazing in the air."

Orsatti grinned. "You sure as hell never talked with no Midway Marine. Yeah, the gooneys are great while they're flying. But you know what? Their landing gear's shot to shit. They come gliding in, they put down their feet—and they crash land every fuckin' time. Ass over teakettle like you wouldn't believe. They're just lucky they don't carry avgas, on account of they'd burn like mad bastards if they did."

"This isn't BS?" Pete was wary of getting his leg pulled.

"Honest to God truth." The gun chief held up his right hand. "So help me Hannah, it is. Like something out of a Disney cartoon, only it's the genuine article."

"I wouldn't mind seeing that for myself." Pete paused, considering. "Well, if seeing it didn't mean going to Midway. Holy Christ, man—talk about the ass end of nowhere."

"There is that," Orsatti said. "But it's probably why the gooney birds go ooh-la-la there. I mean, who's gonna bother 'em? Till we got there, there wasn't anything *to* bother 'em."

"I guess." Till that moment, Pete hadn't worried about where albatrosses went to make whoopee. For all he knew, they checked into hotels like everybody else. But thinking about Midway made him think about other islands, too. "I wish like hell the Japs hadn't grabbed Wake and Guam."

"Guam was gonna catch it. That was in the cards. Look at a map— it's the meat in a Jap-island sandwich," Orsatti said. "Wake . . . Yeah, Wake's a bitch. They hit it when we were still jumping up and down from the raid on Pearl. So now it's their forward outpost instead of ours."

"Uh-huh. That's what worries me. You gotta figure the slopes're flying planes outa there now," Pete said. "So what happens when they spot us? They let the rest of the Buddhaheads know, right?"

"Listen to your Uncle Joe," Orsatti said seriously. "First thing is, the Wildcats aren't just flying over us. They're out ahead of us, too. So they may knock down the Jap snoops before any word gets back. But even if they don't, so what? We *want* to do for the Japanese navy, right?"

"Well, sure, when you put it that way," McGill replied. "Only I don't like it when they know what we're up to while we go in blind."

"Won't matter when the shooting starts." Orsatti spoke with serene confidence.

If Admiral Kimmel, the man in charge of the American fleet, shared that confidence, he didn't let it go to his head. Men on the *Boise* got called to battle stations at all hours of the day and night, and it was bound to be the same on every other ship. Pete's heart pounded whenever he ran to the gun. Would this be the time it wasn't a drill? Or this? Or . . . ?

News crackled out of the intercom: "It is reported that an enemy reconnaissance seaplane has been attacked and shot down. It is not known whether the personnel were able to signal that American aircraft were in the vicinity."

If the Japs hadn't been able to radio a warning . . . The Pacific was a big place, the biggest place in the whole world. An airplane alone on the ocean was far smaller by comparison than a single mosquito buzzing around an elephant. So many things could go wrong. A plane that didn't come back wouldn't necessarily be blamed on enemy action.

Necessarily. That was an interesting word, wasn't it?

Then a Japanese sub fired a torpedo at one of the destroyers out ahead of the fleet. The torpedo missed. The destroyer did its damnedest to sink the submarine. It also failed. But the cat was out of the bag.

Were American submarines prowling way the hell off to the west? If they spotted the oncoming Japanese fleet, would they send back a warning? Would they try to thin out the herd, so to speak? The answer to the first question was obviously yes. To the second . . . The fewer warships flying the Rising Sun Pete had to worry about, the happier he'd be.

First things first, though. The first thing the fleet had to worry about was reclaiming Wake Island. Admiral Kimmel approached the flyspeck on the map by night. His ships ringed it when the sun came up. As soon as the Japs in the garrison spotted them, they opened up with field artillery.

Big guns answered them. So did dive-bombers flying off the carriers. In spite of all the hell coming down on their heads, the Japanese managed to get a few planes of their own into the air. As Pete had seen in Manila, their dive-bombers looked old-fashioned. Like German Stukas, they had fixed landing gear.

Also like Stukas, they could be deadly if they got a chance—or even half a chance. One of them swooped down on a heavy cruiser that was in the same task force as the *Boise.* Curtains of antiaircraft fire rose above the big ship. As far as the enemy pilot was concerned, they might as well not have been there. If something got him, it would get him. He didn't seem to care one way or the other. And he dropped his bomb from no more than fifty feet above the cruiser's stacks.

Something *did* get him as he roared away just above the waves. His plane cartwheeled into the Pacific. He wouldn't have had anywhere to land on Wake, anyhow. But he made the Americans pay an enormous price for shooting him down. That bomb must have reached one of the cruiser's magazines, because the ship's whole bow blew off. What was left sank hideously fast.

The *Boise* hurried over to help pick survivors from the water. There weren't many. Most of them were hurt. All seemed stunned. "I'm handing Dave a shell, an' next thing I know he ain't there no more an' I'm in the drink," one guy said, which seemed to sum it up for everybody.

Clumsy landing barges waddled toward Wake. Jap shells fell among them. One scored a direct hit. Bodies flew through the air as the barge sank. Most of the men were bound to be Marines like Pete. All the same, he wished he were riding in one of those barges. Landing on enemy-held beaches was what leathernecks were for. A sailor could do the job he had now. He could imagine nothing worse to say about it.

"HEY, HARCOURT! Yeah, I'm talking to you. Get your sorry ass over here."

That rasp always made Luc wonder what he'd done wrong now—no, what he'd got caught doing wrong now. It always made him feel he was a private just out of basic, and Sergeant Demange had nabbed him with his hand in the cookie jar. No matter that he was a sergeant himself now, and Demange an officer. The old feeling didn't go away. Luc didn't suppose it ever would.

"What do you need, sir?" Luc almost called Demange *Sergeant*. It wouldn't have been the first time. Habit died hard.

"C'mere, I said, dammit." The cigarette in the corner of Demange's mouth twitched as he talked. Luc wondered if he kept that Gitane there even when he got laid. It wouldn't have surprised the younger man one bit. Demange gestured peremptorily. "Walk with me."

"Whatever you want, sweetheart," Luc said. Demange didn't rise to the bait. He just stomped away from the French encampment. Luc's legs were longer, but he had to hustle to keep up. The air smelled of dust. No human habitations lay anywhere near. Luc had never dreamt how vast Russia was. The last Frenchmen who'd got this deep into the country marched with Napoleon. He hoped he'd come out better than they did.

He still carried his rifle. Demange had one, too, along with an officer's sidearm. You didn't want to let the Ivans catch you, no matter how enticing their safe-conducts seemed to jerks. The front was supposed to lie a few kilometers off to the northeast, but one thing you could always count on was Russian infiltrators.

"What's up?" Luc asked after a little while.

"Keep walking," Demange answered. "I don't want any of those *cons* to hear this." He spat out the latest Gitane's mortal remains, ground them under his bootheel, and lit a fresh one.

"Am I in trouble?"

"No more than any of the rest of us." Lieutenant Demange paused to blow out a stream of smoke, then hurried on. "Some crazy shit is going on, that's all, and I want to talk to somebody about it. You've got your head on pretty straight, and you don't run your mouth when you aren't supposed to."

"Gee, thanks." Luc's sardonic tone couldn't hide how pleased he was. He would rather have got that kind of praise from Demange than to have won a medal and brushed cheeks with General Weygand. To Weygand, he would be just another *poilu*. Demange knew him well enough for his judgment to mean something.

"Any time, kid." Demange paused and looked back. No, none of the other French soldiers would overhear them now.

Off in the distance, artillery rumbled. *German guns,* Luc thought, recognizing the reports. He was glad those 105s would come down on the Ivans' heads, not on his. Of course, the Red Army had plenty of artillery of its own, but getting shelled by the *Boches* still struck him as the definitive experience.

"So what's the crazy shit?" He tried to keep his voice as casual as he could.

"It's political, that's what." Demange couldn't have sounded more disgusted if he were talking about syphilis. "You're not one of those crazy Reds, or I wouldn't say boo to you. But you don't wish you were wearing a German helmet, either."

"I should hope not! Those fuckers are heavy." Luc had handled them plenty of times, dealing with dead or captured Fritzes. He preferred the lighter Adrian helmet he had on right this minute. But that was beside the point. "What do you mean, political?"

"If you had your druthers, who would you rather fight, Hitler or Stalin?"

"If I had my druthers?" Luc echoed. Demange nodded. Luc spoke without the least hesitation: "If I had my druthers, sir, I'd take off this uniform and burn it. Then I'd go home and try and forget everything that's happened to me the past going on three years."

"*Salaud!* You don't get that many druthers. The Nazi or the Communist? Who's in your sights first?"

He was serious. Seeing him serious made Luc think it over harder than he'd expected to. At last, he said, "The Germans live right next door. That makes them trouble no matter who's in charge in Berlin.

When it's a *cochon* like Hitler . . . I mean, Stalin's no bargain, either, but he's way the hell over here. The *Boches* are the ones who can really do us in."

"There you go! I knew you weren't as dumb as you look," Lieutenant Demange said—praising with faint damn, certainly, but praising even so. "That's how it looks to me, too."

"But so what, Lieutenant? Here we are in the middle of Russia. If we don't go after the Ivans, they'll sure kill us."

Demange got rid of another dead Gitane. This time, he gave Luc one after lighting up himself—another sign he was pleased. "Suppose a little bird told you they're quietly working on stretching the Maginot Line from the Belgian border all the way to the Channel?"

"Where'd you hear that?" Luc asked. If Demange met a little bird, he'd clean it and pluck it and roast it, preferably stuffed with mushrooms.

"Never mind where. What you don't know, nobody can squeeze out of you." Demange might have been talking about interrogation by the enemy, not by his own side. He went on, "What you do need to know is, this isn't somebody who talks out his asshole. Or I don't think so, anyway."

"Huh," Luc said, and then, "What do the Germans say about that?" One of the big reasons the Nazis had invaded France by way of the Low Countries was that they hadn't wanted to bang their heads against the works of the Maginot Line. France had figured Holland and Belgium and Luxembourg would make shield enough. Now that France knew better . . .

"If the Germans know what we're up to, they haven't said anything about it," the veteran replied. "That's what I hear."

"Huh," Luc said again, more thoughtfully this time. "Why aren't they screaming their fool heads off? Quiet Nazis? It sounds unnatural."

Demange rewarded him with a twisted grin. "It does, doesn't it? Here's the best answer I can give you: I don't know why. If I was Hitler, me, I'd be having kittens."

"Yeah, me, too," Luc agreed. If somebody who showed he'd gone over to your side by sending several divisions to help you fight your other enemies suddenly started strengthening his border against you,

you had to have something wrong with you if you didn't wonder why. Didn't you?

Luc looked around. Yes, he was glad none of the other soldiers could overhear them. "So what happens now? Do we cross over to the Russians' side of the line the way the Tommies did? Or do we wait till somebody counts three and then turn our guns on the *Boches*? I mean, I wouldn't mind, but. . . ."

"What happens now? We keep on doing what we've been doing till somebody with clout tells us to do something else. Then we fucking well do that instead." Demange paused, considering. "And you never heard word one about this crap from me, understand? Try and say anything different and you won't live to enjoy it."

"I'm no rat," Luc said, genuinely affronted.

"Yeah, yeah. I know that. I wouldn't've said anything at all if I thought you were," Lieutenant Demange replied. "But this is dynamite. You've got to remember it's dynamite. Otherwise you'll get your hands blown off, and you'll be standing there bleeding and wondering what the hell happened to you."

A Russian machine gun opened up, not close enough to worry about. A few seconds later, a French machine gun answered. Maybe the diplomats were doing mysterious things behind the scenes. The men who fought and died were still fighting and dying.

Demange listened to the dueling murder mills with his head cocked to one side and that wry grin still on his face. "It's all *merde*, you know," he said. "Every goddamn bit of it."

"Uh-huh." Luc nodded. All he wanted was to keep from getting ground between the gears. He'd managed so far. Another Russian machine gun started firing. Pretty soon, the artillery would join in. How long could he stay lucky?

BE CAREFUL what you ask for. You may get it. Hideki Fujita must have heard that before he requested a transfer away from Pingfan. Sadly, though, it hadn't stuck. And Captain Ikejiri had wasted no time in ridding the bacteriological-warfare unit of someone who'd screwed up.

When Fujita heard he was being transferred to Yunnan province, he'd assumed he would travel down through China to wherever the devil Yunnan was. As things turned out, the province lay in the far, far south, on the border with Burma. He couldn't simply hop on a train and go there, because Japanese control in China stopped well north of the area.

No, things weren't that simple. The train took him from Harbin to Shanghai. From there, he took a ship to Hong Kong. In Hong Kong, newly seized from the British, he had to wait two days for a plane to Hanoi, newly taken from the French. After another flight, he landed at the airport in Mandalay: Burma, too, had belonged to England till the war got rolling. Then he took the train up to Myitkyina, near the Chinese border.

The train trip was an adventure all by itself. Even before the fighting started, the line must have been an afterthought of empire. During combat, English soldiers had sabotaged it here and there. And the Japanese broom of conquest hadn't come close to sweeping clean. Englishmen with rifles and mortars still roamed the countryside. So did Burmese bandits. Fujita fired out the window several times. He wasn't always sure at whom he was shooting. He didn't much care, either. Nobody who was shooting at him was likely to be friendly.

Myitkyina lay in the middle of steaming jungle. Snow-capped mountains corrugated the horizon to the east and north. Signs at the train station were written in characters he couldn't read. He grabbed the first Japanese soldier he saw and asked—almost begged—to be taken to the local army headquarters.

Since the soldier he grabbed was only a private, the fellow couldn't tell him to get lost. He didn't look happy, though. "Well, come on, then," he said gruffly. Four other Japanese soldiers who'd got off the train with Fujita eagerly followed. They seemed just as lost and confused as he was.

Not surprisingly, the functionaries who made Southern Army go had claimed the best hotel in town. It was a fourth-rate copy of a third-rate hotel in a second-rate city in some happier English colonial possession. Getting shelled in the conquest did nothing to improve it. The clerks there rapidly dealt with the other newly arrived Japanese soldiers. Each of those men had a slot, and they fit him into it. No one seemed to have any idea what to do with Fujita.

"From the Kwangtung Army? From Manchukuo? To here?" A senior sergeant shook his head in disbelief. "*Eee!* Someone's played a dirty trick on you, Corporal, or maybe on us."

"You don't have any records that show where I'm supposed to go?" Fujita asked.

"You might as well have fallen from the moon. For all I know, you did." The sergeant seemed to think he was a funny fellow.

"But that's crazy." If Fujita sounded desperate, it was only because he was. They not only didn't have a slot for him, they didn't even have a board with slots to find out where he fit. And here he was, lucky not to have got killed before he made it to this miserable place. He'd thought Captain Ikejiri was doing him a favor. Ikejiri must have hated his guts.

"Well, let's try a different angle," the sergeant said. "What did you do when you were in Manchukuo?"

Before Fujita could answer, several more soldiers from the train found their way to the hotel. The military bureaucrat dealt with them and seemed to forget about Fujita. The other soldiers were easy. He wasn't. And he had to be careful about what he said. "Well, before I got here I served in Colonel Ishii's unit," he replied when the senior sergeant had time for him once more.

"*Zakennayo!*" that worthy exclaimed. "Who in blazes is Colonel Ishii? What does his damned unit do—besides sending people all over the Co-Prosperity Sphere, I mean?"

Fujita wondered how he should answer that. He feared he shouldn't answer it at all. He also feared he would end up in trouble if he didn't. But when the senior sergeant shouted Colonel Ishii's name, a skinny little superior private with glasses pricked up his ears. "Please excuse me, Sergeant-*san* . . ." he said, and drew the noncom off to one side. They talked together in low voices for a couple of minutes.

"Oh," the senior sergeant said loudly. "He's with *those* people?" He turned back to Fujita. "Why didn't you say you were with *those* people?"

Again, Fujita didn't have to answer because the bespectacled senior private did some more urgent murmuring. The senior sergeant threw his hands in the air. He made as if to clout the younger man, who flinched.

Frightening someone seemed to make the sergeant feel better. Fujita knew that feeling. "Security!" the sergeant said, as if it were the filthiest word he knew. Maybe it was. He glowered at Fujita. "If you don't tell us what you're good for, how can we send you where you need to go?"

"If I do tell you, I violate the orders I got to keep that work secret," Fujita answered unhappily.

"Bah!" The senior sergeant sounded disgusted. "Go to Yanai, then." He pointed at the senior private. "He'll write you orders to get you out there."

Out where? Fujita wondered. Well, he'd find out.

And so he did. Superior Private Yanai wrote out the orders, saying, "This will take you out to Unit 113, in the 56th Infantry Division. There's a shed next to the train station. You get your transport there."

"A shed? Next to the train station?" Fujita knew he sounded dismayed—or maybe furious. A kilometer back to where he'd just come from, in this heat and humidity? He wasn't looking forward to that.

"*Shigata ga nai*, Corporal. I'm sorry." Yanai spread his hands in what looked like real sympathy. Whether it was or not, he was right: it couldn't be helped. Wearily, Fujita slung his rifle over his shoulder and trudged away from the hotel. Unfamiliar gaudy birds chirped in the bushes.

The shed smelled like a barn. Both soldiers on duty there were drunk. Fujita had to shout at them to discover what they called transport: a creaking ox cart. They were in charge of a dozen or so carts, with the oxen to haul them hither and yon. The oxen no doubt explained the smell. The first driver the men in charge of the shed hunted up had no idea where Unit 113 was stationed. They swore at him, but he insisted he'd never been there.

Things had been ragged out on Manchukuo's border with Soviet-backed Mongolia. Here, they would have had to shape up to seem ragged. This was the raw edge of conquest. That Japanese soldiers ruled here near Burma's Chinese frontier should have been inspiring. That the soldiers actually at the frontier were less than the shining lights of the Japanese Army shouldn't have been surprising. Fujita had traveled too far too fast to stay tolerant. He screamed at the stablemen. One of them was a corporal, too. He didn't care. If the other fellow felt like fighting, he intended to maim him for life.

He was almost disappointed when the other corporal quailed instead. Even a drunk could tell he had murder in his eyes. And the next driver the stablemen hunted up did know about Unit 113. "I've been there before," he said. "I can find it again." He eyed Fujita. "Keep your piece handy while we go, though. You might want to fix your bayonet, too. Things can get pretty hairy around here."

"I found out about that on the way up." Fujita unsheathed the bayonet and snapped it into place under his Arisaka's muzzle.

He could have walked to Unit 113 as fast as the ox cart brought him there. He would have had to work harder, though. The trail they followed wasn't much wider than the cart. Anything or anyone might have burst out of the jungle before Fujita or the driver could do anything about it. The oxen took their own sweet time splashing across streams.

It was almost sunset when they reached the clearing that held Unit 113. No fancy compound here—nothing but tents. No officer of rank higher than captain, either. And nobody, from that captain down to the almost toothless old Burmese woman who cooked for the unit, had the slightest idea that Fujita was coming or what to do with him now that he was here.

"Demons take it," the captain said at last. "You're really from Unit 731?" He might have been a skinny little would-be wrestler talking about someone from a famous sumo *dojo.*

"Yes, sir. I really am," Fujita said.

"How about that? I'm sure you'll do a lot of good here, then, with all the things you're bound to know. For now, get some rice, pour some of the old gal's stew over it, and find somewhere to unroll your blanket or sling your hammock. We've got a lot going on here. I'm sure you'll fit right in."

"Yes, sir. Thank you, sir." Fujita knew better than to argue with an officer. He also knew better than to ask the Burmese woman what all went into the stew. It didn't taste half bad, even if it was spicier than he fancied. Better not to wonder where the meat came from. He'd had stews like that before. As long as it filled him up, he wouldn't complain.

LA MARTELLITA LOOKED daggers at Chaim Weinberg. If this was the kind of love wives were supposed to show husbands, he sure didn't want to see how she'd act when she was pissed off at him. (As a matter of fact, he had seen that, and more often than he wanted.)

Her hands cupped her bulging belly. "You did this to me!" she screeched, more or less accurately.

They were walking along a street in Madrid. La Martellita didn't care. She let him have it any which way. Other people within earshot turned to listen. Street theater was the best, and cheapest, entertainment in town. It was a hell of a lot more interesting than the crap either the Republicans or the Nationalists put on the radio.

Chaim knew about street theater. Growing up in New York City's Lower East Side, he couldn't very well not know about it. But he enjoyed watching and listening to other people more than being watched and listened to.

"Take it easy, Magdalena," he said, trying to soothe his inamorata till they got to some place where she could scream at him in something resembling privacy.

"And don't call me by that name!" she told him, still at top volume. "Don't you dare call me by that name! You've got no business knowing that name! I'm the Little Hammer! Do you hear me?"

"*Sí,* Magdalena," Chaim answered easily. If she was going to work like a Stakhanovite to piss him off, the least he could do was return the disfavor.

She said something so incandescent that a little old woman with a face like a Roman bust that was starting to crumble crossed herself. In the aggressively anticlerical Spanish Republic, that was shock indeed. Someone might denounce you for showing you believed.

As for Chaim, he understood most of what his very pregnant sweetheart called him. He would have murdered any man who said a quarter of that to him, and not a jury in the world would have convicted him, either. Plenty of Spaniards would have decked a woman who talked to them like that. (Some would have got a shiv in the ribs after decking them, too. Spain was a lively country.)

He'd already proved he was a soft American—and no one who tried belting La Martellita would have had joy of it afterwards. So, instead of making a fist and playing the goon, he gave her his blandest, stupidest smile. "*¿Qué?*" he said sweetly.

She started to explode. Then she saw he was waiting for that. She sent him a glare acid enough to etch glass. Instead of shrieking, she asked, "Are you playing games with me?" in a deadly quiet voice.

"You're the one who's been playing all the games," Chaim answered. "Yes, you're going to have a baby. I didn't rape you. I did marry you. What else do you want from me?"

Unfortunately, he knew what else she wanted. She wanted him not to be so short and stumpy. She wanted him to have a handsomer face. He wouldn't have minded a handsomer face himself, but he was stuck with the mug he'd been issued. His looks weren't the real problem, though. Even his being Jewish wasn't the real problem, though in a way it came closer. The real problem was, he wasn't a good enough Communist to suit her.

Maybe that had something to do with his being Jewish. It sure as hell had something to do with his being American. He was so used to thinking for himself, he did it without thinking, so to speak. La Martellita was made for knocking unorthodoxy flat. She would have been great in the Inquisition—she had the full measure of Spanish zeal. If he'd really wanted to hurt her, he would have told her so.

"You didn't rape me," she agreed, and well she might—any man who tried to have his way with her without her consent would leave his *co-jones* behind. "But I wasn't sober when you did me, either."

"Neither was I, the first time," Chaim said, which was at least partly true. "But we both were the next morning."

"There wouldn't have been a next morning if there hadn't been a first night."

Chaim sighed. That was also true, dammit. He spread his hands. "All we can do now is try and make the best of it. Yelling at me all the time doesn't help. It just gives me a headache."

"I don't yell at you all the time," La Martellita said. "When you're up at the front, I can't."

"No, all they can do up there is kill me," Chaim said. She looked at him in incomprehension. It wasn't his Spanish, either; he'd said what he meant. But she didn't get it.

She was beautiful. She was dangerous. The combination was irresistible to Chaim, much as a tiger's terrible beauty had to be to a beast-tamer. One split second of inattention, one tiny mistake with the chair, and you'd be lying on the ground in the middle of the center ring bleeding your life out, and all the marks in the bleachers would go *Oooh!* Life with La Martellita was a lot like that.

Too much like that? For what had to be the first time, Chaim wondered. Yes, she was beautiful. Yes, she was dangerous. Yes, the combination was intoxicating. But, when you got right down to it, how bright was she really?

Intoxicated, Chaim had never stopped to worry about it. He'd never stopped to think it might matter. *Not* thinking was most unusual for him, and telling testimony to just how head over heels he was about her. Most of the time, he thought convulsively, propulsively, continuously. If he hadn't turned Red, he would have made a *yeshiva-bukher* to be remembered for generations. If he thought about La Martellita instead of remembering what touching her felt like . . .

"Why are you looking at me like that?" she asked.

"Like what?" Chaim feared he knew like what, but he didn't want to acknowledge it, even—especially—to himself. For a while, you imagine that something broken will put itself back together by magic. But magic is in desperately short supply in the material world.

"Like the way you're looking at me, that's like what." It was obvious to La Martellita. "Like I just died or something."

"No, not you," Chaim said sadly. He'd never imagined himself a prophet, but he could see the future all too clearly now. It was a future where he didn't see the son or daughter swelling in La Martellita's belly. It was a future where he didn't see her, either, and probably one where she told the child nothing but bad things about its father. He'd just watched his love die, and he had no idea what he could do about it.

"What, then?" she demanded. It wasn't obvious to her. He could see why not, too. She'd never been in love with him. If he'd thought she was, it was only because he'd made her reflect what he most wanted to see.

He could tell her. What difference would it make? Not much, which was part of the problem. But, like a wounded soldier who won't look to see how badly he's hit, Chaim didn't want to bring out the fatal words. He said "Never mind" instead, hoping against hope the wound wasn't mortal after all.

Chapter 16

Nothing in Central Europe or France had braced Vaclav Jezek for summer outside Madrid. Dust. Blazing sun. Air that sucked moisture from your body like a vampire. The only thing that hadn't changed was the stink of death. That stayed the same everywhere. It was bound to be the same in hell, assuming this battlefield wasn't one of Satan's ritzier suburbs.

Vaclav wasn't the only one to feel the heat, either. Several of his countrymen got carried off the field with sunstroke. He heard later that one of them had died.

Through it all, Benjamin Halévy went about his business as calmly as if it were an April day in Paris or Prague. He might have been made of metal. Whatever he was made of, the savage Spanish heat couldn't melt him.

"Why aren't you baked like the rest of us?" Vaclav snarled. The weather left him short-tempered, too.

"It's hot," Halévy said. "But my people came out of the desert, remember. I guess the memory of it's still in my bones."

He sounded serious. As Jezek had seen, though, he often sounded that way when he was anything but. "Desert, my ass," the sniper said.

"Well, if your ass seems cooler than the rest of you, maybe it came out of the desert, too." Halévy eyed him. "Have to say you don't *look* like you've got any Jews in the woodpile."

What first sprang to Vaclav's mind was something about Halévy's mother. But he could see for himself how Halévy would parry that. You didn't want to get into a manure fight with a guy who ran a fertilizer factory. Halévy thought faster and nastier than he did, and that was all there was to it. Instead of being bitchy, Jezek asked, "Have you heard anything about when Marshal Sanjurjo will inspect the trenches again?" He waved toward the Nationalist lines, taking care not to raise any part of his arm above parapet level.

Benjamin Halévy grinned crookedly. "I've finally sucked you in, huh? You want him?"

"Bet your sweatless ass I do," Vaclav answered, and the Jew laughed out loud. Undeterred, Vaclav continued, "If I pot the fat old bastard, they'll pin a medal on me. They'll promote me, so I get some extra pay for real and more besides in promises. They'll send me back to Madrid and let me drink and fuck as much as I want. Maybe they'll even pay for the spree. So, yeah, if Sanjurjo shows up, I'll punch his ticket for him."

"You've got all kinds of good reasons," Halévy allowed. "And, on top of it, it might even help the war effort."

"That, too," Vaclav agreed. The damned Jew started laughing again. Vaclav couldn't see why. If it had provoked him enough, he might have taken a swing at his buddy. Halévy was an officer now, so that could have been a capital crime. Worrying about it wasn't what held Vaclav back. The sensible concern that he'd wake up in the bottom of the trench with a sore jaw and maybe a couple of broken teeth had much more to do with it.

Instead of decking the Jew, Jezek lugged his antitank rifle down the line and spied on the Nationalist positions. The enemy soldiers carried on in plain sight of him. He could have killed some of them, but to what end? They'd tighten up and get more wary. That was the last thing he wanted.

Almost the last thing . . . A Spanish sharpshooter had hunted him for a little while. The would-be marksman was now of concern only to his next of kin. It wasn't that he hadn't been brave. It wasn't even that he hadn't been a good shot. But he must have got what he knew about concealment out of some badly translated manual from the last war. The Nationalists wore German-style helmets, which made them familiar-looking enemies. Those helmets were pretty good. But they wouldn't stop an ordinary bullet, let alone the fat ones Vaclav used. That sniper got only one lesson in the art, a very final one.

There were steel loopholes along the line from which Vaclav could inspect the enemy's trenches. As was his habit, he stayed away from them. An ordinary soldier couldn't put a bullet through one except by luck, and from what he'd seen Spanish soldiers were often less than ordinary. But you never could tell. The Nationalists might have a few real experts. Or they might talk to their Italian allies or to the Germans of the *Legion Kondor*. For someone who knew what he was doing, a loophole was a challenge, not something too tough to bother with.

He crossed into the trenches the International Brigades held. They greeted him in several languages, some of which he understood. A— probable—Magyar spoke in German: "Haven't seen any elephants around here for a long time."

"I keep snapping my fingers—that's why," Vaclav answered in the same language. The International made a horrible face. Vaclav trudged on down the line.

The Americans in the Abe Lincoln Battalion (or maybe it was a brigade; even they didn't seem sure) had more trouble talking to him than most of the other Internationals. They knew English, and some of them had picked up enough Spanish to get by. Neither of those did him much good, and they were unlikely to speak any other tongue.

One exception was—surprise!—a Jew from New York City. Chaim understood Vaclav's German, and Vaclav usually managed to cope with his Yiddish. The Abe Lincoln didn't look very happy right now.

"What's up?" Vaclav asked.

"My girl and me—it's gonna go down the drain." Chaim mimed a little whirlpool in case Vaclav didn't get it.

But he did. "It's gonna go down the drain?" he echoed. "It hasn't happened yet? Maybe it won't."

"It's gonna," Chaim repeated gloomily. "Some stuff you see coming way ahead of time. You can't stop it, not unless you're Superman. Maybe not even if you are."

"Not unless you're who?" Vaclav asked.

"Superman. *Übermensch*, it'd be in German, but the English doesn't make you sound like a fucking Nazi. The guy's a comic-book hero. Lemme show you—a buddy sent me a couple from the States, and they honest to God got here, would you believe it? They're pretty good." Chaim rummaged in his pack till he grunted in victory and pulled out a gaudily printed comic book.

The text was in English, of course. Vaclav knew even less English than Spanish—he could get beer and some food in Spanish now, and was starting to be able to swear when he didn't get them fast enough to suit him. But there wasn't a whole lot of text, anyway. The pictures carried the action, and pictures were a universal language. For what he couldn't get from them, Chaim made an enthusiastic translator and explainer.

"See, Metropolis is pretty much like New York City," the American Jew said. "Not exactly, but pretty much. I'm from New York City, so I should know, right?"

"New York City is like *that*?" Vaclav pointed to one of the panels. Superman was rescuing a scantily clad girl with one hand and picking up an enormous locomotive in the other. The bad guys' Tommy-gun bullets ricocheted off his chest as if he were armored like a tank.

"Well, not exactly." Chaim sounded a little embarrassed. "But the look of the place—the skyscrapers and the cars and the clothes and all—that's pretty close. And the newspaper office where Superman works when he's being Clark Kent, that looks like a newspaper office. I mean, it's bigger and cleaner than a real one—I've been in 'em, so I know—but it's got the idea right, anyway."

Vaclav had been in a newspaper office in Prague. It was tiny and airless and dark, housed in some building left over from the eighteenth century. It smelled of ink and beer and tobacco and unwashed people. How it turned out a newspaper every day, God only knew; the editor plainly had no idea. Next to that, even a rougher version of what the comic book showed seemed very much like heaven.

"America must be a strange place," Vaclav said.

"Man, you got no idea," Chaim answered.

"If you lived there, why did you come here?"

"For freedom. For adventure. For love." The Jew's face twisted. "And I got 'em all, and they ain't worth shit. Women are crazy, you know? You can't live with 'em and you sure as hell can't live without 'em."

Not much originality there, but great feeling. Carefully, Vaclav said, "You aren't the first guy who ever found this out."

"I guess not, but that don't make it hurt any less," Chaim replied, and Vaclav found himself without a comeback for that.

WILLI DERNEN SEWED his pip onto a patch with a chevron, then sewed the chevron onto the left sleeve of his uniform tunic. Not just a *Gefreiter*—an *Obergefreiter*. The promotion gods had smiled on him again, presumably because he'd stayed lucky enough not to stop anything. He was a very senior private indeed.

He found it obvious that, if and when a bullet finally found Arno Baatz, he could step right up and do Awful Arno's job better than Arno did himself. Corporal Baatz, unsurprisingly, held a different opinion. "You think you're such hot shit, don't you?" Baatz said. "Well, puff and blow all you want. They won't make you an *Unteroffizier* if you live to be a million."

Blow me, Arno, Willi thought. Aloud, he said, "How about that?" It was a pretty safe phrase any old time.

"Well, they won't, dammit," Awful Arno insisted. "You have to go to noncoms' school to learn to do all the stuff an *Unteroffizier* has to do. It takes weeks. You'd never hack it—no way in hell."

As far as Willi was concerned, if Awful Arno had made it through noncoms' training school, anything this side of Hans the counting horse could probably do the same. Telling him as much was a great temptation. Regretfully, Willi held back. Life was too short . . . he supposed.

So all he said was, "I notice you're wearing your shoulder straps upside down so the Ivans don't spot the pips on them."

"I should hope I am," Baatz said importantly. "Most noncoms do, you know. The Reds understand that we're what makes the army tick. They'd sooner shoot a corporal than a private any old day."

Willi had never dreamt he would sympathize with the Red Army, but all of a sudden he did. Again, letting Baatz know everything on his mind struck him as less than a good idea. He hoped he sounded patient as he answered, "I understand that. But my pip's on my sleeve, where I can't hide it. And the chevron only makes it stand out more."

"Shall I cry for you?" Awful Arno said, and Willi sympathized with the Russian sharpshooters more than ever. Luckily not understanding that, Baatz went on, "Anyway, you've only got it on one side. From the right, the Russians will just figure you're an ordinary, miserable, no-account private."

"*Wunderbar*," Willi said. At least Baatz hadn't added *instead of an ordinary, miserable, no-account* Obergefreiter. He was probably thinking it, though, the same way Willi was having unexpected kind thoughts about the Ivans.

No matter what he thought about them, they didn't love the *Wehrmacht.* Several batteries of 105s opened up on the German positions southwest of Smolensk. Willi and Corporal Baatz both dove for a foxhole. It was big enough to hold the two of them, though Willi would have bet Baatz was no happier about being cheek-to-cheek with him than he was smelling Awful Arno's stale sweat.

If a shell came down on top of them, they'd both head for the Pearly Gates at the same instant. Willi looked forward to passing through while demons with pointy pitchforks dragged the *Unteroffizier* down to a warmer place. He would cherish the look on Baatz's face, damned if he wouldn't. That was an un-Christian thought; he knew as much. Knowing and caring were two different beasts.

Somebody a couple of hundred meters away shrieked for an aid man. That sobered Willi. No, he didn't want a 105 round to come down on them after all, not when he had no guarantee of dying instantly. He'd seen too many slow, anguish-filled ways of passing to want to experiment. Baatz's cheese-pale face said he wasn't thrilled about what was going on, either.

"Damn Russians have too many guns," Baatz yelled through the din.

"Too right they do!" Willi agreed with great feeling.

And then things got worse. He hadn't dreamt they could. *Something* screamed down out of the sky, trailing a tail of fire. No, not one *something*, but dozens of them spread through a square kilometer or so, all screaming the way Willi'd imagined Arno Baatz's damned soul doing.

And then, over no more than a few seconds, they all slammed into the ground and they all exploded.

"*Gott im Himmel!*" Willi shouted, as loud as he could. He hadn't a prayer of hearing himself. Awful Arno's lips were moving, too, but Willi couldn't hear him, either. He had trouble breathing, and tasted blood when he coughed to try to clear his ears. He suspected he was lucky—if he *was* lucky—the blast hadn't finished him altogether.

He looked around. The Russian rockets—he supposed they couldn't be anything else—had left the ground a smoking moonscape. Bodies and pieces of bodies lay scattered at random across it. And the German soldiers who survived were panicking like a bunch of Dutchmen suddenly up against panzers.

Mouths wide open to let out cries of terror Willi couldn't hear, *Landsers* raced toward the rear. Some still carried their rifles or machine guns. Others had thrown them away so they could run faster—or else just forgotten all about them. Here and there, officers and *Feldwebels* tried to stem the tide. They had as much luck as King Canute.

Willi might not have heard those frightened yells, but even his battered ears caught the rising screams in the air to the northeast. "Oh, no! Not again!" he wailed, and curled up in a ball like a pillbug.

The second rocket salvo caught too many panicked Germans out in the open. Between shattering blasts and scything shards, a man standing up without shelter didn't have a chance. Side by side with Willi, Arno Baatz also tried to squeeze himself into as small a space as he could. Willi could read his lips as he howled, "Make it stop, Jesus! Make it stop!"

Jesus, unfortunately, wasn't in charge of that. The Soviet high command was. The rockets didn't come again. But a wave of Red Army foot soldiers surged out of their trenches and swarmed toward the battered German line. Willi supposed they were yelling *"Urra!"*—they always did when they charged. He sure as hell couldn't hear them, though.

If they got close enough, they would kill him. No matter how blast-stunned he was, he could see that. His fine new sniper's Mauser found its way to his shoulder without his quite realizing how it got there. He could hear the report, and the kick helped bring him back to himself. An Ivan fell over. Willi swung the rifle a little to the left. He potted another Russian.

Arno Baatz uncoiled and started shooting, too. So did other *Landsers* here and there. The rockets hadn't taken out or terrorized everybody. But that khaki Russian wave kept coming. There weren't enough Germans left to stop it, and wouldn't have been even if the discombobulated ones were still able to fight.

Willi could see that. Could Awful Arno, or would he get sticky? Mouthing exaggeratedly, Willi shouted, "We've got to get out of here!"

"What?" Baatz mouthed back. Willi repeated himself. The corporal's eyes showed white all around the iris. Baatz bit his lip. Then he nodded.

They both scrambled out of the foxhole and staggered toward the rear—toward a place where, God willing, things like this didn't happen. They weren't the only ones, either. Something in Willi's chest loosened when he saw Adam Pfaff. He first recognized his buddy by his rifle's gray paint job. Pfaff himself was too filthy to put a name to. Willi guessed he was no cleaner himself.

Pfaff waved. A Russian bullet cracked past, between him and Willi. They both ducked. Pfaff said something. Willi held a cupped hand to his ear to show he couldn't hear. Pfaff mimed shock, horror, and disbelief. Then he turned and fired a couple of shots to slow down the oncoming Ivans. That struck Willi as a brilliant idea. He did the same thing himself. Corporal Baatz also sent a round their way. Arno might be awful, but he did have balls.

Then a chattering machine gun really slowed the Russians. Cannon shells burst among them, too. Panzers to the rescue—and Willi hadn't even realized they were around till they started firing. He wondered if his hearing would ever come back. Or had the rockets scrambled it for good?

Right this minute, he didn't care. It looked as if he might get out of here pretty much in one piece. Next to that, nothing else mattered.

IVAN KUCHKOV HAD NEVER gone to the Ukraine before. Now that he was here, he wouldn't have minded getting the devil out. The locals talked funny. A lot of them were anti-Soviet, and hardly bothered to hide it. They seemed to be waiting for the Nazis to run the Red Army out of their neighborhood. As far as Kuchkov was concerned, they could all go . . .

For once, he and the *politruk* were on the same side. "Show traitors no mercy!" Lieutenant Vasiliev said furiously. "Think what they'll do to you if they get half a chance. And don't give it to them!"

The men listening to the political officer nodded. By their wide eyes, some seemed not to have had any such notions on their own. Were they really so wet behind the ears? Kuchkov feared they were. Milk-fed, too damn many of them. If you didn't learn to watch out for yourself, you could bet somebody would jump on you. With both feet, too. In hobnailed boots.

And Vasiliev added, "One thing you don't need to worry about. The victory of the glorious Soviet Union over the debased and degenerate jackals who nibble at her is certain. Certain, I tell you!"

Was it? As far as Kuchkov was concerned, the only certain thing was that, sooner or later, somebody would screw you. Or sooner *and* later, more likely. And, if victory was so bloody certain, why had his division been shipped south to try to slow down the Nazis here? And how come all the fighting these days was on Soviet soil? Shouldn't things be moving the other way?

"Questions?" the *politruk* added.

One of the reasons he asked was to see what kind of questions he got, and from whom. Kuchkov kept his right arm down by his side. What kind of idiot were you if you gave them extra rope to hang you with? They could build a case against you out of nothing if they wanted to. It was a million times worse if they really had something. The Germans would kill you. But so would the people you were supposed to be fighting for.

That had to be why so many Ukrainians were ready to raise a hand in the Nazi salute. Ivan Kuchkov grunted to himself. Well, at least now it made sense. He knew he still had to plug the worthless bastards without hesitation if he thought they had anything to do with the *Feldgrau* boys.

There were Romanians in the neighborhood, too, but he didn't worry about them. The Poles farther north hadn't had as much fancy equipment as the Germans, but they meant it when they fought you, and that counted for more. Marshal Antonescu's swarthy soldiers? Nah. The only reason they were here was that they'd get it in the neck if they tried to bail out. You did have to be careful not to mistake them for your own guys, because they wore khaki, too. But their uniforms had a different cut, and they used funny helmets, easy to recognize since they were so long fore and aft.

The Germans were the trouble, though, and the Ukrainians, and his own superiors. *Fuck it,* he thought. *Nobody's done for me yet.*

He and half a platoon of soldiers cautiously entered a village the next day, not long after sunup. The peasants stared at them with expressionless faces. Ivan didn't quite point his submachine gun at a guy with a cloth cap and a big, bushy white mustache. "How you doing, Grandpa?" he said. "Seen any Fritzes around here?"

Grandpa came back with a paragraph of Ukrainian. For all the good it did Kuchkov, it might as well have been Portuguese. He glanced at his own men to see if any of them made sense of it. Some Russian dialects were closer than his to the crap they spoke down here. A private said, "I *think* he says there haven't been any around."

That was what Ivan thought the old geezer'd said, too, but he hadn't been even close to sure. He nodded—unpleasantly. "Search the houses, boys. We find any Nazi propaganda shit, we'll clean out this whole whore of a place." He rather looked forward to it.

One of the Ukrainian women screeched like a cat after a door got slammed on its tail. Grandpa put his head together with some of the other old farts. Only a couple of young men here. Maybe the rest were in the Red Army. Or maybe they'd run off to join the Hitlerite swine. You never could tell.

All at once, though, Grandpa spoke Russian an ordinary human being could understand: "Pavel here, he says maybe the Germans are that way, not too far." He pointed west, then toward one of his drinking buddies. Pavel looked as if he didn't need to be singled out.

Too bad, cocksucker, Kuchkov thought. "How do you know?" the sergeant growled. Pavel looked blank. That failed to impress Kuchkov. "How do you know, cuntface? You better sing out, 'cause you'll be fucking sorry if you don't."

Pavel did: "In the fields yesterday afternoon, I saw dust from their tanks and trucks. Had to be theirs. None of yours in that direction."

Yours should have been *ours.* Ivan could have nailed him for that. He would have, too, but he had bigger worries. "Just dust?" he snapped. "No soldiers?"

"*Nyet*," Pavel said. "No soldiers."

Ivan considered. If there had been Fritzes in eyeball range then, chances were his half-platoon would have had to clear them out of this pissy hole in the ground—or would have walked into an ambush, one. So chances were the local wasn't bullshitting: not right this minute, anyhow.

"All right." Kuchkov turned back to his men. "Georgi, you and Avram go half a kilometer out that way, see what the fuck you find. Go on. Get your sad asses moving. If you see Fritzes, Georgi, you come back and tell us. Otherwise both of you hang on there."

Avram sent him a wounded look. Ivan pretended not to notice. Avram was a Hebe. You could count on him to fight the Germans. And he made a damn good point man, not least because he was so jumpy. If anybody could stay out there and not draw the enemy's notice, he was the guy. Georgi was pretty good in the field, but not as good as the Jew. If the Nazis *were* coming up, Avram was the man to keep an eye on them.

Off they went, both glum. And well they might have been, because a Mauser barked almost as soon as they left the village. One of them—Ivan didn't see which—fell. The other dove for cover. "We'll fight 'em in here," Kuchkov declared. "House to house if we have to. Misha, go back and tell the captain we need help doublemotherfucking quick. Scram!"

The Ukrainians started screeching again. They didn't want their village smashed up. Well, how often in this lousy old world did you get what you wanted? He wanted to have a mortar team here, for instance. Wouldn't *that* make the Fritzes howl!

He dashed into a tavern at the west end of the village. As soon as he did, he grabbed a bottle. This was a hell of a lot better than the Red Army's daily hundred grams. He swigged and whistled. The vodka was better than the gasoline-tasting stuff the army issued, too.

He peered out through a knothole. Sure as hell, the Germans were coming up. Life sucked sometimes. He sucked, too, at the vodka bottle. Best thing in the world, except maybe a pretty girl's tit. Smooth fire ran down his throat. He grabbed another bottle, just in case. In case of what? The Nazis had a Panzer II with them. Maybe he could turn the virgin bottle into a Molotov cocktail. Or maybe he'd go ahead and drink the son of a bitch.

The Panzer II sprayed the village with machine-gun bullets. Kuchkov had hoped the Fritz commanding it would be dumb enough to drive inside, but no such luck. One of his men fired at the tank from another house. The round clanged off steel, but so what? The enemy tank's cannon fired several rounds into that house. No more rifle fire came from it. Maybe the soldier had learned his lesson. Maybe he wouldn't need to learn any more lessons from now on.

But you couldn't *not* shoot, not with the German foot soldiers advancing. They'd sure as hell shoot you. Kuchkov stuck the muzzle of his PPD-34 out through the knothole and gave them a burst. Then he threw himself flat on the rammed-earth floor.

Sure as shit, machine-gun bullets stitched through the woodwork half a meter above his head. Vodka bottles shattered noisily. "Fucking waste," Ivan mourned.

Then he heard a noise like an accident in a machine shop—a bad accident. He put an eye up to one of the brand new holes in the wall. The Panzer II was blazing as if it had just gone to hell. The Fritzes on foot had stopped and were staring in the same horrified dismay he'd felt a moment earlier. Machine-gun bullets stitched through them from right to left. They all went down, some dead or wounded, others just sensibly hitting the dirt.

Sometimes your officers actually knew what they were doing. Sometimes you got lucky instead. A pair of brand new T-34s stopped the German advance on the village. The Nazis couldn't do anything against the latest Soviet tanks. A Panzer II was nothing but a snack for their 76mm guns. The Fritzes who could legged it back to the west at top speed. And Ivan Kuchkov drank from his liberated vodka bottles till the newly ventilated tavern spun dizzily around him.

THE NAZI OFFICIAL at the Münster *Rathaus* couldn't have looked more disgusted if he'd found rotten, stinking fish on his supper plate and been compelled to eat it. Sarah Goldman didn't care. If anything, she enjoyed seeing that look on his face. She wasn't rash enough to show what she was thinking, of course.

Beside her stood Isidor Bruck. His features also stayed carefully blank. Behind him stood his parents, as Sarah's mother and father stood behind her. Despite everything the *Reich's* bureaucracy could do to make things difficult for them, Sarah and Isidor had finally finished all their paperwork. They'd won the state's very grudging permission to marry.

"Moses Isidor Bruck and Sarah Sarah Goldman"—the pen-pusher with the swastika armband used the first names the Nazis had forced all Jews to adopt (Sarah's renaming with her own name never failed to make her giggle, at least inside)—"you have conformed with the requirements the *Reich* and the National Socialist German Workers' Party place on marriages for persons of the Hebrew religion. You have also paid all the necessary fees to complete the process."

Sarah somehow felt her father stir behind her. She could tell what he was thinking. It wasn't on account of the fees, which were fat. The professor in him wanted to correct the Nazi flunky for calling the religion "Hebrew." For a heartbeat, she feared he would. He didn't. Odds were no Jew in the *Reich* would have been so rash. But she knew he wanted to.

Scowling, the official went on, "This being so, the *Reich* recognizes and permits the marriage." He glanced Sarah's way. "You are now Sarah Sarah Bruck. Your identity card and records will be altered to reflect the new situation."

She made herself nod. She made herself hold her face straight while she did it. Beside her, Isidor nodded, too. He even smiled a little. That was more than she had in her.

She waited for the man in the armband to congratulate them. She should have known better. He seemed surprised to discover the half-dozen Jews were still standing there in front of him. With a brusque, impatient nod, he said, "That is all. You may go." It wasn't quite *Now drop dead,* but it might as well have been.

They left in a hurry, before the fellow changed his mind. Isidor pulled something out of his pocket—a thin gold band. He put it on the index finger of her right hand, the place where Jewish women traditionally wore wedding rings. She took it off and put it on the fourth finger of her left hand. Both her mother and Isidor's kept their rings there, too. They wanted to fit in with the German majority. That wasn't so easy when you wore a yellow star that screamed *Jew!* at the world.

"I love you," Isidor said.

"I love you." Sarah wondered if she really did. This wasn't a fairy tale where you got married and lived happily ever after. But it was a world where you had to grab whatever happiness you could. If you didn't, you knew you'd never see it again. She added, "Let's go home."

From now on, home would be the flat over the Brucks' bakery. Her folks had made the mistake of asking for permission to put that door through between her room and Saul's abandoned one. New construction? For Jews? Impossible! The arrangement wouldn't be ideal, but nothing in Münster was ideal for Jews.

There should have been a reception, with music and dancing. There should have been more food than a regiment could eat, and more liquor than a division could drink. There should have been all kinds of things. There was . . . a loaf of bread from the bakery, and a couple of stewed rabbits Samuel Goldman had unofficially and expensively obtained from one of the other men in his labor gang. The way things had gone for Jews in Germany the past couple of years, that would do for a feast.

And there was schnapps. Somehow there was always schnapps, no matter how bad things got. It wasn't the best schnapps, perhaps—it wasn't the best schnapps, certainly—but it was schnapps.

Sarah drank enough to let her know she'd been drinking. She evidently drank enough to let other people know she'd been drinking, too. Isidor's father said, "You don't want to get too *shikker,* you know."

He laughed in a peculiar, almost goatish way. To Sarah's surprise, and to her mortification, her own father's laugh sounded identical. Her mother, and Isidor's, sniffed at their husbands. But then they laughed, too. Sarah stuck her nose in the air. That only made the older people laugh harder. Isidor put his arm around her, as if defending his new bride. Their parents laughed some more.

It wasn't as if the older Goldmans and Brucks weren't drinking with her and Isidor. She couldn't remember the last time she'd seen her father's cheeks turn pink. His hard work and bad diet usually left him sallow. Pink he was, though. And the meat he cut from the rabbits made him looked remarkably content. Sarah understood that. She had trouble remembering the last time her own belly had felt so happy.

"Well . . ." Puffing on a pipe charged with the same kind of nasty tobacco her own father smoked, David Bruck stretched the word out. He gathered his wife and Sarah's father and mother by eye. "What do you say we go downstairs for a while, maybe take a little walk, hey?"

"Now why would we want to do that?" Samuel Goldman said, for all the world as if he couldn't think of any reason. Everybody except Sarah laughed again. She was sure her cheeks weren't just pink—they had to be on fire.

All the older people left. Isidor stared as the door closed behind them. "This is the first time I've ever seen my mother go out after we eat without washing dishes first," he said.

She looked at him. "Do you want to think about your mother now?" she asked. Then she blushed again. Had that really come out of her mouth? As a matter of fact, it had.

And the way Isidor looked at her left her with no doubts his mother wasn't the first thing on his mind. She thought she would blush one more time, but the warmth spreading through her started lower down. "Come on," Isidor said.

When they got to the doorway to his room, he picked her up and carried her over the threshold. She squeaked. He silenced that by kissing her as he put her down. Then he shut the door behind them, even though they were alone in the flat. The door had a hook and eye to keep it from being opened from the outside. Isidor fastened that, too.

He looked on what he'd done and found it good. In very short order, he and Sarah were officially man and wife. "You're squashing me," she said.

"Sorry." Isidor didn't sound sorry. He couldn't have sounded much happier if he'd tried. Sarah was pretty happy, too—maybe not quite so happy as she'd imagined she would be on her wedding day, but her imagination hadn't taken into account the way things were for Jews in Germany these days.

After apologizing, Isidor rolled off her. That also made her happy.

He didn't roll far. He couldn't, not without falling off the narrow bed. They would have to get a bigger one . . . somewhere, somehow, sometime.

His hand roamed her. She let it happen. Pretty soon, she started enjoying it and the other things he did. Before long, they were making things official again. Sweat beaded on Sarah's skin. She was doing a warm thing, it was a warm summer's day, and the room was above the ovens.

After a while, she said, "Again?" in surprise.

"Again," Isidor answered proudly.

"What if they come back?"

"What if they do? The door's shut. They won't come barging in. And even if they break down the door or something, you're my wife, right? We don't have to sneak any more."

He sounded like a boy with a new toy. Too much like that? Sarah wasn't sure. She liked the new toy, too. But . . . three times? Things wouldn't go well if she said no on her wedding day. She turned toward him and kissed him instead. That seemed to be the right thing to do, at least for the moment. And three times it was, even if the third round wasn't so easy as the first two had been.

If he tried for four, she *was* going to tell him no. Enough was enough, and she was getting sore. He didn't. He fell asleep instead, quite suddenly and quite deeply.

Sarah was miffed—till she fell asleep herself, even though she hadn't expected to. When she woke up, she and Isidor were entangled almost as intimately as they had been before. Noises outside the closed door said Isidor's parents—and, she recognized a moment later, hers as well—were back.

What do I do next? she wondered. For now, *nothing* seemed a good answer. Her new husband—her new husband!—was still snoring. But her life had just changed forever. Much too soon, she'd find out how.

Chapter 17

Something was wrong. Peggy Druce knew that. She also knew she was afraid she knew what it was. The complicated, inside-out reasoning should have made her laugh. Instead, it left her more afraid than ever.

Most of the time, she would have taken the bull by the horns. She had a low tolerance for bull generally, as even the Nazis came to understand. Without that low tolerance, she knew she would still be stuck in Europe. But going nose to nose with somebody you couldn't stand was one thing. Going nose to nose with the man you loved more than anyone else in the world was something else again. Boy, was it ever!

Most of the time, Herb also spoke freely, at least when he was talking with her. He might be (might be, hell!—he was) more circumspect than she was in public, but she always got to find out what was on his mind. Or she had, till she got back from England.

Of course, if this went wrong it would blow up in her face. She knew that, too. Did she ever! And what was liable to happen if it did . . . What was liable to happen if it did was plenty to make her keep her big trap shut for months. *Not* talking about something, though, could prove as toxic as talking about it obviously was. That silent poison might be slower-acting, which didn't mean it wasn't there.

And so, one Thursday evening after dinner and a couple of high-balls, Peggy said, "Herb, I think we need to talk."

Her husband neatly folded his copy of the *Daily News* (the evening paper, so he and Peggy wouldn't have to depend on the radio or wait for tomorrow morning's *Inquirer* to keep up with what was going on), stubbed out his cigarette in the pocket of a bronze ashtray shaped like a baseball glove, and said, "What's cookin'?"

Even though Peggy was sitting down, her knees wanted to knock. All the same, she said, "I think you know. About us."

Herb made a small production out of firing up another Pall Mall. He held out the pack to her. She got up, took one, let him light it for her, and retreated to her chair. He dragged deeply, then blew a long stream of smoke toward the ceiling. He looked up at the smooth plaster as if watching for enemy bombers, but all there was to see was the smoke disappearing little by little.

His sigh might have come straight from *Camille*. "Damn," he said without heat. "Who told you?"

"Who told me what?" Peggy echoed foolishly.

"I figured you were bound to hear sooner or later. I thought you must have already. Otherwise, you wouldn't have said 'We need to talk' like that." Herb sounded resigned, and a bit mad at himself. "Or maybe you would. Who the . . . Who knows? But people do gossip."

"And what do people gossip about?" Peggy chose to rephrase that: "Why would people gossip about you?" Listening to herself, she thought she sounded resigned, too. She didn't think she sounded mad at Herb, which was good.

He sighed again, even more deeply. He knocked ash into the bronze glove and set the cigarette down. Then, staring down at the comfortably shabby Persian rug under his slippers, he said, "You know, you were away from home a lot longer than we thought you would be when you headed for Europe."

"I sure was," she agreed. "What about it?"

He kept looking at the rug, which wasn't like him. "Even then, I told myself I'd tell you if you ever asked me. Dammit, I messed around with one of the girls from the typing pool for a month or so. It didn't mean anything, and I'm sorry I did it, but it happened."

"You're sorry now," Peggy said. "What about then?"

"Then . . ." He looked up—he seemed to make himself look up—with a familiar crooked smile on his face. "Then I got so sick of playing with myself, I might've ended up in bed with somebody a lot homelier than Gladys."

Peggy knew she couldn't have picked Gladys out of a police lineup of clerk-typists, assuming there was such a thing. That was probably just as well. She also knew Herb had just handed her the moral advantage. If she wanted to hang on to it, she could. But she realized that was another kind of slow-acting poison. The idea was to air things out on both sides . . . wasn't it? That seemed to be their only chance of getting back to where they had been.

And so she let out a sigh of her own. "Well . . ." she said, and then bogged down. This was even harder than she'd expected. Herb was a *man*, dammit. How would he take what she was about to come out with? She hadn't got up on her high horse, but that didn't necessarily mean he wouldn't. If he did . . . she'd deal with it as best she could, that was all. "Well," she repeated, and then made herself go on: "Well, it's not like you were the only one."

There. It was out. Now—would the sky fall? Herb's eyes widened. He started to say something, then shook his head and visibly swallowed it. As she had, he tried again a moment later. He managed one word: "You?"

" 'Fraid so, hon." Peggy didn't want to look at him now.

"I'll be—" Whatever Herb would be, he didn't want to finish it. Peggy didn't suppose she could blame him. "How'd that happen?" he asked after a long, long pause.

"It was after the opera in Berlin. I got smashed. I thought the guy who took me was a fairy, but he turned out not to be. Not all the time, anyway." Peggy still felt like a jerk about Constantine Jenkins, which did her no good whatsoever.

"Only the once?" Herb asked.

"Yeah," Peggy said, and left it right there. It was true. She would gladly have told him she'd swear on a stack of Bibles, but she knew her man. That would have left him more inclined to doubt her, not less.

"How about that?" he said, more to himself than to her. He looked at his cigarette. Most of it had burned away while they were talking. So had most of Peggy's. Herb put his out. She did the same. He started to take another one, then stuck the pack back in his pocket instead. He gathered himself. "I guess you've got the edge on me, 'cause I did it more than once. Not a whole lot more than once, but I did, dammit."

"You don't sound exactly proud of it," Peggy said.

"Nope." Herb eyed her. "Neither do you."

"I was snockered," Peggy said. "And I was dumb. I don't *want* to mess around. It's more trouble than it's worth."

"Amen!" Herb said, as if responding to a sermon from Father Divine. He might have had the same thought, for he added, "You can sing that in church."

Peggy said, "Maybe now we can quit looking at each other out of the corners of our eyes, the way we have been."

"That'd be good." Herb lit another Pall Mall after all. Peggy made a small pleading noise, so he gave her one, too. He went on, "I wondered if you'd noticed we were doing it."

"Uh-huh." Peggy nodded. This felt like going to the dentist. Any minute now, the novocaine would wear off. And how much would things hurt then?

"It ought to get better now that it's out in the sun and air," her husband said. "As long as it stayed covered up, it was going to go bad. And there isn't much worse than gas gangrene." Such glancing references were as close as Herb came to talking about things he'd seen Over There.

The only thing Peggy knew about gas gangrene was that it sounded horrible. No. She knew something else: she didn't want to think about it, not right this minute. She had something else in mind. "We ought to celebrate getting it out in the open," she declared.

"Celebrate, huh?" Herb gave her another crooked smile. She nodded back. The smile straightened—some. "The wench grows bold," he said.

"Damn right," Peggy answered.

Up the stairs they went. Peggy didn't know if it was a celebration, but it was pretty good. Better than it had been while they both kept secrets? She thought so. She hoped so. She also hoped it would keep getting better again. That was the point to all this, wasn't it?

She also wondered if she could find some way to do Gladys a quiet bad turn, whoever the round-heeled little chippy was. And there was one more thought Herb didn't need to know anything about.

ALISTAIR WALSH WANTED to fight the Germans. That was the point of putting on the uniform again, wasn't it? The only trouble was, he—and the rest of the British Army—had no convenient place to do so. Land in the Low Countries or France and they'd get slaughtered. Land in France they couldn't. England and France weren't at war with each other—and a good thing, too, as far as Walsh was concerned. Even RAF planes avoided French airspace when they flew off to bomb Hitler's towns.

Would French fighters really rise to try to help the *Luftwaffe* shoot down English bombers? If they did rise, how hard would the French pilots fight? Nobody seemed to want to find out, or to have the nerve.

"By God, your Excellency, I wish Churchill were still alive," Walsh told Ronald Cartland in the pub near Parliament. "He'd make the froggies show whether they meant it or not."

"Nothing halfhearted about Winston," the MP agreed, draining his whiskey and waving to the barmaid for a reload. He was catnip to the female of the species, no two ways about it. Walsh knew she wouldn't have come over half so fast for *him*. He drank whiskey or brandy or anything else he could find on the Continent. When he could get a pint of decent bitter, he liked that better.

Sooner or later, Parliament would start working again. The provisional government kept promising elections soon, and also kept pushing back the day. People were starting to grumble. Walsh worried lest creeping Chamberlainism reassert itself when the votes were finally cast. If that happened, then what? Another *coup d'état*? He wouldn't have been a bit surprised.

Cartland asked, "Did you catch Musso's speech on the shortwave last night?"

"Afraid I didn't," Walsh admitted. "Wouldn't have done me much good if I had, either. When I go to one of those restaurants with the red-and-white checked tablecloths, I can tell the dago with the pencil behind his ear I want a plate of spaghetti and meatballs. My Italian starts and stops right there."

"Ah," Cartland said politely. "I should have thought of that. Can't say I ever studied it myself, not in any formal way. But I speak French and I did endless Latin, so I can muddle along after a fashion."

I'll bet you can, Walsh thought, without either rancor or envy. The MP would have picked up his education at some posh public school, and then at Cambridge or Oxford. Walsh often thought he'd got his own, such as it was, at a jumble sale. Considering how easily he might have spent his whole life grubbing coal out of a seam, he hadn't done too badly for himself.

And . . . "So what did the bugger with the big chin say, then?"

"Called us traitors to the cause of Europe, if you can imagine the cheek." As any aristocrat might have, Cartland seemed more affronted than anything else. "He said that, since Hitler was busy giving Stalin what-for and didn't have time for puppies like us—"

"Puppies?" Walsh broke in. "Musso has the gall to call us puppies?" He wanted to laugh and to haul off and punch somebody, both at once. He would have felt that way if a waiter in one of those checked-tablecloth eateries had called him the same thing, too.

"He did indeed," the MP replied, sipping from his fresh drink. "He said he'd have to go on and let us have a proper hiding himself, since Adolf was busy."

"And then you wake up!" Alistair Walsh exclaimed. "The Fritzes, now, they're proper soldiers, say what you will about the bleeding *Führer*. But the Italians?" It came out of his mouth as *Eye-talians*, which only made his pique plainer.

"Quite." Cartland spoke with the same frozen disgust a society matron might have used in carrying a dead rat from the drawing room by the tail.

In his mind's eye, Walsh studied a map. The clearer the mental picture got, the more it enraged him. "He's mad as a balloon, he is," the Welshman said, with the air of a judge sentencing a bungling burglar. "Barking mad! How does he propose hiding us when we hardly even touch?"

"He could cause trouble for Egypt from Libya, I suppose, and for

Malta from Sicily. He might even use Abyssinia and Italian Somaliland to go after British Somaliland—assuming he's balmy enough to want British Somaliland, I should say." Ronald Cartland, plainly, had been eyeing mental maps longer than Walsh and spreading them wider.

Walsh had never been stationed in British Somaliland. He knew several regulars who had, though. From everything he'd heard, Cartland was spot-on. Chances were not even the Somalis wanted to drive their sheep and camels through land so miserable—not that Italian Somaliland was any improvement.

He wasted no more time worrying about the Horn of Africa. Even if Mussolini's legions there carried all before them, all they would have was the goddamn Horn of Africa. Egypt, on the other hand . . . "Wouldn't be so good if the bloody Italians"—he pronounced it the same way he had before—"paraded through Alexandria or took the canal away."

"No. It wouldn't." If Cartland's laconic agreement wasn't British understatement at its best, Walsh didn't know what would be.

The veteran noncommissioned officer did some more considering. Ronald Cartland was better suited to the General Staff than he would be himself if he lived to be a hundred, which didn't mean he couldn't cope at need. His calculations were quick and, he thought, accurate. "Musso'd need more than luck to bring it off. He'd need a miracle, or as near as makes no difference."

"I've heard that before from others," Cartland said. "I like it better from you. I respect your judgment."

"Thank you very much, sir." Walsh suspected pleasure was making his ears turn pink. He was happier—prouder, anyhow—than he would have been had the pretty young barmaid whispered a suggestion that they go find a room together. He didn't despise animal pleasure—far from it. But the opinion of a man he admired was a weightier business altogether.

"For what? For telling the truth?" Cartland waved his gratitude away as unnecessary.

"For thinking it is the truth." Walsh wasn't about to let the aristo get away with that. He was going to be grateful, dammit, and that was all there was to that.

"Have it your way, Sergeant." Now the MP spoke in a way Walsh understood completely, like a junior officer addressing a senior non-com. Officers had rank and class on their side. Sergeants had experience and the knowledge that came with it. More often than not, that left the advantage with them. Senior officers knew what their juniors often didn't: sergeants were more important to the army than subalterns.

"If I had my way, sir, I'd go to Egypt right now. That's the kind of thing Mussolini would try, and I'd love to be there to help give him what he deserves," Walsh said.

"Is that truly what you want? If it is, I daresay I can arrange it."

Walsh felt like whooping and turning handsprings. All he did was give back a small, dignified nod. He didn't even smile, not where Ronald Cartland could see him do it. But what was the point to having well-connected friends if you didn't make the most of it once in a while?

"Egypt . . ." Cartland said in musing tones. "Have you been there before?"

"I spent a year—well, not quite—in Cairo in the Twenties." Walsh remembered the amazing heat and the crowding and the smells, which made your nose sit up and take notice even after you'd been on a battlefield. "Not much like good old Blighty, but we need to hang on to it even so."

"That we do. Lord knows how we'd manage without the Suez Canal," Cartland said. "My sister and I visited once. I'll never forget the Pyramids. That was in the Twenties, too: well before the Depression. Perhaps we were there at the same time."

"Yes, sir. Perhaps we were." *Long odds,* Walsh thought, but so what? Keeping your officers happy and interested in you was yet another skill sergeants needed to cultivate. And getting back into action would be good, even if he was only going up against the dagos.

THEO HOSSBACH STILL had trouble getting used to the radioman's position in a Panzer III. For two and a half years, he'd stayed hidden away from the war. The radio set in a Panzer II lent itself to that. Now, all of a sudden, he could see out. He not only could, he had to. Along with the radio, he had an MG-34 to take care of.

How many Ivans had he done for by now? He'd lost track. In a way, that embarrassed him. When your occupation was something as serious as killing people, shouldn't you remember how many you were responsible for? But to do that properly, he should have started counting as soon as the original Panzer II rolled across the frontier separating Germany and Czechoslovakia. He'd been part of a killing team since 1 October 1938, after all. The score from the obsolescent machine's little cannon and machine gun went partly to his credit—or to his blame, depending on how you looked at things.

The only trouble was, any kind of count along those lines was impossible. Because he hadn't been able to see out, he didn't even know where to begin. He couldn't very well ask Ludwig Rothe or Fritz Bittenfeld, either. They were both dead, as was Heinz Naumann.

Adi Stoss might be able to give him an approximate score for the second Panzer II, and for this newer, larger machine. Theo didn't plan to ask him about it. If they ever did talk seriously, they had other things to hash out first. Besides, *might be able to* wasn't the same as *could*. Theo didn't know—he'd never asked—whether Adi was running his own tab.

And, the way things worked these days, keeping track of how many Russians you slaughtered wasn't the only game in town, or the most important one. Making sure the Russians didn't slaughter you had become much more urgent. Their light tanks were nothing German panzers couldn't handle. Even in a thinly armored Panzer II, Theo hadn't worried about them much.

But the KV-1 was a whole different kettle of cabbage. Yes, it was clumsy and slow, but it was about the size of a whale. A Panzer III, the *Wehrmacht*'s main battle machine, could hurt it only by luck or from behind. Had the Ivans had more of the damned things or used them with greater skill, the KV-1s could have been even worse news than they were anyhow.

As for the T-34 . . . It was hot inside the Panzer III, but thinking about the Reds' newest and finest panzer made Theo shiver all the same. It had all the KV-1's virtues—a powerful engine, thick armor, and a big gun—and, so far as he could see, none of the other beast's vices. T-34s weren't slow and clumsy. Anything but, in fact. And whoever'd come up with their armor scheme deserved the biggest, gaudiest medal Stalin could pin on him.

German engineers had never considered armor shape, except perhaps insofar as the simplest shapes were also the easiest to manufacture. If you needed more protection in a particular place, you made your steel plates thicker there. But all those plates were pretty much vertical. Czech, French, and English designers worked from the same basic principles. It wasn't as if there were any other way to go about things.

Except there was. Relying on the Russians' inborn simplicity and fondness for the brute-force approach didn't always pay. Some Soviet designer had had a better idea—a much better idea, as a matter of fact. If you sloped your panzer's armor at, say, a forty-five degree angle, a lot of shells that would have penetrated vertical plate ricocheted away instead. And even the ones that did dig into the armor had to go through more of it to do damage: for shots coming in from most directions, sloped plate was effectively thicker than the same amount of vertical armor would have been.

Once you saw the stuff in action—once you watched your best shots bounce off a T-34 without hurting the metal monster—the idea seemed obvious. Everything seemed obvious after you banged into it nosefirst. But if it was so goddamn obvious, how come no German engineer in a clean white lab coat had twiddled with his slide rule till he came up with it first?

The Russians were *Untermenschen,* weren't they? Hitler and Goebbels loudly insisted they were. If they were *Untermenschen,* though, and the swastika-following Aryans were *Übermenschen,* why did the Red Army have better panzers? If the Ivans just had more panzers (which they also did), that wouldn't have been so corrosive to Nazi ideology. The USSR was a hell of a big country. Having seen more of it than he'd ever wanted to, Theo knew that right down to his toes. And he also knew the T-34—and, to a lesser degree, the KV-1 as well—made every German panzer look like a model from the year before last.

He said as much to Adi. The Panzer III's layout put them side by side at the front of the hull. Not only that, Theo trusted Adi further than he trusted . . . well, just about anybody else. You couldn't count on people to keep quiet if security forces started hurting them. Short of that, Theo was sure Adi would never betray him. He was pretty sure Sergeant Witt wouldn't, either, but only pretty sure. The new guys who fattened up the crew? He hadn't made up his mind about them yet. It wasn't as if there was any hurry.

Adi nodded. "They're mighty good, all right. Not perfect, but mighty good."

"Not perfect? Close enough!" Theo was stung into volubility, or as close to it as he came. "The gun? The armor? *Der Herr Gott im Himmel*, the armor! The diesel engine, so they don't burn the way our beasts do?"

"*Ja, ja.*" Adi sounded like a man indulging a little boy. That infuriated Theo till the driver went on, "The commander's up in the turret all by himself, though, the way Hermann was with the Panzer II. He's got to shoot the cannon, fire the machine gun, *and* command the panzer. And he's got more panzer to command than Hermann did with the II."

"Oh." Theo thought that over. He didn't need long. With a sheepish shrug, he admitted, "You're right."

Stoss shot him a sour look. "How am I supposed to have a proper argument with you when you go and say things like that?"

"Sorry," Theo answered. "But I'm not going to lie."

"Too bad. We could probably keep wasting time till sundown if you did," Adi said. "Now we've got to find ourselves something else to talk about instead." Irony glinted in his dark eyes. He could come out with something like that, confident Theo wouldn't take him seriously. Plenty of soldiers would have.

They didn't need to look for a new topic for very long. Off to the left, at the edge of an apple orchard, a Russian machine gun snarled to malignant life. The water-cooled Russian gun was much heavier and clumsier than a modern, air-cooled MG-34. It didn't shoot as fast, either. Once in position, though, it made a more than adequate murder mill.

"Panzer halt!" Hermann Witt's voice traveled the speaking tube from the turret to the front of the hull.

"Halting," Adi answered as he hit the brakes. Witt traversed the turret—smoothly and quickly, with the hydraulics. In case of battle damage, he could also use a hand wheel and gearing to crank it around. It was too big and heavy for him to wrestle it into place with handles, as he could have in a Panzer II.

The cannon spoke twice. After a moment, though, the Russian machine gun spat more defiant death at the Germans. Back in the turret, Sergeant Witt swore. Theo would have, too. He presumed the panzer commander knew what he was aiming at and had hit it. If the machine-gun crew was still in business, it was operating out of a concrete emplacement.

Witt snapped, "Armor-piercing!" The cannon fired twice more. This time, Witt grunted in satisfaction. "*Got* the fuckers!" he said. "Some poor, sorry shithead lugging a flamethrower won't have to try to fry them before they puncture him instead. Forward, Adi!"

"Forward," the driver echoed, putting the Panzer III back in gear. In a low voice—too low for Witt or either of the new guys in the turret to hear—he went on, "Who knows what all else is lurking in the trees? Our foot soldiers will find out. Oh, won't they just!"

That same thought had occurred to Theo. He wouldn't have said it out loud, not even quietly to a friend he trusted. There lay one of the big differences between him and Adi Stoss. They had others, of course, but the fact that Adi *would* speak his mind seemed the most important. It did to Theo, anyhow.

TO HANS-ULRICH RUDEL, the woods southwest of Smolensk looked like, well, woods. They were less manicured than a carefully maintained German forest would have been. The Ivans had so much land, they had forests coming out of their ears. They had everything coming out of their ears, from iron and coal to wood to people. That was the only possible reason they were giving the *Reich* so much trouble.

From 3,000 meters overhead, Hans-Ulrich wouldn't have been able to tell that the panzers in front of the woods belonged to the *Wehrmacht* if some of them hadn't draped themselves in swastika flags as an identification symbol. Even seeing the banner that united Party and *Reich* didn't leave him a hundred percent sure. The Reds sometimes captured those flags and used them as shields against the *Luftwaffe*.

Hans-Ulrich chuckled, there alone in the cockpit. A swastika flag might keep German planes from bombing Soviet panzers. But how many of the enemy panzer outfits that used it had suffered attacks from the Red Air Force? That kind of crap happened too often even to Germans who'd carefully briefed their air support about the ruse of war they were using. Given the Russians' slipshod procedures, they were bound to go through it even more.

"These are the right woods, aren't they?" Rudel asked through the speaking tube. He wanted to make certain he didn't do anything idiotic.

Sergeant Dieselhorst's quick "You bet, sir" went a long way toward reassuring him. Dieselhorst might not respect the *Führer* as much as he should, but he was the kind of man who went to extraordinary lengths to keep from endangering anybody on his own side. Sure enough, he went on, "The river curls behind the trees and then goes into them, just like it does on the map. For a change, the map and the landscape match up great. We're where we ought to be, all right."

"Good. If I put the bombs in amongst the trees, then, they'll come down on top of the Russians," Hans-Ulrich said. Using Stukas for a job ordinary bombers might have done wasn't efficient. A blind man could see that. But if no ordinary bombers could be spared, bombs from Stukas were better than nothing—as long as they landed where they were supposed to.

He yanked hard on the bomb-release lever. The explosives under the Ju-87's wings and attached to the fuselage's midline fell away. He watched the bombs tumble down toward the treetops—but only for a moment, because Sergeant Dieselhorst's rear-facing machine gun suddenly gave forth with a long burst. "A *Rata*! A fucking *Rata*!" Dieselhorst yelled.

The names Marshal Sanjurjo's soldiers and their German allies had hung on Russian fighters in the Spanish Civil War stuck, even if the Germans were facing them thousands of kilometers from Spain these days. Biplane Polikarpovs were *Chatos;* the shape of the cowling for their radial engines made the nickname fit.

Later Polikarpov monoplanes also had flat noses, but the Spaniards and *Legion Kondor* flyers called them *Ratas*—Rats—to distinguish them from the biplane fighters. They were no match for a Bf-109. When you flew a Ju-87, though, that seemed much less comforting.

Bullets slammed into the Stuka from behind. The *Rata* flashed past and swung into a tight turn, obviously intending to make another pass, this time from dead ahead. No matter how grossly inferior to a 109 the Polikarpov fighter was, it could outrun and outmaneuver a dive-bomber as if the Junkers plane were nailed in place in the sky.

Rudel did everything he could. He fired bursts from his twin forward-facing 7.92mm machine guns. He tried to turn away from the ugly little monoplane with the big red stars on its green-painted fuselage. The *Rata* looked as if it were homemade, possibly by someone who didn't know much about airplanes. But Hans-Ulrich might have been trying to fly a rooster against a hawk.

A bullet scarred the Stuka's windscreen. If that hadn't been made of thick armor glass, the round would have scarred Rudel, too, or more likely left him too dead to heal and scar. More rounds hit the armored engine compartment and the wing. Even if the engine was armored, the instrument panel screamed that the Ju-87 was losing fuel at a hideous rate and overheating even faster. Some of those rounds got home despite the protection.

The engine coughed, farted, ran smoothly for a few seconds, and then coughed again. Smoke started pouring out of it.

"You there, sir?" Sergeant Dieselhorst sounded worried, and with good reason, too.

"I'm here," Hans-Ulrich answered. "I was hoping you were."

"We going to have to bail out?"

"Well . . ." Hans-Ulrich didn't want to say yes. German parachutes left a lot to be desired, even if merely having a parachute would have made a pilot from the last war jealous. The idea of coming down near— or maybe among—the Ivans didn't thrill him, either. But the engine coughed one more time, then crapped out altogether. A Stuka glided better than a brick, but not a whole lot better. Sometimes the outside world answered questions for you. "Yeah, Albert, we've got to bail out."

Dieselhorst tried to make light of it. "Not like we've never done this before, right?"

"Right." Rudel's voice sounded hollow, even to him. They'd been shot down once before, over France. Had the *poilus* caught them, they probably would have been taken prisoner. No guarantees with the Ivans, none at all.

But if they didn't get out now, they were guaranteed dead. Pilot and rear gunner had separate sliding cockpit canopies. Maybe that wasn't such a terrific design feature. If one of them got stuck . . .

They didn't, not this time. And neither Hans-Ulrich nor Dieselhorst mashed himself to strawberry jam by hitting the tail as he scrambled free of his enclosure. Nothing left to do but fall, yank the ripcord, and hope. Later, Rudel realized he should have done some praying while all that was going on. He consoled himself by remembering he was just a trifle busy at the time.

Whump! When the chute filled with air, it felt as if a mule kicked him right in the chops. His vision grayed out for a moment. Then color and motion came back to the world.

He floated downward. Off to his left, Sergeant Dieselhorst waved to him from under another silk canopy. Hans-Ulrich waved back. He yanked on the lines to spill wind from one side of the canopy and steer himself away from the Red-infested woods. He also anxiously looked around for that *Rata.* Russian fighter pilots had the charming habit of machine-gunning helpless parachuting German flyers. It wasn't sporting, but they didn't care. To his relief, the *Rata* was nowhere in sight.

Russian soldiers on the ground did fire at him and Dieselhorst. A bullet thumped through the taut silk above him. If the hole turned into a tear . . . He'd regret that all the way down, but not afterwards. He didn't worry about a bullet thumping through him till he'd almost reached the ground. He wondered why the devil not. Stupidity came to mind.

As the ground rushed up below him, he had to worry about his landing. He'd sprained an ankle—only luck he hadn't broken it—the last time he came down in a chute. He didn't want to be out of action for weeks now. He bent at the knees and at the waist, as training suggested. Another Russian bullet cracked past him, too close for comfort. Training never talked about distractions like that.

Thud! He made it. Not a pretty landing, but the moving parts all seemed to work. He cut himself free of the parachute, then grabbed for his Luger—soldiers were loping toward him. But his hand fell back: they wore *Feldgrau,* and helmets of a familiar shape.

Now—did they realize *he* was a countryman? "Good job!" one of them yelled, waving. Hans-Ulrich grinned and waved back—they did. He looked around. Albert Dieselhorst was free of his chute and on his feet, too. They'd be flying again as soon as they got a new bus.

Chapter 18

Stas Mouradian's latest airstrip lay not far in front of Smolensk. The Germans and their allies kept coming forward, despite everything the Red Army and Air Force could do to stop them. If Smolensk fell . . . Stas wasn't a member of Stavka, the Soviet General Staff, but he could see how bad that would be. Smolensk was the great bastion on the road to Moscow.

If Moscow fell, the game would be up. He could see that, too. Maybe Stalin would find refuge somewhere beyond the Urals. Having traveled the width of the USSR, Stas knew how vast the country was. But could you keep fighting with your capital gone? Would anyone follow your orders if you tried?

But that was a worry for another day, probably a worry for another year. The red flag with the gold hammer and sickle still flew over Smolensk. The swastika was still hundreds of kilometers from Moscow. That Stas could wonder what would happen if the capital fell said things weren't going the way Soviet authorities wished they would.

It wasn't that serious yet. Maybe it wouldn't get that serious. But if Stalin hadn't been greedy, if he hadn't decided he could take Wilno away from Poland on the cheap, the war between the USSR and the *Reich* might well have stayed a war in name only. Till Smigly-Ridz asked Hitler for help, the Soviets and the Nazis couldn't get at each other without violating some buffer state's neutrality. That would have been more dangerous than it was worth.

Would it have been more dangerous than thinking that Stalin's greed had led him into an enormous mistake? Now there was an interesting question for any Soviet citizen to contemplate! As long as you kept your mouth shut, you had a chance of staying safe (from the NKVD, anyhow; the *Luftwaffe* was a different story). But Mouradian had heard—as who in the Soviet Union had not?—of people arrested for no better reason than an expression some Chekist didn't fancy. Those people went into a camp as readily as the ones brave or crazy enough to criticize the regime out loud. They came out of the camps as readily, too: which is to say, just about never.

The distant rumble of artillery distracted Stas from such gloomy reflections. He cocked his head to one side, listening. Those were Russian guns. That was good. No—it was better. He would really have had something to worry about if he heard German guns from here.

But the squadron had been flying out of this airstrip for only about a week. When the Pe-2s got here, you couldn't hear anybody's guns. Stas had been used to fields farther forward. He'd been used to, if not happy about, the sound of guns. Once or twice, he'd had to fly off a runway enemy artillery was suddenly able to reach. Being out of earshot of the front had felt relaxing.

Now he wasn't any more. He wasn't so relaxed, either.

At the edge of the airstrips, a technician wearing earphones manned a sound detector that looked like nothing so much as half a dozen enormous hearing trumpets. They could pick up approaching enemy planes at distances greater than the naked eye could reach. They could some of the time, at any rate. When everything went just right. When other noise didn't distract or confuse the technicians.

There has to be a better way, Stas thought. If he knew what that way was, they'd pin a Hero of the Soviet Union medal on him in a flash. At a guess, it had something to do with radio. Everything modern and scientific seemed to. His guesses stopped right there. He was a pretty good pilot, but he'd never make an electrical engineer.

The technician jerked off the earphones and ran to a bell mounted on a nearby post. He rang the bell as if his life depended on it. And his life was liable to, for he shouted, "They're coming! They're coming!"

A kicked anthill would have shown more chaos, but not a lot more. People ran every which way. Antiaircraft gunners manned their cannons and pointed them west. The technician was pointing in that direction, but Stas couldn't tell whether the gunners followed his lead or simply knew German planes were most likely to appear from that direction. Pilots and groundcrew men jumped into zigzagging trenches to shelter from the expected attack. Some of them had rifles. If they fired at the *Luftwaffe* planes, it might make them feel better. It was unlikely to do anything else.

Stas realized he was the only man just standing there. He wasn't running. He wasn't jumping. He wasn't training an antiaircraft gun in the desired direction or chambering a round in his Mosin-Nagant.

Now he could hear the ominous drone of German airplane engines without the fancy sound detector. Their note was different from that of Soviet powerplants. It seemed deeper, and somehow imbued with sinister purpose. Maybe that was Stas' imagination. On the other hand, he knew he was far from the only Soviet fighting man who imagined the same thing.

"What the hell are you doing there, you stupid fucking idiot? Growing roots like a beet?" a groundcrew sergeant shouted. "You don't get your cock in gear, they'll plant you, all right!"

Where the rising drone from those bombers hadn't unfrozen Stas, the sergeant's profanity did. That might have been because it was aimed at him personally, unlike the bomb loads that would come whistling down any second now. He sprinted toward the closest trench.

He hadn't even got there before the antiaircraft guns started pounding away for all they were worth. He jumped in. Somebody down below caught him and steadied him. "Thanks," he said, without noticing who.

"Any time." Lieutenant Colonel Tomashevsky didn't even sound sarcastic. Squadron commanders caught on the ground in a bombing raid needed to run for their life like anybody else. When they jumped into a trench, they had to hope somebody would grab them and keep them from falling on their face. It was, of course, simply an application of the Golden Rule, no matter how much scorn a good Marxist-Leninist would heap on the book from which that Rule came.

During the last war, someone had claimed there were no atheists in the trenches. Stas didn't know if he would have gone that far. He did know he had to make a conscious effort to keep from crossing himself when the *Luftwaffe* bombers came overhead. You didn't dare reveal too much. His hand twitched, but that was all it did, even when the bombs started bursting on and around the strip.

"Lord, have mercy! Christ, have mercy!" A man in mechanic's coveralls was too scared to worry about what he gave away. He crossed himself again and again, as if possessed. He was only a corporal. Maybe he thought he was too small a fish for the NKVD to care about. If so, he was an optimist. Or maybe he believed none of the other frightened men in the trench with him would betray him to the NKVD. Well, he had a chance of being right about that. How good a chance? Stas wasn't willing to risk it.

Something not far enough away blew up. "The ammunition store for one of our guns—maybe for a battery," Lieutenant Colonel Tomashevsky said.

Mouradian nodded. That was what it had sounded like to him, too. Something else was on his mind: "Where are our fighter planes, Comrade Colonel?"

He didn't think they could possibly be where Tomashevsky suggested. For one thing, he'd always supposed the Devil was male. But wherever they were, they weren't here. And that was a crying shame. Of all the German bombers, only the Ju-87 had anything close to the Soviet Pe-2's performance. The Do-17s and He-111s overhead would have been easy meat for even biplane Polikarpov fighters, let alone their monoplane cousins or the hotter, faster new MiGs. Would have been . . . Some of the saddest words in Russian or any other language.

At last, after doing what they'd come to do, the Germans went away. Soviet fire had brought down one of them. The shattering roar when its whole bomb load blew as it hit the ground almost shook Stas' fillings loose. But when he stuck his head up to look around, he grimaced. For all the destruction the Nazis had worked, they hadn't paid much of a price. Most of the buildings around the airstrip were either gone or burning. The strip itself was cratered like photos of the moon. And four columns of greasy black smoke marked Red Air Force bombers' funeral pyres. Stas hoped none of them was his. Without revetments, it would have been worse. Even with them, it was plenty bad enough.

And Stas had no idea if any bombs had come down in the trenches where men huddled. He also had no idea where the squadron would fly its next mission from. He was sure of only one thing: it wouldn't be from here, not for a while.

LITTLE BY LITTLE, Narvik improved as a U-boat base. As far as torpedoes and diesel fuel and repair facilities went, there had never been anything wrong with it. You couldn't take on as much fresh food there as you could at a base in Germany or even farther south in Norway. That made the ratings grumble—it made Julius Lemp grumble, too—but it wasn't the end of the world.

But a U-boat base, a proper U-boat base, didn't just tend to the boats. It also took care of the men who sailed them. When sailors came back from a long, uncomfortable cruise where, like as not, their lives had been in deadly danger, they wanted to blow off steam. They *needed* to blow off steam. They wanted good booze and bad women. Bad booze would do in a pinch, but good women were right out.

In Germany and the Low Countries, of course, there were brothels in towns full of sailors. People in those towns might not have been proud of that, but they understood it was part of the way things worked.

Norway was different. The locals didn't even approve of drinking. Like America, the country went through a spasm of prohibition after the last war, though Norway gave up on it in 1926.

As for friendly fornication, or even fornication for hire . . . Narvik wasn't a big city like the ports farther south. You couldn't be a whore here without all of your neighbors knowing and most of them disapproving. Narvik was probably a nice place for kids to grow up (assuming they didn't freeze to death or go berserk during a long winter night), but the town had never heard of privacy.

Drinking at clubs supported by the *Kriegsmarine* took the edge off the one problem. The authorities didn't seem to know what to do about the other.

"I'll tell you what to do, by God," Lemp said to the base commandant after the U-30 came back from its latest cruise in the Arctic Ocean. "Bring in enough girls from Germany to keep the crews happy."

The commandant was a commander named Robert Eichenlaub. He outranked Lemp, but the U-boat skipper was irked enough not to care. And being sure they'd never promote him again because of his earlier foul-ups gave him an odd advantage. He was free to speak his mind. Unless he got himself chucked in the brig, they couldn't do anything to him worse than what they were already doing.

Commander Eichenlaub looked pained. "It's not so easy as you make it sound, *Lieutenant.*" He bore down on Lemp's rank, trying to put him in his place.

Lemp was in no mood to let him get away with that. "Why not, *Commander*?" He bore down on the commandant's rank just as hard. "You can get volunteers in Kiel or Wilhelmshaven and ship them up. Or you can just grab some. They're only prostitutes, for heaven's sake." By the way he talked about them, they might have been gaskets or valves or anything else you requisitioned from the quartermaster. That was how he thought of them, too.

"It wouldn't work. We don't even have female secretaries here—and if we did, they wouldn't want to associate with the working girls," Eichenlaub said. "Neither would the Norwegians."

"I'll bet some of them would," Lemp retorted shrewdly—and lewdly.

"No doubt—but that doesn't help us, either," Commander Eichenlaub said.

"So you're worried about keeping the whores comfortable and happy, then," Lemp said.

"They may be whores, Lieutenant, but they're also human beings," Eichenlaub answered.

"How about worrying about keeping my men comfortable and

happy, then?" Lemp snarled. "They may be U-boat sailors, Commander, but they're also human beings, too. I'm pretty sure about most of them, anyway."

They glared at each other. Maybe Commander Eichenlaub wasn't sure why Lemp seemed immune to disapproval from on high, but he could see that the junior officer was. He didn't like it, either. "I know the U-boat service takes wild men, Lemp, but you go over the line," he said, his voice starchy with distaste.

"Why? Because I'm trying to make my men think this is a place they might want to come back to, not Dachau with polar bears?" Lemp said.

"That will be quite enough, Lieutenant Lemp. A note on this conversation will go into your file," the commandant snapped.

Lemp left. But he left laughing, which was bound to delight Eichenlaub all the more.

The U-30's diesels were getting an overhaul. That, the base at Narvik could handle. Lemp went out to the docks to see how things were going. He found that another U-boat had come in while he was having his useless discussion with Commander Eichenlaub. He'd known the skipper, a short—and short-tempered—fellow named Hans-Dieter Kessler, for a long time.

"Here we are. Happy day!" Kessler said. "This place is a goddamn morgue. It's an icebox even in the summertime—it sticks us on a shelf and freezes us out of the fun."

"What fun?" Lemp asked.

"Good point!" Kessler agreed. "They ought to do something about it. Either that or they ought to give us enough leave so we can go down to some place where they remember how to have a good time."

Julius Lemp smiled a slow, conspiratorial smile. "Why don't you go tell the commandant exactly what you think, Hans-Dieter?"

Kessler cocked his head to one side and studied his fellow skipper. "What? You think I fucking won't? You think I don't have the balls?"

"No, I think you will, and I know damn well you've got the balls," Lemp answered truthfully. "And I think Commander Eichenlaub needs to know I'm not the only guy who figures his men get a raw deal every time they have to put in here. He may not want to listen to you once you get going."

"Aha!" Kessler pounced. "So you just reamed him out, did you?"

"Who, me?" Lemp said. Kessler laughed. He headed off toward Eichenlaub's office with purposeful strides. Of course, he had more of a career to lose than Lemp did. He'd never been so careless as to sink an American liner by mistake. The powers that be might still visit higher rank upon him.

Lemp climbed the iron ladder to the top of the U-30's conning tower, then descended into the submarine's hull. They'd had all the hatches open for days, airing the boat out. They'd cleaned in there as they never could at sea. And she still stank. The reeks of diesel fuel and puke and sour piss and unwashed men and stale food were in her paint, or more likely in her steel.

He liked the mechanics working on her engines. They reminded him of his own ratings: they were utterly indifferent to spit and polish, foulmouthed, and damn good at what they did.

An enormous brawl broke out that night in one of the taverns the *Kriegsmarine* maintained. For a while, it was touch and go whether the shore patrolmen would be able to put it down. One of them had to fire a shot in the air to make the drunken, riotous sailors pay attention to him and his comrades. Not a few men from the U-30 distinguished themselves—if that was the word—in the action.

Commander Eichenlaub wasted no time summoning Lemp back to his office. "Do you know how much damage your, your hooligans— your barbarians—have done?" the commandant snarled.

"Not to the pfennig, sir," Lemp answered. "I do know"—expecting the summons, he'd made a point of ascertaining—"they weren't the only U-boat's crew in the scuffle. Are you calling in the other skippers, too?"

"Scuffle? Sweet Jesus Christ! It was about three centimeters this side of an insurrection! And never mind the other skippers. I'm talking to you." But Eichenlaub suddenly didn't sound so self-righteous. Lemp knew he'd made a shrewd guess.

"Yes, sir," he said, his voice mild as boiled milk.

Eichenlaub told him he was a bad boy, and that he commanded a pack of savages. Lemp nodded, not without pride. The commandant fretted and fumed till he got it out of his system. Lemp knew it wouldn't come to anything in the end. He saluted and left. As far as he was concerned, the unhappy sailors had made his point for him better than he could have done himself.

"IT'S A BOY!" Chaim Weinberg passed out cigars—harsh, twisted, coal-black cheroots, which were what he could get—to the Abe Lincolns in the trenches northwest of Madrid. The news had just come up from the city. He swigged from a flask of brandy, too, and offered it to his buddies along with the stogies.

"What are you gonna name the little bastard?" Mike Carroll asked.

"He's no bastard. We did it by the numbers, La Martellita and me," Chaim said.

"If you didn't do it by the numbers, you wouldn't've knocked her up," Mike said. "And I don't care if you and her did tie the knot. Any kid of yours is bound to be a bastard, right?"

"Ahh, your mother," Chaim growled, and started on down the trench. He would have tried to murder a lot of guys who said anything like that. But he and Mike had been in Spain together a hell of a long time. If anybody'd earned the right to razz him, Carroll was the guy.

"Hey, wait a second!" he called after Chaim. "What *are* you gonna name him?"

"Carlos Federico Weinberg," Chaim answered. "Isn't that the god-damnedest handle you ever heard? His mother wanted to name him for Marx and Engels, and how could I tell her no?"

"Wouldn't be easy," Mike agreed. Unspoken in the air between them floated the thought that you'd probably get purged if you tried to tell a Party functionary she couldn't name her son for Communism's founding fathers. Carroll did ask, "What would you have called it if it was a girl?"

"Carla Federica." Chaim spread his hands, as if to say *What can you do?* When La Martellita made up her mind, it was by God made up. Nothing this side of the end of the world would make her change it—and maybe not that, either.

"Well, *mazel tov*," Mike said. Where did he pick up the Yiddish? Probably from Chaim. He found one more question before his buddy went away. "How come you don't look happier, man?"

"Oh, I'm happy. I just didn't tell my face about it." As if to prove as much, Chaim took a big gulp from the flask. Then he got out of there in a hurry, before Mike could ask him anything else he didn't want to answer.

La Martellita hadn't married him because she loved him. No matter how drunk he got, he knew better than that. She'd married him so her kid would have a name—a curiously Catholic notion in a staunch Red, but there you were. And here Chaim was. Carlos Federico Weinberg had his name, all right.

Which meant . . . what? Chaim knew too goddamn well what it meant. It meant La Martellita didn't need him for anything at all any more. Divorce had been next to impossible in pre-Republican Spain. In the parts of the country Marshal Sanjurjo ruled, it still was. In the Republic, it was easy as pie.

So Chaim figured the next piece of news he got from Madrid would be that La Martellita was dropping him like a live grenade. If she hadn't got so drunk she needed him to get her back to her flat, if she hadn't been so drunk she didn't say no when things went on from there . . .

Ah, c'mon, you shlemiel. *You knew this wasn't gonna have a Hollywood ending even while you were* shtupping *her.* Chaim nodded. Yeah, he'd known, all right. He just hadn't given a rat's ass. And he couldn't think of any man who would have when he poised himself between her open legs, either.

So this is what you bought, dumbfuck. He nodded again, and answered his scolding self: *Yeah, yeah, yeah, but now I'm doing the paying, goddammit.*

Well off to the left, an enormous report rang out. Chaim nodded again, this time in mere recognition: that was the crazy Czech who went sniping with his antitank rifle. He was a pretty good guy, which didn't mean he wasn't *meshuggeh*. You had to be nuts to lug that huge, heavy hunk of almost-artillery across half of Europe. All the same, Chaim hoped he'd hit whatever he was aiming at. He also hoped the Fascist on the receiving end was at least a major.

The bastard must have been, and that Czech must have blown his reactionary head off, too. The Nationalists didn't get their knickers in such a twist when a sniper exterminated one of their ordinary assholes. Machine guns sprayed sudden death toward the Republican positions. A moment later, Sanjurjo's big guns started shelling the Republican trenches. The Fascists wanted payback, and they wanted it bad.

Chaim didn't want to be part of the payback. He dove into a scrape someone had dug in the forward wall of the trench. It wasn't a proper bombproof, but it was better than nothing. If a 105 came down right on top of it . . . Chaim made himself not think about that. Getting buried alive wasn't the way he wanted to cash in his chips.

If the Nationalists followed up the shelling with an infantry attack, he was in more trouble than he knew what to do with. He didn't have his rifle with him. He had the brandy and cigars instead. Would one of Sanjurjo's men take a cigar in exchange for not bayoneting him? They didn't make deals like that, sad to say.

But the Nationalists would have taken casualties in an infantry attack. They didn't want that. They wanted to dish them out so they could avenge whichever officer the Czech had potted with his honking big rifle.

They got what they wanted, too. Wounded Abe Lincolns screamed and moaned. Some were Americans, some the Spaniards who filled out the ranks of all the International Brigades these days. All wounded men sounded pretty much the same, regardless of country or politics.

In a rational world, something like that would convince people all men were brothers. They wouldn't try to kill one another any more. But who ever said the world was rational? And even being brothers might not make men like each other any better. Look what Cain did to Abel, after all.

Chaim shook his head. The Bible was just another book of myths and superstitions. There never were any such people as Cain and Abel. He had no trouble believing that with the top part of his mind. The part with roots down to the core of him, the part that wasn't Marxist-Leninist, had other ideas.

If La Martellita heard about this bombardment, would she hope a shell killed him? Then she wouldn't have to go through the paperwork of divorcing him. She could get on with her life as the widow of a heroic soldier. She could milk it for all it was worth.

After a moment, Chaim shook his head. His ladylove was no hypocrite. If she wanted him dead, she'd come right out and tell him so. She might do him in herself.

No, she just wanted to be rid of him. He hated that. And he hated the certain knowledge that he couldn't do anything about it even more.

Almost everybody went through life wishing he could get what he most wanted. From the moment Chaim set eyes on La Martellita, she was what he most wanted. He'd got her, too, even if she was so smashed the first time he did that she hardly knew he was doing it.

And he'd made the all too common discovery that getting exactly what you wanted could hurt even worse than mooning after it forever. As long as you kept on mooning after it, you always thought it was perfect. Once you got it, you were much too likely to discover what a jerk you were for wanting it to begin with.

Beautiful women were there to be wanted, of course. To men, they often seemed to be there for no other reason. But how many of the men who actually got one stayed happy afterwards? Not many, unless Chaim missed his guess. He knew too well he wasn't.

What were you supposed to do? Turn into a queer? Even if you could, wouldn't you get into the same kind of stew about gorgeous guys? Besides, he wasn't a queer. He liked women. He liked the beautiful kind better than the homely ones, too. He didn't know anybody who didn't. You couldn't win. You didn't have a chance.

The Czech with the antitank rifle fired again. Some Fascist shithead probably discovered *he* didn't have a chance. Whether he laid beautiful women or homely ones, he'd be laid out now. *Hasta la vista, fucker,* Chaim thought.

No barrage followed. Maybe this time the sniper just blew out a corporal's insides. If ever a movement prided itself on class consciousness, it was Sanjurjo's, but for all the wrong reasons. Or maybe the Czech missed. Stranger things had happened. *Damn right!* Chaim thought. *I've got me a kid named Carlos Federico!* He swigged from the brandy flask again.

IN RUSSIA, the sky seemed wider than it did anywhere else Willi Dernen had ever seen. That might have been because the countryside seemed—

and was—wider, too, but Willi wasn't so sure about it. He wasn't sure about anything any more. He'd been here too long and done too much, and victory still looked as far away as whatever lay under the far end of that vast Russian sky.

He had other reasons for keeping an eye on the clouds drifting across the wide sky, too. Adam Pfaff noticed him doing it as they tramped along a dirt road—once you got out of the cities, Russia had no other kind. "What's up?" Pfaff asked. "You can't do anything about the weather."

"My ass, I can't," Willi said. "I can worry about it, and I damn well do. It'll start pouring rain pretty soon, and all these shitty roads'll turn to glue. Then we freeze our nuts off for the next six months. Some fun, huh?"

"Well, sure. What would you rather be doing?" Pfaff said.

"Drinking and fucking. What else is there?" Willi sounded honestly surprised.

His friend considered. "Well, there's . . ." Pfaff shook his head. He thought some more. "Or there's . . ." Another rejection, this time with a thumbs-down. "Nah." More thought still. He grinned ruefully. "You're right. That's about all there is that's worth doing. Oh—maybe filling up on mutton stew, too."

"There you go," Willi said. "But we get to do this crap instead. Aren't we lucky?"

"We're lucky if we come through alive," answered the man with the gray Mauser.

"Dernen!" Arno Baatz shouted. "Are you lowering Pfaff's morale?"

"Not a bit of it, Corporal," Willi said. "He's lowering mine." Beside him on the dusty road, Pfaff giggled softly.

Awful Arno didn't. "Think you're funny, don't you? Well, you listen to me. Just because nobody's made a charge stick on you yet doesn't mean nobody will. You mark my words."

Willi was about to tell Baatz where to put his words—sideways— when the section point man came trotting back toward the main body of men. Johann Stallinger made a good point: he was short and skinny and anxious. He nodded ahead, in the direction from which he'd just come. "Something's in those fields," he said. "The way the grain was moving, it's not from the wind."

"Are you on the rag again, Stallinger?" Awful Arno asked.

"If you don't like the job I do, Corporal, you can put somebody else up there," the point man answered. Whatever else he might have thought, his pale, pinched face didn't show it.

You could watch Baatz working through it. You could, and Willi did. Arno did want to go forward. "If you're having vapors . . ." he growled. But he knew Stallinger might not be. Johann was point man for a reason. If the fields were full of Russians, the section was asking to get bushwhacked. Baatz's pudgy features cleared as he made up his mind. "Braun!"

"Yes, Corporal?" Gustav Braun's face said he wished he were a thousand kilometers away from here.

"You got that big drum on your machine pistol. Let Stallinger take you up to the fields he's having spasms about, and you shoot the whole thing off. If that doesn't flush the Ivans, nothing will, on account of there won't be any there," Baatz said.

Willi blinked. The order actually made good sense. He wouldn't have thought Awful Arno had it in him. Braun carried a Russian PPD-34 submachine gun instead of a Schmeisser. The Russian piece came with a drum that held seventy-one rounds. It took 7.62mm cartridges instead of 9mm, but the Germans had captured plenty. The big magazine made it heavy to cart around. Every once in a while, though, you needed the extra firepower. This looked to be one of those times.

Even Braun could see as much. "Right, Corporal," was all he said. If he didn't sound thrilled . . . Well, Willi wouldn't have been thrilled with an order like that, either, no matter how much sense it made.

Stallinger did have a Schmeisser. A point man often found himself in positions where he needed to spray around a lot of lead in a hurry. He also seemed less than delighted about going back to where he'd sensed trouble, but hey, there was a war on. You did all kinds of things you weren't delighted about.

The rest of the *Landsers* spread out into a loose skirmish line. Nobody told them to. No one needed to tell them. They knew what was what. Willi knew he had a round in the chamber. He knew it, but he made sure anyway. He noted the best place to dive for cover, and also the next best place.

Stallinger and Braun went forward. If the Russians had a machine gun in amongst the barley . . . If they had a machine gun in there, hell was out to lunch, because they could mow down the rest of the section, too.

Braun knew his business. He didn't just squeeze off one long burst as he fired. The muzzle would have pulled up and to the right, and he would have shot over what he was trying to flush out. He fired two, three, four rounds at a time. Willi didn't know exactly when he hit something. The Ivans might have been disciplined enough to keep quiet when they got shot. But one fellow couldn't help making the grain around him sway in unmistakable fashion as he toppled over. Tiny in the distance, Stallinger waved urgently.

Awful Arno waved back. *Get away!*, that meant, but giving the order was easier than following it. The Russians figured out that they weren't going to be able to take the whole section unawares. They grabbed what they could get, and opened up on Stallinger and Braun. Both men went down. Maybe they weren't dead, but Willi didn't like the odds.

He was already trotting forward before Awful Arno told him to. So were the rest of the *Landsers.* You didn't let the Russians take your buddies alive, not if you could help it. You didn't even want them grabbing German corpses. They mutilated them for the fun of it, and to intimidate live Germans who came upon their handiwork.

Bullets reached out toward the advancing men in *Feldgrau.* One cracked past Willi, viciously close. He had to make himself keep moving by main force of will. His body, animal thing that it was, wanted to throw itself flat, or else to run. The barley still concealed the Ivans.

But not perfectly, not as he got closer to them. He spotted khaki through green going gold. When he raised his Mauser to his shoulder, the Russian showed plainly through the telescopic sight. He fired. He got a split-second glimpse of most of the man's face contorted with pain. Then he worked the bolt, lowered the rifle, and trotted on. That enemy soldier wasn't likely to trouble them any more.

Ambush spoiled, the rest of the Red Army men slipped off to the east. Their rear guard kept firing to make sure the Germans didn't chase them too enthusiastically. If they wanted to retreat, Willi was ready to let them. Awful Arno kept yelling for the section to push harder.

Then he yelled again, wordlessly this time. He held his rifle in his right fist. His left arm hung uselessly, blood darkening the field-gray sleeve. "I'm hit!" he said. Disbelief filled his voice. And why not? He'd stayed lucky for going on three years—he must have thought nothing could bite him. Well, that showed how much he knew.

The *Landser* next to him slapped a wound bandage on his arm. "Go back, Corporal," the fellow said. "The aid men will patch you up. Can you manage on your own, or shall we send somebody with you?"

"Send somebody." Willi wasn't sure he was the senior *Obergefreiter,* but he spoke up anyway. "He can't handle his weapon one-handed. If we've bypassed any Ivans, they'll do for him if he's by himself."

They took his orders. Baatz and a protector headed for the rear. Willi didn't know what he'd do without Awful Arno to goad him on. He looked forward to finding out, though.

When the Germans got up to the point man and his comrade, they found Braun dead but Stallinger still very much alive, though down with a leg wound. More men hauled him off to the rear. They buried Braun in a shallow grave and set his helmet on it. They might have marked the grave with a bayoneted Mauser, too. The PPD-34 was too valuable. Another *Landser* grabbed it and brought it along.

Chapter 19

The farther south and east into the Ukraine the Germans and Romanians drove the Red Army, the more familiar things became for Ivan Kuchkov. More of the people spoke Russian, for instance. It was Ukrainian-accented Russian, with guttural h's replacing proper g's, but he could more or less make sense of it. Real Ukrainian hovered right at the edge of comprehensibility for him, which pissed him off.

People farther south and east here didn't seem so ready to prick up their ears and whinny at the sound of a crappy German oompah band, either. They remembered they were Soviet citizens. Maybe the NKVD had left them too scared to forget. Kuchkov wasn't inclined to be picky. As long as they didn't give the Hitlerite swine a helping hand, he didn't care why.

He wished more T-34s would come into the fight. "The Fritzes shit their drawers every time they see one of those fuckers," he said as his section cooked this and that around a fire built from the planks of a blown-up barn. "The pussies'd all run for home if we had enough."

His men nodded. For one thing, he was obviously right. For another, arguing with him was a losing proposition. He backed up his words with fists, knees, teeth, a knife he carried in his boot, and anything else that might come in handy. Even the *politruk* had quit agitating that he should join the Party. In the middle of a war, a political officer could meet an untimely end just like anybody else. And chances were the authorities would be too busy with bigger stuff to ask a whole lot of questions.

Off to the north, a Soviet machine gun fired a couple of short bursts. No German machine gun answered, so maybe the guy at the trigger was shooting at shadows. Or maybe he'd scragged a Nazi. Kuchkov hoped so.

All of his men had cocked their heads in the direction of the gunfire. When it petered out, they nodded or smiled and went back to whatever they'd been doing. So did he. That wasn't trouble. It wasn't trouble for his section, anyhow, which was the only kind of trouble he worried about. The smart fuckers with the fancy rank badges on their uniforms cared about how the whole front was going. This tiny piece of it was plenty for him.

One of the soldiers turned coarse tobacco from a pouch and a strip of old newspaper into a cigarette. He lit it with the tip of a burning twig. After blowing out a long, gray smoke stream, he said, "Maybe we'll get to stay here awhile."

"Watch your dumb cunt of a mouth, Vanya," Kuchkov said without heat.

"Huh?" Vanya wasn't the brightest star in the sky. But even he got it after a couple of seconds. "Oh. Sorry, Comrade Sergeant."

"*Sorry*'s all right for me. There's plenty of pricks who'd stick *sorry* right up your sorry ass, though," Kuchkov growled, more to make the soldier remember than because he was really angry. Officers went on and on about squashing defeatism wherever it stuck up its ugly head. The NKVD squashed people it imagined to be defeatists, usually for good. If somebody here ratted on poor, slow Vanya . . . Kuchkov didn't know there was an informer in his section, but he would have been surprised if there weren't. Unlike the poor jerk with the roll-your-own, he understood instinctively how the system worked.

He had his own reasons for hoping the Red Army could hold the line in these parts, even if he wasn't dumb enough to come out with them. There was a village maybe a kilometer and a half behind this campfire, and his eye had fallen on one of the girls there, a cute little blonde named Nina.

She'd smiled back at him, too, damned if she hadn't. Some women liked handsome. Kuchkov didn't have a prayer with them. He knew it. He didn't like it, but what can a guy do about his own mug? Some women, though, some women liked strong. And with those broads he had a fighting chance. He wasn't pretty and he wasn't smart, but he could break any two ordinary jerks over his knee like skinny sticks.

A smile, the right kind of smile, was all it took. If he could get Nina alone, especially if he had some vodka along, he knew damn well he'd be able to slide his hand under her skirt. The war was won as soon as you did that.

But if the Germans drove the Red Army back before he got the chance, some Nazi son of a bitch with broad shoulders would end up balling her instead. That would be a waste, nothing else but.

Kuchkov tore off his own strip of *Pravda*. Or maybe it was *Izvestia* or *Red Star*, the Army paper. Since he couldn't read, he didn't care. He wiped his ass with newsprint. And he rolled smokes with it. "Let me have some of that *makhorka*, Vanya," he said.

"Sure, Comrade Sergeant." The soldier passed him the pouch. Vanya might be dim, but he was as eager to please as a dog. With deft fingers, Kuchkov formed a cigarette. He lit it the same way the other man had. He had food, he had smoke in his lungs, he might get laid before too long, the Germans seemed pretty quiet. . . . Life could have been worse.

Since the Germans stayed quiet through the night, at sunrise the next morning he made up an excuse to go back to the village. No one asked him any questions. An ugly mug and a strong, hairy back made other people mind their own business. He knew what they called him when that back was turned. When he overheard it, he broke some heads. That worked. Let them mock, as long as they feared.

He reached the place just as the peasants were going out to their chores. Waving, he called, "Nina! Come here!" He didn't go *Come here, you bitch!* For him, it was the height of suavity.

She waved back, which made his hopes—among other things—rise. "What do you need, Sergeant?"

You. But that would be for later. He pointed to a nearby stand of brushy woods he'd noticed—the best privacy you could find around here. "Let's talk about you whipping up a big tub of stew for my guys, hey?"

"Where do I get the stuff to put in it?" she asked. The obvious answer was *from your village.* That would leave the people there hungry.

But he just said, "Well, we can talk about that." He hopped over a bush and walked into the woods. Nina followed. He offered her his water bottle. "Here. Have a knock of this first, sweetie."

Calling it a knock warned her. Her eyes didn't cross when she swigged Red Army vodka. Calling her sweetie probably warned her, too. But she was smiling when she handed back the water bottle. "You should drink some."

"Fucking right I should." He titled his head back. Fire slid down his throat and exploded in his stomach like a 105. He held out the vodka. "Have some more."

"Sure. Best way to start the day." Nina was a Russian, all right.

"Almost the best way." Kuchkov grabbed her. She squealed and she giggled and she made a token try at pushing him away, but then they were rolling on the ground together and kissing. When he did reach under her skirt, she laughed again and then she purred. Who ended up on top was a matter of luck. She undid his fly, sucked him for a minute to make him even harder than he was already, and impaled herself on him. His hands clutched her meaty backside while they thrashed. She had plenty to hold on to.

She threw her head back and mewled. A moment later, he grunted as joy shot through him. A moment after that, before he could decide whether to slide out or start again, German shells started landing on the Russian line and reaching back toward the village.

That made up his mind, and in a hurry. He threw Nina off him, even his rude chivalry forgotten. She let out an indignant squawk. He didn't care. He scrambled to his feet, shoving his cock back into his pants and doing up the buttons. Then he took off on the dead run, back toward his section. Fun was fun, but killing the fucking Fascists really mattered.

He ignored the shell bursts. If one got him, it got him. None did. He wasn't as fast as an Olympic track man getting back, but an Olympic track man didn't run in boots and carry a submachine gun. He reached his men before the barrage stopped and the ground attack came in.

"Hold on to your dicks, boys," he called when the artillery let up. Nina'd sure had hold of his. "We'll slaughter the clapped-out cunts."

They didn't. The Germans were veterans, and didn't assume the shelling would make their advance easy. They came cautiously, by small groups, firing and moving. Where they met strong defensive fire, they held up and started digging themselves foxholes. They weren't going to let their officers get them killed if they could help it. If they hadn't been Nazis, they would have been sensible men.

For a wonder, Russian tanks showed up before the Germans brought up any armor. The Fritzes retreated sullenly. *Maybe I can fuck Nina again tomorrow,* Kuchkov thought. You never knew till you tried.

PETE MCGILL PASSED five-inch shells as fast as he could. The Japs had more dive-bombers than Carter had little liver pills. Sweat poured down his bare back. He'd be sunburned like nobody's business if he lived, but that was the least of his worries. He'd got way too hot and sticky to stay in his shirt.

Most of the guys at the gun wore nothing but a helmet above the waist. You needed a helmet. You needed one bad. What went up eventually came down, and lots and lots was going up. Fragments rained down all over the Pacific. You'd feel like a jerk if one of them smashed your unprotected skull—but not for long, worse luck for you.

The five-incher bellowed again. Pete heard it as if from very far away. If he had any ears at all left by the time this got done, he'd count his blessings. A shell casing clanged on the deck. Somebody kicked it out of the way to keep from tripping over it. It didn't roll far. Too much other brass had already been kicked. Pete grabbed the next round and passed it to the loader. Into the breech it went. The gun lowered a little to bear on the dive-bomber. *Blam!* The cycle began anew.

The Jap plane didn't give a damn about the *Boise.* It was swooping down on a heavy cruiser. Shells burst all around it, black smoke puffs soiling the clean, moist Pacific air. The pilot ignored everything but his target. He released the bomb and zoomed away bare yards above the ocean. A shell clipped his wing then. His plane broke up as it went into the drink. Fire floating on the sea was the only grave marker he'd ever get.

Too late came the hit. The bomb burst right alongside the American ship. It wasn't a killing blow. But blast and fragments would do their worst, and their worst was no damn good. The *Boise* had taken blows like that, and suffered from them yet.

"One fucker won't be back!" Joe Orsatti shouted. Everybody at the five-inch mount yelled as loud as he could. It was the only way the Marines had a prayer of making themselves heard. Even as things were, Pete might not have understood if he hadn't read the gun chief's lips.

"How many more have they got?" he yelled back. Orsatti didn't answer. By the nature of things, he couldn't know. Neither could Pete. But that was *the* question.

All the guys with the fat gold stripes on their sleeves who'd made up the American attack plan seemed to have missed something: the Japs had turned their mid-Pacific islands into unsinkable aircraft carriers. They had sinkable carriers, too; the Americans had sunk one. But no American carriers remained afloat, and the U.S. fleet had yet to see any Japanese naval craft at gun range. (No, that wasn't quite true. One Jap sub incautiously surfaced near a battleship whose big guns happened to be trained its way. A few seconds later, nothing was left of that sub but paper clips.)

No twilight-of-the-gods super-Jutland here, no matter what the planners—and Pete McGill—had figured this fight would look like. No Joe Louis–Max Schmeling. Instead, the Japs were making like some superfast lightweight. Hank Armstrong on benzedrine, maybe. They jabbed and jabbed and jabbed, and when you tried to hit back they weren't there. And they wore you down, one punch at a time.

Pete had guessed the big free-for-all would happen somewhere near the Philippines. And it might have, if the U.S. fleet had been able to get that far. But even Guam still lay far to the west. And reaching Guam would be no cure-all; the Stars and Stripes didn't fly there any more. How many Japanese planes would come up from all their islands and attack the remains of the American force? How long before they'd be more than all the antiaircraft guns aboard the surviving ships could hope to knock down? If the admirals went on being stubborn, that day might come soon.

If it did, Pete probably wouldn't even get a brief patch of fire on the Pacific to mark where he'd gone down. An oil slick would be about it.

He didn't want to die. Not yet. He didn't have nearly enough revenge for Vera. Four red rings circled his five-inch gun's barrel, each one signifying a plane Orsatti was sure they'd killed. The rings, and the rest of the paint on the barrel, were blistered and scorched from the heat of all the shells that had gone through. It took a hell of a lot of firing to knock a plane out of the sky: way more than anybody'd figured before the war got rolling.

The *Boise*'s engines picked up. Pete felt the new vibration through the soles of his shoes. The light cruiser swung into a long turn, carving a white wake into blue water. When the turn ended, she was heading east.

"Now hear this!" blared from the loudspeakers. "At the orders of the fleet's commanding officer, we are withdrawing toward Hawaii. I say again—at the orders of the CO, the fleet is withdrawing from these waters."

So it wasn't just the *Boise*. It was everybody. Everybody who was left, anyway. Pete wasn't even sure of the current CO's name; Admiral Kimmel went down with the *Arizona* when she sank, probably figuring that was easier than having to explain failure back home.

Well, if the new guy was throwing up his hands and hightailing it back toward Pearl, his name was also likely to be mud whoever the hell he was. The Secretary of the Navy and the President would blame him for not blowing the Japs out of the water. After all, if another admiral fell on—or was pushed onto—his sword, less blame would stick to his superiors.

Then again, if the Americans kept pushing forward no matter what, it wouldn't be long before they had nothing left to push with. Going into this war, everybody'd wondered how sea power stacked up against air power. Now that the returns were in, they didn't look encouraging for the poor bastards in ships. It had been a running fight between airplanes all the way west across the Pacific. Now that the U.S. Navy was out of carriers, the fleet went on taking it on the chin no matter how much antiaircraft fire the ships threw up.

Pete nervously scanned the sky. Just because the fleet was on the lam, that didn't mean the Japs would leave it alone. *Kick 'em while they're down* was good advice in bar brawls and in war. If the other guy didn't think he'd almost licked you, he wouldn't jump on you again any time soon. Now the U.S. Navy was trying to get up off the floor and brush away the sawdust and the spilled beer.

Some of the other ships were still firing—maybe at Japanese planes, maybe at nothing. Around the *Boise,* it was quiet for the moment. Pete suddenly realized how very stiff and sore and weary he was. "Fuck," he said.

Orsatti must have read his lips, because he didn't say it very loud. The gun chief nodded. He looked like hell: unshaven, bags under his eyes, his face thin and drawn. Pete probably looked the same way, but he hadn't seen himself any time lately. He'd been living on coffee and sandwiches and snatching sleep curled up on the deck next to the gun like a dog since . . . He couldn't work out since when. It had been a while now. He knew that.

One of the other guys pulled a crumpled pack of Luckies from his dungarees and gave everybody a cigarette. Pete took his gratefully. The nicotine seemed to help a little with the haze of fatigue that dogged him. "Fuck," he said again. This time, the rest of the crew nodded in mournful agreement.

"Didn't never figure we'd get licked," Orsatti said, speaking slowly and loudly. "Not by the Japs."

Pete could have said *I told you so.* He'd known the Emperor's finest were tougher than most Americans wanted to believe. He kept quiet. Sometimes being right cost more than it was worth.

But then he did say "Fuck" one more time. After another drag on the Lucky—some luck!—he amplified it: "What's gonna happen to the poor sorry assholes stuck on the islands we took away from the slanties?"

"Maybe we'll make pickup while we go," Orsatti said. But he didn't sound as if his heart was in the words. Pete could see why. If the fleet was doing its goddamnedest to get away from the Japs, would it want to stop for anything? That was asking to get worked over again.

But to leave leathernecks behind to try to hold off Hirohito's bastards with whatever they happened to have . . . That was the worst kind of losing proposition. Sweet Jesus, was it ever!

Or was it, really? Wasn't getting killed trying to take them off and then leaving them stuck for the Japs anyway worse still? An admiral was bound to think so. The admiral in charge of the fleet *did* think so. Pete was a Marine. For two cents' change, he would have torn the goddamn admiral's head off and pissed in the hole.

MARRIED. When Sarah Goldman (no, she was Sarah Bruck now; she had to keep reminding herself she was Sarah Bruck) had thought about being married before she actually was, she hadn't thought much about what came after she went through the ceremony. Oh, she'd thought about some of it, but you couldn't do that all the time even when you were newlyweds and very young. She hadn't thought about what her *life* would be like after the wedding.

She had expected she would eat better, and she did. The Brucks were bakers, after all. Even if they were Jews, even if the Nazis watched them three times as hard as the Aryan bakers in Münster, they found ways of making flour silently vanish from the official allocation. Some they baked into stuff they ate themselves. They traded the rest with other people who dealt in food. Nobody—nobody below the rank of *General-major,* anyhow—ate well in the Third *Reich*. But the Brucks did very well for Jews, and better than some Aryans.

Sarah hadn't expected she would work so much harder. Isidor might have got himself a wife. His mother and father had got themselves a brand-new employee they didn't have to pay. They made the most of it. She knew next to nothing about baking when she started sharing Isidor's little room. They set about giving her a crash course.

To be fair, they started her on simple things, as if she were a child. She could tell time, obviously. They could trust her to open the ovens and take out the loaves after half an hour (they could also smear oint-ment on her hands when she burned herself doing it—it wasn't as if they'd never got burned).

They could let her mix the various flours that went into war bread. "No, none of them is sawdust," David Bruck assured her, amusement in his voice.

"Was there any in the last war?" she asked. "People always say there was."

"There were things nobody talked about. The government issued them to us, and we used them. It was use them or not bake anything." Isidor's father no longer sounded or looked amused. "That was . . . a very hard time."

"This isn't?" Sarah's flour-covered hand reached for but didn't touch the six-pointed yellow star on her blouse.

David Bruck wore a star, too. He considered. "We were hungrier then, but we were happier, too. People weren't banging on the tea kettle at us all the time because we were Jews."

Sarah smiled. Her mother would use that homely phrase for rais-ing a ruckus every now and then. Her father always looked pained when Mother did. It wasn't the kind of thing *Herr Doktor Professor* Goldman was used to hearing, his expression said. *Herr Doktor Profes-sor* Goldman was doing all kinds of things these days that he hadn't been used to.

And so was Sarah. Besides the burns, unfamiliar work made her arms and shoulders ache. Her feet hurt because she was on them so much. She was tired all the time. She sometimes wondered if this was what she'd signed up for.

It would have been worse if she hadn't seen that all the Brucks, Isidor included, drove themselves harder than they drove her. That made her feel silly about complaining. But she slept as if someone hit her over the head with a boulder as soon as she lay down.

When she slept. As the hours of darkness got longer, RAF bombers started showing up over Münster more often. There weren't many of them, and they didn't drop a lot of bombs, but they wrecked the nights when they appeared.

She and Isidor and his parents would go downstairs and huddle under the counters. It was no better than hiding under the dining-room table had been at her parents'. If a bomb knocked the building down on top of you, you'd get squashed. If one blew out a side wall, it would blow you up, too. The Aryans in the neighborhood, like the Aryans in her old neighborhood, had proper bomb shelters. *Verboten* for Jews, of course. Jews took their chances.

Isidor took his chances in the blackout darkness. She'd never got felt up during an air raid before. She wanted to laugh and she wanted to belt him, both at the same time. She couldn't do either, not without giving away what he was up to.

Every couple of weeks, she and Isidor would walk over and see her folks. She enjoyed that more than she wanted to show. The Brucks talked about bakery business and neighborhood gossip and the music on the radio, and that was about it. At her own house, talk ranged all over the world and across thousands of years. She'd thought it would be the same for everybody—till she discovered it wasn't.

Coming back to such talk felt wonderful. She said so once, while Isidor was using the toilet. Her father's smile twisted a little. "The Brucks are nice people. They are—don't get me wrong. But they're not very curious, so they might not seem very exciting, either."

"Not very curious!" she echoed, nodding. That was it, all right. That was exactly it. The Brucks knew what they knew, and they didn't worry about anything else.

Socrates talked about people like that in the *Apology*. If she tried to tell Isidor so, he would look at her as if she'd suddenly started speaking ancient Greek herself. It wasn't that knowing all the strange things she knew ever did her much practical good. But it gave her things to think about she wouldn't have had otherwise. When she was with other people who had the same strange set of mental baggage, it also gave her things to talk about that she wouldn't have had otherwise.

When she was with the Brucks . . . A flush from the bathroom said Isidor would be coming out. She put that one on the back burner.

Was this what marriage was about? Giving up part of yourself you hadn't even been aware you had in exchange for love? She had no doubt that Isidor loved her. She loved him, too. It wasn't that he made her abandon that part. But he didn't have its match, so showing it to him seemed pointless.

But he had points of his own. As he sat down beside her, he said, "I heard this one from an Aryan the other day, if you can believe it. Hitler, Goebbels, and Göring are on a plane that crashes. Everybody aboard gets killed. Who is saved?"

Something in the way her father's mouth twitched told her he already knew the joke. But all he said was, "*Nu?* Who?" She was glad, because she hadn't heard it, and she didn't think her mother had, either.

"The German people," Isidor answered, and exploded into laughter.

If there were microphones in the house, they were all in trouble. Sarah knew as much. She laughed anyway. So did Mother. "An Aryan told you that?" Father asked Isidor. He was also laughing, even as he went on, "Was he an SS man, seeing if he could land you in trouble because you thought it was funny?"

"No, no." Isidor shook his head. "Not like that. It was one old guy talking to another one on the street. I heard it walking by."

"*Ach, so.*" Samuel Goldman relaxed. "That should be all right, then. Nobody seems happy with the way things are going."

"'We continue the advance on the important Soviet citadel of Smolensk.'" Isidor amazed Sarah. She hadn't dreamt he could imitate a self-important newsreader so well.

He surprised Sarah's father, too. Samuel Goldman let out a sudden bray of laughter, then looked at Isidor as if he'd never really seen him before. Maybe he hadn't. And maybe now he saw some little piece of what Sarah saw in the baker's son.

Walking back to their little room after the visit, Isidor said, "I like talking with your mother and father. They're . . . interesting."

"Peculiar but fun?" Sarah's voice was dry.

Isidor kicked a pebble down the sidewalk. "You said that. I didn't."

You sure meant it, though, Sarah thought. She cocked her head to one side—a gesture her father might have used—and asked, "Do you think I'm . . . interesting, too?"

This time, Isidor didn't hesitate for a second. "Darn right I do!" He was undressing her with his eyes.

"Not like that, *Dummkopf*," she said, though the eager stare warmed her. "Like my folks, I mean."

"Oh." To him, that seemed less important. But he nodded after a moment. "Yeah, I guess so. You . . . kind of think lefthanded, if you know what I mean."

If Sarah hadn't thought that way, she wouldn't have. As things were, she batted her eyes at him and murmured, "You say the sweetest things." If you couldn't always leave them happy, sometimes confused worked almost as well.

THE IVAN STRUGGLED out of his hole. Blood from a small wound to his ear dripped onto his baggy khaki tunic. He left his rifle behind and kept his hands over his head. "*Freund!*" he said hopefully. "*Kamerad!*"

Luc Harcourt's lip curled in scorn. "You stupid sack of shit, I'm no fucking German," he answered in his own language.

"*Mon Dieu! C'est vrai! Vous-êtes français!*" To Luc's amazement, the Russian—corporal, if he was reading the rank badges the right way—spoke a French as near perfect as made no difference. The fellow went on, "The *Boches* were in this sector yesterday, and I did not even think to look at your uniform. A thousand apologies, *Monsieur*. Ten thousand!"

Sure as hell, German tanks had passed through here the day before. The French infantry was helping to clean up the pocket the armor had carved out. "If I was a *Boche*, odds are you'd be dead right now," Luc said.

"*Vous-avez raison*," the Russian agreed. "Once more, I thank you for your mercy."

Luc didn't know how long he'd stay merciful. Prisoners were a pain in the ass. But a prisoner who spoke French as if he were educated at the Sorbonne might be worth something. Intelligence sure wouldn't have any trouble interrogating him. Luc gestured with his rifle. "Well, c'mon. Get moving."

"But of course." The Russian put a hand to the side of his head. Naturally, it came away bloody. "How badly am I hurt?"

"Just an ear. Those always bleed like mad bastards, but it's only a little wound," Luc answered with rough sympathy. Then he said, "Hang on. Take off your belt—nice and slow. Don't do anything stupid. You can hold up your pants with one hand afterwards."

"*Oui, Monsieur.*" The Ivan obeyed. The belt had several grenades on it. Only after it lay on the ground and the prisoner had straightened up again did Luc relax—a few millimeters' worth, anyhow.

"*Now* get moving," he told the guy, and the Russian did. After a few steps, he asked, "How come you speak such good French?"

"It is the language of culture—and I am, or I was, a student of French history. Yevgeni Borisovich Novikov, at your service." The POW made as if to bow, but didn't follow through.

Culture. Right, Luc thought. The so-called student of French history looked like any other captured Russian: dirty, whiskery, in a baggy tunic and breeches. The splatters of blood from his ear were just accents. (But for the blood and the cut of his uniform, Luc didn't look much different himself.)

After a few steps, he did ask what was on his mind: "If you're so educated and everything, how come you're only a crappy corporal and not an officer?" Why should he worry about offending a prisoner he'd never see again?

"Only a corporal?" Novikov barked bitter laughter. "For me, getting promoted was a miracle. I come from a kulak family. Do you know what kulaks are? Were, I should say—not many of us are left alive."

"Kulaks are rich farmers, right?" Luc hoped he wasn't confusing the Russian word with something else altogether.

But the captured, cultured corporal nodded. "Rich enough to have a few cows, anyhow. Richer than the ordinary *muzhik.* Richer because they worked harder than the ordinary *muzhik* and didn't drink as much. Rich enough that they didn't want to get herded into collective farms and give up more than they got. Rich enough to get called enemies of the state and go to the wall." He grimaced. "I'm lucky to be alive, let alone a corporal."

He might have thought that would impress Luc. And it did—but only up to a point. "Happy day, buddy," Luc said. "Doesn't mean you wouldn't've shot me if you got the chance. I've been in this shit since '38. Tell me about lucky to be alive."

"It could be, though, that you were allowed to be a human being before the war began," Novikov replied.

Allowed to be a human being. Luc chewed on that till he spotted Lieutenant Demange. If anyone ever stood foursquare against the notion of letting people be human beings, Demange was the man. He waved to Luc. "What the hell you got there?" he called, as if Luc had brought in some exotic animal instead of an ever so mundane POW.

"Russian who speaks French better'n you do, Lieutenant," Luc answered sweetly.

Demange said something about Luc's mother that he was unlikely to know from personal experience. Luc grinned; he'd got under Demange's skin, which he didn't manage to do every day. The lieutenant glowered at Yevgeni Novikov. "So what the fuck you got to say for yourself, prickface?"

"I am glad your sergeant here did not kill me when he could have," Novikov told him. "I hope you will not, either."

He knew what could happen to captured soldiers, then. Well, who didn't? And Demange looked comically amazed. "You *con!*" he said to Luc. "The asshole *does* speak better French'n me. Better than you, too."

"I'm not arguing," Luc said. "The guys who question him won't have to fuck around with German." There were French interrogators who spoke Russian, but only a very few. But lots of Frenchmen could get along in German, and so could lots of Russians. Conducting an interrogation in French would be a luxury.

Lieutenant Demange nodded. "You're right. I bet he speaks better French than the clowns who squeeze him, too." He chuckled unpleasantly. "And a whole bunch of good that'll do him. Go on and take him back, Harcourt."

"Will do." Luc would have taken Novikov back any which way. Any excuse to move away from the front line where people were liable to shoot at you was a good one. *Now I only have to worry about shells and bombs,* Luc thought with perfectly genuine relief. Had he tried to imagine that before the war, he would have decided he was nuts.

He had to give Novikov up at regimental headquarters: a scattered handful of tents any self-respecting Boy Scouts would have laughed at. They would, at least, unless a French picket plugged them before they could get close enough to laugh. The picket was invisible till he called a challenge. He'd definitely earned his merit badge in foxhole digging.

Luc didn't know the headquarters password. A rigid Russian or German might have shot him for that. The sentry laughed at him and then passed him through. The guy could see and hear he was a Frenchman.

The officers at the HQ weren't thrilled to see Yevgeni Novikov. *One more POW—just what we don't need,* their attitude declared. Then he opened his mouth. They fell on him with glad cries after that, especially when they discovered he would sing like a skylark. They even gave Luc a cup of good burgundy—not *pinard,* heaven forbid; they were, after all, officers—and a pack of Gauloises as the bringer of good news.

Thus fortified, he started up to the front again. He took his own sweet time getting there. If Lieutenant Demange didn't like it, too damn bad. But Demange wouldn't care, not about something like this. Back when he was a sergeant, he would have taken his time returning, too. Anybody would. Who in blazes wanted to come straight to the killing zone?

That thought made Luc stop again. When you were heading to the front, any excuse was a good one. So it looked to him, at any rate. But there were a few white crows who were never happier than when they were mixing it up with the Nazis or Reds or whoever the enemy happened to be.

Most of the time, dumb *cons* like that didn't last long. They got too eager, and somebody on the other side—probably some scared fuck who would rather have been in an *estaminet* somewhere with a barmaid in his lap—took them out. Not many people missed them once they were gone, either. They tended to get their comrades killed, too.

Every once in a while, though . . . By all accounts, Hitler had been that kind of ferocious loner. He'd spent just about all the last war as a runner at the front, and he'd come through with hardly a scratch. You couldn't begin to figure the odds on that. The way it looked to Luc, God had dropped the ball there.

He laughed at himself. "Fat lot anybody can do about it now," he said, and lit one of his new Gauloises.

Chapter 20

Instead of flying out of an airstrip in front of Smolensk, Stas Mouradian was flying out of one east of the city. That suggested that the fighting wasn't going the way the Politburo and General Secretary Stalin had in mind.

Of course, other such hints had appeared long before this. When the war started, Stas had flown out of an airstrip in Slovakia. Slovakia lay a long way west of where he was flying from now. So did Poland. So did Byelorussia. He'd flown from airstrips in those places, too.

Looking at that progression (even if you ignored his detour to the Far East, which also hadn't turned out well), you might start to suspect that Soviet leadership left something to be desired. As a matter of fact, Stas had started suspecting as much even in Slovakia.

He'd also suspected he'd better keep quiet about it. The enemy could kill you. So could your own side. Defeatism was a capital crime. If the Nazis shot you down, you at least had a chance of getting things over with in a hurry. Once the Chekists started in on you, they'd take their time and really make you sorry.

He wondered how long his squadron would be able to keep flying.

Lately, days had been dawning with clouds massing in the northwest and drifting across the sky, covering it ever more thickly. The fall *rasputitsa* was coming. Airstrips, roads between towns, and everything else would turn to mud.

He also wondered why Red Air Force engineers hadn't built more paved airfields around here. They might have given the Soviet Union a vital edge in its fight with the Fascists and their allies. Maybe the engineers had had other things to do, things they found more important. What those things might be, Stas couldn't imagine.

Even saying there should be paved runways near Smolensk, or wondering aloud why there weren't, was one more thing that might make the NKVD notice you. Stas knew they had a dossier on him. Well, they had a dossier on everybody. But the folder with his name on it would be thicker than most. Every so often, he couldn't stop himself from hinting that not all the men who led the Union of Soviet Socialist Republics were grand and towering geniuses.

The squadron took off from its dirt runway and flew north and a little west toward Velizh, another town threatened by the Nazis. If the enemy swung around behind Velizh, the fortress might fall even if it wasn't immediately overrun. The Germans had shown how good they were at biting off pockets with their armor and then using guns and infantry to chew up the Soviet forces still inside.

Lieutenant Colonel Tomashevsky stayed in the clouds as much as he could. He had to be navigating by compass and dead reckoning and perhaps a little un-Soviet prayer. All the same, Stas thought he would have flown the same way were he leading the squadron. Unlike the SB-2, the Pe-2 was no clay pigeon for the Bf-109. It was about as fast as the German fighter. But the Messerschmitt could outclimb, outdive, and outturn it. Dogfights with 109s remained a bad bet.

When Tomashevsky ordered the Red Air Force bombers down below the cloud layer, down to where they could see—and be seen—once more, Stas expected them to have to grope around for Velizh. Russia was full of fields and forests. He'd traveled all the way across it to the Far East. He knew how enormous it was, and how lucky you had to be to find anything on the first try.

"*Bozhemoi!*" Ivan Kulkaanen exclaimed as the last rags of mist blew away from the windscreen and the horizon stretched out to kilometers. They were right over the town their bomb loads were supposed to defend.

"I couldn't have put it better myself," Mouradian said. Was the squadron commander that good a navigator, or had he filled an inside straight? Stas didn't think he could do it again, but he'd done it once, and nothing else mattered for this mission.

The war was laid out below them, as if on a situation map. Soviet trenches in front of Velizh kept the Nazis from storming in. But the Red Army had to defend long lines, and its strength was spread thin. The Germans were forming assault columns. If one of them broke through, the Soviet soldiers in the trenches would have to fall back to keep from being bypassed.

Lieutenant Colonel Tomashevsky's static-distorted voice resounded in Stas' earphones: "We will bomb the central Fascist column. Acknowledge."

"Bombing the central column—plane eight acknowledging," Mouradian replied. Other pilots also showed they'd heard. Again, Stas would have made the same choice. That German force looked thicker and more muscular than either of the other two. How would it look after a good many tonnes of high explosives came down on its head?

As a matter of fact, Tomashevsky didn't bomb the head of the column. He released his presents several kilometers to the west. The other Pe-2s followed him in. They were supposed to bomb the same place he did. But followers never did. They didn't want to hang around any longer than they had to. The Nazis were already throwing up fierce antiaircraft fire.

Because of all that, the Pe-2 pilots following the squadron commander didn't drop their bombs right where he had. They bombed short—and progressively shorter as plane after plane unloaded. Stas was no more immune than anyone else. He'd seen—and been part of— the effect on every mission he'd flown.

What he'd never seen before was someone taking advantage of it. Lieutenant Colonel Tomashevsky understood ahead of time what his flyers would do. Their bombs fell ever more toward the front of the German column, and probably smashed the hell out of it. If he'd blasted the head of the column himself, most of the rest of the squadron's bombs would have landed short. Some of them might have come down on the poor bastards defending Velizh.

Doctrine, as Stas knew, was for the squadron leader to put his bombs exactly where they belonged. Doctrine decreed that the other pilots would of course place their loads right where he had. In the Red Air Force no less than the Red Army, doctrine carried the weight of holy writ.

What Lieutenant Colonel Tomashevsky had done worked better than doctrine. It couldn't have been an accident or an error. Stas admired the squadron commander's cleverness. He thought it was a shame Tomashevsky wouldn't be able to spread the improvement to other officers who led squadrons. When he submitted his report, he would have to say he'd conformed to orders in every particular. Officers who did anything else wound up explaining themselves to the NKVD, which no one in his right mind wanted to do.

"Back to base," Tomashevsky ordered. Again, Stas acknowledged. He was never sorry for permission to get the hell out of there.

Kulkaanen peered down at the German column as Mouradian turned the Pe-2 toward the neighborhood of Smolensk once more. He shook his head in pleased surprise. "Boy, we walloped the snot out of them, didn't we?" he said.

"We sure did," Stas agreed dryly. Did his copilot have the slightest idea of how they'd walloped the snot out of the Nazis? If he did, he was doing his best to hide it.

That thought brought Mouradian up short. Ivan Kulkaanen might be doing his very best to conceal any surplus intelligence he owned. Maybe you would get promoted if you showed you had more on the ball than the other junior lieutenants around you. Or maybe you'd get . . . what was the word farmers used? Culled, that was it. A sunflower that stood taller than the others in the field almost begged for the scythe.

Marx said Communism's doctrine should be *From each according to his abilities, to each according to his needs.* But what if your abilities were of the sort that made your superiors nervous? You'd be sorry, that was what. Or you'd turn into a chameleon, so they'd look right at you without seeing you, or at least without noticing you were any different from the rest.

Was that what Kulkaanen was up to? Stas didn't think so, but he hadn't imagined even the possibility till now. And something else occurred to him. Was that something he should be doing more of himself? He knew he was brighter than most of the other pilots in the squadron. His superiors likely did, too. All of a sudden, he wondered whether that was good or dangerous.

No NKVD men waited to haul him off to a fate worse than combat when he landed the Pe-2. The Chekists had plenty of other things to worry about. If he was on their list, he hadn't yet come to the top. Since his own side didn't feel like killing him yet, the Germans would get another chance one day soon.

TO AN ENGLISHMAN, Egypt, even in what should have been autumn, came with only two settings on the thermostat: too hot and much too bloody goddamn hot. Alistair Walsh donned khaki drill shorts that showed off his pale, hairy legs. Even in tropical uniform, he sweltered.

He started out wearing a solar topee: a fancy name for a pith helmet. But another veteran sergeant who'd had a go at the half-arsed desert warfare with the Eyeties set him straight about that. "Go any place where they might shoot at you and you want a proper tin hat, pal," the other man said. "That ugly thing you've got on your head—"

"You mean my face?" Walsh broke in. They were pouring down pints in a makeshift sergeants' club somewhere between Sollum, which was in Egypt, and Tobruk, which was in Italian-owned Libya. Just a big tent, actually, and the beer came from bottles, but it could have been worse.

The other sergeant laughed. "I've seen worse mugs. My own, for instance. But you do want a tin hat. Even if it's already khaki, paint it again and throw sand on the paint while it's still wet. That kills sun glare better than anything else we've found."

"Nice." Walsh nodded appreciatively. "I wouldn't have thought of that."

"Nor I," his drinking partner said. "I've heard we nicked the notion from Musso's boys, but I can't swear to it."

"Interesting. How much in earnest are they, really?"

"Well, it depends," his new chum answered.

"It often does," Walsh agreed, his voice dusty.

The other fellow chuckled. "And isn't that the bloody truth? They were brave enough against the Austrians the last go-round."

"Not exactly the first string on either side in that match," Walsh said.

"Too true. They haven't covered themselves with glory in Spain. By all accounts, most of them never wanted to go there, and they've fought that way. Here . . . It depends more on the unit and the officers with the Eyeties than it does with the Fritzes," the other sergeant said.

"With the Fritzes, they always mean it," Walsh said with feeling. "You know what you're getting with them, same as with Navy Cuts." In aid of which, he lit a cigarette and offered his new friend the packet.

With a nod of thanks, the other man took one. "I'm Joe Billings," he said, and stuck out his hand.

Walsh shook it and gave his own name. "And just as much a Taffy as you'd expect from the handle," he added. If he said it first, the other fellow couldn't use it against him.

But Billings only nodded. "Heard it in the way you talked," he said, and no more. By his own accent, he came from England's industrial Midlands. He went on, "Some of the Italian regiments, they aren't worth tuppence ha'penny. Others . . . Others'll give you everything you want and more besides. For a while, I should say. They're all short of staying power."

"Not the men, by what you say." Walsh was trying to put pieces together.

"Not in those outfits. Some damn fine soldiers there," Billings said. "Rifles, machine guns, grenades, that kind of thing, one bloke's kit is about as good as the other's. But they're short on artillery, they're woefully short on tanks, and the ones they've got are old-fashioned junk."

"Heh." Walsh drained his pint. "Back in France, I would have said the same thing about ours. The Germans chased us a deal more than we chased them, and that's the truth."

"You aren't fighting the Germans any more, though," Billings said. "This is a different business."

How different it was Walsh discovered anew when he ducked out of the tent to ease himself. A million stars blazed down on him. The Milky Way was a pearly mesh cast across black, black sky. You never saw night skies like this in England or France. Too much moisture in the air, and, till the blackouts, too many lights sullying the darkness. Oddly, the only place he'd ever known the heavens like this before was in Norway, on a few of the rare clear winter nights.

But this wasn't Norway, either. He'd frozen his ballocks off there despite a sheepskin coat. Nights got cold here—you did want your greatcoat—but not cold like that. The wind smelled different. You didn't breathe in ice and pine trees here. You smelled sand and dust and petrol and exhaust. English forces here were far more motorized than they had been in Norway.

Walsh sniffed again as he did up his trousers. He didn't know what he was sniffing for. Camel shit? Something like that, he supposed. He'd seen a few camels since he got to Egypt. The natives used them. So did the English and the Italians—when they ran short of lorries. You could also eat them if you had to. Walsh hoped like hell he'd never have to. Could anything that ugly possibly taste good?

He went back into the tent. Joe Billings had bought them both fresh pints while he was outside. Pretty soon, he'd buy a round himself. They'd both be pissing all night long.

He was nursing a headache the next morning. That didn't keep the personnel wallahs from sending him up to his new slot: senior underofficer for an infantry company. All the young lieutenants eyed him as if he were a leper. And well they might. They had the seniority of rank, but he had that of experience. They could order him around, and they didn't have to do what he told them to do—not by military law they didn't. But they might land in worse trouble for ignoring him than he would for ignoring them.

One of them asked him, "Did you go through it the last time around?"

"Yes, sir." Walsh tapped his leg. "Bought part of a plot, but not the whole thing." He grinned crookedly. "Weather's better for it here than it is back in Blighty—I'll tell you that. Hardly aches at all."

The subaltern nodded. His name was Wilf Preston. He had a sunburned, wind-chapped face full of freckles, and he looked hardly old enough to have escaped from public school: his posh accent said he'd likely gone to one. He hesitated before continuing, "Speaking of Blighty, were you, ah, in London when the government, ah, changed?"

"Yes, sir," Walsh repeated. By the way Preston asked the question, he already knew the answer. *That's . . . interesting,* Walsh thought. *My reputation goes before me. They aren't leery just because staff sergeants are supposed to eat second lieutenants without salt.*

He wasn't used to having that kind of reputation. For the rest of his life, he would be the man who'd brought in Rudolf Hess, the man who'd known Winston Churchill, the man who'd helped topple Horace Wilson in a military coup. He might be a lowly staff sergeant, but people with far more power than lowly lieutenants would look sidelong at him from here on out. *Who are your friends?* they'd wonder. *What can you do to me if I cross you?*

If he shouted "Boo!" young Wilf Preston would probably jump right out of his skin. It was tempting—damned if it wasn't. Instead, he pointed west and asked, "Could you tell me what Musso's lads are up to, sir?"

"They're just patrolling for the time being," Preston answered with transparent relief. "So are we, mainly. They haven't shown a great deal of push since we drove them back over the border. We have the feeling that the only reason they attacked at all was so Benito could show Adolf he was strafing us for ducking out of the alliance against Russia."

"Pity he can't be his own fool instead of Hitler's," Walsh said.

Up at the front, a mile or two from where they talked, gunfire started up. Walsh began to unsling his Lee-Enfield, but noticed Preston wasn't getting excited. "They always open fire around this time of day," the subaltern said. "We think they have orders to shoot off so many rounds every morning, and this is how they make their quota."

"War shouldn't be about work rates," Walsh said. "If it were, all the soldiers would unionize—and likely go out on strike. Then you'd need to hire blacklegs if you wanted any killing done."

Preston looked at him in yet another new way. "You're quite daft, aren't you?" he said.

"Who, me?" Walsh shrugged. "I do my best."

HANS-ULRICH RUDEL WOKE to a soft drumming against the canvas of his tent. He was afraid he knew what that was, but he might have been wrong. He stuck his nose outside to see. Said nose, and the rest of his face, met raindrops. He didn't take the Lord's name in vain. Even now, he remembered he was a minister's son. But he did say something that never would have come out of his mouth before he joined the *Luftwaffe*.

The rain poured down from a pewter sky. Hans-Ulrich squelched over to the mess tent. Some of the flyers in there had already started drinking. One of them raised a flask in salute to him. "Have a snort, Rudel!"

"You know I don't do that," Rudel answered.

"You may as well. We sure as hell aren't going up for a while." Peter took a long pull at the flask. Did his cheeks and nose turn redder, or was that only Hans-Ulrich's sanctimonious imagination?

Preferring not to dwell on it, Rudel said, "It may stop. The ground may dry up again." He didn't believe himself, either. He'd been in Russia the autumn before. He knew what these rains were like.

So did Peter, who laughed raucously. "Go talk to a virgin, pal! This weather's fucked us before, and it's fucking us again."

Since Hans-Ulrich feared he was right, he walked over to see what the field kitchen had turned out. It was a thick stew of boiled buckwheat groats—kasha, the Ivans called the stuff—and onions and carrots and bits of flesh. Pointing to one of those bits in his mess tin, Hans-Ulrich asked, "What is it?"

"Meat." The fellow who'd ladled out the stew gave back a laconic answer.

"I figured *that*," Rudel said with exaggerated patience. "But will it neigh when I bite down? Or bark? Or meow?"

"As long as it doesn't ask you for a loan, *Herr Oberleutnant*, odds are you're better off not knowing," the cook replied.

Sighing, Rudel decided he was likely to be right. He sat down on a bench and spooned up the stew. They'd never serve it at the Adlon— although food inside the *Reich* was nasty these days, too. The meat had been boiled so long, he couldn't tell what it had started out as. It tasted . . . meaty. He emptied the tin tray faster than he'd expected. He would have gone back for seconds if he hadn't worried that the cook would laugh at him.

There was a strange thing. Around his neck hung the Knight's Cross, proof that he didn't fear anything enemy flak might do to his Stuka—or to him. Yet the thought that an enlisted man who needed a shave might mock him kept his behind glued to the planking.

Courage, and then again courage. Before the war started, he hadn't understood that it came in different flavors. And what kind of courage was required for an Aryan holder of the *Ritterkreuz* to sleep with a half-Jewish barmaid? To love her? Hans-Ulrich shook his head. It wasn't like that—quite. Even having anything to do with her, though, took bravery unlike either bearding a cook or diving on an enemy panzer. It took a certain amount of moral courage, though Rudel himself was unlikely ever to see it in that light.

Colonel Steinbrenner ducked into the mess tent. At a training base in Germany, no doubt, the flyers would have stopped shoveling in kasha and mystery meat. They would have put down the vodka jugs (no, they wouldn't have had any vodka jugs to begin with). And they would have leaped to their feet, stiffened into attention, and saluted the squadron commander.

A couple of them nodded. One man paused in lighting a cigarette long enough to wave. The rest went on with what they were doing. Steinbrenner took that for granted. He shed his officer's cap and scowled at the drops of water on the patent-leather brim. "Fucking wet out there," he remarked.

"Too right it is," said the pilot with the cigarette.

One of the men passing around the jug held it out to the colonel. He laughed, shook his head, and went over to the pot full of stew. The cook filled his mess kit. Then Steinbrenner caught Hans-Ulrich's eye, wordlessly asking, *May I sit next to you?*

Hans-Ulrich nodded and did his best to look eager and inviting. Discipline at the front didn't work the way it did in the *Reich* during peacetime, but you needed some mighty good reason to tell your squadron commander to get lost, and he had none.

"How's it going?" Steinbrenner asked as he parked himself.

"In this weather, sir? It's not going anywhere," Rudel said.

"You've got that right, anyway. The *Landsers*'ll just have to live without air support for a while. Well, so will the Russians." Steinbrenner dug into breakfast. He chewed thoughtfully before delivering his verdict: "I've had worse, but I've sure had better. What's the meat?"

"Don't know," Hans-Ulrich admitted.

"Didn't you ask?" Steinbrenner said.

"Yeah, but the cook said I'd be better off not finding out," Rudel answered.

The squadron commander turned and shouted at the guy behind the cauldron: "Hey, Klaus, what did you kill before you dumped it into this slop?" He didn't worry about the enlisted man's precious sensibilities.

And Klaus didn't worry about his, either. "Sir, I believe that's your granny," he replied. The mess tent erupted with laughter.

Colonel Steinbrenner spooned up some more meat. His jaws worked again. He shook his head. "Nah. Granny'd be tougher than this no matter how long you stewed her." More laughter. The cook held up the ladle in salute, acknowledging the hit.

Hans-Ulrich knew he couldn't have done anything like that. He could sass Sergeant Dieselhorst that way, and maybe a couple of the other flyers he felt comfortable with, but not a cook he didn't care a pfennig for one way or the other. Yes, Colonel Steinbrenner was older than he was, but Rudel suddenly realized more than age and rank went into running a squadron.

He didn't go on from there to realize Steinbrenner had asked to sit next to him for a reason. He was a gear with a worn-down tooth or two, and didn't fit smoothly into the squadron's mechanism. Had he realized something like that, he would have taken another step toward being ready to lead such an outfit.

"So what are you going to do now that flying gets tricky?" Steinbrenner asked him. Then the colonel shook his head once more. "Now that flying gets stuck in the mud, I should say."

"Oh, I don't know, sir. Maybe I'll see if I can con a furlough out of my squadron commander," Rudel said blandly. "Some people can drink so that weeks seem to go by in days. If you don't drink, though, weeks stuck in the mud seem more like years."

"Best argument for drinking I've heard lately," Colonel Steinbrenner remarked. Hans-Ulrich hadn't intended it as anything of the kind, but he could see how the older man might hear it that way—and jab him with it. Steinbrenner went on, "If you did get a furlough—by some miracle, you understand—where would you go? What would you do? And 'Anywhere away from here' isn't a good enough answer."

Now Hans-Ulrich chose his words with care: "Well, I might take a train back to Poland to get away from the war for a bit. To, ah, Bialystok." Why deny it? Steinbrenner knew about Sofia.

He nodded. Yes, he was unsurprised. "And how's your girlfriend there?"

"That's what I'd like to find out, sir. She, ah, she doesn't write much," Rudel said. In point of fact, Sofia didn't write at all. He'd never told her not to, but she knew getting love letters—or any letters—from a *Mischling* wouldn't be good for him.

Colonel Steinbrenner nodded. "That may not be the worst thing in the world," was all he said, but it told Hans-Ulrich he not only knew about Sofia but also about her racial makeup.

If they wanted to make a case against me, they could. The weight of the Knight's Cross on his neck felt most reassuring to Rudel. But that kind of thing wouldn't stop them if they decided you were disloyal. It might slow them down, but it wouldn't stop them. The only thing that would stop them was obvious, unswerving loyalty to the *Reich* and to National Socialism. Hans-Ulrich had it, in abundance. He also had a half-Jewish girlfriend. Would that make them doubt the other? All he could do—if he didn't want to give Sofia up, and he didn't—was hope not.

YOU EXPLAIN HOW you messed up. You promise not to do it again, and you mean what you're saying from the bottom of your heart. After that, the sun's supposed to come out and everything's supposed to be wonderful: just the way it was before. It's straight out of a Hollywood script.

Peggy Druce was discovering that real life didn't work out the way movies did. It was nothing she hadn't suspected before. But, despite confessions, she and Herb couldn't seem to go back to the way they'd been before she sailed for Europe in late summer 1938. They could talk about forgiving each other. Meaning it was harder—harder than she'd ever expected.

It wasn't anything showy or dramatic. He didn't haul off and belt her one. She didn't smash crockery over his noggin. They still enjoyed each other's company, at the dining-room table and even in the bedroom. They weren't going to end up in divorce court. Nothing like that.

But all the king's horses and all the king's men couldn't put Humpty together again. Peggy felt the lack, the way she'd felt it when she woke up from the ether without her wisdom teeth. She could still go back there with her tongue and remember when she'd had them. She could remember this other thing that was missing now, too.

They'd given her codeine to keep the extractions from hurting so much. She wished there were also a pill for this. She tried bourbon, but that seemed to make matters worse, not better.

Herb was drinking more these days. He wasn't drinking what anybody would call a lot, but he was drinking more. Peggy wondered if she should say something about it: at least let him know she'd noticed. In the end, she kept her mouth shut. She also wondered whether she should have done that about their adventures while apart.

She didn't think so. This was better than the looming thing in the room with them that neither had wanted to admit was there. The trouble was, she'd thought that better would turn out to be the same thing as what kids called all better. Nope. And the difference between the one and the other was enough to tempt her back toward the Old Grand dad bottle again.

Then one dreary, rainy, early-darkening afternoon Herb came through the door with more bounce in his step than she'd seen since she got back from Europe. "Ha!" he said as he hung his topcoat on a peg so it would drip on the tile floor.

"Ha?" Peggy asked.

"Ha!" He said it again, even more emphatically. For good measure, he added, "Hoo-hah!" Then he lit a cigarette.

"Okay, now I get it," Peggy said. "You're all excited because Glenn Miller just took you on as a scat singer."

He coughed, blowing out ragged puffs of smoke. "Don't do that," he wheezed. "You'll make me choke to death."

"Sorry." She did her best to sound properly contrite. It wasn't easy; she still wanted to laugh. "Maybe I wouldn't need to if you'd tell me what's really going on."

"Well, I was going to." Herb took another, cautious, drag on the coffin nail. This time, he didn't try to explode when he exhaled. "Needed more finagling than I ever thought it would, but I finally did it."

"That's nice," Peggy answered. "Did what?"

"Persuaded Uncle Sam I could do something that would help give the war effort a kick in the pants." Her husband looked proud enough to bust the buttons on his vest.

And well he might have. He'd been trying to do something for the country ever since Japan attacked the Philippines and tried to hit Hawaii the January before. The trouble—or at least part of the trouble—was, the government was deluged with middle-aged men offering their services. Most of them were too old and too far from war service to be worth anything with weapons in their hands. Getting men to fight and giving them the tools they needed to fight with had to be Washington's top priority.

Even that wasn't going so well as people wished it would. Stories about waste and inefficiency and fraud and profiteering showed up in the papers almost every day and in the news magazines almost every week. But the War Department's worries about everything else ran only a distant second—when they ran at all.

"What will they want you to do?" Peggy asked. It might have been *Will I ever see you again?* That wasn't even close to fair, not when she'd gallivanted all over Pennsylvania and beyond, telling eyewitness tales of how nasty Fascism was, so prosperous people—and those not so prosperous—would fork over the cash to let the government take care of whatever it decided needed taking care of.

"Make things run smoother," Herb said. "Efficiency expert, is what it boils down to. Only they'll pay me more than a run-of-the-mill efficiency expert, 'cause I won't be dealing with stuff on the shop floor. I'm supposed to make whole factory systems run better."

"How much is 'more'?" was Peggy's natural next question. Herb named a number. She whistled softly. That was pretty good, all right. Then she asked, "Are they going to draft you so you can do it?"

"Unh-unh." He shook his head. "They'd have to make me a colonel or something to give me enough clout to do the job, and they don't want to make colonels out of guys who were corporals the last time around and got out of the Army as fast as they could afterwards. Can't say I blame 'em, either. So I'll be a civilian with a fancy letter from the Secretary of War—or maybe from the President; dunno yet—that says I have the power to bind and to loose."

Peggy looked suitably impressed. "Wow! Can I touch you?" She reached out as if to tap him gently with the very tip of her forefinger.

He grabbed her and squeezed her. "You darn well better, babe."

She squeezed back. She liked being in his arms. It felt like the right place to be. She only wished there weren't that little something in the back of her mind. Once upon a time, Gladys the clerk-typist had been in his arms, too. And, once upon a time, Peggy herself had wound up in that American diplomat's arms.

None of that would happen again. If she hadn't been sure of it, she wouldn't have liked being in Herb's arms any more. All the same, the shadow lingered.

Countries in Europe remembered slights and defeats at the hands of their neighbors that went back centuries. Sometimes, even in this day and age, they chose their allies—and their wars—on account of them. That had always struck a sensible, no-nonsense, apple-pie American like Peggy as insane. Once something was over, it was over.

Wasn't it?

Well, as things turned out, that depended. She and Herb were finding out for themselves that memories weren't always so easy to shove aside. And if people who loved each other had trouble doing it, how much harder was it for countries that hated and feared and mistrusted one another?

Peggy started to tell Herb that all at once she understood why European nations went off the rails every generation or two. But she didn't go ahead and do it. It would have involved reminding him they'd gone off the rails themselves. They were both doing their best to forget that. Whose fault was it that their best didn't seem to be good enough?

It probably wasn't anybody's fault exactly. It—

"Did you say something?" Herb asked, so she must have made a noise after all.

She shook her head. "Not me. Must have been the goldfish."

"We haven't got a goldfish," Herb pointed out. They grinned at each other from a distance of about six inches. How many times had one of them or the other—or, as here, both of them in collusion—made that same silly joke? It was one of the things they shared, one of the things that made them a couple.

Gladys wouldn't have known how to finish it. Neither would Constantine Jenkins. *We're like an old sock and a shoe, Herb and me,* Peggy thought. *We fit, and we're comfortable together.* That wasn't such a bad thing, not when you considered the alternatives.

Chapter 21

If anything was more fun than changing a panzer track in mud and rain, Theo Hossbach had trouble imagining what it might be. The job resembled nothing so much as a bout of all-in wrestling, with the added chance of getting squashed if you were careless.

Having a five-man crew instead of three did help. More hands couldn't make this work light, but they did make it a little lighter. And the gunner and loader complained just as much as the three men who'd come out of their little Panzer II together.

Which didn't mean those three didn't complain. "These fucking things better work, is all I've got to say," Adi Stoss growled, plying spanner with might and main.

"This beast should have come with them," Lothar Eckhardt said. The gunner wiped a wet sleeve across his equally wet forehead and went on, "I mean, they knew all along what things in Russia would be like, right?"

Adi and Hermann Witt both laughed raucously. Even Theo snorted. Sergeant Witt said, "Lothar, they didn't know their ass from their elbow. Highways on the maps are horrible dirt tracks on the ground. Secondary roads on the maps aren't there at all. They didn't realize we'd need wider tracks on our panzers till we screamed at 'em that the Russians could keep going where we bogged down. And it's taken a fucking year to get the *Ostketten* out to us so we could dance like this."

Ostketten: East tracks. Panzers hadn't needed wider tracks in Czechoslovakia or the Low Countries or France. They sure did here in Russia. This wasn't much of a civilized country, or much of a civilized war.

Eckhardt stared at Hermann Witt. "But hasn't the General Staff come out and looked at this ground?"

"Don't bet anything you can't afford to lose," Adi said.

"Son of a bitch!" Eckhardt said with feeling. "If they haven't, somebody ought to stick 'em in a penal battalion. Maybe they'd learn some sense if they lived through that. And if they didn't, who'd miss 'em?"

Penal units were a Soviet idea the *Wehrmacht* had borrowed. Take a bunch of guys who'd disgraced themselves by cowardice or some other mortal sin. Give them a chance at redemption—throw them in where the fighting is hottest. If they try to retreat, shoot them yourself. If they die in action, oh, well. Chances are they'll shake the enemy doing it. And if they happen to live, you can turn them back into ordinary soldiers again. Or, if you're so inclined, you can fill up the holes in the penal battalion with new fuckups—there are always new fuckups—and throw it into action somewhere else.

The system had an elegant simplicity. Theo was surprised the Nazis hadn't thought of it for themselves. But then, they'd never been shy about stealing ideas from other people. Instead of talking about that— which might have made him learn more about penal battalions than he'd ever wanted to know—Theo went on manhandling the *Ostketten* into place on the road wheels and the idlers and, most important of all, the drive sprocket.

After close to two hours, they finished. A couple of them had vodka in their canteens instead of water. Say what you would about vodka, but it didn't give you dysentery. The haves shared with the have-nots. Socialism was real at the front. Everywhere else, as far as Theo could tell, it was only a sour joke.

Smacking his lips, Adi said, "No dumb cop's gonna write me a ticket for drunken driving, not today."

"If anybody tries, mash him like a potato," Hermann Witt said. He eyed their backbreaking handiwork. "Let's see if we can go mash some Ivans now."

Ostketten wouldn't keep out shells from a T-34 or a KV-1, of course. But the panzer crew had lashed the old, narrow tracks to the glacis. They might help turn an enemy round there. Or, of course, they might not. But it was worth a try. Theo had seen several other Panzer IIIs similarly decked out. More and more crews would improvise improved armor as more *Ostketten* arrived.

At least the panzer's engine started up right away. Hard freezes hadn't begun yet, let alone the kind of weather that made a mockery of German antifreeze and motor oil. Mechanics swore this year's antifreeze and lubricants were better than the stuff the *Wehrmacht* had used the year before. Theo hoped that meant they wouldn't have to build a fire under the engine compartment to thaw things out enough to start. He hoped . . . but he didn't really believe it.

He dripped on his seat when he took his place inside the panzer. The radioman and bow gunner was as far from the engine compartment as he could get. In the Panzer II, Theo's station had been right on the other side of the fireproof—everyone hoped!—bulkhead. He'd warmed up in a hurry there. No such luck in this machine.

Over on the other side of the centrally positioned radio sat the driver. At Sergeant Witt's command, Adi put the Panzer III in gear. It rattled and clanked ahead. The engine's grinding growl seemed a long way off to Theo, who'd been used to listening to it right at his elbow.

Theo glanced over at his comrade, but Adi was paying attention to what he was doing. "How does it seem?" Theo asked. If he wanted to find out, he had to spend some words.

"Feels . . . a little better, maybe," Adi answered after a judicious pause. "I don't want to charge into the thickest slop I can find, you know, just to see if the *Ostketten*'ll pull us through it. They're liable not to, and then you'd have to call a recovery vehicle to fish us out. Everybody'd love me for that."

If by *love* he meant *scream at*, he was right. Otherwise . . . Otherwise, he was a sarcastic, cynical veteran panzer man, just like thousands of others in the *Wehrmacht*. Well, almost just like thousands of others. As long as the authorities didn't notice the difference, everything was fine. It had been fine for quite a while now. Theo hoped it would stay that way.

German authorities weren't the only ones who could foul things up, of course. The Russians weren't thrilled about having other people's tanks gallivanting across their landscape. Theo wondered why. Now that he could see out, he could see what a broad, bleak country this was. It might not have looked so bad when the trees had leaves and the grain was greening toward gold, but the harvest was over and cold and rain had done for the leaves. The word that crossed his mind for the land hereabouts was haunted.

If you were a German panzer man, the landscape damn well *was* haunted. Russians wore mud-colored uniforms to begin with. And they took camouflage very seriously: more seriously than the Germans did, for sure. They wouldn't mind rolling in the mud and rubbing it on their faces to make themselves harder to spot. They'd daub mud on their panzers, too, or drape netting over them to disguise their outlines. You might not suspect they were around till a shell slammed into your side armor from a direction you hadn't worried about.

Adi hit the brakes. Hermann Witt's voice came through the speaking tube: "Why'd you stop?"

"Ground up ahead doesn't look quite right," Stoss answered.

"What's the matter with it? Just looks like ground to me," the panzer commander said.

"I'll go ahead if you want me to, but I'd sooner back up and go around," Adi told him.

"Do that, then," Witt said. "You don't usually get the vapors—and if you have 'em this time, well, shit, you're entitled once in a while."

"Thanks, Sergeant. You're all right, you know that?" Adi put the panzer into reverse. Theo wondered what would have happened were Heinz Naumann still in charge here. No, he didn't wonder; he knew. Naumann would have ordered Adi to go straight ahead, just to show him who the boss was. And then they would have seen . . . whatever they would have seen.

As Adi was making his loop, another Panzer III did head straight across the stretch of ground he hadn't liked. It did fine for about thirty meters. Then it hit a mine that blew off its left track. Curses from the other panzer's radioman dinned in Theo's earphones. Now those guys would have to wait for a recovery vehicle, or else come out of their steel shell and try to repair things well enough to limp away. If the Reds aimed an antipanzer cannon at them while they were stuck . . . That would be hard luck. For them.

Hermann Witt's voice came through the speaking tube again: "Good job, Adi."

"Thanks, boss," the driver answered. Theo wondered what Naumann would have said after they charged into the minefield at his orders. Since the other commander had stopped one with his head, nobody would ever know now. And maybe that was just as well for everyone—except Naumann, of course.

VACLAV JEZEK SPRAWLED under a battered chunk of rusting corrugated iron between the Republican lines northwest of Madrid and the Nationalist positions. Rain drummed down on the iron. The ground around the Czech's hidey-hole was getting muddy. No, by now it had already got muddy. Every so often, a little chilly rill dribbled in with Vaclav. Summer was over. Spanish autumn warned that Spanish winter was coming.

Some yellowing bushes concealed where the muzzle end of Vaclav's antitank rifle stuck out from under the sheet iron. The bushes also made it harder for him to peer through the telescopic sight, but he didn't mind. A sniper's first commandment was *Don't let them spot you.* If you didn't honor that commandment and keep it wholly, you wouldn't live long enough to learn the second one.

And, naturally, the rain also cut down on visibility. That blade also had two edges. Yes, Vaclav had more trouble finding likely targets. But Marshal Sanjurjo's men would also have more trouble noticing him if he made a mistake.

He gnawed on a chunk of spicy Spanish sausage. His tongue thought Spaniards put peppers and garlic in everything this side of ice cream. They were even worse than Magyars for hotting up their food. The sausage, actually, wasn't too bad now that he'd got used to it.

He wished for a cigarette. He had a pack in his pocket, but lighting one now would be a king-sized mistake. Even through the rain, an alert Nationalist might spot smoke leaking out from under the iron sheet.

Some of the American Internationals chewed tobacco when they got into a spot where they couldn't light up. Vaclav thought about it, but not for long. The idea seemed too disgusting to stand. He could deal with the no-smoke jitters till night fell. Then he could either have a careful cigarette here—making sure the struck match and the coal didn't show—or go back to the trenches and smoke his head off.

In the meantime . . . Waiting was a big part of the sniper's game. If you weren't patient, you wouldn't last. One of these days—one of these years—Vaclav wanted to go home to a free Czechoslovakia. Letting some Spanish Fascist asshole pot him before he could wasn't in his plans.

He moved the antitank rifle a few millimeters. Through the scope, he eyed a new stretch of the Nationalists' rear entrenchments. It seemed no more interesting than the old stretch had. The Spaniards there were more careless than they were at the front, where an ordinary rifleman could pot anybody who unwarily stuck his head up over the parapet. They thought they were far enough away to be safe.

The hell of it was, they were right. He could have blown some of their brains out, sure. Seeing them in helmets so much like the ones the Nazis wore made him want to do it, too. But he wasn't about to waste his precious ammo on ordinary Josés and Jorges. If you were going to snipe at long range, you wanted to get rid of the officers, the high-powered guys whose loss hurt the enemy out of proportion to their numbers.

Like this bastard, for instance. He wore an officer's cap with a high crown and a brim, not a helmet or a service cap. The brim helped keep the rain out of his eyes, but it also told the world what he was. There were stars above the brim. How many? Small or large? That would say how big a fish Vaclav had in his sights. At this range and in this weather, he couldn't be sure.

Whoever the jerk was, he pointed a finger at one of the ordinary soldiers and told him off in no uncertain terms. That decided the sniper watching him from afar. Anybody who thought he was such a big shot deserved whatever happened to him. Vaclav took careful aim, inhaled, exhaled, and pressed the trigger.

The elephant of a gun slammed against his shoulder. The stock was padded, but that helped only so much. And the report, always fearsome, seemed four times as loud under the sheet of corrugated iron. But the Nationalist officer fell over, which was the point of the exercise.

Vaclav quickly chambered another round. Had the Nationalists seen the muzzle flash when he shot their officer? If they had, would they come after him and try to pay him back?

No one came. He wouldn't have wanted to hunt snipers in the rain, either. You never could tell, though. Sometimes people got upset when you murdered their officers. Sometimes, no doubt, the regular guys in the trenches hoisted one in your direction when you blew the head off some jackass they couldn't stand. That was the kind of thing you were unlikely to hear about, which had always struck Vaclav as too damn bad.

He kept watching through the sight. He didn't intend to fire two in a row from the same spot, not unless he got a terrific target. He'd think twice even then; shooting two in a row without moving felt almost like signing your own death warrant.

After a while, he took a small swig from his canteen. Cheap Spanish white wine tasted different from cheap French white wine, but no better. With regret, he kept it to the one small swig. The less you drank, the less you needed to get rid of. He didn't have much room to piss under here unless he wanted to lie in it.

Some more sausage, some chewy barley bread . . . This wasn't the Ritz or the Adlon, no two ways about it. Where was the barmaid with the big tits to bring him another bottle of bubbly?

Wherever she was, she wasn't anywhere around here. He didn't find any more overbearing officers to shoot at. You could peer through a sight for only so long. Once he decided he wouldn't spot anything more, he pillowed his head on his arms and fell asleep.

It was dark when he woke up. Under the iron sheet, it was black as Hitler's heart. He needed a second or two to realize he hadn't died or been buried alive. He had a way out, a way back to his friends.

"Fuck!" he muttered. He had to give his own heart stern orders not to try to pound its way out of his chest. His hands shook. Of course, that was partly because he hadn't had a cigarette in much too long.

He carefully backed out of the little artificial cave where he'd sheltered. It was still raining. No one in the line challenged him till he was clambering over the parapet.

"Good going, guys," he said as he dropped down into the forward trench and fumbled for his cigarettes. "I could have been a Nationalist with a machine pistol. You never would have known the difference till I opened up." He cupped his hands so he could strike a match in spite of the waterworks from on high.

"Nah. You would've made more noise getting through stuff if you were," one of the other Czechs answered.

"You hope I would," Vaclav said. "Some of those guys know what they're doing, though." It started coming down harder. He kept a hand over the cigarette so the raindrops wouldn't put it out. After so long without, he needed more than just a drag or two to feel right.

"We heard you fire," the other Czech said. "Get the guy you were aiming at?"

"Bet your ass," the sniper said, not without pride. "*He* won't be telling anybody what to do again."

"So some other jerk will do it instead." That cynicism came from Benjamin Halévy.

With exaggerated patience, Vaclav answered, "The idea is, if we kill enough of them, they'll run out of men—or the ones they have left won't be worth shit."

"Yeah, that's the idea, all right," the Jew agreed. "Sure is taking it a long time to work, though."

Vaclav looked at him—looked through him, really. "If you don't like it, you can always go back to France. The rest of us, we're fucking stuck here. We aren't going back to Czechoslovakia—that's for goddamn sure." The Nazis held—held down—two-thirds of what had been his country. Slovakia, the remaining chunk, called itself independent. It might be able to sneeze on its own. It couldn't wipe its nose afterwards, though, till Hitler countersigned the order.

"Bite me, Jezek," Halévy said without heat. "I'm not going anywhere, and you know it. I volunteered for this shit, same as you."

"Maybe that proves you really are a dumb sheeny after all. You don't usually talk like it, though," Vaclav replied. They swore at each other in a companionable way. Nobody would be going anywhere much till the rain quit for a while, and they both knew it.

RAIN. SLEET. A little snow mixed in for good—or bad—measure. Julius Lemp wondered why he'd brought the U-30 up to the surface. He could hardly see the U-boat's bow from the conning tower, let alone anything farther away. Stumbling over a target in the storm-tossed Barents Sea would be purely a matter of luck.

True, the boat could go faster surfaced than submerged. Again, so what? If all he saw was this tiny circle . . . Yes, he'd sweep out more area cruising along at fifteen knots, but enough to matter? He doubted it.

Still and all, that didn't mean he didn't try. He wore oilskins over his peacoat, and a wide-brimmed, waterproof hat. He was soaked anyhow. Sleet stung his cheek whenever he faced into the wind, which seemed to have come straight down from the North Pole. The waves that slapped the submarine had taken a running start from that wind, too.

One of the ratings on the conning tower with him tried to clean salt spray off binocular lenses for the third time in ten minutes. He looked through the Zeiss glasses again, then let them thump down to his chest on their strap with a disgusted growl. "Lousy things are worse than useless," he complained to Lemp, or possibly to God.

God didn't answer. Lemp did: "I know, Franz. I'm not using mine, either, not right now."

"We don't have to worry about planes, anyway, not in this crap we don't," Franz said. "You'd have to be nuts to take off to begin with. If you didn't kill yourself doing that, you'd never spot a U-boat. And if you did spot one, you'd lose it again before you could do anything about it."

"We hope," Lemp said. And Franz had to nod to that, because you never could tell. Life was a bitch sometimes. You just never could tell. The Russians were nuts enough, or stubborn enough, to put planes in the air regardless of the weather. And they were used to operating in awful conditions, more used to it than the Germans were. If one of their seaplanes came out of nowhere, it might be able to deliver an attack before the U-30 vanished in the swirling snow and mist. U-boat skippers who didn't stay nervous all the time didn't come home again.

U-boat skippers who *did* stay alert all the time, and who insisted their crews do the same, were iron-arsed sons of bitches. All you had to do to know that was talk to any sailor who'd served under Julius Lemp. He'd recite chapter and verse—and book, too, if you gave him time and fed him a couple of seidels of beer.

Normal watches up on the conning tower lasted only two hours. You could sweep your field glass across the sky just so long before you stopped noticing things. As Franz had seen, sweeping field glasses across the sky on a day like this was a losing proposition. Lemp sent the ratings below at the appointed hour. New men, also dressed in foul-weather gear, took their places.

Lemp stayed topside himself awhile longer. He made and enforced the rules; he could break them if he chose. A gull scudded by. He would have sworn its golden eyes bore a fishy look that had nothing to do with herring or cod. *What's this crazy human doing out here in weather like this? Why isn't he back on land where he belongs?*

A big wave slapped the U-30 when the boat was already rolling to port. The crest tried to throw Lemp and the ratings on the conning tower with him into the sea. He grabbed the rail and hung on tight, spitting frigid salt water. More seawater cascaded down the hatch. Along with the U-boat's usual foul smells, volleys of foul language poured out of the hatch a moment later. The men in the pressure hull would have to get rid of the water as best they could—and fix whatever the unexpected bath had shorted out.

"*Alles gut?*" Lemp called down, rubbing at his stinging eyes.

More profanity from below made it clear that *nichts* was *gut*. The diesels didn't miss a beat, though. Whatever the sudden flood had done, it hadn't soaked the engine room.

Which turned out to be a good thing, because a rating let out a horrified squeal: "Ship dead ahead!"

Too many things were happening too fast. Lemp spun like a man suddenly hit from behind. If it was a destroyer, they were dead. No matter how alert you were, you couldn't hope to fight it out on the surface taken by surprise.

But it wasn't a warship. It was a big, rusty freighter, maybe a straggler from a convoy on the way back to England. "Hard left rudder! Emergency full power!" Lemp screamed down the hatch at the same time as the freighter's whistle blared a warning. Peter was down there. He would obey instantly. Whether instantly was fast enough to do any good . . . they'd know much too soon.

The steam whistle shrilled again. If the freighter turned with the U-30, the U-boat was sunk—literally. Sailors at the ugly old ship's bow pointed at the submarine. They were close enough to let Lemp see their open mouths and staring eyes as the U-30 and freighter slid past each other. Then one of the sailors caught sight of the U-30's wind-whipped ensign. His eyes got even wider. Lemp thought they'd bug right out of his head.

He must have figured we were Russians, the U-boat skipper realized. The freighter's captain must have thought the same thing, or he would have rammed the boat. Some English admiral—maybe even the First Sea Lord—would have pinned a medal on his chest. That wasn't going to happen now.

One of the sailors up on the conning tower asked, "Are we going to track that damned pigdog and do for him, Skipper?"

No one would have claimed Julius Lemp was not aggressive. Certainly no one from the torpedoed *Athenia* would have claimed any such thing. All the same, Lemp wasn't sorry to see the freighter vanish into mist and spray and sleet as abruptly as it had appeared.

And the more he thought about pursuing it, the less he liked the idea. "No, we'll throw this one back," he answered. "Her skipper will be dodging and zigzagging for all he's worth—and chucking every gram of coal he's got into the furnace, too. We'd only find the rustbucket by luck . . . and who knows how far away the convoy escorts are?"

None of the ratings said anything more. Lemp would have been astounded if they had. Commanding the U-boat was his job, nobody else's. Did the sailors up there with him seem unusually subdued, though? Did they think he should have gone after the freighter?

More to the point, would they, or one of them, report him for not going after the ship? Would some *Kriegsmarine* board decide he'd shown defeatism or lack of fighting spirit or whatever the hell they called it these days? Would Party *Bonzen* court-martial him on account of it, or put him on the beach?

He hated to have to think that way, which didn't mean he didn't do it. Bad things happened to politically naïve people. Then again, bad things also happened to politically pushy people—at least to the ones who didn't shoot up the ladder at top speed. You had to be aware without making the people who paid close attention to such things aware that you were aware. It could be a tightrope act.

And so, when he finally did go below, he logged the incident in the most particular detail, noting every detail of bad weather and dreadful visibility. That might—likely would—save his bacon if he had to try to explain himself to the *Kriegsmarine*.

But if he had to explain himself to the SS? He grimaced. The black-shirts listened when they felt like it. When they didn't, they went ahead and did whatever they would have done anyhow.

In his tiny cabin—separated from the rest of the boat by a curtain, which made him the only man aboard to enjoy (if that was the word) so much privacy—he listened to what was going on around him. No cries warning of other ships came from the watchstanders on the conning tower. That was his biggest, most immediate worry. Everything else sounded pretty much normal, too, which came as a relief. If the ratings who had a brief from one security service or another to spy on him were plotting with one another, they were doing it where he couldn't hear, and they weren't doing it where they were disturbing the rest of the crew.

Nice of them, Lemp thought. He hadn't fretted about security men when the war started. In those innocent days, he'd only cared about fighting the enemy. He wished things were still so simple now.

HIDEKI FUJITA HAD been through the fringes of a couple of typhoons in Japan. Till he got to Burma, he'd thought that meant he knew something about rain. Now he had to admit he'd been nothing but an amateur.

In the monsoon, water poured down by the warm bucketload. You could stand outside naked and wash off. Men did, whenever they felt the need. What you couldn't do was dry off again afterwards. Water dripped through thatched roofs and pounded off galvanized iron. Even when the soldiers of Unit 113 weren't being deluged, the stifling humidity made sweat stick to them so they felt as if they were.

Quite a few soldiers wore nothing but loincloth and zoris in the rain. Before long, Fujita was one of them. Leaving on a uniform, even a tropical-weight uniform, only ensured it would rot faster. It would rot anyway, but you could make things take longer.

Despite the ghastly weather, the war went on. Now that Japan was fighting England in Asia, the English suddenly were doing everything they could to help China keep the Emperor's forces busy. Supplies came from India to Yunnan Province in southern China by road and by air. They were no more than a trickle, but a trickle that annoyed the Japanese.

Occupying the Chinese end of the supply line was impossible. The Empire was stretched too thin. She didn't have enough soldiers, and too many of Chiang Kai-shek's troops stood in the way. Making it hard for the Chinese to collect the supplies or do much with them . . . That was a different story.

And that was the kind of thing Unit 113 could help with. Fujita helped load porcelain bomb casings full of cholera bacilli and rodents infected with plague. Whenever bombers could take off, they carried the germ bombs over the mountains into China. The town of Baoshan, in western Yunnan, was a special target because of the rail lines to Kunming, the provincial capital, that ran through it.

Before long, reports came back that Baoshan was suffering from disease outbreaks. That was the signal for more bombers to attack the place. These carried ordinary high explosives and incendiaries. Hideki Fujita didn't think Baoshan would burn very well if it was as wet up there as it was down here, but—surprise!—none of his superiors asked for his opinion.

Some of what they did worked, even if Fujita couldn't find out exactly which part. They wanted the people who lived in Baoshan to flee from the town and spread sickness through the Chinese countryside. Japanese soldiers monitoring radio signals from Yunnan reported that Unit 113's officers were getting what they wanted.

They were so pleased by their results, they gathered the unit's enlisted men together so they could brag about what they'd accomplished. A major named Hataba stood on a table to let everyone see him. "It is now established that Chinese forces have had to evacuate Yunnan Province," he declared. "They take sickness with them wherever they go. And they cannot gather the goods England tries to give them."

A sergeant standing by Fujita clapped his hands. "Good!" he said. "That's good! That's very good!"

"*Hai!* Very good!" Fujita agreed. He really did think it was. But he would have agreed even if he'd thought it was a disaster. Now that he'd been demoted to corporal, he'd quickly relearned the necessary art of sucking up to sergeants. They'd make you sorry if you didn't, and you couldn't do anything about it. All you could do was grease them up and try to keep them happy.

The sergeant's noise and his own servile reply made Fujita miss a little of what Major Hataba was saying. When he could pay attention again without the risk of getting thumped, what he heard was, "—not just in China. Our illustrious unit, and others working on related projects, can punish the English in India the same way. Everyone knows India has been full of disease since the beginning of time. It's even filthier and more backward than China. Who there would realize why an epidemic started where the English were loading up their goods to send them on to the Chinese bandits?"

He paused, waiting expectantly for an answer. The assembled soldiers gave him the one he wanted: "Nobody, Major-*san!*"

"Nobody. That's right." Up on his rickety table, Hataba nodded. "I am obtaining the authorization we will need to give the English and the Indians everything they deserve. And we will!"

"*Hai!*" the soldiers shouted, and, "*Banzai!*"

One hot, wet, sticky day followed another. No planes from Unit 113 dropped disease bombs on India, though the attacks against China continued. Fujita was less surprised than some of the men he worked with when Major Hataba's sought-for authorization proved slow in coming. Up in Manchukuo, Unit 731 had always worked in the darkest secrecy. Why wouldn't it be the same for the germ-warfare units down here?

And even if the Chinese figured out what Japan was doing to them, well, who cared about the fuss Chinamen kicked up? They sounded like a bunch of hysterical geese when they got excited. It would be different if England realized the Japanese were waging germ warfare against her. When England said something, the whole world listened.

England might not just talk, either. She might hit back. China hadn't a prayer of matching Japan's science. But England was one of the places from which Japan had learned science to begin with.

What kind of bacteriological-warfare program did England have? Fujita had no idea. Did his superiors know? All he could do was hope so.

Whether they knew or not, his superiors—or rather, his superiors' superiors—refused to issue the order Major Hataba craved. Perhaps they feared to break secrecy. Or perhaps they just weren't inclined to take any chances they didn't have to.

Gradually, the men in Unit 113 quit talking about India. They pretended no one had ever said anything about it. Had they done otherwise, Major Hataba would have lost face. If that happened to an officer, what could he do but make everybody who served under him sorry?

Fujita settled in. Myitkyina had a military brothel staffed by Burmese comfort women the Japanese had recruited—or just grabbed. The one Fujita mounted started crying as soon as he finished and got off her. He didn't care. Why should he? He was happy. And a comfort woman was only a convenience, like a rubber rain cape.

The day after he got back from his leave in Myitkyina, Major Hataba summoned him. Ignoring his hangover, he stood at stiff attention and saluted like a machine. "Reporting as ordered, sir!" he said, wondering how much trouble he was in and whether he could wiggle out of it.

But the major wasn't in a mood to pull the wings off flies. He said, "At ease, Corporal." Fujita relaxed . . . fractionally. Hataba went on, "You're a good man. I'm glad to have you here. The people at Unit 731 were stupid to let you go, if you want to know what I think. You're wasted as a corporal. I'm making you a sergeant—let's see how you do."

He handed Fujita two silver metal stars—one for each collar tab. "Put these on. You'll help us more with two stars on each tab than with one."

"*Domo arigato,* Major-*san!*" Fujita bowed low, grateful inferior to superior. The joy he felt at getting his rank back made coming inside the unhappy Burmese comfort woman seem as nothing beside it.

"You're welcome, Sergeant. And you're dismissed." Major Hataba might promote him, but he wasn't about to waste a whole lot of time on him.

So what? Fujita bowed again, almost as deeply. He didn't think his feet touched the ground as he left the major's presence. As soon as he could, he affixed the new stars to the red tabs with the yellow stripe across the middle. The tabs looked so much better now that they had their second stars back! He thought so, anyhow.

People noticed when he walked around the little base. "Congratulations, Sergeant-*san!*" a private said, and gave him a cigarette and a light. Even as a corporal, he could have knocked a private around. But a sergeant could do it with more flair. A sergeant could do anything with more flair. And all the corporals who'd been senior to him would need to watch themselves from here on out!

Chapter 22

When you came out of the line here, you couldn't toddle off to an *estaminet* to soak up some wine and chat up the barmaid. This was war without distractions, and Alistair Walsh missed them.

Even the Italians weren't much of a distraction. That was the only good part of the fighting here. As Sergeant Billings had said, some of their units weren't too bad. Most, though, didn't really have their hearts in the fight. When English forces outmaneuvered them, they would surrender with smiles on their faces. It happened again and again, because the English had more tanks and far more lorries than Mussolini's boys.

"You have to understand, sir, it doesn't work this way all the time," Walsh told Lieutenant Preston when another band of Italians waved white flags after the briefest exchange of fire. "For those dagos, it's nothing but a game. You come up against Fritz, though, and you'll find out he means it."

The subaltern nodded, with luck in wisdom. "Quite," he said. "It is a bit like playing football when the other side's down to nine men, isn't it? Hardly seems sporting."

"Bugger sporting . . . sir," Walsh said earnestly. "You lose men here, they don't get up again after the referee blows his bleeding whistle. It'll take the Judgment Trump to set 'em on their pins again."

Wilf Preston stared at him. The youngster's eyes were blue as sapphires. They were also red-tracked with weariness, just like Walsh's. Sun and wind and sand had burned and chapped Preston's fine, fair skin. "I do grasp the difference, Sergeant," he said, his voice starchy with indignation.

Devil you do. But Walsh couldn't say that. "Yes, sir" would have to do.

"Besides," Preston went on, "wouldn't you sooner have it easy than rough?"

Maybe he wasn't a complete twit. Walsh sketched a salute. "Now that you mention it, sir," he answered, "yes."

Only later did he wonder how true that was. Had he asked Ronald Cartland to stay in England and help turn young hooligans into proper soldiers, the MP would have arranged that as effortlessly as he'd seen to this. And Walsh would have done something useful to King and country, something where he could have lived comfortably and where he would have been most unlikely to catch a packet.

Instead, he'd requested service here, and here he was. A fat black fly landed on the back of his hand. He squashed it before it could bite him. It had a nasty smell, like shit mixed with blood. And you couldn't kill them all. There were just too many. Beelzebub—lord of the flies. He'd had the Bible pounded into him when he was a boy, same as most Welshmen. Till this campaign, though, he'd never realized what a dark and terrible god old Beelzebub must have been.

Lieutenant Preston wasn't immune to the flies, either. Could you bring the bugs up on charges? *Officers, disrespect to*—something like that? Preston didn't try to smash his flies. He just waved his hands over them so they buzzed away. That might have been a better idea. He didn't need to fret about the mess and the stink. Of course, the bloody things would come back. . . .

He still had his pecker up: "If we keep going the way we are, we'll take Tobruk away from Musso's lads before long. What will they do then?"

"They'll be in even more trouble than they are already, that's what,"

Walsh answered, liking the notion. Tobruk was the big Italian base in eastern Libya. If it fell, the enemy might have to fall back to Benghazi, or maybe all the way to Tripoli. Without it, the dagos sure as dammit wouldn't be able to mount another attack on Egypt.

They seemed to know that, too. Some of them even seemed to care. Their resistance stiffened as they pulled back into the works surrounding the Mediterranean port. No doubt about it, they were better at fighting a static campaign than one that called for movement.

And now they had ships bringing supplies straight in to them. That beat the stuffing out of the English truck convoys that started way the hell back in Alexandria. Italian tanks might be laughable, but one army's 105mm howitzer was about the same as another's. If the other buggers could bring in more ammo than you could . . .

In that case, you dug trenches and laid barbed wire in a ring around his trenches and barbed wire and you settled in as best you could, because grabbing Tobruk was liable to take a while after all. But for the weather and the scenery, it might have been 1918 over again.

In 1918, biplanes had dueled above the trenches. And so they did again here in 1941. RAF Gloster Gladiators fought Fiat CR-42s high overhead. Planes and pilots seemed evenly matched. When one side or the other won a dogfight, a cheer went up from its troops on the ground.

These days, pilots wore parachutes. They mostly hadn't in 1918. God, what a long, hard way down! Every time Walsh saw a silk canopy blossom in the sky, he remembered Rudolf Hess bailing out of his Bf-110 over Scotland. What a mess that had made! Not for the first time, Walsh thought, *I should have bashed his brains in with a rock.*

Both RAF flyers and their Italian foes were sporting. When a pilot hit the silk, they didn't machine-gun him while he floated helplessly. The same courtesy had been observed most of the time in Western Europe. From things Walsh had heard, the Russians and the Japanese didn't play by those rules. Neither did the Fritzes in Russia. Fair play? *Verboten!*

Italian bombers sometimes came over the English lines by night. They weren't very accurate—they cost the Tommies more in lost sleep than in damage or casualties.

Little by little, the besiegers assembled a striking column to try to break through the Italian lines. The Italians had to defend everywhere, so they spread themselves thin. Without tanks, an attack on their position would have been suicidal (remembering 1918, Walsh knew that might not have stopped the donkeys with the red collar tabs from ordering one anyway). With tanks, a breakthrough had a chance. That was one of the things tanks were for: punching holes in positions too tough for infantry to crack by itself.

The Italians didn't do much to hinder the English concentration. Walsh got the idea that, like a tortoise bothered by a dog, they weren't going to stick their heads out of their fortified shell unless and until they had to. The English generals must have got the same idea, because they took their own sweet time readying their attack.

As things turned out, they waited too long. Walsh's regiment wasn't in the main striking column. It went to a smaller one that would deliver a feint to make the Italians commit their reserves to the wrong part of the semicircle around Tobruk.

Just after dawn two days before the feint was supposed to go in, he heard unfamiliar engine noises in the air. Then, all of a sudden, they weren't the least bit unfamiliar—only unexpected and out of place, which, unfortunately, wasn't the same thing.

He grabbed Lieutenant Preston's arm. "Sir—that's the bloody *Luftwaffe*—109s and Stukas, heading this way!"

"What? You're daft!" the subaltern exclaimed . . . perhaps five seconds before the Messerschmitts started strafing the feinting column. A few seconds after *that,* Stukas dove down out of the sky like ugly falcons, their Jericho Trumpets screaming fit to jolt a man's soul right out of his body. And in case the Jericho Trumpets fell down on the job, 500kg bombs weren't half bad for spreading terror around, either.

Walsh dove under a lorry—the best cover he could find. He would roll out to fire a shot or two at the planes overhead, then duck back again. Those weren't Italian pilots flying German planes. Black crosses and swastikas declared who was at the controls. For reasons of his own, Hitler had decided to jump into the war in Africa.

With both feet, too—manmade thunder off to the east said the real striking column was catching hell, too. Tobruk might fall, but it sure as the devil wouldn't fall day after tomorrow.

RAIN IN RUSSIA meant panzers went nowhere fast. Theo Hossbach knew that as well as any German soldier in the USSR. With the wider *Ost-ketten*, his Panzer III was less likely to bog down, but swift thrusts and dashes were a thing of the past.

The Ivans slowed down in the mud, too. Their ponderous KV-1s had as much trouble with it as any German panzer. T-34s, though, chugged through goop Theo wouldn't have wanted to try even with *Ostketten*. Adi was right—the T-34 wasn't a perfect panzer. But it was kilometers out in front of whichever machine ran second.

And so, for the time being the *Wehrmacht* would try to hang on to what it had already gained instead of pushing deeper into Russia. Maybe, once a hard freeze came, the *Panzertruppen* could have another go at Smolensk. In the meantime, units settled down in villages and on collective farms to wait out the mud time.

A couple of platoons from Theo's company based themselves on a *kolkhoz* southwest of Smolensk. A few of the buildings remained more or less in one piece. The Ivans who'd fled the farm had slaughtered some of their livestock and driven the rest with them when they headed east. Hitler planned on turning European Russia into Germany's breadbas-ket. No one in the *Reich* had seemed to realize Stalin would have plans of his own. The Germans might gain ground, but they'd draw as little benefit from it as the Russians could manage.

Like any sergeant worth the paper he was printed on, Hermann Witt believed idle hands were the Devil's playground. "If our panzer isn't going anywhere for a while, then by God we'll make sure it goes like anything when we do start moving again," he declared.

Theo wasn't the only one who had no trouble containing his enthu-siasm. "What? Stand in the rain and sink into the mud while we screw around with the engine?" Adi Stoss said.

"In a word, yes," Witt answered. "Do you think I won't be there with you, passing you spanners and pliers and fan belts and whatever else you happen to need? I'll be messing with the ironmongery, too, you know."

Adi nodded—reluctantly, but he did. So did Theo. Sergeant Witt was not a man to stay dry where his crew got wet, nor a man to stay clean where they got dirty. He made a good panzer commander, in other words. That didn't mean he couldn't be a pain in the fundament.

The new guys were no more enamored of busting their humps in the rain and the ooze than the crew's old-timers. "If I had a pretty girl there with me, now, not some hairy, smelly old sergeant—" Kurt Poske said.

"You'd come down venereal in about a minute flat," Witt broke in.

Affronted, Poske shook his head. "I can last a lot longer than that."

Once they got the bitching out of their systems, they fell to work. They tore down the engine, rain or no rain, mud or no mud. They bore-sighted both machine guns. Lothar Eckhardt calibrated and adjusted the sights for the main armament. They checked every link of their tracks, and got the track tension left and right to just where Sergeant Witt and Adi wanted it.

And Theo serviced his radio set. It still worked all right, but a couple of the tubes plainly wouldn't last much longer. He swapped in a spare for one, but couldn't match the second. To his annoyance, none of the other half-dozen radiomen at the *kolkhoz* had—or would admit to having—that tube, either. He'd gone and talked to all those relative strangers, and they hadn't been able to help him? It hardly seemed fair.

Unhappily, he reported his difficulty to Sergeant Witt. Witt rubbed his chin, considering. "How long will the old one last?" he asked.

Theo shrugged. "A day? Six months?" He shrugged again. As usual, he talked as if he had to pay for each word expended.

"All right. Next time a *Kettenrad* comes along, hop a ride back to regimental HQ and snag a new one," Witt said. "Snag more than one, if you can. Maybe we can swap some of the spares for other stuff we need."

Muttering didn't count as words. Neither did Theo's resigned sigh. Most of the men at regimental headquarters were real strangers, not the relative kind. He would rather have tackled a T-34 with a Panzer II than have anything to do with them, no matter how much sense Witt's order made.

Two days later, a *Kettenrad*—a motorcycle with a track instead of a rear wheel—brought mail up to the *kolkhoz*. When it started back, Theo sat in the sidecar. He carried his Schmeisser. You never could be sure the *Wehrmacht* had cleared out all the Indians (the common German name for enemy soldiers).

He didn't have to use the machine pistol on the way to the village the regimental bigwigs had taken as their own. *Babushkas* cooked for the headquarters staff. Old men with Tolstoyan beards cut their firewood. Younger women probably served them other ways.

Theo didn't have to ask questions to find the machine shop. Following his ears toward a smithy's clangor got him there. He stood and waited to be noticed. Eventually, one of the mechanics asked, "Well, what do you need?" He held out the failing tube. The mechanic turned and yelled, "Hey, Helmut! Here's a guy for you!"

The bespectacled Helmut plainly cared more about radio sets and their parts than about his fellow human beings. Theo got on fine with him, in other words. And he had and could spare four tubes of the model Theo needed. Theo stowed them in his greatcoat pockets.

He wondered how he'd get back to the *kolkhoz*. Witt hadn't said anything about that. He was walking up the village's muddy main street (all the other streets were muddy, too) when someone called, "Hey! Yeah, you—the goalkeeper!"

That made Theo stop. He turned. At first, he didn't recognize the *Landser* coming toward him. Then, to his dismay, he did. It was the fellow who claimed he'd seen Adi play football before the war. Theo would rather have met up with a Russian ambush.

"How are you doing?" the guy asked, as if they were old friends. Theo doled out a shrug. He didn't want to talk to this fellow, who was nothing but trouble—and worse trouble because he had no idea how much trouble he was. Sure as hell, he went on, "And how's your buddy, the footballer?"

Several possibilities ran through Theo's mind. The truth was among them, but he didn't let it bother him for long. Saying Adi'd been killed seemed better, but Mr. Snoopy here might suspect that and try to check it out. How about some play-acting instead?

With a guttural growl, Theo raised the Schmeisser and pointed it at the *Landser's* belly button. The safety was still on, but he didn't figure the other guy would notice fine details. "You fucking son of a bitch!" he ground out. "So you're the asshole who tipped him to the blackshirts, and now you're here to gloat? I ought to blow your balls off—if you've got any."

The guy in *Feldgrau* went whiter than skim milk. "N—N—N—" He couldn't manage a *"Nein!"* till the fourth try. Desperately, he went on, "I didn't do that! I *wouldn't* do that! I'm no rat! On my mother's name, I swear it."

What Theo said about his mother would have got him murdered if he weren't the one holding the machine pistol. "And that's bullshit, too," he added.

"It isn't! Honest to God, will you listen to me?" the *Landser* said. "That time after the game, I just wanted to say how good he was. How was I supposed to know he'd get his long johns in a twist?" That was what Theo thought he said, anyhow. To a man from Breslau, the other guy's broad Bavarian dialect came within shouting distance of being a foreign language.

"*Somebody* reported him. You sure looked like a good bet." Theo let his synthetic anger cool. He lowered the Schmeisser—a little. "Why don't you just fuck off? I still don't trust you. And if I ever see you again, you'll wish I hadn't."

Gabbling thanks and apologies and who knows what, the other fellow beat it. Theo spotted another *Kettenrad*. He'd *been* talking. A little more wouldn't hurt . . . much. Damned if he didn't get himself a lift back to the *kolkhoz*. Every once in a while, words had their uses.

And Sergeant Witt beamed when he displayed the four tubes. "There you go!" He clapped Theo on the back. "And you'll save the one that's going bad, too, right? If it isn't all the way dead, you can get a little more out of it." Theo nodded; he'd already thought of that. Witt went on, "Anything else going on at HQ?"

"Nah." With a slow smile, Theo squeezed out the one word.

HONOLULU AGAIN. Pete McGill hadn't wanted to see it. He'd hoped to see Manila once more instead. No such luck, though. The U.S. Navy would have had to win the big Pacific slugfest to make that happen. Far from winning, the great fleet the USA sent west from Hawaii had barely got to play. The planes that rose in swarms from Japanese-held islands and from Japanese carriers didn't give the American ships the chance to close with the Imperial Navy's battlewagons.

Wildcats buzzed above Pearl Harbor now. Like the Jap-occupied islands farther west, Hawaii made an enormous, unsinkable aircraft carrier. If anything was going to hold the Japanese Navy away from Pearl, it would be air power.

Meanwhile, Pete and the other Marines aboard the *Boise* joined her sailors in repairing battle damage and getting her ready to go out again and do . . . well, something, anyhow. The damage wasn't anything big—metal dented and torn by near misses from Japanese bombs. The light cruiser hadn't been a major enemy target. No light cruiser would storm into Tokyo Bay or anything like that. Sensibly, the Japs had gone after the American ships that could do them the most harm.

More planes—fighters, bombers, reconnaissance—came into Hawaii almost every day by ship. So did more tanks, more soldiers, and more everything else. If the United States had to fight Japan starting from San Diego and San Francisco and Seattle, the war would be far longer and harder—if it could be won at all.

But no new Japanese attack on Pearl Harbor came. Word got back that planes from Japanese carriers were helping to bombard Singapore. Besieged and isolated, the British bastion at the southern tip of Malaya seemed likely to fall. Everything else from Guam to the border between Burma and India already had.

"I bet the Aussies are sweating bullets," Joe Orsatti remarked as he and Pete lugged five-inch ammo aboard the *Boise*. The light cruiser had replenished at sea from the *Lassen*—ammunition ships, fittingly enough, were named for volcanoes—but she'd shot off almost all of what she'd taken aboard then. Her main armament, by contrast, hadn't fired a shot.

"I bet you're right. I sure would be, anyway," Pete said. His leg and his shoulder still pained him when he worked hard. He wondered if they always would. Every time something in either place twinged, he thought of Vera. If the aches lasted the rest of his life, so would his memories of their time together in Shanghai.

"Gettin' more stuff through to them, it's like running the gantlet," Orsatti said. He set a wooden case that held two shells down on the deck.

With a grunt of relief, Pete laid his burden down, too. Something in his back clicked when he straightened. That had nothing to do with his injuries, or he didn't think it did. It simply came from hard work.

As other leathernecks knocked the casings apart and stowed the shells, he said, "You're right twice running. You ought to quit while you're ahead."

"Funny. Funny like a dose of the clap," Orsatti said.

"I ain't seen your mother lately," Pete retorted. Orsatti flipped him the bird while they walked down the gangplank to pick up more shells. Neither man hurried. The job would get done, but it didn't have to get done right away. The *Boise* wasn't heading into action again any time soon. Pete went on, "We've got to try it, though. They're screwed if we don't."

"Yeah, I guess." Orsatti picked up another two-shell case: a hundred pounds of brass and explosives, plus the weight of the wood. He lugged it back toward the cruiser.

Pete did the same. His shoulder and his leg really complained. He didn't listen to them. He could do the work. He'd proved that aboard the *Boise*. If he hurt, he hurt, that was all. He had a bottle of aspirins he'd bummed off a pharmacist's mate in sick bay. When he got especially sore, he took a couple. Sometimes he thought they helped. Sometimes they didn't seem to do anything.

After he set down his next crate, he said, "We could use some liberty, you know?"

"What? You'd rather drink and fuck than haul shit around like a draft horse? What kind of Marine are you, anyhow?" Orsatti demanded in mock anger.

"One with my head on straight, that's what," Pete answered.

"They don't pay you to drink and fuck," the other sergeant pointed out.

"They don't pay me enough to do this shit all the goddamn time when I'm in Pearl," McGill said. "When I'm on board ship, okay, fine. I'm stuck there. I ain't stuck here—except I need a pass."

"People in hell need mint juleps to drink," Orsatti told him. "You had all that soft China duty, where you could eat like a pig and screw like a lord. You aren't in a good place to piss and moan, you know?"

Pete shut up. China duty *was* soft, especially to somebody who'd spent most of his time in the Corps on one ship or another. Servants, good food all the time, cheap whorehouses—what more could a Marine want? But when it went bad, it went as bad as it could. He wondered how many of the leathernecks he'd served with in Peking and Shanghai were still alive. He hoped they'd made the Japs pay a high price for bagging them.

A few days later, he did snag a pass into Honolulu. He got drunk, he went to Hotel Street, and he got laid. Then he drank some more and got laid again. In the course of drinking more still, he knocked an Army sergeant cold with a left to the belly and a right to the jaw. He walked out of that joint before the Shore Patrol showed up, leaving the Army three-striper on the floor. The jerk would be sadder when he woke up, but probably no wiser.

He made it back to the *Boise* on time. Next morning, it was black coffee and some of those aspirins. He hardly remembered coldcocking the Army guy. Nor was he the only man just back from liberty who seemed a little the worse for wear.

For his sins, the *Boise* steamed out into the Pacific later that day for live-fire exercises with towed targets. Aspirins or no aspirins, when the guns started going off he thought his head would explode with them. Before long, he hoped it would.

The other guys at the gun razzed him every time he flinched. Since he flinched a lot, he got several weeks' worth of razzing all in the space of a few hours. "Hangovers and big booms don't mix," Joe Orsatti observed.

"Thank you, Albert Einstein," Pete replied. After a moment, he added, "Fuck you, Albert Einstein."

His jimjams didn't keep him from passing shells to the loader when planes brought targets overhead. If slow-moving strips of orange cloth had dive-bombed the *Boise*, the Marines at her secondary armament would have blown them out of the sky.

A Navy lieutenant warned, "Keep an eyeball peeled for submarines. We aren't within safe waters."

He outranked the leathernecks—a two-striper was the equivalent of a Marine Corps captain. So they couldn't say much while he was in earshot. Once he'd gone . . . That was a different story.

"What? He thinks we're too dumb to look if he don't tell us to?" Orsatti groused.

"He must figure we're like ordinary swabbies," Pete put in. That got some laughs. Marines were convinced sailors were idiots in training to be morons. Of course, it worked both ways, which was one of the reasons sailors and Marines from the same ship sometimes brawled when they got liberty at the same time.

One of the other guys in the gun crew just said, "Whistleass peckerhead." That summed things up as well as any other two words Pete could have thought of.

No one saw a periscope, or even imagined he saw a periscope. The hydrophones didn't report any contacts. There was talk that the *Boise* would get a fancy new version as part of her refit. Sonar was the name Pete had heard. He didn't know much about it, but he was in favor of anything that would help keep them from stopping a torpedo.

They made it back to Pearl undamaged. That young lieutenant seemed convinced they got back for no other reason than his own enormous heroism. The leathernecks laughed behind their hands. Otherwise, they kept their opinions to themselves.

IVAN KUCHKOV HATED squelching through the mud. He hadn't had to do that when he was in the Red Air Force, or not nearly so much of it, anyhow. But his only other choices were falling behind and letting the Nazis capture him (a bad bet) or getting wounded or killed (a worse one). So squelch he did.

Ukrainian mud seemed particularly oozy and bottomless, too. Everybody said Ukrainian soil—the famous black earth—was fertile beyond compare. He supposed that was so: this country was all *kolkhozes*. But, when the *rasputitsa* came, the black earth also turned goopy beyond compare.

"Avram!" Ivan called. Then he raised his voice to yell "Avram!" again, louder this time. The point man was well out ahead of the section, the way he was supposed to be.

He stopped when he finally heard Kuchkov. "What do you need, Comrade Sergeant?" he shouted back. He could afford to make some noise, as Ivan could; no Germans were in the neighborhood. Or if the Germans were, things were even more fouled up than the brass wanted to admit. Kuchkov guessed—no, on second thought he was sure—that was possible, maybe even likely.

He slogged forward through the muck to catch up to Sasha Davidov. If there were Fascists around, he didn't want to call the point man back. Then the whole section might run into them without warning. That *he* might run into them without warning occurred to him only when he'd almost reached the Jew. He hung on to his PPD-34 a little tighter once it did.

And the first question out of his mouth was, "Any fucking sign of the pricks?"

Avram shook his head. "Not around here, Sergeant." He pointed ahead. "Once we get over that swell of ground, we'll be able to see farther. Of course, if there are any Germans on the far side of it, they're liable to spot us, too."

Ivan grunted. Normally, he would have had no more use for a skinny, swarthy little kike than any other Russian of peasant stock did. But times weren't normal—not even a little bit. The game had changed as soon as the USSR and the Nazis actually came to grips. Some Russians and more Ukrainians and people from the Caucasus liked Hitler better than Stalin. They'd desert if they got the chance. Not even the *politruks* could stop them all the time.

You didn't need to worry about the Jews, though. They were in the fight to the last bullet. They had to be. If the Nazis caught them, they'd get a bullet, all right. A Russian might be able to surrender. No guarantees, but he might. *Zhids* didn't have a prayer. The Germans casually murdered them, the same way they got rid of the political officers who fell into their hands.

Pointing to that same swell of ground, Kuchkov asked, "Can you haul your sorry ass to the top and over without letting the Fascist pussies spot you?"

Avram was no braver than he had to be. But then, people who were braver than they had to be had a way of not living long. He tossed a *papiros* into the mud—he didn't want some alert Fritz noticing the coal or the smoke. He nodded: not with any great enthusiasm, but he did. "I can do it."

"All right. You go ahead, then. But some of the clumsy cuntfaced bitches in our outfit, you know they'd trip over their dicks if they tried, right?" Ivan said. He waited for the Jew to nod again before he went on, "So I'm gonna lead our assholes around to the left. If it's clear, you fucking meet up with us there. Got it?"

"*Yob tvoyu mat'*, Sergeant," Davidov assured him.

Ivan burst into raucous laughter and slapped him on the back. Literally, what the Jew said meant *Fuck your mother*. In a different tone of voice or at a different time, it might have made Kuchkov try to murder him. But the filthy phrase lay at the bottom of *mat*. It could have a multitude of meanings, foul or fair. What Avram was getting across here was *You bet your ass*.

Fair enough. He was betting his own ass that he could do what he said he could do. "Go on, then," Ivan told him. "You get into trouble, I'll send some of the shitheads after you."

Davidov nodded and went on. If he got into trouble, Ivan's promise probably wouldn't do him any good. He had to know that, but he moved up anyhow. He might be a kike, but he was all right.

The rest of the section took its own sweet time catching up to Kuchkov. The men weren't fools. They could tell they were pretty safe where they were. The farther ahead they moved, the better—or rather, the worse—their chance of bumping into Nazis with guns.

Kuchkov profanely explained how they were going to skirt the swell of ground ahead. He also told half a dozen soldiers to rush to Avram's rescue if the point man's luck ran out. "You fuck that up, you better be more scared of me than you are of those German walking foreskins," he added. The soldiers nodded. Anyone who wasn't afraid of Ivan didn't know him very well.

It had been drizzling. The rain started coming down harder as he took his section where it needed to go. In a way, that was good: the Germans would have more trouble noticing them. In another, not so good: the Red Army men would have more trouble spotting the Fascists.

Avram carried a PPD-34, too. You wanted to be able to throw a lot of lead at the bad guys in a hurry if you came across them when you didn't expect to. Ivan kept his head cocked toward the top of the low hillock. He'd hear that snarl through the rain's plashing.

It didn't come. He got the rest of the section where they needed to go. Then he waited. Avram Davidov materialized as if out of thin air. "I think there are some Germans in the trees along the stream up ahead," he said.

"You sure?" Ivan asked him.

"Pretty sure, Comrade Sergeant," Davidov answered. "I don't have any field glasses, but they looked like Germans, sure as the devil."

"Bugger the cocksucking Devil," Kuchkov said. He turned to another Red Army man. "Yuri!"

"*Da*, Comrade Sergeant?"

"Go back and tell the company CO that we've bumped into the fucking Fascists. Ask him if he wants to reinforce us for a proper attack or if we should just sit tight and keep an eye on the pussies. You got me?"

"*Da*," Yuri said again, and accurately gave back what Ivan had said. Like his sergeant, he could no more read and write than he could fly. He relied on his memory in ways people who could write never did. He was also pretty good at traveling cross-country—not so good as Avram, but good enough. Off he went, at the fastest clip the mud allowed.

Ivan didn't need to order his men to start digging foxholes and camouflaging them. The soldiers automatically did that when they saw they wouldn't be moving up for a while. The foxholes here would be nasty places, and would start filling up with water soon. The men dug anyhow. If German machine guns or artillery were going to probe for them, they wanted somewhere to hide.

Yuri probably wouldn't make it back for a couple of hours. It might be dark by the time he did, which would put things off till tomorrow. Ivan didn't mind; he was in no hurry to get shot at. He just hoped the Nazis weren't readying their own onslaught. They might not need to wait hours to set up something good-sized. The bastards had radio sets falling out of their assholes.

Night came before either Yuri or a German attack. Yuri did manage to find his way back in the dark, and the jumpy sentries managed not to shoot him when he did. "Reinforcements will come up in the morning," he reported. "The captain wants us to sit tight till then."

"*Khorosho*," Ivan said. The order let him to what he already wanted to, which suited him fine.

But, as Avram discovered, the Germans reinforced under cover of darkness. The Soviet attack never went in. Instead, the Red Army pulled back another kilometer or two and tried to draw a firm line in the mud.

Chapter 23

Hans-Ulrich Rudel shivered. Snowflakes swirled through the air. His breath smoked. The ordinary *Luftwaffe* greatcoat wasn't defense enough against the Russian winter. He'd have to go back to wearing his flying togs all the time, the way he had the year before.

The *Wehrmacht* had been caught short last winter. Even the Germans' Polish allies laughed at them or, worse, pitied them because of their inadequate cold-weather gear. Nothing could embarrass German national pride worse than pity from a pack of slovenly, hard-drinking, wife-beating Poles.

Things were better this year. Proper winter clothing was reaching the *Landsers* who needed it most in something like adequate quantities. They wouldn't have to steal lousy, flea-infested sheepskin jackets from Russian peasants, the way they had before. They wouldn't have to tailor bedsheets into camouflage smocks for the snow, either. There were proper snowsuits, reversible between white and *Feldgrau*. Progress, of a sort.

But only of a sort. As a lot of invaders had discovered before Germany tried it, Russia was easy to get into. Getting out was a lot harder.

You could win victory after victory . . . and then what? The Red Army kept throwing in fresh divisions as if it manufactured them in Magnitogorsk. And there were always more kilometers of broad, flat Russian terrain ahead of the men from the *Reich*.

Nobody talked much about having a bear by the ears. Get labeled a defeatist and you'd soon envy men who'd only been captured by the Ivans. Hans-Ulrich was sure, though, that if he'd started having doubts about what Germany could hope to accomplish here, other people had worse ones and had had them longer. He was automatically loyal to the *Reich*, to the Party, and to the *Führer*. Others tried to separate the idea of Germany from the people actually running the country.

And there were other worries. Not long after the ground got hard enough to let them start flying again, Albert Dieselhorst sidled up to Rudel on the airstrip and spoke in a low voice: "What have you heard about the French?"

"Huh?" Hans-Ulrich blinked. "What do you mean, what have I heard about them? They eat frogs' legs and snails. They make good wine, too, though you'd care more about that than I do. What else am I supposed to know?"

His radioman and rear gunner breathed out twin gusts of exasperation through his nostrils. "In a military sense . . . sir." The military honorific plainly took the place of something more like *you donkey*.

"Well . . ." Hans-Ulrich chose his words with care, even with Dieselhorst. If he talked about the way the French had held the *Reich* out of Paris two wars in a row, he could still end up in trouble. So he stuck with the obvious: "They're holding a stretch of the line not too far south of here."

"Yes. They are." The sergeant exhaled again, not quite so extravagantly this time. "How hard are they holding it?"

"Huh?" Hans-Ulrich repeated. This time, though, he didn't stay a blockhead long. Even an innocent like him began looking for plots when the war wasn't going so well. "What? Do you think they're going to try and pull an England on us?"

"It's . . . possible." Dieselhorst seemed happier that his superior did have some kind of clue after all. "Are you ready to fly against them if we have to?"

"I'm always ready to fly against the enemies of the *Reich*," Rudel answered, now without the least hesitation.

Sergeant Dieselhorst grinned crookedly. He reached out and set a hand on Hans-Ulrich's arm. It wasn't the kind of thing a noncom was supposed to do with an officer. It was, though, the kind of thing an older man might naturally do with a younger one he liked. "There you go, sir. I should've known you'd come out with something like that."

"Well, what else do you expect me to say?" If Hans-Ulrich sounded irritable, it was only because he was. He was a falcon. Fly him at something, and he'd kill it for you. What it was didn't matter, as long as you wanted it dead. He didn't think of himself in those terms, of course. But then, chances were a true winged, taloned falcon didn't think of itself in those terms, either.

"Not a thing, sir. Not a goddamn thing." Dieselhorst paused, perhaps wondering whether to go on. After a few seconds, he did: "If the froggies screw us over, we've got a two-front war for real."

"God forbid!" Rudel burst out. That had been the nightmare in the last fight, one that Germany hadn't had to face this time around. If she did . . . Well, the war got harder.

"God won't forbid it. God doesn't work that way." Dieselhorst spoke about God with as much assurance and conviction as Hans-Ulrich's father ever had. He went on, "People are going to have to take care of it. One way or another, it'll be people. It always is."

He sketched a salute and ambled off. No one, not even a National Socialist Loyalty Officer, could have made anything of the conversation if he didn't overhear it. They'd been flying together since the start of the war: more than three years now. Of course they'd have things to talk about.

If France went bad, the *Luftwaffe* would have to fight back out of Germany itself. Well, out of the Low Countries, too. But all that seemed small consolation for so much fighting, so much treasure, so much blood. And if France let England back onto the Continent while the war against the Russians ground on . . . That could be very bad. Hans-Ulrich didn't need to be a General Staff officer to see as much.

Two days later, he got up the nerve to ask Colonel Steinbrenner, "Sir, just how loyal are the French?"

The squadron commander blinked. *"Et tu, Brute?"* he said.

"Sir?" He might as well have been speaking Latin. After a moment, Hans-Ulrich realized he was.

Sighing, Steinbrenner dropped back into plain old *Deutsch:* "So you've heard the rumors, too, have you?"

Rudel also realized that, if he had, odds were everybody else in the squadron had been buzzing about them this past fortnight, or maybe longer. *There* was an encouraging thought. Not even winning the Knight's Cross had made him less of a white crow. "Yes, sir. I've heard them," he mumbled.

"Well, now that you have, you know as much as I do," Steinbrenner said. "If they turn out to be true, we've got some new troubles. If they don't, we've got our old lot. Any *other* questions?"

What came out of Hans-Ulrich's mouth then surprised him: "Can I get a little bit of leave, sir? Long enough to go back to Bialystok? If things turn bad, I'd like to have the chance to say good-bye to Sofia."

"You know, you ask so few favors, it makes me nervous sometimes," Steinbrenner said. "Yes, I'll give you leave. What you do with it is your business, not mine. Enjoy yourself, though."

"Thank you very much, sir!" Hans-Ulrich stiffened to attention and saluted. Colonel Steinbrenner's answer was more a wave than a salute, but that was a superior's privilege.

Three days later, Hans-Ulrich was back in Poland. It was snowing in Bialystok, too. He didn't feel so cold there, though. The tavern where Sofia worked wasn't far from the train station. German and Polish soldiers crowded the place, drinking as if they didn't want to think about tomorrow—and they probably didn't.

The bartender stuck his head into the back room and shouted something in Polish that had Sofia's name in it. She came out a moment later, trim and neat as always. The bartender pointed toward Hans-Ulrich, who sat at a small table against the wall.

She walked over to him. "You again. So they haven't shot you down yet?"

"As a matter of fact, they did, but I managed to bail out," he answered, which sobered her. He went on, "Bring me a coffee, will you?"

"You'll make us rich!" she exclaimed, snippy as ever. Her pleated skirt swished around her legs as she went off to get it.

When she set it—almost slammed it—down on the tabletop, Hans-Ulrich said, "I don't know how much longer I'll be able to keep coming back here. We're liable to get transferred." He didn't say anything about the possibility of flying from Germany again. Let her think he was going to the Ukraine or something. He assumed she was no spy, but he took no chances.

He waited for one of her patented zingers to come back at him. She surprised him by gnawing at her lower lip and not saying anything for a little while. Finally, she murmured, "Well, it was fun while it lasted, wasn't it?"

"It's not over yet," he said quickly.

"You want to lay me some more, you mean." That sounded like her, all right.

He quirked an eyebrow. "You'd be amazed."

"It's been more fun than I ever figured it could be, so maybe you'll get another chance," she said. "Maybe—if you wait like a good boy till I come off my shift."

He clasped his hands on the table in front of him, as if he were eight years old and sitting at a school desk. Laughing, Sofia swirled away again.

CARLOS FEDERICO WEINBERG YOWLED lustily in Chaim's arms. The baby had La Martellita's blue-black hair—a startling amount of it, when so many little tiny guys were bald. Telling who newborn babies looked like was a mug's game—they mostly looked squashed. Chaim hoped this one would end up taking after its mother.

Carlos screwed up his face and started to cry. "Hey, I'm not *that* ugly," Chaim said, first in English and then in Spanish.

La Martellita rolled her eyes. She hardly ever thought his jokes were funny. "Give him to me. He's hungry," she said. "When he cries like that, that's what he means."

Chaim handed her his son. She handled the baby with practiced efficiency, where he was as careful as if he were taking a detonator out of a land mine. As soon as he settled Carlos in the crook of her left arm, she unbuttoned her blouse and gave the baby her breast.

She saw Chaim eyeing her. He could no more help it than he could help breathing. "They're for this, too. They were for this before they were for men to stare at," she said pointedly.

"I guess so." Chaim didn't want to argue with her. He just wanted to keep looking. Were women's tits really for milking before they were for ogling? If men didn't admire them and grab them and lick them and suck at them, how many babies would get born to nurse from them? Not many, by God!

It was like the chicken and the egg, only a hell of a lot more fun to think about. If he brought it back to the Abe Lincolns, they'd argue about it for days, if not for weeks. It was more interesting than what the lousy Nationalists were liable to try next, no two ways about it.

Deftly, La Martellita switched Carlos from one side to the other. He ate like a pig. If he didn't know when he had a good thing going, he was no son of Chaim's. When she put him up on her shoulder and patted his back, he belched as if he'd been drinking Coca-Cola instead of milk.

She reached a finger inside his diaper. "Wet again," she said resignedly, and set about fixing that. Chaim would have been afraid he'd stick the kid with a pin. La Martellita wasn't, and she didn't.

Carlos wasn't circumcised. Chaim had never seen a Spaniard who was. He felt a pang of tradition flouted. Jews had had that covenant with God for thousands of years. Never mind that the top of Chaim's mind made a point of not believing in God. He felt the pang even so.

He didn't say anything about it. If he were going to take Carlos and La Martellita back to the States, he might have. But they'd stay in Spain. Carlos would have to fit in as best he could. A funny-looking cock wouldn't help.

He tried something less likely to cause trouble: "Thanks for letting me visit you. Thanks for letting me see my son." Technically, they remained man and wife. She hadn't divorced him yet. Having a baby probably kept you too busy to worry about something you could take care of any old time. He knew too well the writing was on the wall.

She nodded as she started rocking Carlos in her arms. The baby's yawn showed off pink, toothless gums. His little crib only cramped her tiny flat even more.

"It's all right," she said. "You aren't the best Communist ever, but it's not like you'd go over to the other side."

She really did think that way. Not whether he was a good guy, not whether he'd make a good father, but how good a Communist he was. Chaim admired such dedication without sharing it. He would have wanted to jump on her adorably padded bones if she were Marshal Sanjurjo's mistress. Hell, he would have wanted to jump on her bones if she headed up Sanjurjo's General Staff.

She hummed a lullaby to ease Carlos down into sleep. Chaim thought the tune sounded oddly familiar. Was it one American mothers used, too? Then he recognized it and started to laugh.

"*Now* what?" La Martellita asked after making sure his silly noises hadn't bothered the baby.

"Nothing—I suppose. But how many kids go nighty-night to the *Internationale?*"

"And why shouldn't he?" La Martellita would have bristled more, but she was easing Carlos down into the crib. He made a little noise as she slid her arm free, but only a little one. Then he kind of sighed and went on sleeping.

"No reason at all," Chaim said. "It did surprise me, though."

A soft answer turned away wrath. Sometimes. When La Martellita didn't feel the overwhelming urge to rip somebody a new asshole. Chaim braced himself for *tsuris*. It didn't come. Instead, La Martellita sat down on the edge of the narrow bed where Carlos had got started. A sigh whistled out of her. "You have no idea how tired I am," she said.

Actually, Chaim thought he did. La Martellita had done a lot for the Republic and the revolution, but he didn't believe she'd ever fought in the line. When you spent most of a week on a couple of hours' worth of snatched catnaps . . . Some battles petered out just because both sides got too goddamn exhausted to keep going any more.

But if, for once, she didn't feel like squabbling, Chaim wouldn't go out of his way to provoke her. All he said was, "I know raising kids isn't easy."

La Martellita nodded. "It would be harder still if I'd had to invent a last name for Carlos, or if he had to do without one."

"I'm glad to give him mine," Chaim said, fearing he knew what was coming next.

"I'll bet you are." La Martellita smiled cynically. "You got the fun that goes along with being married."

Got. Past tense. Chaim's Spanish wasn't perfect—nowhere close—but he understood that, all right. He felt as if he were defending the Ebro again, back in the days before England and France went to war with Germany. Not much hope, but he was damned if he'd retreat. "Bits of it," he said, "when I could come back into Madrid. And if you didn't have some fun with me, you ought to be in the movies, on account of you sure acted like it."

She flushed. He'd managed to hit a nerve, even if that was all he'd managed. "There were . . . moments," she admitted.

"There could be more." Chaim wanted like anything to sound debonair and suave. He had the bad feeling he seemed horny and desperate instead. Well, he was—both.

"No. It's over." La Martellita, by contrast, sounded altogether sure of herself. When didn't she, dammit? "I have gone to the Palace of Justice to register the dissolution of our marriage."

In the Republic, that was all you needed to do. Very simple. Very clean. Very civilized. "Aw, shit," Chaim said in English. He'd known all along it was coming. That should have made it easier when it got here. Somehow, it didn't. La Martellita didn't speak English. He translated for her: "*Mierda.*"

"I don't mind if you want to keep seeing the baby," she said—she really was trying to be civilized. "But . . ." She didn't go on, or need to. If he tried to touch her again, he'd leave without his *cojones.*

"Shit," he said again. No, it didn't hurt any less. More, if anything. He got to his feet. "Take care of yourself, *querida.* You could do worse than me." He couldn't help a little vinegar: "And I bet you do."

"My worry. Not yours." La Martellita looked toward the door. Out Chaim went. He headed for the bar a few blocks away, the one from which he'd taken her on the night they started Carlos. He brawled with a guy half again his size, and left him moaning and bloody on the floor. *El narigón loco*—the crazy kike—was on the loose again.

VACLAV JEZEK LISTENED to the impassioned Yiddish pouring out of the American International. The Czech guessed he was getting maybe two words out of three. That was plenty to understand what was wrong with the other guy.

"Women," he said in his own slow, clumsy German when the American finally paused for breath. "Nothing better than a woman to drive a man nuts."

He hadn't cared about any one woman since he had to leave Czechoslovakia. When he got the urge, he went to a whorehouse and laid his money down. It was easy and quick. If it didn't give him everything he might have wanted . . . Well, what did? Especially in wartime?

"Man, you got that right," Chaim said. "I never thought I'd get this one to begin with. To get her and then to lose her like that—it's a bastard and a half."

"You had her for a while. That's better than not having her at all," Vaclav said.

"Is it? I fucking wonder," the American replied.

Was it? Wasn't it? Vaclav was trying for sympathy, not philosophy. He didn't know. He didn't think anybody could know. And, right now, it wasn't his worry any which way. He unbuttoned his breast pocket and pulled out a pack of cigarettes. "Here. Have one of these."

"Thanks. You're a *mensh*, you know?" Chaim had an American lighter he fueled with brandy these days. Its blue flame was almost invisible, but lit his cigarette and one for Vaclav. They smoked together, and both stashed their tiny butts in tobacco pouches—waste not, want not. Chaim went on, "That was good. Not as good as pussy, but good."

"You do what you can," Vaclav answered with a shrug.

"Yeah. And when you can't, you don't." The International reached out to touch the long barrel of Vaclav's antitank rifle. "I hope you do, pal. I hope you blow that cocksucker Sanjurjo's head from here to Bilbao, you know?"

"You do what you can," Jezek repeated. People kept telling him to finish off the Nationalist leader. Nobody told him how, though. *Wait till he shows up, then shoot him.* That was what it boiled down to. If it were so easy, by now Sanjurjo would have as many holes in him as a colander. But only another sniper would understand that.

Or maybe not. "You can do it," Chaim said. "Honest to God, you can. That Big Bertha you carry, it can reach farther than those Nationalist *tukhus-lekhers* really imagine."

"If he shows up, I'll try." Vaclav didn't know how many times he'd said that since reaching the Madrid front.

"Kill him. If you can't fuck, killing's the next best thing." Chaim thumped him on the back and mooched away. Vaclav scratched his head. He didn't get any kind of charge from shooting Fascist officers. The most he took from it was an artisan's satisfaction at a difficult job done well. Some people had other ideas, though.

Trenches got muddy in fall. Rain made them even less livable than they were when it was dry. Rain also made sniping with the elephant gun harder. Yes, you could still kill somebody two kilometers away. Rain didn't bother bullets a bit. But if you couldn't *see* anybody two kilometers away, how were you supposed to kill him?

Vaclav still went out to one hidey-hole or another between the Republican lines and those of the Nationalists. If he had more trouble finding targets, the enemy would have more trouble finding him. Sometimes he would come back after dark without firing a shot. Better not to fire if you couldn't do anything worthwhile. He told himself as much over and over again. It was frustrating all the same.

"Don't worry about it," Benjamin Halévy said after he blew off steam in the Jew's ear.

"Easy for you to say," Jezek snarled.

"Probably." By refusing to take offense, Halévy only annoyed him more. "But you aren't obliged to get yourself killed by being stupid. You've lived through another day. Maybe the chances tomorrow will look better. As long as you're still here, you can find out."

"Well . . ." Vaclav looked at that from every angle, trying to get angry at it. Try as he would, he couldn't. "Do you have to be so sensible all the goddamn time?"

"I'm sorry. I'll do my best not to let it happen again," Halévy said.

Vaclav wondered if Jews were usually that way. Then he thought about Chaim the American. Whatever else you could say about him, sensible he was not. Jews probably differed as much from one another as anybody else. From where Vaclav had started before the war, that made a pretty fair leap of tolerance and understanding.

It started raining harder. Halévy had a shelter half. He draped it over his shoulder for a poncho. "I hate winter in the field, you know?" he said.

"Tell me about it." Vaclav's shelter half dated back to the Czechoslovakian Army. He shrugged it on, too, but wondered why he bothered even as he did it. A lot of the rubberized fabric once coating it was long gone. That meant it let in water just like any other piece of cloth. "Next time we fight a war, let's do it in Panama or the Belgian Congo or somewhere like that." He named the places he could think of that were least likely to be afflicted with winter.

"There you go." Benjamin Halévy nodded. "Good to see you've got it all figured out."

"My ass. If I had it all figured out, I'd be lying on the beach on the Riviera or somewhere like that, next to a girl with hardly any clothes and even less in the way of morals."

"Sounds good to me," Halévy said. As a Jew in the French Army, he could have left the service when France threw in with the Nazis. Had he headed down to the Riviera, he could have found a girl like that. From everything Vaclav had seen, France was full of them. But Halévy chose to come to Spain and leave his life on the line. When you looked at him like that, who said he was so goddamn sensible?

Like animals, they both curled up and got what sleep they could. Vaclav woke before dawn—again, like an animal. He gnawed on garlicky sausage and hard bread, then went out into no-man's-land. There were ways through the wire, if you knew them. Vaclav did—he'd made some of them.

What was left of a smashed house out there didn't offer a whole lot of cover, but Vaclav didn't need much. Most important were concealing the outline of his helmet and making sure the Nationalists couldn't spot the antitank rifle's long barrel. The ruins let him do both well enough.

He draped the shelter half over the big gun's telescopic sight. Keeping it dry mattered more than keeping his carcass that way. War was at least as much about tools as about the men who wielded them.

As dawn poured thin gray light over the landscape, Jezek suddenly jerked as if a scorpion had stung him. That was a summertime worry here, but not in weather like this. The Nationalist soldier crawling toward this wreckage, however, was. He'd fixed bushes to his Nazi-style helmet with a strip of inner tube, a trick Vaclav also used. And his rifle had a telescopic sight, so he was probably a sniper on his way out to see what harm he could do the Republicans.

But he'd had a mild case of *mañana,* the common Spanish ailment. He'd had it, and he'd never get over it. Jezek shifted the elephant gun's barrel so the massive piece bore on the oncoming Spaniard's track. At less than a hundred meters, he hardly needed the sight. He used it, though. He didn't want to miss.

When he fired, the gun almost took his shoulder off, as it always did. The Spaniard sank down like a punctured tire. He twitched a few times, even after a hit from a round that could pierce three centimeters of hardened armor plate. Human beings were damned hard to kill. Vaclav chambered another round, just in case. He quickly decided he wouldn't need it.

He thought about crawling over and getting the enemy sniper's rifle. It would be a good weapon to bring back. *Not while it's light out,* he thought. Somebody might be watching. After darkness would be time enough. You had to be patient if you were going to play this game.

ANOTHER TRIP out of town to raise funds for the war effort—and, on the side, for the Democratic Party. Peggy Druce was more relieved than not to get out of Philadelphia. She never would have felt that way before she went to Europe.

It wasn't her fault. She understood that. It wasn't Herb's fault, either. It wasn't anybody's fault. It was just one of the things that happened when two people, even two people who loved each other a lot, got separated from each other for years at a time.

Maybe things would get better pretty soon. Peggy kept hoping so.

She had no doubt Herb did, too. Till they did . . . Sometimes, she was just more comfortable when she didn't feel that mild awkwardness, that slight constraint, while she was in the same room as her husband.

Carbondale was north and east of Scranton, not very far from the border with New York. It was exactly what its name declared it to be: a coal town, one of perhaps 20,000 people. Most of them were Welsh and Irish—the primarily Slavic mining towns lay farther west. As their ancestors had since the early nineteenth century, the breadwinners went down under the ground to grub out anthracite.

US Highway 6, the main drag, twisted like a snake with a bellyache. What Peggy could see of where people actually lived looked to be on the grim side. Even so, the man who met her at the train station—a plump druggist named Vernon Vaughan—had his own small-scale civic pride.

"Carbondale's come through the Depression better than a lot of places," he declared, watery sunlight glinting off the silver rims of his bifocals. "The mines always stayed open. They had to cut back some, but they didn't shut down. Most people had some money most of the time. That meant the merchants didn't go under, either."

"Good for you," Peggy said, and she meant it. Plenty of towns Carbondale's size, all across the country, might as well have closed up shop for good after the market crashed in 1929. Since she was here on business, she felt she had to add, "I hope that means you'll reach for your wallets when it comes time to buy your war bonds."

"Well, I figure we will." Vaughan's double chin wobbled when he nodded. "People here are proud to be Americans. They work hard, sure, but they know they're better off than they would be if Great-Grandpa stayed in the old country. The Irish, now, they got out 'cause Great-Grandpa was starving. My folks didn't have it quite so bad, not from the stories I've heard, anyway. But I went Over There in 1918, and I was proud to do it."

"Good for you," Peggy said again. "My husband was the same way." She didn't tell him that she and Herb had lived more than comfortably enough even when the country hurt worst. She didn't tell him she'd had enough money to stay in Europe for a couple of years, either. The way things worked out, she wished she'd never boarded the liner to begin with.

"There you go," Vaughan said. "Let me grab your overnight bag there, and I'll take you to your hotel. It's only two, three blocks away. And the Rotarians' hall where you'll talk is right next door."

"That all sounds great," Peggy said, again most sincerely. Some places were better organized, some not so well. Vernon Vaughan seemed to have things under control.

The hotel would never make anyone forget the Ritz Carlton. But it would do. She'd stayed in plenty of worse places on the other side of the Atlantic: she didn't have to trot down the hall to the bathroom, for instance. And she wouldn't have to scramble for the shelter when air-raid sirens started shrieking.

She talked about that when she went next door to speak. "They're still having air-raid alerts on the West Coast, though," she said. "We have to make sure no enemy can ever strike at us at home. Not ever! When I was in Europe, I saw for myself how horrible that was."

People applauded her then. But they sat on their hands when she talked about helping England now that she was back in the fight against Germany. Carbondale wasn't the ideal place for that line, even if she realized as much half a minute later than she should have. What had Vernon Vaughan said? The town was full of Irish and Welsh. And why had their ancestors crossed the ocean? To get out from under their English landlords and overlords.

Time to ad-lib, then. "You may not love England," she said, "but if you think Hitler's a better bargain, I'm here to tell you you're out of your ever-loving minds. If you get on England's bad side, she'll break you if she can. If you get on Hitler's bad side, he'll kill you—and as many of your friends and neighbors as he can catch, to make sure they don't get any nasty ideas like freedom on their own."

That drew a little handclapping, but not much. Peggy went back to laying into Japan. Sooner or later, she expected, there *would* be a reckoning with the Nazis. But it would probably have to be later. People like the ones in the Rotarian hall here showed why FDR couldn't go and declare war on Germany. If old Adolf had declared war on America, now . . .

Well, it hadn't happened. The best thing the USA could do now against the evil day was strengthen herself as much as she could. If that meant whipping up hatred against the Japs, okay, she'd whip it up. We were fighting them, after all. And we weren't doing any too well against them right this minute, either.

"Show your hearts with the red, white, and blue!" she finished. "Everybody talks about being a patriot, but patriotism takes more than talk. Put your money where your mouth is, folks. You can't fight a war with nothing but talk. I wish you could, but you can't. It takes cash, too."

She hadn't expected much. This wasn't a big city, or even a medium-sized one. And Welshmen, at least, had almost the same kind of name for stinginess as Jews.

But she did great. The bonds the men of Carbondale bought wouldn't mature for years. Washington could spend the greenbacks they forked over right now. Both sides seemed to think it was a good bargain.

Afterward, Mr. Vaughan took her to dinner at an Italian place down the street. The tablecloths were red and white checks. There was a poster of a Venetian gondolier on one wall, and of the Leaning Tower of Pisa on another. Despite the clichés, the spaghetti and meatballs were fine. Peggy could see the cook. He looked more like a mick than a wop, but he knew what he was doing.

And he had the advantage of American abundance. With plenty of food and plenty of fuel, if you screwed up the food it was your own damn fault, not that of your ingredients the way it might be in screwed-up Europe.

As they ate and drank red wine, Vaughan did his best to put a move on her. Peggy pretended not to notice. He wasn't her type—not even close. Still and all, getting noticed that way felt good. It reminded her she was alive. It wasn't that Herb never acted interested. Even so . . .

"Well . . ." The druggist put a fin on the table, which made him an extravagant tipper. He climbed to his feet. "Let me walk you back to the hotel."

"Thanks." Two glasses of ordinary Chianti didn't make Peggy susceptible. She was more amused that he kept pitching than anything else.

She had no trouble shedding him in the hotel lobby. That behind the front desk stood a large, strong-jawed maiden lady who plainly disapproved of everything enjoyable under the sun only made it easier.

Up in her room all by herself, she pulled out a mystery story and read till she got sleepy. What with the wine and all that filling food, it didn't take long. Vernon Vaughan wouldn't have had much fun with her even if he had got past the dragon downstairs—not unless he enjoyed necrophilia, he wouldn't.

He was there to take her back to the station the next morning. "Sorry if I got out of line last night," he said.

"Don't worry about it," Peggy told him. "I'm heading home, that's all."

So she was. And before long she'd look forward to getting out into the boondocks again. How smart had she been to ignore him, then? That she could wonder said not everything in Philadelphia was the way she wished it would be.

Chapter 24

arvik again. Julius Lemp was not a happy man. Namsos would have been better. Wilhelmshaven would have been wonderful. But it was Narvik, so the U-30 could get back up to the Barents Sea as soon as possible. More fuel for the diesels, more eels for the tubes, more food for the crew, and away they'd go again.

He'd already complained to the powers that be here about Narvik's shortcomings as a liberty port. His crew had already tried to take the place apart—and they weren't the only gang of U-boat sailors to join the rising against authority.

Predictably, authority didn't forget. When the U-30 tied up, she was greeted at the pier by a squad of shore patrolmen, all of them wearing *Stahlhelms* and all of them carrying Schmeissers.

"Well, this is a fine crock of herrings," Lemp growled at the chief petty officer in charge of the squad. "You'd think we'd put in at Aberdeen by mistake." He shook his head. "No, by God! The Royal Navy'd give us a better hello than this, to hell with me if it wouldn't."

The steel helmet's beetling brim only made the CPO's features seem even more wooden than they would have otherwise. He saluted stiffly.

"Sir, I have my orders," he said. "No one is going to tear Narvik up again—that's what the people here have in mind."

Daylight was already leaking out of the sky, though it was only midafternoon. Before long, arctic night would fall: Narvik lay north of the Arctic Circle. "Disgraceful," Lemp snarled.

"Sir, if you didn't lead such a pack of hooligans, there wouldn't be a problem," the shore patrolman answered in a gruff monotone.

"If this place weren't a morgue—" But Lemp could see this was an argument he'd lose. The shore patrol didn't just have the firepower. The bastards had the backing of the bigger bastards here, the ones with all the gold stripes on their sleeves.

His crewmen had been glaring at their natural foes. They reminded him of cats snarling at sheep dogs. Then one of them tipped him a wink. Did that mean they'd stay out of trouble or that they'd dive into it headfirst? Lemp didn't know, not for sure, but he was afraid he could guess.

He let the shore patrolmen lead the U-boat sailors off to whatever passed for fun in Narvik. Then the mechanics fell on his submarine. He was glad to see them. Unlike either the high command or the shore patrol, they seemed to be on the same side as the men who actually did the fighting.

He thought about staying away from the officers' club in sympathy for the way his men were being treated. He didn't think about it long, though. The alternative was staying cooped up in his tiny, curtained-off cabin in the stinking, claustrophobic pressure hull.

He did make a point of repairing to the club in his grimy working togs instead of putting on a proper uniform. No one there said a word about it, though. The shorebound officers were evidently used to U-boat skippers' eccentric ways.

Those shorebound men did let him know that plans actually were in the works for an officers' brothel, and one ratings could patronize as well. That plans were in the works didn't mean the brothels were working yet. Lemp thought that was a damn shame. He was a few years older than the men he commanded. He didn't burn quite so hot as most of them. But that didn't mean he didn't burn at all. Oh, no—nowhere close. He would have welcomed a grapple with a nice, warm girl, even if it was purely a business transaction.

Since he couldn't screw, he drank. He'd got to the bottom of his third stiff schnapps, hoping they would improve his attitude. All they succeeded in doing was making him dizzy. They were strong, and he was tired; they hit him hard. Only later did he stop and wonder what would happen when the U-30's ratings started drinking. That was when he remembered the one sailor's wink. As such things have a way of being, that was also just exactly too late.

A burst of submachine-gun fire brought silence smashing down in the officers' club. A moment later, another burst rang out. "Good God!" somebody said. "Have the Royal Marines landed, or what?"

There was a cheerful thought. If English raiders were swooping down on Narvik, they could do a hell of a lot of damage. Most of the German forces here belonged to the *Kriegsmarine.* The only reason they were here at all was to go after convoys bound for Russia. Shore patrolmen wouldn't stand much of a chance against cold-blooded professionals.

One of those shore patrolmen rushed into the officers' club. He looked around wildly before his gaze fixed on Lemp. "Come quick," he shouted, "before those maniacs of yours tear this whole base to shreds!"

Just what it deserves, Lemp thought. The words almost came out— such were the dangers of three strong drinks. But he managed to stifle them. Instead, he said, "If they had more ways to blow off steam without getting in trouble, they'd do that. They wouldn't brawl."

"They're a pack of criminals, nothing else but," the shore patrolman retorted. "If you don't calm them down, they'll get courts-martial for making a mutiny. That's a capital crime." By the way he spoke, he thought the U-30's men deserved no better than a blindfold and a cigarette.

"Take me to them," Lemp said. He had to pay close attention to where he put his feet when he followed the shore patrolman out of the officers' club.

It was cold outside, cold and dark. The northern lights' wavering curtains danced in the sky, now red, now gold. Lemp spared the aurora a glance, no more. It wasn't as if he didn't see it on a lot of frigid winter nights.

He could have found the fighting without his guide. Men were yelling and screaming. Whistles blew frantically. Things broke—often, by the sound of it, over somebody's head. Two shore patrolmen dragged a wounded buddy from the fray. "Making a mutiny," the man with Lemp repeated grimly.

"They're just drunk and disorderly, and they hate this miserable place," the U-boat skipper answered, hoping he was right. If the lads had got the bit too far between their teeth, they'd be in big trouble in spite of anything he could do. To try to convince himself things were as he wanted them to be, he added, "I do, too. Who wouldn't?"

"You weren't smashing up the officers' club when I found you, though . . . sir," the shore patrolman said. Lemp judged a discreet silence the best response to that.

From out of the gloom ahead came a shout: "Halt! Who comes? Friend or foe?"

It wasn't the kind of challenge the shore patrol would issue. Not only that, Lemp recognized the voice of the rating doing the shouting. "It's me, Willi—the skipper," he called back. "Playtime's over. You boys have had your fun—and you've made your point, too."

He waited. If Willi and the other sailors rejected his authority, they really were on their way to military courts and the brig, if not worse. Several men up there argued back and forth. When the chain of command broke, you had to figure out who had authority. At last, Willi said, "Well, come ahead, sir. You can help us pick up the pieces."

"Enough is enough," Lemp said as he advanced, trying to pour oil on troubled waters.

"Enough is too much," the shore patrolman beside him put in, trying to make a bad situation worse. Lemp contrived to step on the man's foot.

As had been true the last time things went arsey-varsey, not all the brawling sailors came from the U-30. But the rioters had done a more thorough job of tearing Narvik to pieces this time around. They weren't brawling for the fun of it; they were brawling because they were furious about what passed for a base up here in the frozen north. Lemp did sympathize, but he had to hope very hard that they hadn't got themselves in too deep.

"If you give it up now, you probably won't land in too much trouble. You're good fighting men, and the *Reich* needs you for the war effort," he told them. "But if you push it even a centimeter further, they'll land on you hard. You haven't just pissed them off this time. You've scared them, and that's worse."

"They treat us like shit when we come in from a patrol, they'd better be scared," growled a sailor from another U-boat. But the fight had gone out of the men. They'd made their point. There wasn't much else they could do, not here at the frigid end of nowhere. They gave it up. Lemp headed back toward the officers' club, hoping the argument he'd used with the sailors would also work on their superiors—and his.

HIDEKI FUJITA LOVED being a sergeant again. He was *meant* to have two stars on each collar tab—he thought so, anyhow. And Unit 113 was a much smaller outfit than Unit 731 had been. That made him seem a much bigger frog.

Unit 113 was also a much less experimental place than Unit 731 had been. Here, they went out and did things. That suited Fujita fine, too. He was no big brain, and knew he never would be. But when somebody pointed him at a job, he would take care of it.

Not only that, he had a knack for getting the most out of the men under him. He'd knock them around when they deserved it, but he didn't give them bruises for no better reason than to show his cock was bigger than theirs. As long as they hopped to it, they didn't need to worry about him.

They went on spreading disease through Yunnan Province. If the Chinese died from the plague and from cholera, they wouldn't be able to do so much with the military equipment England sent them. Even more to the point, if the Chinese feared they would die from those dreadful diseases, their panic helped Japan at least as much as real illness would.

Major Hataba assembled the men in the unit to say, "We have received an official commendation from the Imperial War Ministry in

Tokyo for our contributions to victory in China. *Banzai* for the Emperor!"

"*Banzai!*" the soldiers shouted, Fujita loud among them. "*Banzai!*"

Hataba did not remind the men of Unit 113 that he'd also wanted to use bacteria against the English in India. No doubt he was doing his very best to forget all about that. Fujita remembered it, but not very often. It hadn't happened, so it didn't matter. Everyone was better off *not* remembering a plan that hadn't come to fruition.

It wasn't as if the Japanese didn't have other things to think about. Fujita came from Hiroshima, in the south. Winters in Mongolia, Siberia, and Manchukuo had left him horrified and amazed. What was alleged to be the approach of winter in Burma left him horrified and amazed, too, but not the same way.

"*Eee!*" he said to another sergeant. They were drinking warm beer together; there was no other kind of beer to drink. "I thought I knew everything there was to know about hot, sticky weather. But this makes the worst August in Hiroshima feel like February."

"*Hai.*" The other man nodded. His name was Ichiro Hirabayashi. He was a career noncom; he'd spent his whole adult life in the Imperial Army. Nothing seemed to faze him much. "Your clothes rot. Your boots rot. You start to rot, too. I've learned more about ringworm and jock itch and athlete's foot and all that crap than I ever wanted to know since I got here."

"You aren't the only one," Fujita said dolefully. "I had jock itch so bad, I thought I'd got a dose from one of the comfort women in Myitkina."

Hirabayashi laughed at that. Fujita didn't think it was so funny. A medical assistant had given him some nasty-smelling ointment to smear on his privates. It helped some. It wasn't a cure, though. He still itched in all kinds of places where he couldn't scratch without being crude.

The other sergeant drank more beer. In reflective tones, he said, "I hate this miserable place, you know? I hate the weather. I hate the rot. I hate the bugs. I hate the sicknesses. I hate the Burmese, too."

"What's wrong with the Burmese?" Fujita asked. He could see why Sergeant Hirabayashi hated everything else about Burma.

"They're lazy. They're shiftless. They're thieving. They don't talk any language a civilized man can understand." Hirabayashi spoke with great

conviction. A British colonial administrator pouring down gin and ton-
ics in Mandalay a year earlier might have said the same thing, even if he
would have said it in English rather than Japanese.

"Well, besides that?" Fujita said.

He set Hirabayashi laughing again. "You're a funny fellow, aren't
you?" the older man said. "That's good. You get up into Burma's asshole
the way we are and there's not a hell of a lot to laugh about."

"It's war. *Shigata ga nai, neh?*" Fujita said.

Sergeant Hirabayashi nodded. "No, you can't do a damn thing about
it—except drink when you get the chance." He suited action to word.

So did Fujita, who said, "One good thing, anyhow. At least the RAF
doesn't bomb us here. When I fought the Russians in Siberia, they were
always trying to drop stuff on our heads. That wasn't a whole lot of fun.
Can't say I miss it."

"All right. There's something," Hirabayashi admitted. "But I'll tell
you, it's not much."

"I won't argue." Fujita poured himself another mug of beer and
downed it, and then another one after that.

He woke the next morning with a headache that pounded behind
his eyes like a piledriver. Strong tea did next to nothing to fix it. One
more mug of beer helped some. The headache dulled, even if it didn't
disappear. Shouting at conscript privates let him work off more of his
discomfort. He wasn't especially proud to remember that the next day,
but consoled himself with the thought that he hadn't slugged anybody.

Odds were Sergeant Hirabayashi wouldn't have been so fussy. Noncoms like Hirabayashi would have led Japanese troops into action in the
Sino-Japanese and Russo-Japanese Wars. Back in samurai days, men
like him would have been loyal retainers to their overlords, even if they
wouldn't have worn collar tabs back then.

If I stay in the Army as long as he has, will I end up like that? Fujita
wondered. He didn't want to be a career noncom. He wanted to go back
to the family farm and spend the rest of his days there. If he never saw
another rifle or another porcelain bomb casing full of germs, that suited
him fine.

No matter what he wanted, though, the Army wouldn't turn him
loose till the war ended, if it ever ended. And even after he escaped its

clutches, he sometimes wondered uneasily how he would fit down on the farm. He wasn't the person he had been before conscription got him. He was harder, tougher, less patient. He'd seen more of the world than he'd even imagined while he was still a civilian. He didn't like a lot of what he'd seen, but that wasn't the point. The point was, his horizons had broadened. A farm off in the middle of nowhere was likely to seem a farm off in the middle of nowhere, not an unquestioned home for the rest of his life.

He didn't know what he could do about that. No, actually he did know; he couldn't do anything about it. Now that he'd seen the wider world, he couldn't very well forget about it, even if he wished he could.

His father had carried a rifle in the Russo-Japanese War. Had he felt some of the same thing after he came home again? If he had, he'd managed to stifle it. Or maybe he'd just never talked about it with his family. He must have realized they wouldn't understand.

I do now, Fujita thought. Young men all over Japan would understand after the war. The country would be different then, because they'd changed. How it would be different, Fujita wasn't sure. But it would be.

Of course, not all of Japan's young men in uniform would go home again. Fujita wasn't thinking about the ones who would die in battle. Their spirits would return to the Home Islands, to live forever at the Yasukuni Shrine. But, after the war was done, how many soldiers would Japan need to protect her conquests in China and Russia and the Pacific islands and Southeast Asia and the East Indies?

Did Japan have that many soldiers? Could she maintain them without ruining herself? Fujita was tempted to laugh at himself. How could he know, when he was just an ignorant peasant bumped up to sergeant? He was surprised even the question had occurred to him.

Then he wondered if it had occurred to the people who were supposed to worry about such things. That, though, was another kind of question altogether.

SARAH BRUCK SOON SETTLED into the routine of marriage and of bakery work. If not much time seemed available for romance, well, she was usually too busy to miss it. And romance during wartime, at least for a Jew in the *Reich,* was a pallid, harried thing to begin with.

She did eat better than she had when she was living with her parents. But, when she wasn't too tired, she missed the talk at their house. All the Brucks ever talked about was baking. Sarah treasured the weekend visits she and Isidor made. She was glad they intrigued her husband, too. He sensed a wider, deeper world there than the one he was used to at home.

She didn't treasure the air raids. As nights got longer, the RAF came over Germany more and more often. Münster, in the far northwest near the Dutch border, took more than its share of pounding: it lay within easy range of England, and bombers didn't need to fly through French airspace to reach it. Sarah could have done without the honor.

Fear iced through her every time the sirens' screams jerked her headlong out of sleep. The Brucks had no proper shelter to go to, no more than her parents or any other German Jews did. They—and Sarah—huddled downstairs, between their shop counter and the ovens. That gave them some protection if a bomb hit above them. If one blew up in the street outside, though . . . She resolutely refused to worry about that. If it happened, odds were she'd be too dead to do any more worrying, anyhow.

Her father gave forth with a gravedigger's good cheer when she and Isidor visited after a raid. "Here for a while I thought they were going to throw me off the labor gang for lack of work," Samuel Goldman said, his eyes twinkling even though he had dark bags under them. "But we've had plenty to do lately."

"I'll bet you have!" Sarah exclaimed. "It's been terrible."

"An awful lot of houses knocked to smithereens," Isidor agreed.

"Well, so there are." Sarah's father didn't sound so cheery when he said that. He paused to light a cigarette. For a moment, Sarah took that for granted—but only for a moment. He didn't roll the smoke himself, with newspaper for a wrapper and tobacco scrounged from other people's dog-ends. No: this one was machine-made, whole and new. Seeing her stare, he nodded. "We clear the wreckage, you know. Whatever we find that we can carry away, we keep. I'm not what you'd call proud of it, but I do it just like everybody else."

"Good for you!" Isidor answered before Sarah could. "If that's the only choice you've got, you have to take it."

"That's what I tell myself." Samuel Goldman nodded again. "I scavenged the same way in the trenches when we went forward. The French and the Tommies always had so much more than we did. We ate better after every advance. Mother and I are eating a little better now, too. But it feels different when you're scavenging from the neighbors, not the enemy."

"What else can you do?" Sarah asked sympathetically.

"I could do nothing. Then we'd starve. This is better—I suppose." Father's cheeks hollowed as he sucked in smoke. He looked up toward the ceiling, or maybe toward whatever lay a mile beyond the moon, as he continued, "A lot of the time, we're the ones who pull the bodies out of the rubble, too. I didn't mind bodies much, you know, when they wore horizon-blue or khaki. I even got used to bodies in *Feldgrau*. Lord knows we saw enough of them. But bodies in pajamas or nightgowns? That's a lot harder."

Sarah and Isidor looked at each other. Neither of them seemed to know what to say to that. At last, Sarah asked, "Have you . . . found anyone you know? Uh, I guess I mean knew?"

"I'm afraid so," he said. "You remember Friedrich Lauterbach?"

"Sure. He studied under you. He's in the *Wehrmacht* now, isn't he?" Sarah left it there. Had the world gone down a different path, she might have been more likely to marry him than the husband she had now. He'd stayed decent even after the Nazis took over, getting Father money for writing articles that would see print under his byline rather than a Jew's. Sarah hoped he hadn't stopped anything.

Her father nodded. "That's the fellow. His older brother was a doctor here. Was." He repeated the past tense. Something in the way his jaw set made Sarah fight shy of asking just what had happened to the luckless Dr. Lauterbach.

Isidor yawned. "I'm sorry, but I don't think we'll stay very late," he said. "You have air raids two or three days in a row, you get so sleepy you can't see straight."

"That's the truth!" Sarah's mother exclaimed; she hadn't had much to say till then. "And the horrible *ersatz* coffee and tea you can get nowadays don't have any kick in them at all." Everybody nodded at that. People grumbled about it all the time.

"They make pills for pilots and other people who've got to stay awake," Father said. "Not the stuff that goes into coffee, but the real strong stuff, benzedrine and the like. Plenty of times I've wished I could get my hands on some of those. I could use them, believe me."

"Who couldn't?" Isidor said. "Dr. What's-his-name—Lauterbach—didn't have any at his house?"

"If he did, somebody else beat me to them. What can you do?" Samuel Goldman spread his hands. Sarah remembered when they were soft and smooth and impeccably manicured, with only a writer's callus on one middle finger. Now they were scarred and battered, with filthy nails and with hard yellowed ridges across the palms. Well, her own hands were a lot harder than they had been, too.

She and Isidor got back to the flat over the bakery well before curfew. In lieu of benzedrine pills, they went to bed early. Sarah thought she could sleep the clock around if she got the chance. Tired by bad food and nighttime air raids, she wanted to hibernate like a dormouse.

She didn't get the chance that night. The RAF came over again, a little before midnight. The sirens wailed like damned souls. Sarah and Isidor and the older Brucks did some heartfelt damning of their own as they stumbled down the stairs in darkness absolute.

Then the bombs whistled down. As soon as Sarah heard them, her terror redoubled. They sounded louder and closer than they ever had before. She tried to burrow into the floor when they started going off.

It sounded as if one hit right across the street. The window in the front of the bakery had survived the whole war. It didn't survive this: it fell in on itself with a tinkling crash. "*Scheisse!*" Isidor's father said loudly, and then, "I beg your pardon."

"Don't worry about it," Sarah said as the building shook from other hits only a little farther away. Now she understood why her own father still sometimes called bomber pilots air pirates even though the name came straight out of Dr. Goebbels' Propaganda Ministry. If they were trying to kill you, they weren't your friends.

After forty-five eternal minutes, the bombers droned away. "That was awful," Isidor said. Sarah couldn't have put it better herself. She shivered, not just from fear but also because the shattered front window was letting in cold air.

It was letting in light, too. The grocery across the street was on fire. Isidor's father started to go out to see if he could help. Stepping on broken glass made him change his mind in a hurry.

There wasn't much water pressure when a fire engine finally clanged up. What had the bombs done to the pipes under Münster? Nothing good—that was plain. Firemen in what looked like *Stahlhelms* with crests did the best they could with what they had.

"He's going to lose everything," David Bruck said gloomily. "I just hope he's alive. He's a *goy*, but he's a *mensh*. The two shops have been across the street from each other as long as I can remember."

"It's terrible," Sarah said.

"It's worse than that," her father-in-law answered. "For him and for us. I know I won't be able to get glass to fix that window. Heaven only knows if they'll even give me wood scraps. I've got to have something, or people will just come in and steal. How am I supposed to stay in business?"

When Sarah decided to marry Isidor, she'd figured that getting into a baker's family would at least mean she had enough to eat. Now even that wasn't obvious any more. She suddenly hated the RAF almost as if she were a genuine German after all.

ANASTAS MOURADIAN LAY in his tent, trying to sleep. He had his flying suit of fur and leather, and long underwear below it. He had two thick, scratchy woolen blankets. He had a cot that kept him off the ground. The tent itself held off the worst of the wind. He was miserably cold even so.

Russian infantrymen learned to sleep in the snow, shrouded by no more than their uniform and greatcoat. Stas was no foot soldier; he was a flyer. He was no Russian, either. He knew what good weather was all about. When it got this frigid, his teeth chattered like castanets.

Then the tent flap flew open. A blast of air straight from the North Pole rushed inside. So did a human shape—no more than a lumpy outline in the darkness. "What the devil—?" Stas said, groping for his service pistol.

"You've got to hide me!"

The voice was familiar. Stas stopped feeling for the automatic. "What do you mean, hide you, Ivan? Hide you from whom?" he asked. Having learned Russian as a second language, he was often more precise in his grammar than men who'd spoken it from birth.

But Ivan Kulkaanen wasn't a native Russian-speaker, either. "Hide me from the Chekists! They're after me!" The Karelian's voice wasn't just familiar. It was desperate. He panted like a hunted animal worn down after a long chase.

Now the ice that ran up Mouradian's back had nothing to do with the arctic air rapidly filling the tent. *"Bozhemoi!"* he burst out. "What did you do? What do they think you did?" The questions were related, but not necessarily identical. And the second was the one that really mattered. If the NKVD decided you'd done something, you might as well have, because they'd hang it on you anyway.

"I wrote in a letter to my cousin that the war wasn't going as well as it ought to be," Kulkaanen answered miserably.

"Bozhemoi!" Stas repeated. This time, his tone was hopeless. "You *wrote* that?" He didn't ask *How could you be such an idiot?* It had already occurred to him that his copilot and bomb-aimer might be playing a part. The NKVD might be building a case against him and using Kulkaanen as a provocateur. It struck him as unlikely—if the Chekists wanted you, more often than not they just grabbed you—but it was possible.

"I wrote it," Ivan agreed. "I wrote it in Finnish. I didn't think they'd ever be able to read it. But they did, and I'm fucked." Karelia lay in the far north, next to the Finnish border. A lot of Finns thought it belonged to them by rights, not least because the only differences between Finns and Karelians were the names and where they happened to live.

Of course the NKVD would have men who read Finnish, just as the Chekists had men who read Armenian and Georgian (hell, Stalin could do that) and Azerbaijani and Kazakh and Lithuanian and every other language under the Soviet sun. The NKVD probably had men who read

Sanskrit, for Christ's sake. Hey, you never could tell when a professor of the ancient languages of India might turn wrecker on you.

"Hide me!" Kulkaanen said again, even more urgently than before. "If I can count on anybody, it's you!"

There was a compliment Stas appreciated—and one he could have done without. "Hide you where?" he asked, doing his best to sound like the voice of sweet reason. "What do you want me to do with you, Ivan? Stick you in my back pocket?" Kulkaanen was both taller and thicker through the shoulders than he was himself.

"There's got to be somewhere!" the Karelian said.

"Under my cot, maybe? That should fool the NKVD for a good second and a half—two if you're lucky," Stas said.

Kulkaanen groaned. "I'm fucked," he said once more: an observation all too likely to be accurate. With yet another groan—or maybe this one was better called a moan—he fled out into the night.

Stas felt like groaning and moaning, too. Now he didn't have to worry about whether the cold would keep him awake. Adrenaline would handle the job just fine. He lay there, trying without much luck to relax, heart thuttering in his throat.

He didn't get to lie there long. Not fifteen minutes after Ivan Kulkaanen disappeared, someone shone an electric torch full in his face and shouted, "Answer, in the name of the Soviet Union!"

Stas answered, all right: "Turn that goddamn thing off, you stupid motherfucking jackass! Do you *want* to bring Nazi bombers down on us?" If you were going to deal with the NKVD, any moral advantage you could grab was precious.

The torch winked off. Except for a wavering purple-green afterimage, Stas could see nothing at all for a little while. The Chekist demanded, "Did the anti-Soviet criminal Ivan Kulkaanen come here?"

"Ivan came here, yes," Stas answered. No matter what Kulkaanen was dumb enough to put in a letter, Mouradian was sure he'd harmed the Hitlerites far more than this blustering Russian ever would. It wouldn't help him, of course, but it was true.

"What did he want? What did you tell him?" the NKVD man barked.

"He wanted me to hide him. I said I couldn't." Stas gave back the exact truth. It couldn't land poor Ivan in any more trouble.

"What did he do then?"

"He ran away. You don't see him here, do you?"

"Never mind what I see," the intruder snapped. "Why didn't you instantly report his treasonous behavior?"

"Because he only just now came and went." That was a lie, but only a tiny one. "And because it's bloody cold out there." Truth again. "And because I expected you people would be on his trail." One more truth.

"Where did he go?" the NKVD man asked, so even a Chekist could see the sense in his response.

"Comrade Investigator, I have no idea," Mouradian said, which was also true. "But wherever he is, he can't have got far."

"Ha! You're right about that. And when we catch him, he'll be sorry he didn't run off to Venus or Mars."

The NKVD man ducked out of Stas' tent and let the flap fall. He shouted obscenity-filled orders to whatever friends he had out there. They'd comb the grounds around the airstrip. Were they moronic enough to turn on their torches while they did it? They probably were. Who was going to tell Chekists they couldn't do something? You could wind up in a camp yourself if you tried.

I did it. I got away with it, too, Stas thought, not without pride. He was still cold—colder now, in fact, with all the icy air his visitors had let into the tent. He huddled under the blankets. Sleep was hopeless. He'd be pouring down tea tomorrow to keep his eyes open, or coffee if they had any.

Or maybe not. He'd need a replacement copilot if he was going to fly. Could they deliver somebody soon enough to do him any good? He'd have to see.

Out at the edge of the encampment, somebody yelled. A moment later, someone fired a long burst from a machine pistol. A moment after that, somebody let out a horrible scream. Was that Kulkaanen? Or were the NKVD brutes mowing one another down? Stas knew where his hopes lay.

As a Karelian, Kulkaanen probably knew even more about snow than the Russians coming after him did. Maybe he could get away. It still didn't seem likely, but it was possible.

It was possible, but it didn't happen. They brought him in near daybreak. They'd beaten the snot out of him for making them work so hard. Odds were he had worse coming. If they didn't execute him, they'd give him twenty-five years in the gulag. They wouldn't bother hanging a mere tenner on him, not after he'd gone and pissed them off.

And the war would grind on, whether run well or badly. Why couldn't he have seen that? Any which way, no matter what he told his cousin, the goddamn war would grind on.

Chapter 25

Lieutenant Demange sidled up to Luc Harcourt and murmured into his dirty and none too shell-like ear: "Be ready."

"Be ready for what?" Luc asked irritably. "I'd sure be ready for a holiday on the beach at Nice or somewhere like that, I'll tell you." The flat Russian landscape he saw at the moment wouldn't have reminded him of the Riviera even if it weren't draped in snow.

"Funny. Funny like the crabs," Demange growled, the usual Gitane in the corner of his mouth jerking as he spoke.

"I don't know if I've got crabs or not. I don't give a good goddamn, either," Luc said. "I've got regular lice, though, and fleas, and bedbugs. So who cares about the *papillons d'amour*?"

"It's war. What d'you expect?" Demange's narrow, bloodshot eyes flicked now this way now that. Luc tried to look every which way at once, too. The Ivans off to the east were supposed to be pretty quiet right this minute. But you'd never live to get old by counting on what the bastards on the other side were supposed to be doing. Demange went on, "Yeah, it's war, but the political wheels are spinning again. That's what you've got to be ready for."

"Oh, God! Are we going through another round of that *merde*?" Luc looked around again, this time off toward the left. His regiment was stationed at the French expeditionary force's left flank. Next to them in the line were the *Boches*. If he suddenly didn't have to worry about the Russians any more, he would have to worry about the Fritzes instead.

"Could be," Lieutenant Demange answered. "What I hear is, Daladier's been talking with the English. If he decides they look like a better bet than Hitler, things here get sticky in a hurry."

"No kidding!" Luc exclaimed. After a moment, he added, "You know, some of the guys in my section really do hate the Russians. You stay here for a while and they keep trying to kill you, that'll happen."

"Sure it will. So what?" Demange said. "We came here on account of some French jackass with a white mustache and fancy embroidery on his kepi told us to. If that same jerk, or another *con* just like him, says Stalin's the hottest lay since Josephine Baker and we should make nice with him from now on, we fucking well will. That's how the game is rigged, and you know it as well as I do."

Luc's sigh brought out fog almost as thick as the lieutenant's cigarette smoke. "Yeah, I guess so," he said unhappily. "You want I should warn the men something may be cooking, then?"

"Hold off a while longer. Like you say, some of the dumb shitheads like the Nazis better than the Reds. Wouldn't do if one of 'em spilled the beans and brought the Germans down on our heads before we were ready to go over to the Russians."

"You're right." Luc sounded more unhappy yet—and he was. "So you don't think I'd do that, huh?"

"If you even thought about it, I'd blow your fucking head off before you got the chance to try," Demange replied.

"Love you, too, Lieutenant." Luc teased a few syllables' worth of sour laughter out of Demange.

If the Red Army knew the French were thinking about changing sides, it didn't let on. The Russians always had—sometimes quite literally—more artillery than they knew what to do with. They also had their horrible new barrage rockets that could lay a square kilometer waste in nothing flat. Winter weather troubled such toys much less than it interfered with infantry actions. The Russians pounded the French positions again and again.

Luc wondered if they were trying to tell the French generals that they could hurt the troops those generals commanded worse than the Nazis could. If they were trying to do that, he didn't think it would work. Yes, the Russians could punish the expeditionary force. But the Germans could invade France—could invade, and had invaded, and might invade once more if France did switch back to England's side.

None of which made him cower any less in the shallow scrapes he hacked out of the frozen ground when the Red Army pounded his countrymen's positions. Shell fragments whined maliciously not far enough over his head. Blast from the rockets picked him up and slammed him down till he felt as if he'd lost a fifteen-rounder to Joe Louis.

The shelling did send one of the most pro-Nazi soldiers in his section away with a nasty thigh wound. Seeing the mess, Luc guessed the poor groaning bastard would lose the leg. He didn't wish that kind of anguish on anybody—and Marcel had been a brave fellow even if he was a Fascist.

Two days after Marcel got hit, Lieutenant Demange quietly told Luc, "Now you can let your guys in on it. They need to know."

"Oh, they do, do they?" Luc said tonelessly. He wasn't at all sure he needed news like that himself. He glanced off to the left again. The closest German detachments were only a few hundred meters away. No barbed wire separated them from the French, as it did from the Russians. They were allies, after all . . . for the time being, anyhow.

Demange's eyes slid in the same direction. He nodded glumly, as if at a question Luc hadn't asked. "Yeah, it's liable to get a little hairy," he said. "We may end up playing flank guards. Doesn't that sound like fun?"

"Fun. Right," Luc said, still with no expression in his voice. Demange chuckled, thumped him on the back, and went off to brief some more noncoms.

Luc spread the word through his section. He quietly told off a few reliable *poilus* to keep an eye on the handful of others who might give them away to the *Wehrmacht*. "It's politics, my dears," he said over and over again. "Nothing we can do about it but roll with the punches." He wished he had a better line. That one reminded him too much of the way the Russian rockets knocked him around.

"We're crossing into the Reds' lines, right?" one of his men asked. "How do we know when we're supposed to do that? If we go too soon, the *salauds*'re liable to machine-gun us instead of letting us through."

"They'll give us the signal to move on." Luc hoped like nobody's business he wasn't lying.

And, as a matter of fact, he turned out not to be. "When it's time for us to go, the Russians'll fill the sky with green flares," Lieutenant De- mange said. "Just like fucking traffic lights, Harcourt. Even the dumb- shits in your section ought to be able to remember that."

"Here's hoping. Some of those dimbulbs wouldn't remember their heads if they didn't have 'em stapled on," Luc said. Demange grunted something that might have been laughter. How many times had he talked about ordinary soldiers the same scornful way? Sure as hell, Luc had got most of what he thought he knew about being a sergeant straight from the horse's mouth.

The Russians shelled the stretch of German line that abutted the French positions. Perhaps for the sake of verisimilitude, perhaps just to remind the French that they weren't buddies yet, they also shelled Luc's regiment. A couple of luckless men got killed; a few more picked up wounds. French 75s and 105s indignantly joined the German guns that gave back counterbattery fire. Luc hoped like anything that they mur- dered some Ivans. He didn't want anybody's artillery coming down on his head.

The Red Army signaled early one frigid morning (there was no other kind in Russia at this season of the year), just as night was giving way to daybreak. One second, the predawn stillness held. The next, it might have been a Bastille Day fireworks show, except that all the stars and rockets and flares flying up in the east were green.

"Let's go!" Luc called. "There'll be ways through the wire. The flank guards will hold off the *Boches* while we move." While France and Ger- many played at friendship, you weren't supposed to call the *Feldgrau* boys *Boches*. It was an order widely ignored—he ignored it himself—

but an order even so. The flank guards still weren't supposed to fire until fired upon, which would probably get some of the poor bastards killed.

Luc carried his rifle at high port as he hurried across the snow-covered fields toward the gaps in the barbed wire that had better be there. No firing came from in front of him. That was encouraging. But, all at once, he heard MG-34s and Mausers open up off to the left. Swearing under his smoking breath, he hunched over and tried to hurry faster.

"GREEN FLARES," *Oberleutnant* Wolfgang Gruber told Willi Dernen and the other men commanding squads in his company. "That's what you've got to look for from the Russian lines. That's the signal for the froggies to try and fuck us over."

"What do we do then, sir?" Willi asked. To his surprise, he found he liked leading a squad. Because Awful Arno had done it for so long, he'd assumed he would hate the job. But no—and he didn't think he was doing it badly. He added, "I mean, I won't be sorry to get the Frenchies off our flank—I was always scared the Ivans would push through them to flank us out. Still . . ."

"When they turn their coats, we've got to make them pay," Gruber answered. "Till then, we have to make nice. I guess there's still some chance the guys in the striped pants and the cutaways can straighten things out again. I mean, I don't want them on our flank any more than you do, Dernen, but I don't want a hole in the line four divisions wide, either."

Willi grunted and nodded. The *Wehrmacht* had managed to patch things up and keep going when the English turned traitor. Maybe the General Staff could figure out how to do it again, especially since they seemed to have some warning. But that wasn't a game you wanted to play once, much less twice.

Gruber looked from one corporal and *Obergefreiter* to the next. "Any other questions?" he asked. Nobody said anything. Willi had asked the only one that mattered. The company CO nodded. "All right, then. Let your men know what's going on."

Adam Pfaff nodded cynically when Willi passed along the news. "No big surprise, is there?" he said. "Anybody who ever counted on a lousy Frenchman was just asking to get his pocket picked."

"That's how it looks to me, too," Willi said. "We got as much as we could out of the no-good pigdogs. Best thing we can do when they fly the coop is remind 'em why screwing around with the *Reich* is a bad idea."

Pfaff nodded again. Most of the other guys in the squad bobbed their heads up and down, too. At the time, Willi thought he'd been plain enough. Later, though, he was faintly appalled at what had come out of his mouth.

Sharing a cigarette with the *Obergefreiter* with the gray Mauser, he explained why: "I sounded just like that cocksucking Baatz! *Just* like him, you hear me?"

"Take an even strain, man," Pfaff said. "If you're a noncom or making like a noncom, you've got to come out with that bullshit every now and then. You couldn't do your job if you didn't."

"I don't want to sound like Awful Arno," Willi said. "Why couldn't I sound like a *good* corporal instead?"

"Because you've had the dumb turd blabbing in your ear since the war started, that's why," his buddy answered. "Some of it's bound to stick, the way shit sticks to the hair around your asshole."

"There you go!" Willi liked the comparison. "Thanks. Now you made me feel better."

"What are friends for?" Pfaff said modestly.

One thing friends were for, as far as Willi was concerned, was staying with you through thick and thin. The French flunked that test. The Germans started unobtrusively patrolling their right flank, where their positions adjoined those of their alleged allies. Willi noticed the froggies doing some unobtrusive patrolling of their own, keeping an eye on what the *Landsers* were up to. When Germans and Frenchmen couldn't avoid noticing one another, they still waved and swapped smokes and rations, but it wasn't the same as it had been.

Willi wondered what would happen if he asked some French noncom about green flares. He figured it was even money whether the guy had kittens or tried to murder him on the spot. Probably just as well he didn't know enough French even to frame the question. Of course, he might run into a Frenchman who could *verstehen* some *Deutsch . . . ?*

He never did so much as find the chance to ask. Patrolling got more dangerous: Russian artillery fire picked up. He noticed that the Ivans were also hitting the French positions off to the right of where the German part of the line ended. He hoped they were killing bunches of the men who were plotting to go over to them. It would serve the French right, by God!

All he really wanted to do was get out of Russia—eventually, get out of the war—in one piece himself. If doing that involved massacring every Ivan from here to Omsk, he would. If it involved sitting on his ass instead, he'd do that. He wasn't fussy. He didn't know anyone who'd been at the front for a while and didn't feel the same way.

So he didn't complain when the Russian artillery fire eased off again. If the Reds were hauling their guns twenty kilometers north to hit the Germans there, that was all right with him. His boys had been taking it in the neck for a while. Now it was some other poor bastards' turn.

And then, one clear, cold morning, a new fish named Erich Something-or-other shook him awake. "Sorry to bother you, *Herr Obergefreiter,*" the kid said: to an ordinary rifleman, even Willi's picayune rank mattered. Erich went on, "They're shooting off green flares. Bunches of them, in fact."

"Ah, fuck!" Willi said, wriggling out of his blanket like a bad-tempered butterfly emerging from its pupa. He looked eastward. Sure as hell, green fire was everywhere. He sighed and swore and lit the day's first smoke. "All right. We're on with the French again, then. Are the rest of the guys awake?"

"Most of them," Erich answered. "We didn't want to bother everybody, in case this wasn't what you warned us about."

"Give the sleepyheads a good, swift kick in the ass, in that case. This sure won't be anything else." Willi grabbed for his scope-sighted rifle. The longer the range at which he could pick off treacherous froggies, the better.

Oberleutnant Gruber spoke to most of the company: "The French figure they can get away with yanking the *Führer*'s mustache. We're going to make them sorry, you hear me? The more *poilus* we kill here, the more we kill right now, the fewer we'll have to worry about on the Western Front later on. So let's go get 'em!"

The *Landsers* raised a cheer. Willi joined it, but he had the feeling he'd heard something most of them had missed. If France was back in the war, there would be a Western Front again, wouldn't there? The *Wehrmacht* had come so close, so goddamn teasingly close, to Paris. Well, close only counted if you were chucking hand grenades. He had a couple of potato-mashers on his belt. He'd use them if he couldn't get rid of the enemy from farther away.

He trudged south and east through the snow, toward the boundary between the German and French sectors. Shooting had already broken out. As he remembered from the fighting in France, it was easy to tell whose machine guns were going off. MG-34s fired a lot faster than the crap the froggies used. French rifles didn't sound the same as Mausers, either. He hadn't had to worry about them for a while, but all that stuff came back in a hurry.

There was a Frenchman, scurrying east to the vodka and borscht the Reds would give him for turning his coat. Willi dropped to one knee, to steady his aim and to make himself a smaller target. Exhale . . . Don't squeeze the trigger. Touch it gently, like a tit . . . The Mauser pushed back against his shoulder. In his scope, the Frenchman staggered, stumbled, and fell.

He worked the sniping rifle's downbent bolt and slogged forward again. He knocked over a couple of more *poilus,* both of them from a range where an ordinary Mauser without a scope probably would have missed. He felt sorry for them. How could he not, when it was a risk he took himself? But he knew they would have shot him without a qualm. Do unto others before they could do unto you. If that wasn't war's Golden Rule, it should have been.

A French noncom up ahead was trying to rally his section. It was another long shot, but Willi didn't hesitate. Down went the noncom. His men scattered like partridges. Willi slapped a new clip into the rifle.

As he did, a bullet cracked past his head. Not all the froggies were running, dammit. He flattened out in the snow. Where was that French son of a bitch? Willi couldn't spot him. That was scary. You always hated it when the guy who was trying to kill you was good at what he did.

ARISTIDE DEMANGE PEERED balefully across the snowy fields. That damned *Boche* had disappeared. With a white snowsuit and a white-washed helmet, he was almost impossible to spot as long as he kept his head and his hands out of sight.

In front of Demange, Luc Harcourt's blood steamed in the snow. The Germans were still well over half a kilometer away. It had taken one hell of a shot to punch Harcourt's ticket for him. Well, punched it was; that one had torn his throat out. He'd lie here till the wolves found him.

Which didn't mean Demange wanted to lie here with him. The veteran glanced back over his shoulder, working out what he needed to do next. The stupidest thing you could do was move before you decided where you were going and how you intended to get there.

He crawled backward, trying his best to keep Harcourt's body between him and the German sniper. Acting as cover was the last favor the kid could do him or anybody else. When Demange had gone about as far as he could go that way, he scrambled to his feet and sprinted for the cover of some snow-covered bushes.

A Mauser bullet snapped past him, viciously close. He dove behind the bushes, his breath harsh in his throat. *I'm getting too old for this crap,* he thought. All those chain-smoked Gitanes . . . He spat out the butt he had in his mouth now. The last thing he wanted was for that fucking Nazi to spot cigarette smoke yelling *Here I am!*

Can I take him out? he wondered. He had a lot of practice with a rifle, but he was only a good marksman, not a great one. And his piece wasn't all that accurate out past three or four hundred meters. If the guy who'd potted poor damned Harcourt wasn't carrying one of their man-hunting fancy Mausers, Demange would have been astonished. All of which meant that, in any kind of long-range duel, the odds were on the other fucker's side.

Then a Hotchkiss machine gun opened up. Puffs of rising snow traced its stream of bullets across the ground. Demange loved machine guns ... when they were shooting at the other clowns. He wasn't nearly so fond of them when they tried to put *his* lights out.

Now the sniper would have to keep his head down, though, unless he craved a round in one ear and out the other. And if he couldn't fire, or would be rushed when he did, now looked like a terrific time to put some more distance between him and the lieutenant's precious, irreplaceable self.

He used the bushes to screen his movements from the *Boche.* The asshole might be willing to pop up for a shot if he got a good target. Best not to give him one, then. All the same, the spot between Demange's shoulder blades, that stretch of skin right above his spine, itched madly as he hustled toward the Red Army lines.

No 7.92mm round ripped through that spot, or any other. Demange thanked the God in Whom he'd long since quit believing. He hadn't stopped anything big in this war, not yet. He sure as hell did in 1918. The more you know about getting shot, the less you wanted to do it again.

A horrible clanking monster rumbled straight at him: a whitewashed T-34. It looked as if it could make canapés out of every French tank ever manufactured. The reason it looked that way was simple: it could. The commander rode with his head and shoulders out of the hatch. Recognizing Demange as a Frenchman, the Ivan waved a mittened hand as the T-34 clattered past.

"Watch out for a sniper up ahead!" Demange yelled. He doubted the Russian heard, or understood if he did hear. He'd tried, though. What else could you do?

He soon discovered he should have warned the driver to watch out for one of the Germans' fearsome 88mm multipurpose guns, but he'd had no idea the damn thing was in the neighborhood. The *Boches* hadn't wasted it on anything so trivial as foot soldiers. A T-34, now, *that* they took seriously. A big armor-piercing round slamming into steel plate sounded like an accident in a steel mill. The T-34 slewed sideways and started burning. A diesel engine didn't go to blazes the way a gasoline-powered one did, but there were limits to everything.

Demange wasted maybe a second and a half feeling sorry for the unlucky *cons* inside the T-34. Then he trotted on toward the Russians' lines. Whatever the tank wouldn't do now that it had been intended to, it had got the Germans off his back for a while. From his point of view, what more could he want?

As promised, there were lanes through the barbed wire. The Ivans had even gone to the trouble of marking them with strips of red cloth. Never a trusting soul, Demange yelled "Friends! We're friends!" as he came forward. He didn't want his new comrades potting him by mistake.

A Russian appeared out of nowhere. One second, he wasn't there. The next, he loomed up in front of Demange, a snowman with a sub-machine gun. Instead of mowing the lieutenant down, he pointed with the stubby barrel. "You go that way," he said in bad, palatal French.

"I will go that way," Demange agreed, speaking slowly and clearly. Afterward, he thought the Red Army man understood his obedience better than his reply.

He spotted a few more Russians as he tramped along. A couple of them gave him and the *poilus* who'd come in more brusque directions. He wondered how many more of the snowsuited *cochons* he wasn't see-ing. The Russians knew things about camouflage other people didn't even suspect. Their strength was like an iceberg: nine-tenths of it hid below the surface.

Finally, he came to an officer—a captain, by his collar tabs—who wore khaki. He relaxed a bit himself then, deciding he was out of any possible sniper range. The captain carried a clipboard and a pencil. His French was pretty fair: "Give me your name, your rank, and your pay number," he told Demange.

"Whatever you want." Demange rattled them off. He assumed half a dozen Russians he couldn't see crouched somewhere nearby, ready to gun down anybody stupid enough to argue or complain.

The captain wrote things down in a language and a script Demange couldn't begin to follow. He also took the information from the enlisted men who trailed Demange. Then he gestured with the pencil, the same way the guy in the snowsuit had with his machine pistol. "Go that way, past the trees, another kilometer. Get into one of the trucks you find."

Demange sketched a salute. "You got it." He turned to his men. "Come on, you lugs. One more lousy kilometer, then we're done march-ing for a while."

"At least they aren't taking away our rifles," one of the French soldiers said.

He was right. Demange found that mildly encouraging, too—but only mildly. If the Russians wanted to slaughter them from ambush, how much would their rifles help?

The trucks gave Demange pause, much the same way as the sight of his first T-34 had some weeks earlier. They were big, sturdy, broad-shouldered machines that made every design engineer in France, Germany, and England look like an amateur, and a half-assed amateur at that. If the Russians made trucks like these and tanks like those, how come they were still such fuckups?

Then he saw letters of his own alphabet on the trucks' grillwork. STUDEBAKER, they proclaimed. The Russians hadn't made these trucks. They'd got them from the Americans. That was something of a relief. The Americans had a real talent for manufacturing things. He remembered that from the last war, that and their puppyish enthusiasm. They were new to the fight, and still eager for it. All the French soldiers left alive then had long since shed such stupidity.

Another moon-faced Ivan with a submachine gun waved him and some of his men into the back of one of the Studebakers. Three or four Frenchmen were already inside. Before long, the compartment was packed as tight as a tin of anchovy filets. "Anybody know where they're going to take us?" asked one of the fellows who'd got there ahead of Demange.

"As long as it's away from the front, who gives a damn?" the lieutenant returned.

He was as grimy and unshaven as any enlisted man. His greatcoat hid his rank badges. The men who didn't know him treated him the same way they would have treated one of their own. That suited him fine; he'd never wanted to be an officer to begin with.

The truck's engine rumbled to life. The driver put the big beast in gear. Wherever they were going, they were on their way.

IN THE SUMMERTIME, the stinking Fritzes pressed forward and Soviet forces fell back. Ivan Kuchkov had seen that in all three summers of the war. During the winter, though, all bets were off. The Nazis weren't such hotshots once snow started coming down. They were soft pussies, the Germans. All the good weather in Western Europe spoiled them rotten.

As far as Ivan was concerned, the Ukraine had pretty easy winters. It got a hell of a lot colder and snowed a hell of a lot more farther north. But even the weather here was plenty to screw up the Fascist bastards. Their tanks didn't want to run. Sometimes even their gun oil froze up.

When you killed a guy who couldn't shoot back because the bolt on his Mauser was stuck tight, you had to feel a little sorry for him. But you blew his head off anyway, and you were a jackass if you felt more than a little sorry while you did it. What was he doing hundreds of kilometers inside your country except trying to murder you and fuck your sister and steal everything you ever had or would have? Ivan was a jackass all kinds of ways—he even recognized some of them—but he wasn't a pitying jackass.

West of Kiev, the German and Soviet positions looked more like interlaced fingers than anything resembling a line. A Stavka officer who planned and proposed dispositions like those would have got sent to the gulag or a punishment battalion in nothing flat. None of this had been planned; like a lot of war, it just happened. The Russians had gone ahead where they could. The Germans hung on to villages, and to the roads that let them keep the villages supplied.

To complicate things even more, Ukrainian bandits in the woods bushwhacked Russians and Germans almost impartially. A lot of them would have been pro-Nazi if only the Nazis gave them the chance. But the Germans liked Ukrainians no better than they liked Russians. More often than not, they couldn't even tell them apart, or didn't bother trying. So the bandits took potshots at them, too.

One of the reasons so many of the bandits would have gone over to the German side if only the Germans wanted them was that they hated Jews even more than most Russians did. Kuchkov had no great love for *Zhids* himself. Guys like Avram Davidov, though, got more useful in this kind of country. Avram knew what to be nervous about. The short answer was, everything. And when the short answer was everything, the long answer didn't matter.

The Ukrainian nationalists' big disadvantage was that they didn't have an actual country on their side. No factories made rifles and mortars and hand grenades just for them. No trains and trucks made sure weapons reached them in—literally—carload lots. They had to make do with hunting rifles and whatever they could steal from the Germans and Russians.

On the other hand, they were desperately in earnest. The only reason most of the Red Army men and their foes in *Feldgrau* wore their country's uniform was that they would have got it in the neck if they'd tried to say no to the fat sons of bitches who'd conscripted them. The bandits went out to fight because they felt like fighting. They didn't have a country on their side, but they sure wanted to. It made a difference.

Right now, Ivan and his men crouched in amongst some trees that wanted to be a proper forest but didn't quite know how. Avram's eyes flicked across a field to some more trees that might have been an orchard before Stalin started tearing the Ukraine a new asshole but had plainly stood forgotten ever since. The little Jew didn't point; the Red Army men's cover wasn't all that great.

"*Somebody's* in there, Comrade Sergeant." Davidov sounded as spooked as a guy wandering the corridors of a haunted castle in some bad horror film.

"German cunts?" Kuchkov asked. That was his first guess because his officers said there were supposed to be Nazis around here somewhere. He let them do his thinking for him. He knew he wasn't real good at it himself.

Unhappily, Avram shook his head. "I *think* they're Banderists." He was hardly ever cheerful. Now he looked and sounded even gloomier than usual. Stepan Bandera was the bandit chief in charge of most—not all, but most—of the jerks who wanted to fly the gold-and-blue flag, stamp their stupid trident on everything that didn't move, and go around grunting in their almost-Russian language.

"Fuck," Kuchkov said. "You sure?"

"Two or three of them showed themselves there for a few seconds." Davidov still didn't point. He did add what he plainly thought was a clincher: "One of 'em was wearing a cloth cap."

"Fuck," Kuchkov repeated. Real soldiers would wear helmets, or maybe service caps or berets. Only a yokel off a farm would dress like a yokel off a farm. Ivan went on, "We don't need this extra fucking shit, you know?"

"Sorry, Comrade Sergeant." Sasha sounded as if he meant it. He was like anybody else: getting shot or ripped to pieces by artillery fire didn't appeal to him one hell of a lot. After a moment, he asked, "What shall we do?"

Ivan only grunted. He had no idea how many Ukrainians were lurking over there. He didn't want to have to attack them across open ground. If they had a machine gun, or maybe even if they didn't, they could murder every one of the men who'd come at them.

He grunted again. Then he picked up a branch not quite as long as he was and tied his snow smock to it by the arms: not much of a flag of truce, but he had to hope it would do. "I'll parley with the bitches," he said. "If they don't turn me loose, or if anything else gets fucked up, send somebody back to regimental artillery and have 'em blast the living shit out of those trees. Got it?"

The Jew nodded. If anybody in this section could be counted on to take care of something like that, he was the guy. Waving the improvised white flag, Ivan started across the field toward the forgotten orchard. It was a long, slow, lonely walk. They could kill him if they wanted to. No—they wanted to kill him, and they could. It wasn't the same thing.

After a while, a shout came from the leafless fruit trees: "Hold it right there, you cocksucking Red!"

"Ah, fuck your mother. You haven't got a cock big enough to suck," Ivan answered without much rancor. But he did stop.

"You've got some nerve, talking like that out in the open." The Ukrainian in the orchard made enough of an effort to speak Russian that Kuchkov could follow him well enough. "What do you want?"

"My guys have a radio." Ivan lied without compunction. "All we have to do is call, and the big guns'll fuck your position over. If you cunts clear out peaceable-like, we won't call. I'll give you half an hour."

"Why should I believe a guy who licks Stalin's balls?" The Ukrainian was almost as foul-mouthed as Kuchkov himself.

"'Cause I'm standing here, that's why," Kuchkov answered. "You think I'd let you shoot my dick off for nothing better'n bullshit?"

"With a Russian, who the hell knows what you'd be dumb enough to do?" the bandits' spokesman said darkly. Ivan stood out there in the cold wind. He'd figured he would have to wait. The bandit couldn't just give orders, the way a proper sergeant could. He had to talk his buddies into doing shit.

Ivan made as if to look at a watch he wasn't wearing. "Twenty-eight minutes now," he called. "Don't sit there jerking off. Get your nuts in gear."

He waited some more, occasionally checking that nonexistent wristwatch. After a while, the Ukrainian said, "All right. Keep your old galoshes on. We're leaving." Ivan chuckled. *Old galoshes* was Russian slang—not quite *mat,* but close—for a used rubber. Hearing it made him think the bandit meant what he said.

When Ivan did wave his section forward, only half his men came out of their positions. If that wasn't Avram's doing, he would have been amazed. You always wanted somebody in reserve. They occupied the orchard with no trouble—the bandits really had gone away. Kuchkov swigged vodka and lit a *papiros* to celebrate. A bloodless victory was the best kind.

Chapter 26

Like the Goldmans, the Brucks had a radio set. If anything, they listened to it more than Sarah's mother and father did. Books meant less to them than they did to the Goldmans. Isidor and his folks used the radio to fill in the spaces where the Goldmans would have been reading.

Which would have been all right, if Dr. Goebbels weren't the fellow giving the orders about what went out over the airwaves. Oh, not even Hitler's club-footed propaganda boss could screw up everything. Sarah had no problems with Handel and Bach and Beethoven. They didn't belong to the Nazis alone. They were part of every halfway cultured person's baggage.

Wagner . . . Wagner was more complicated. Sarah had been a girl in the days back before the *Führer* came to power. She remembered her father playing records of Wagner's operas then. And, after the direction in which the Nazis were taking Germany grew unmistakably clear, she remembered him smashing those records one by one and throwing the pieces in the trash.

That didn't mean he, or anyone else in the Third *Reich*, could escape

Wagner altogether. Naturally, Hitler's favorite composer was on the radio all the time. Samuel Goldman had usually turned it off or found another station when that happened. Sometimes, though, Sarah had caught him listening, hardly seeming to realize he was doing it. The Germans made it plain that liking Wagner was a big part of being one of them, and her father'd always wanted nothing more than to be, and to be seen to be, a good German himself.

Besides, some of what Wagner wrote—not all, not to Sarah's ear, but yes, some—was ravishingly beautiful.

These days, more French treason and French betrayal were on the radio than Wagner. German commentators screamed that France had broken her commitments as an ally and a friend.

David Bruck was nowhere near so sophisticated a man as Samuel Goldman, but did you need to be a weatherman to know which way the wind was blowing? "It'll be two fronts going full blast, same as it was in the Great War," he predicted. "It didn't work then. What are the odds it will this time?"

"Do you want it to?" Sarah asked him. "If this regime goes down the drain, maybe whatever comes along next won't blame everything on the Jews."

The baker looked startled. "I hadn't even though of it like that," he confessed. Turning to his son, he went on, "See what a smart girl you married, Isidor?"

"Oh, yeah?" Isidor said. Sarah was about to throw something at him when he added, "If she's so smart, how come she married me?" That self-mockery was very much his style. This time, he dragged her into it, too.

"Must be your good looks," David Bruck said. They all laughed. Isidor looked a lot like his father. The older Bruck gave his attention back to Sarah. "I hadn't even thought about no more Nazis. I just remember how hard things were during the last war, and what a horrible mess everything was afterwards."

The Nazis had sprung from that horrible mess. What might spring from the next one, if there was a next one? Whatever it was, it couldn't possibly be worse than Hitler's party. Sarah was sure of that.

She wondered if her father would be so sure. The Nazis had surprised him with their virulence. Had they gone as low as people could go? Sarah thought so. If she was wrong, she didn't want to find out about it.

"Well," Isidor said, "let's get these into the ovens." And into the ovens the dark loaves went. He and his father complained all the time about the horrible brown coal with the lumps and chunks of worthless shale they had to use for baking these days.

Sarah understood why they complained: they were used to better. Jews all over Germany were used to better all kinds of ways. Here, though, Sarah wasn't inclined to *kvetch* along with them. Before long, the baking bread would smell wonderful. And the ovens, even if they burned the cheapest, most adulterated coal around—and what else would a Jewish bakery get?—kept the place warm. In earlier war winters, she'd shivered till spring finally came. No more.

The war bread came out of the ovens right at the top of the hour. David Bruck turned on the radio to catch the news. "It'll all be lies," Sarah said.

"Nah." He shook his head. "Not all. Just most of it." She nodded; he was right. If you listened carefully and knew how to read between the lines, you could sometimes glimpse the real moving figures that cast the enormous, blurry shadows the newsreaders talked about.

The latest broadcast started out with a bang: "The Jews are our misfortune!" the announcer shouted, slamming his fist down on a tabletop. "So our beloved *Führer,* Adolf Hitler, said twenty years ago, and, as usual, history has proved him right."

At that point, Sarah's father would have given forth with a derisive snort. Since he wasn't there, she did it for him. Her husband and father-in-law made identical shushing noises.

"Now the Bolshevik Jews of Moscow conspire with the plutocratic Jews of Paris to try to smash the German *Reich* between them," the newsreader went on. "For a little while, it seemed the degenerate French would have will enough to resist the poisoned honey the Jews poured down their throats. Sadly, though, this was not to be. As a result of base French treachery and deceit, we are punishing the enemy soldiers who seek to desert to the Bolsheviks."

They'd said the same thing after England decided she'd had enough of the fight in Russia. Maybe it was true. Maybe it was sweet syrup designed to make the radio audience feel better about what was going on. Here, Sarah couldn't know for sure without going to Russia herself. There weren't many places she wanted to be less than in Münster, but the Russian front was one of them.

"Fighting has resumed in France," the announcer said in portentous tones. "Displaying their usual cowardice, the French were pushed back several kilometers in the skirmishes. No sign of English troops on the Western Front has yet been detected. As always, England talks a better game than she plays."

Sarah would have looked across the street at the bombed-out grocery there, only she couldn't. The bakery's front window was repaired—after a fashion—with scraps of plywood and cardboard. The RAF played all too good a game.

"In other news relating to the changed war situation, unlimited U-boat warfare in the North Atlantic has resumed," the announcer said. "If America's Jew capitalists think they can get rich shipping arms to increase Europe's woe, we will hurt them in their pocketbooks. Wait and see how loud they scream!" He laughed a most unpleasant laugh.

After that, home-front reports took over. Then the radio started playing *Tristan und Isolde*. David Bruck smiled. He liked Wagner. He hadn't quit liking the composer because the Nazis liked him, too, the way Sarah's father had. She wondered what that said. Most likely, no more than that he liked Wagner even better than Samuel Goldman did.

Isidor said, "I bet the *Wehrmacht* is jumping up and down with joy because they get to fight a two-front war again."

"Bet you're right," his father agreed. "They've already tried to toss out our beloved *Führer*"—he laced that with sarcasm, not the newsreader's *schmaltz*—"a couple of times. How long before they take another shot at it?"

Sarah looked from one of them to the other. No, they weren't sophisticates like her father. But, as she was coming to realize, that didn't make them dummies, either. They could see what was going on in the world.

Hitler would be able to see it, too. How far could he trust the *Wehrmacht*? If he didn't trust it, what would keep the French and English out of Germany? For that matter, what would keep the Russians out of the *Reich*? There was a thought to make any good National Socialist's blood run cold!

Sooner or later—probably sooner, the way Isidor grabbed her every chance he could steal—she was going to have a baby. What kind of world would it grow up in? In a world that didn't look a whole lot like this one? In a world without Nazis? A few weeks earlier, that would have looked impossible. Now? Now she could hope, anyhow.

"YOU *CAN* GO HOME AGAIN," Vaclav Jezek said, contradicting the title of a new novel he'd never heard of.

Benjamin Halévy shrugged. "Yeah, I guess so. But unless we all go back to France to fight the Germans, I'm staying right here with you guys."

"You're a French citizen. You're a French soldier," Vaclav said. "What if your government orders you back?"

Halévy told him what the French government could do about it. Vaclav didn't think governments were equipped to do such things, especially not sideways. He laughed all the same.

"One thing," he said when he got done laughing. "Now that France and Germany are on the outs again, they'll open up the supply spigot here."

"There you go. That *is* something." Halévy sounded enthusiastic all at once. "Let the fucking Fascists get thirsty for goodies for a change. With France and England back in the war, I'd like to see Hitler and Mussolini ship Sanjurjo any toys."

"It's funny. The Nationalists are Fascists, and I can't stand them on account of they're dumb enough to be Fascists, but I don't hate them the way I hate Germans," Vaclav said. "I wonder why."

"All the Spaniards have done is try to kill you," Halévy said. "They haven't raped your country and stolen it from you. Besides, I bet you didn't have much use for Germans even before the war. What Czech does?"

"You are a smart Hebe," Vaclav said, less ironically than he'd intended. Every word of that rang true.

"Hey, I love you, too." Halévy made as if to kiss him.

Laughing some more, Jezek pushed him away. "Leave me alone, you fairy!" he said, and laughed again.

"Not guilty." Halévy shook his head. "I'm a French Jew fighting for the Czechoslovakian government-in-exile in Spain. I've got to be normal some kind of way. I like girls. They don't always like me, but I like girls."

"Girls don't always like anybody," Vaclav said. He and Halévy went on from there. When everything else failed, you could always talk about women.

Vaclav slipped out through the wire before dawn the next morning. If you were in place by the time the sun rose, the bastards on the other side wouldn't notice you moving. The Nationalists' would-be sniper had discovered the error of his ways about that, but he'd never get the chance to do it over and do it right, not now he wouldn't.

The Czech crawled into a shell hole whose forward lip helped shield him from the prying eyes of Sanjurjo's men. They wouldn't find him easy to spot any which way. Twigs and branches torn off bushes broke up his helmet's outline. More camouflaged the antitank rifle's long barrel. His greatcoat was dun-colored to begin with, and muddy on top of that. He'd smeared streaks of mud on his face, too. They had chameleons in the far south of Spain. He did his best to impersonate one of the goggle-eyed lizards.

Since he lacked goggle eyes of his own, he peered through the scope on his rifle instead. The Nationalists behind the lines seemed busier than usual, hustling here and bustling there. He wondered if they were getting ready to attack in this sector. That wouldn't be so good, neither for the Republic nor, more relevantly, for his life expectancy.

After a while, though, he decided it wasn't that kind of hustle and bustle. It seemed more as if they were getting ready to receive a VIP. In spite of himself, excitement coursed through him. People had been telling him to blow Marshal Sanjurjo's head off ever since he crossed the Pyrenees. What if he really got the chance?

Don't blow it, that's what, he thought. One shot, probably out close to 2,000 meters. He could hit at that range. He'd done it before. He'd missed, too, but he refused to dwell on that. Footballers missed all the time, but they kept playing even so. And strikers shrugged off misses and put the ball in the net the next time. Without false modesty, Vaclav knew he was one of the best strikers in this game. He was still here, wasn't he?

He'd smoked a cigarette just before he emerged from the Republican trenches. The next one would have to wait. As usual when he was out between the lines, he didn't want to do anything that might give him away.

Time dragged on. If you didn't know how to wait, you had no business sniping. He ate some sausage. He took a leak. He'd improved the bottom of the shell hole by digging a little trench so he could deal with such things without needing to lie in a puddle of piss afterward.

A Nationalist officer in one of those almost-German helmets surveyed no-man's-land through field glasses. The nerve of the son of a bitch! Vaclav almost killed him to discourage the Fascists from doing that kind of thing again. They knew that he was out here, or that he was liable to be, anyhow.

He would have disposed of the officer had those binoculars paused while they were pointed his way. He might have done it on general principles if he weren't after bigger game. He'd never known the Nationalists to do that kind of thing before. Maybe they were trying to make sure their precious big shot would be safe.

Vaclav ducked down before he shook his head. *Sorry, boys,* he thought. *I'm here, whether you see me or not.*

He waited some more. Clouds rolled in and turned the day gloomy. He hoped it wouldn't rain. That would screw up everything. He needed a clear shot if he ever got a target.

A few drops fell. "Come on, God! Quit screwing around!" Vaclav grumbled. "Whose side are you on, dammit?" The rain stopped. Either God was on his side or the rain just stopped. He remembered a day when he would have figured it was God. Now he would have bet it just happened.

Any which way, after a while he spotted a Nationalist general haranguing a bunch of assembled officers. It wasn't Marshal Sanjurjo. Vaclav knew what he looked like; the Fascists slapped posters of his jowly mug on anything that didn't move. This guy was younger and skinnier.

A good thing, too: if you were fatter than Marshal Sanjurjo, you were too fat to be a general, and probably too fat to live.

Well, this shithead was too Fascist to live. He had an oval, rather disapproving face and a neatly trimmed dark mustache. By the way he gestured, he wasn't the most exciting speechifier God ever made, no matter on whose side God turned out to be.

He wasn't quite so far away as Vaclav had thought he might be: no more than 1,500 meters. The Czech aimed with his usual meticulous care. He took a couple of deep breaths. As he let out the second one, he fired.

Muzzle brake or not, padded stock or not, the antitank rifle always tried to break his shoulder. He'd have a fresh purple bruise tonight, to go with the ones that were fading to yellow. But the Nationalist general stopped in the middle of one of his jerky gestures and fell over. As far as Vaclav was concerned, that counted for more than the bruises.

The Fascists started running around like chickens suddenly minus their heads. The guy with the field glasses popped up again. Except for Vaclav's rule against shooting twice from the same place, he would have nailed him for his presumption. Sitting tight wasn't easy, but he did it.

His pals back in the Republican trenches were on the ball. They started shooting rifles and machine guns at the Nationalist lines. That made Sanjurjo's men decide against going out to hunt for him. He appreciated the gesture. Any heirs he might eventually have would, too.

More waiting, then. Once darkness fell, Vaclav crept back to the little stretch of trench the Czechs held. They pounded him on the back and plied him with harsh Spanish brandy and even harsher Spanish cigarettes. "Do you know who you got?" they yelled. "Do you?"

Since Vaclav didn't, he answered, "Tell me, for Christ's sake. All I know is, it wasn't the big cheese."

"Next best thing, by Jesus," one of them said. "It was that Franco asshole who's given us so much grief."

"Hey! That was worth doing!" Jezek said. Francisco Franco was— no, had been—one of the Nationalists' better generals. He had balls even if he was a Fascist, and he had a tenacity few on either side showed. What he grabbed, he held on to.

Well, all he'd grab from here on out was a plot of earth two meters long, a meter wide, and two meters deep. In the end, that was all any-body ever grabbed, but when you got it mattered.

The Republicans hadn't put an enormous price on his head, the way they had with Sanjurjo. All the same, Vaclav bet they'd give him some leave and some cash to have a good time in Madrid for potting Franco. And if you couldn't have a good time in Madrid, you weren't half trying.

BATTLE DAMAGE REPAIRED, the *Boise* steamed out of Pearl Harbor and headed west, looking for trouble. Pete McGill was happy about that. Any chance to give the Japs one in the slats—or, better, one in the nuts— looked good to him.

He wished he were on the six-inch guns instead of the secondary armament. Then he could have fired at enemy ships, not planes. If you sank a destroyer or another light cruiser, you could give yourself credit for hundreds of Japs instead of the lousy one or two you got for hitting a fighter or a bomber. Vera still needed more revenge. No matter how much he tried to take, it could never be enough. That didn't mean he didn't want to up his score, though.

Along with the *Boise* came three destroyers, a heavy cruiser, and the *Ranger*. All the other ships were along to protect the carrier. The *Ranger* wasn't the ideal carrier to go after the Japs. She was just arrived from the Atlantic, and she'd been more a training ship than a combat vessel. But the fleet carriers that had been in the Pacific now lay on the bottom. If the USA was going to hit back at all, it needed to grab whatever it could get its hands on.

"Two years from now, none of this shit'll matter," Joe Orsatti said as the gun crew stood by their piece looking out over the wide, empty ocean. "Two years from now, we'll have so fuckin' many carriers, they'll fly out our nose when we sneeze. Tojo'll see 'em in his bathtub, for Chrissake. Little tiny Wildcats'll strafe his fuckin' mustache."

Everybody laughed. "You're outa your goddamn tree, you know that?" Pete said, not without admiration.

"Yeah, well, I have fun." Orsatti looked around some more. "Except when I gotta put up with youse guys, I mean."

"Boy, you talk even more New York than I do," Pete said, again more admiringly than not. "I didn't figure anybody could."

"Comes of bein' a dago," Orsatti said with pride of his own. If the wrong guy had tried to slap that label on him, he would have decked the bastard, but he could stick it on himself. He pointed at McGill. "Now you, you're just a regular paddy. If you came from Minnesota, you'd sound like a fuckin' squarehead. But a guinea like me, don't matter where he's from. He still sounds like Hell's Kitchen—or Jersey at the most." Inevitably, that came out *Joisey.*

"Talking about Jersey"—Pete pronounced it much the same way—"who's that kid who's been singing with Goodman and now with Dorsey?"

"Sinatra." Orsatti spoke with assurance. "Yeah, he's from Hoboken. My folks know his folks some kinda way. I *think* one of my cousins went out with a gal who's kin to him—like second cousin or something—but it didn't stick."

"Too bad for your cousin," Pete said. "The way the dames scream for that guy, he's gonna end up with more money than Henry fuckin' Ford. Probably enough so some even sticks to a second cousin."

"Wouldn't surprise me a bit," Orsatti agreed. "But it's water under the bridge now. And Vito's in the Army, poor sap, so he's got more to worry about than trying to make it with Sinatra's cousin."

"My ass, he does. The Army's safe as houses." Like any halfway decent Marine, McGill looked down his nose at the larger service. He had his reasons, too: "What's he gonna do besides train and look cute? Army can't fight the Japs, not till it gets delivered, and that won't happen any time soon. If we were fighting the Germans, too, he might have to work for a living. Way things are, though? Forget about it."

"It's coming. You gotta think so, anyway," Orsatti said. "Now that France and England are over their fling with the Nazis, we're shipping 'em stuff again. That'll piss Hitler off—hell, it'd piss me off. So he'll start torpedoing freighters, and we'll jump in, same as we did against the Kaiser."

"Could be," Pete allowed. "He's turned his subs loose again over in the Atlantic."

Idly, he wondered what it would be like to be a kid from Hoboken with girls screaming for you wherever you went. There sure had to be worse ways to make a living. Back when he had Vera, he wouldn't have cared if all the other girls in the world were screaming for him. (And if that didn't prove he'd been head over heels, what would have?) Since he couldn't have the one he'd wanted most, being able to pick and choose from all the rest didn't seem half bad.

The *Ranger* and her shepherds steamed south and west. Nobody'd said where they were going: not to the likes of Pete McGill, anyhow. He didn't care. As long as it was toward the enemy, that suited him fine.

Wildcats from the carrier flew a combat air patrol over the task force. Floatplanes from the heavy cruiser buzzed ahead of the American ships to make sure they weren't running into trouble facefirst. Little by little, the USA was learning to fight a mid-twentieth-century war. No matter what kind of super-Jutland the admirals had imagined, it probably wasn't going to happen. Admirals' imaginations hadn't encompassed airplanes and submarines. Battleships turned out to be dinosaurs: huge and ferocious and armored, with mouths full of big, sharp teeth, but doomed to extinction all the same.

Klaxons hooted almost every day. Swabbies and leathernecks dashed to battle stations. It always turned out to be a drill. Men swore when the all-clear sounded. But they didn't swear too loud or too hard. Most of them had been aboard the *Boise* when the big American fleet tried to run the Japanese gantlet. Only now was Pete coming to realize how dumb the admirals had really been.

Joe Orsatti laughed at him when he said so. "I bet you still believe in the tooth fairy and the fuckin' Easter Bunny and Santa Claus, too," Orsatti said. "But don't sweat it. Sure, our big guys are dumb. But you bet your ass the Japs are, too."

Pete *was* betting his ass. Everybody in this flotilla was. If he'd had any doubts, they were erased when one alert was followed by an iron-throated shout of "This is no drill!" from the intercom speakers. The officer at the mike went on, "Japanese planes incoming from bearing 240. I say again, this is no drill!"

Grunting, Pete grabbed a shell and handed it to the loader, who slammed it into the five-inch gun's breech. Joe Orsatti trained the gun to bear on the enemy planes' expected track toward the *Ranger*. Pete stood ready to pass as many fifty-pound shells as might be needed. His shoulder complained every time he did it, but he'd long since quit listening.

Overhead, the Wildcats tangled with a swarm of Japanese Zeroes. Wildcats had a chance against Zeroes, but not usually a great chance. One of the American planes splashed into the ocean as Pete watched. "Shit!" he said.

And the Zeroes kept the Wildcats too busy to do what they should have been doing: going after the dive-bombers that followed the fighters in. Japanese naval dive bombers—Vals was the U.S. code name for them—were ugly and old-fashioned. Like German Stukas, they had fixed landing gear. Also like Stukas, they could put a bomb down on a silver dollar if you gave them the chance.

Four of them pulled away from the main bunch and buzzed toward the *Boise*. A Wildcat that broke off from the big mêlée shot one of them down. A moment later, a Zero shot down the Wildcat. The rest of the Vals droned on.

All the light cruiser's antiaircraft guns, large and small, started going off at once. Pete jerked shells like a man possessed. Bursts blackened the air all around the enemy planes. One took a direct hit and turned into a fireball. The other two dove.

Joe Orsatti frantically swiveled the five-inch gun. "Aw, fuck!" he said, again and again. "Aw, fuck!"

Bombs fell free. One of them hit fifty feet to starboard of the *Boise*. The other caught the cruiser just abaft the bridge.

Pete flew through the air with the greatest of ease. Next thing he knew, he was in the blood-warm Pacific. He was amazed how far from the ship he'd been thrown. A good thing, too, because the *Boise* was already starting to settle in the water. Pete looked around for a life ring. He could dog-paddle for a while, but. . . . Off to his left, a dark gray dorsal fin sliced the sea. It was the oldest shipwreck cliché in the world—except when it happened to you. And it was happening to Pete.

THEO HOSSBACH HUDDLED with the rest of the panzer crew around a little fire in a peasant's hut in a tiny village whose name, if it had a name, was written in an alphabet he couldn't read. He wished for hot coffee thick with sweet cream. Yes, he was from Breslau, but Viennese-style would have suited him fine.

They'd found some tea in the hut. Water was boiling in a dented pot over the fire. No sugar. No milk. An Englishman probably would have killed himself before he drank such *Scheisse.* Theo looked forward to getting outside of anything warm. He would have drunk plain old hot water just then, and been glad to have it.

Hermann Witt took the pot and filled everybody's tin cup. The loose tea in the bottom of Theo's cup smelled great when the water hit it. He had to make himself wait before he drank so it would brew some in there.

"The Tommies would laugh at us." Not for the first time, Adi Stoss' way of thinking paralleled his.

Everybody swore at the Tommies—everybody except Theo, who as usual kept his ideas to himself. "Lousy bastards ran out on us, same as the French fuckers," Lothar Eckhardt growled. The gunner scratched without seeming to notice he was doing it. Odds were he was lousy himself. Theo was pretty sure *he* was, too. You came into one of these places, you'd pick up company whether you liked it or not.

"Next time we see Englishmen, it'll be through our sights," Kurt Poske agreed.

Adi said, "Well, the good news there would be, we'd be seeing Tommies instead of Ivans. That'd mean we'd got out of Russia in one piece."

Theo sipped his tea. By now, it was plenty strong. The caffeine made his heart beat faster. It sure held more than the ersatz coffee that came with German rations. He wondered if that crap had any at all. You could get benzedrine tablets. He'd used them once in a while—who didn't, when you needed to keep going?—but he didn't like them. They were too much like squashing a cockroach by dropping a building on it. Caffeine, now, caffeine was just right.

"Two-front war," Witt said, and not another word. With just Theo and Adi there, he probably would have talked some more. Neither Kurt nor Lothar had ever given the slightest hint they would bring anything to the National Socialist Loyalty Officer, but the panzer commander didn't take needless chances in combat with the enemy or with his own side.

"That's what screwed us the last time. I just hope it doesn't screw us again," Adi said. Maybe he trusted the two new guys further than Witt did. Maybe he had his reasons, too. If Eckhardt or Poske ever reported him to the powers that be, odds were they wouldn't do it for anything so trivial as a few ill-chosen words. He had bigger things than that to worry about.

"I wouldn't mind getting the hell out of Russia. I mean, who in his right mind would?" Eckhardt said, a sentiment that certainly had its points. He went on, "I don't want to get my sorry ass *run* out of Russia, though, know what I mean? We get run out of Russia, things aren't going so good."

Adi nodded. So did Theo; that was plainly true. But Adi said, "You know what this miserable country is? It's a swamp with no bottom, that's what. We throw in panzers and planes and people, and then we throw in some more and some more and some more after that, and the swamp just kind of goes *glup!*, and it's like we never did anything to begin with."

"*Glup!*" Theo echoed. He liked that.

"There's got to be a bottom somewhere," Hermann Witt said slowly. "The Ivans have to run out of land and soldiers and machines sooner or later." He grimaced. "Only thing I wonder is whether the *Reich*'s pole is long enough to reach that bottom."

Sooner or later. People had been saying the Russians were bound to run out of people and stuff ever since the Germans started fighting them in northeastern Poland. Now the Germans (and the Poles and Romanians and Magyars and Slovaks, but—dammit!—not the English or French any more) were halfway to Moscow. All the same, *sooner or later* was looking more and more like *later*.

The fire dwindled down toward extinction. Like the other guys in the crew, Theo glanced around for more wood to throw on it. He didn't see any. There wasn't any to see; they'd burnt the last of it. Sergeant Witt said, "Lothar, go on out to the woodpile in the square and bring back some more fuel."

Eckhardt picked up his Schmeisser. Everybody kept a weapon handy all the time. You never could tell when some Reds would sneak past the German pickets and raise hell. But the gunner couldn't go out without pissing and moaning first: "I just fetched firewood like two days ago. Why don't you send the Hebe instead?"

It hadn't been noisy inside the hut before. Now silence seemed sudden and absolute. The wind still howled and whined, but that might have been a million kilometers away. "What did you call me?" Adi asked softly. His machine pistol lay beside him. He wasn't holding it, the way Lothar held his. All the same, Theo would have bet on Adi if shooting started. And shooting didn't seem very far off at all. Theo glanced down at his own Schmeisser—*just in case,* he told himself. In case of what, he didn't want to think about.

For a wonder, Lothar actually got how far he'd stuck his foot into it. "Hey, take an even strain," he said, making no quick or herky-jerky moves. "I didn't mean anything nasty by it. Honest to God, Adi, I didn't. But, so you know, everybody in the company calls you that when you aren't around to hear it."

Theo hadn't heard anyone call Adi that. Which proved . . . what? Not much, probably. If self-sufficient Adi had a best buddy, it couldn't be anybody but Theo. People wouldn't say anything Adi didn't fancy where Theo was around to overhear it. If it got back to Adi . . . Theo wouldn't have wanted him for an enemy. Nobody with a pfennig's worth of sense would.

"Lothar, first things first. You'll get the wood 'cause I told you to," Witt said. "If I wanted Adi to fetch it, I would have sent him. Hear me?"

"Yes, Sergeant," Eckhardt said, his voice uncommonly solemn.

Witt nodded, recognizing that. "*Wunderbar.* Now, about the other thing . . . If people do call Adi that, tell 'em for Christ's sake to cut it out. We need the SS sniffing around us like we need an asshole where our mouth ought to be. You hear me there?"

"Yes, Sergeant," the gunner repeated, more formally yet.

"All right. Now get the hell out of here and bring back that wood before we freeze to death. Go on—scram!"

Eckhardt went. "You didn't need to make a big deal out of it, Sergeant," Adi said after a moment. "I shouldn't've got pissed off."

"People talk too goddamn much," Witt said, a sentiment Theo heartily agreed with. The panzer commander went on, "That's a dangerous nickname to have. It'd be dangerous for a fat blond Bavarian."

He left it there. He didn't say *It's really dangerous for somebody who kind of looks like a Jew, and who just happens to be missing his foreskin.* Adi was no dummy. He could work that out for himself. After another pause, he said, "A while ago, Theo told me the guys knew. I'd kind of got used to that."

"Knowing is one thing. Blabbing's something else," Witt said. "If things were different, you'd probably be a major by now, and ordering all of us around."

"I don't want to tell anybody what to do," Adi said. "I just want people to leave me the fuck alone."

Words burst from Theo: "No wonder I like you!"

The other crewmen laughed like loons. "No wonder at all," Adi agreed.

"Enough, you lovebirds," Witt said, and the panzer men laughed some more. "Getting through the war in one piece—like you said before, Adi, that's the only thing that counts. The rest is just bullshit. So let's get through, and if the other stuff needs sorting out we can always do it later."

Lothar came back with an armload of wood to build up the fire. Theo fed in a few little skinny chunks. When they were burning well, he added some bigger ones. After a while, they caught, too. Like wall lizards basking in the sun, all five panzer men leaned toward the flames, soaking up the wonderful warmth.

THE WAR THAT CAME EARLY

Two Fronts

HARRY TURTLEDOVE

PUBLISHED BY DEL REY BOOKS

Chapter 1

Marine Sergeant Pete McGill lay in the *Ranger*'s sick bay. He had a cut from bomb shrapnel along one rib and another in the side of his neck. A couple of inches there and he would have been nothing but a snack for the shark that had circled him after he got blown off the *Boise*'s deck and into the tropical Pacific.

He knew he was lucky to be alive. A lot of good men hadn't made it off the light cruiser before she sank. The bomb from a Jap Val that flung him overboard broke her back, and she went down fast.

That blast also flung him clear of the fuel oil from her shattered bunkers. You swallowed some of that crap, you were history even if they did fish you out of the drink. And, even though his cuts must have been bleeding like billy-be-damned, the dorsal went away instead of slicing in for the kill. Maybe he was an off brand.

He'd managed to stay afloat, then, till the *Ranger* came over and started picking up survivors. That must have been a couple of hours. By the time he got rescued, he'd kicked off all his clothes so he could tread water better. And every square inch of him that had been above the surface for even a little while was sunburned to a fare-thee-well. The sunburn would have troubled him worse than his little wounds if they hadn't had to put about a dozen stitches in the one on his ribcage. They'd used novocaine when they sewed him up, but it had long since worn off.

The Japs had dive-bombed the *Ranger*, too, but the carrier, unlike the poor damned *Boise*, must have carried a rabbit's foot in her back pocket: all the bombs the Vals dropped missed, though none missed by much. She had some sprung seams, and blast and fragments had swept men from her flight deck. But she could still make full speed, and she still answered her helm. What more did you want—egg in your beer?

From what the other wounded men in the sick bay said, right this minute the *Ranger* was making full speed back toward Hawaii. The little task force of which she'd been the centerpiece had aimed to make life miserable for the Japs on some of the Pacific islands they held. What you aimed for and what you got, though, unfortunately weren't always the same critter.

A pharmacist's mate came through. Some of the guys in there were a lot worse off than Pete. Two or three of them, he feared, would go into the ocean shrouded in canvas, with a chunk of iron at their feet to make sure they didn't come up again.

"How you doing, uh, McGrill?" the pharmacist's mate asked.

"Hurts," Pete said matter-of-factly. He knew more about pain than he'd ever wanted to learn. On that scale, this wasn't so much of a much. But it *did* hurt. Without rancor, he added, "And it's McGill."

"Sorry." The Navy file sounded more harassed than sorry, and who could blame him? He went on, "I'll slather some more zinc oxide goop on where you cooked. You want a couple of codeine pills?"

"I'll take 'em." Pete knew they'd help a little, and also knew they'd help only a little. As he had experience with pain, so he also had experience with pain medicine. He wasn't bad enough off to need morphine: nowhere near. They'd want to save what they had for the poor, sorry bastards who really did need it.

"Here you go, then. Can you sit up some?"

Pete could, though moving made him hurt worse. He swallowed the pills, gulping all the water in the glass the pharmacist's mate handed him. He felt as if the salt water of the Pacific had sucked the moisture right out of him.

Whatever was in the ointment besides zinc oxide, it smelled medicinal and vaguely noxious. It soothed the skin on his cheeks and neck and shoulders and the top of his back. "I wish you could rub it in my hair, too," Pete said. That was, of course, cut leatherneck short, so he had himself a sunburned scalp.

"I will if you want me to," the pharmacist's mate said.

"Nah. It'd be too messy," Pete decided after a moment's thought. He asked, "Can your scalp peel?"

"Fuckin' A it can," the Navy man said. "I've seen some bald guys who toasted their domes. It ain't pretty, man. Like dandruff, only more so."

"Hot damn," Pete said resignedly. "So I've got something to look forward to, huh?"

"'Fraid so, McGrill." No, the pharmacist's mate hadn't been listening. And how big a surprise was that? He had bigger things to worry about than Pete's name. Off he went, briskly, to the guy in the next bed, who'd lost a sizable chunk of meat from one buttock, and who'd sleep on his stomach—if he slept at all—for the foreseeable future.

They got Pete out of the sick-bay bed a day later. Since he'd come aboard the *Ranger* with not even the clothes on his back, they had to give him everything from skivvies on out. Nothing fit real well, and his shirt chafed his tender hide. But clothes make the man. Once he had on even these hand-me-downs, he felt like a Marine again.

Ranger's Marine detachment figured he was a leatherneck, too. They'd lost a few men to the Japs' near misses, and had several others worse off than Pete. He got to be low man on the five-inch-gun totem pole again, for the same reason as before: he was a new guy, and had no established place of his own. He didn't fret over it the way a more reflective man might have. It was useful duty, and duty he knew he could do.

His gun chief was a tobacco-chewing Okie sergeant named Bob Cullum. He had a narrow, ferrety face, cold blue eyes that seemed to look every which way at once, and hands with slim, almost unnaturally long fingers: a surgeon's fingers, or a fiddler's. He guided the dual-purpose gun with a delicacy and precision Joe Orsatti would have

envied. Unless some other ship had plucked Joe out of the Pacific, he
was dead. Pete hoped for the best there, but expected the worst.

Cullum's long, slim fingers had another talent, too. He could make a
deck of cards sit up and beg. Since Pete came into the *Ranger* naked as
the day he was born, that didn't matter much to him. Cullum said, "Hey,
if you want to play I can front you. If you end up losing it, pay me back
when we get in to Pearl."

"Thanks, but I'll pass," Pete said. "Never been much of a gambler,
and I don't want to do it on borrowed money." That wasn't strictly true.
He didn't add that Cullum seemed a little too eager, though. Anybody
who could set the cards jitterbugging like that could probably make
them behave in all kinds of interesting—and profitable—ways.

He must have sounded sincere, because the other sergeant didn't get
mad. "Well, maybe you ain't as dumb as you look, then," he said. His
drawl and Pete's adenoidal Bronx accent were halfway toward being
foreign languages to each other.

"Up yours, too, Mac," Pete said. He didn't sound—and wasn't—
especially pissed off. But if Cullum wanted to make something of it, he
was ready. Sometimes you had to go through crap like that when you
found yourself in a new place. He figured Bob Cullum was faster than
he was, but he had two inches and at least twenty pounds on the other
leatherneck. Things evened out.

Cullum thought it over. Pete must have said it the right way, because
he seemed willing to let it alone. "And the horse you rode in on," he replied, also mildly. He eyed Pete. "You look kinda like a raggedy-ass
scarecrow, you know?"

"Only things that fit are my shoes," Pete agreed. He spread his hands.
"Shit, what can you do, though?"

"Let me work on it," Cullum said. "I've been on the *Ranger* since she
was commissioned, and if I ain't the best scrounger aboard I dunno
who the hell would be."

"Okay," Pete said, which committed him to nothing.

But Bob Cullum proved as good as his word. By the time the carrier
did get to Hawaii, Pete had clothes that fit better than approximately. He
had a wallet with five dollars in it. He had an obligation, too, and he

knew it. When he and Cullum got some liberty, he'd be doing the buying.

He didn't mind. The other sergeant was plainly a guy with an eye for the main chance. If Cullum figured Pete might be connected to the main chance one way or another . . . *What am I supposed to do?* Pete thought. *Hope the son of a bitch is wrong?*

HANS-ULRICH RUDEL'S FLYING suit was made from fur and leather. No matter where you took off from, up above 5,000 meters the air was not only thin but far below freezing cold. In Russian winter, that flying suit came in handy when you were still down on *terra firma*. Rudel all but lived in it from first snowfall to spring's grudging arrival months later.

He sat in the cockpit of his Ju-87 at the end of a runway made by flattening out a long, narrow strip of wheatfield. The fall rains and the thick, gluey mud they brought were over. The ground under the Stuka's landing gear was frozen as hard as Stalin's heart.

He spoke into the voice tube: "Radio behaving, Albert?"

"Seems to be, sir," Sergeant Dieselhorst answered, voice brassy through the tube. Along with the radio, he was in charge of a rear-facing machine gun. Both he and Hans-Ulrich always hoped he didn't have to use it. The Stuka was a fine dive-bomber, but it had been in trouble against even the Czech biplane fighters it faced at the very beginning of the war. Fighters these days were a lot nastier—although the Ivans still threw biplanes at the *Luftwaffe*. The Ivans, from everything Hans-Ulrich had seen, threw whatever they could get their hands on at their foes. If not all of it was top quality, it could still do some damage before it went down in flames. That was how they seemed to think, anyhow.

A groundcrew man yanked at the starting crank in front of the port wing. The crank was hard to move; another mechanic joined the first fellow in coveralls. The Junkers Jumo engine roared to life. Smoke and flame belched from the exhaust pipes. The prop blurred into invisibility. The groundcrew men carefully stepped away from the plane. If you weren't careful around a spinning prop, it could cost you your head—

literally. At least one groundcrew man had been shipped home from Russia in a coffin sealed tight because of a split second's inattention.

"Everything look good, *Herr Oberleutnant*?" Dieselhorst asked—shouted, really, because the racket was terrific even inside the sound-proofed cockpit. Outside . . . Like artillerymen, a lot of the *Luftwaffe* troops in the groundcrew wore earplugs to try to save some of their hearing.

Hans-Ulrich checked the instrument panel. "All green, Albert," he answered, and gave the guys outside a thumbs-up to let them know the Stuka was ready to take off. They waved back.

The dive-bomber lumbered down the unpaved airstrip (as far as Rudel knew, there were no paved ones this side of Warsaw). When it reached takeoff speed, Hans-Ulrich hauled back on the stick, hard. The Stuka's nose came up. It sedately started to fly, rather like a fat old man doing a slow breaststroke across a public pool.

No Ju-87 ever made was or would be or could be a hot performer. All the same, Hans-Ulrich wished that particular comparison hadn't occurred to him. The weight and drag of the twin 37mm panzer-busting cannon under his wings only made his Stuka even more of a beast than it would have been anyhow. He'd used guns like this pair to blast enemy panzers here and, earlier, in France. He'd even knocked down a couple of fighters with them, more from desperation than tactical brilliance.

And he'd been shot down twice, once in France and once here in Russia. He and Sergeant Dieselhorst had both managed to bail out twice, and hadn't hurt themselves too badly either time. No enemy pilot had machine-gunned them while they hung helpless under their big silk canopies, either. The Frenchman who'd got Rudel's first Stuka must not have thought that was sporting. Victorious German pilots also didn't murder defenseless French flyers.

The Ivans . . . There were no guarantees with the Ivans, none at all. Hans-Ulrich knew how lucky they were not to have got perforated when the Russian pilot shot them down.

He spiraled slowly upwards. He wanted to gain altitude before he crossed the front and went hunting on the Soviet side. You couldn't die of old age waiting for your altimeter to unwind. It only seemed as if you could.

"Three thousand meters," he said at last to Dieselhorst. "Oxygen time."

"I'm doing it," the rear gunner/radioman answered. "Delicious."

"Well, that's one word," Hans-Ulrich said with a laugh. Sucked in through a rubber hose, the bottled oxygen always reminded him of gnawing on a tire tread.

He flew north and east, in the general direction of Smolensk. If everything had gone the way the *Führer* and the General Staff wanted, the city would have fallen to the *Wehrmacht* before the fall rains slowed everyone's operations to a crawl. (Of course, if everything had gone the way the *Führer* and the General Staff wanted, Paris would have fallen to German blitzkrieg before winter 1939 turned to spring. You had to deal with what you got, not with what you wanted.)

Other Stukas droned on in the same general direction. They spread across the sky too loosely to be in anything worth dignifying by the name of formation. They had no set target. If someone spotted something that seemed worth going after down on the snowy ground, he'd attack it. If not, he'd keep going.

If someone spotted something. . . . The Russians had forgotten more about the art of camouflage than Germany knew. That was one of the reasons the hammer and sickle still flew above Smolensk: one of the reasons Smolensk still shielded Moscow from attack. The *Wehrmacht* had got more than its share of bloody noses on the way east from forces whose existence it hadn't suspected till it ran into them face-first.

"Hello!" Rudel exclaimed. "What's that?"

"What's what?" Sergeant Dieselhorst asked. Like Epimetheus in the myth, he could see only what already lay behind him.

"Train heading north," Hans-Ulrich said. "They've whitewashed the cars and the locomotive, but you can't whitewash the smoke plume coming up out of the stack." He spoke into the radio, too, alerting his squadron CO to what he'd found and where he thought it was.

"Go get it, Rudel," Colonel Steinbrenner answered. "Somebody may show up to give you a hand, too. Here's hoping it's a troop train full of French traitors on their way up to Murmansk or Arkhangelsk."

"Yes, sir. Here's hoping." Rudel switched off the radio and called into the speaking tube: "I'm going to shoot up the cars and then give the engine a couple of 37mm rounds through the boiler."

"That ought to do it, by God," Dieselhorst declared.

"It had better. And when I pull up, give the train a burst from your machine gun, too," Hans-Ulrich said.

"It'll be a pleasure," the rear gunner replied.

Hans-Ulrich didn't have to stand the Stuka on its nose to attack the train. He came in at a shallow angle, flying slowly, and shot it up from back to front and from only a few meters above the cars. Then, as he'd promised, he blasted the locomotive the way he was in the habit of shooting up enemy panzers through the thin engine decking that didn't do enough to protect them from attack from the air.

As he pulled back the stick to climb for another attack if he needed one, Dieselhorst did rake the train with a long burst from his MG-34. "That engine's blowing steam like a whale," the sergeant reported. "They won't be able to keep going like that for long. . . . *Ja,* the fucker's already slowing down."

"Good," Hans-Ulrich said. "I'll make another pass and chew up whatever's in the cars one more time. With luck, I'll start some fires."

What was in the cars were soldiers—Russian or French Rudel couldn't tell, since both wore khaki when not in winter white. They spilled out as he climbed for the new attack. By the time he dove again, muzzle flashes warned that they were shooting back.

Well, they could try if they wanted to. A Stuka was a tough target for a rifleman. Even if a bullet or two did hit, the Ju-87's cockpit and engine were armored against small-arms fire. Infantrymen, poor fools, weren't. Rudel's thumb came down on the firing button. His forward-facing machine guns chattered. The enemy soldiers ran every which way through the snow.

Sergeant Dieselhorst gave them a parting burst as the dive-bomber climbed away from the stricken train. "They're froggies, I think, *Herr Oberleutnant,*" he said. "I'm pretty sure some of them were wearing the helmets with the crest."

"Good," Hans-Ulrich said savagely. "They need to know they can't play those games without paying the price."

"Damn straight, sir." But then Dieselhorst went on, "What kind of price will *we* have to pay when the war in the west starts cooking again?" Since Hans-Ulrich had no good answer for that, he pretended not to hear, but droned on back toward the airstrip west of Smolensk.

LIEUTENANT ARISTIDE DEMANGE had traveled in cattle cars before. In the last war, the French Army used them all the goddamn time: often enough to make stencils for painting the legend 8 HORSES OR 36 MEN on their sides. In the last war, the French Army'd used anything and everything it could find. Things hadn't changed much in the generation since, either. If it was there, you grabbed it. Legalities and other details would wait till later.

But the Red Army made Demange's countrymen look like a bunch of pikers. Fighting against the Russians, he'd seen they were in grim earnest. Now the French expeditionary force was in Soviet hands. The Ivans wanted them the hell out of their country. What they wanted, they got. And they didn't worry about legalities even a little bit. Legalities were whatever the commissars said they were. Anybody who didn't like it headed for Siberia or got a bullet in the back of the neck.

When Demange was a sergeant, he'd always tried to make his men more afraid of him than they were of the enemy. He'd done a damn good job of it, too. But, from everything he could see, all of Red Russia worked that way.

No doubt the generals and colonels who'd led this force in the biggest French invasion of Russia since Napoleon's day were riding north in the same kind of luxury high Soviet officers enjoyed when they weren't at the front, classless society or no classless society. No doubt. People who weren't generals or colonels headed north however the commissars wanted them to. And if the commissars felt like getting some of their own back . . . They might be godless Communists, but they were also human beings.

So Demange and too many men from his company were sardined into a cattle car the French Army would have been ashamed to use in the most desperate hours of funneling men forward into the Verdun charnel house. You could watch the sleepers go by through spaces between the floorboards as the train rattled up the tracks toward . . .

wherever the hell it was going. Nobody'd bothered to tell Demange where that was.

Nobody'd bothered to muck out the car, either. As far as Demange could tell, nobody'd bothered to muck out the car since Tsar Nicholas was running things, or maybe Tsar Alexander before him. The Frenchman would never again doubt what bullshit smelled like.

Sanitary arrangements were a couple of honey buckets with covers. When somebody needed to crap, Demange told a *poilu* to stand in front of his chosen bucket and hold up a greatcoat to give some rudimentary privacy. By what Demange had seen in the USSR, the covers on the buckets represented no small concession to French sensibilities from the Red Army.

His men were hardened to Russian conditions. They bitched about the stinks in the cattle car, but if you put a bunch of *poilus* fresh from the front in heaven they'd bellyache about that. Demange discounted it. Besides, some of the soldiers had vodka in their canteens instead of *pinard* or—God forbid!—water. They were the ones who pissed and moaned the loudest, and who fell asleep first. Hearing them snore, Demange wouldn't have minded a good slug of liquid lightning himself. He knew how to hold his booze. He wouldn't go out like a flashlight with a used-up battery.

Two French soldiers played piquet. Four more made what would have been a bridge table if only they'd had a table. One fellow leaned against the filthy boards of the cattle-car wall with a pocket New Testament a few centimeters in front of his nose. How anybody could go through more than five minutes of combat and still believe in God was beyond Demange, but Maxime was a long way from the worst man in his company. As long as that stayed true, the lieutenant didn't care how stupid he was every other way.

Demange stubbed out the tiny butt of one Gitane and lit another. While he was awake, he smoked. His cigarettes dangled from the corner of his thin-lipped mouth. Alert *poilus* gauged his mood by the angle of the dangle. Of course, the gamut of those moods ran from bad to worse. He wasn't about to waste his rare happiness on his men, the *cons*. He inhaled deeply. Gitanes were good and strong. The smoke helped him ignore the other foul odors in the cattle car.

He'd just blown out a long stream of gray when he cocked his head to one side. He was trying to hear better—which, in its own way, was pretty goddamn funny, considering how often he'd fired a rifle right next to his ear. If by some accident he lived through the war, he'd be deaf as a horseshoe five years later. And this train, clunking along over a railroad that needed way more maintenance than it ever got, didn't exactly make the ideal listening platform.

All the same, this new background noise didn't sound like anything that belonged with the train. It was getting louder, too, as if coming up from behind. It sounded like . . . "Fuck!" he said softly when he realized what it sounded like. He didn't get the chance to yell before machine-gun bullets tore through the cattle car's back wall and roof.

Something stung his cheek. Automatically, his hand went up to it. His fingers came away bloody. For a bad second or two, he wondered if he'd got half his face shot away and just didn't feel it yet. His hand rose again. No: he was still pretty much in one piece. Either a round had just grazed him or he'd got nicked by a flying splinter or something.

Not all of his men were so lucky. The iron tang of blood suddenly warred with the rest of the stinks. One of the bridge players was down. With most of the left side of his head blown off, he wouldn't get up again, either. The *poilu* beyond him clutched at his leg and howled like a wolf. The same bullet might have got them both.

Other wounded men added their shrieks to the din. At least one other poor bastard looked to be dead, too. And, to add insult to injury, a bullet had holed one of the honey buckets below the waterline. Only the goddamn thing didn't hold water.

The train slowed, then stopped. At first, Demange swore at the engineer. Why wasn't he going flat out, damn him? But that was a question with an obvious answer. If the German Stuka—Demange thought it was a Stuka, anyhow—had shot up the locomotive along with the cars behind it, the train wasn't going anywhere because it couldn't.

And if it couldn't . . . Demange knew what he would do if he were flying that ugly, ungainly bastard. "We've got to get out of here, dammit!" he yelled. "That cocksucker'll come around again for another pass now that he's got a target he can't miss." That he hated Germans didn't keep him from giving them the professional respect they were due.

There was a seal on the door. The Ivans didn't want their guests wandering around. They just wanted them out. He'd been told there would be hell to pay if that seal got broken. Well, too bad. There was already hell to pay, and his men were doing the paying. He broke the seal and slid the door open. He supposed he should have counted himself lucky that some subcommissar hadn't nailed it shut.

"Out!" he ordered. "Grab your rifles, too. Maybe we can fuck up the lousy Nazi's aim if we make him flinch or something."

Out went the French soldiers. The hale helped the wounded. Demange waited till everybody else had left the cattle car before he jumped down himself. He still carried a rifle. No officer's pantywaist pistol for him. If he spotted something half a kilometer away that needed killing, he by God wanted the proper tool for the job. He was damned nasty with the bayonet, too, and didn't flinch from using it: more than half the battle right there.

Here came the Stuka again, machine guns winking malevolently. It flew low enough and slow enough to let Demange see the pilot's face for a couple of seconds. He fired two shots, neither of which did any perceptible good. The plane's bullets kicked up puffs of snow. They thocked into the train. A couple hit with the soft, wet splat that meant they were striking flesh.

Some of the *poilus* fired at the Ju-87, too. It buzzed off toward the southwest. Demange looked around. Nothing to see but the shot-up train, snowy fields, and distant, snow-dappled pines. If he wasn't in the exact middle of nowhere, he sure as hell wasn't more than a few centimeters away.

And how long would the Russians need to figure out that this troop train was well and truly fucked? Would they get it before the French soldiers stranded here within a few centimeters of the middle of nowhere started freezing to death? All Demange could do was hope so. In the meantime, he lit a new Gitane and bent to bandage a man with a bullet through his forearm.

"MERRY CHRISTMAS, SERGEANT!" Wilf Preston said, and handed Alistair Walsh a tin of bully beef.

"Well, thank you very much, sir," the staff sergeant said, surprised and more touched than he'd dreamt he could be. The young subaltern was a decent enough sort. He might even make a good officer once he got some experience to go with all his Sandhurst theory.

Till he acquired that experience, he had Walsh as his platoon staff sergeant. Walsh had been in the Army since 1918, around the time Preston was born. The junior lieutenant had the rank, but men higher up the chain of command were more likely to hearken to Walsh. At a pinch, the British Army could do without subalterns, but never without sergeants. So it had been for generations. So, the admittedly biased Walsh suspected, it would be forevermore.

He hadn't thought to provide himself with a Christmas present for Preston. Truth to tell, he hadn't remembered it was Christmas. Well, there were ways around such difficulties. He took an unopened packet of Navy Cuts out of a breast pocket of his battledress tunic.

"Here you go, sir," he said. "A happy Christmas to you, too." He'd scare up more smokes somewhere. He could always cadge them from the men. They knew he didn't welsh on such small debts.

Even thinking the word made him swallow a snort. He *was* Welsh, as his last name suggested. He proved as much every time he opened his mouth; to English ears, his consonants buzzed and his vowels were strange. If he hadn't stayed in the service after the last war ended, he would have gone down into the mines instead. Chances were he'd been safer in uniform than he would have been had he taken it off with most of the Great War conscripts.

For all he knew, he was still safer here in North Africa than he would have been grubbing coal out of rock. As long as the Italians were England's only foes on this side of the Mediterranean, he'd reckoned his odds pretty good. Musso's boys made a feckless lunge into British-held Egypt, then retreated into Libya. Tobruk, their main base in the eastern part of the colony, had looked like falling soon.

But it hadn't fallen, and now it wouldn't—not in any kind of future Walsh could see, anyhow. The main reason Mussolini'd tried pushing forward was to punish England for backing out of its alliance with Germany against the Russians. With *il Duce* in trouble, Hitler had sent in planes and tanks and men to pull his chestnuts out of the fire. Who would have guessed that the *Führer*, always so ready to double-cross most of his neighbors, would prove loyal to this strong-jawed son of a bitch who didn't come close to deserving it?

At this season of the year, Libya wasn't so bad. Rain made the hillsides and even the desert green up a little. It wasn't blazing hot, the way it had been and the way it would be again before long. Even the flies and mosquitoes and gnats and midges were only annoying, not pestilential.

The Fritzes, now, the Fritzes were pestilential the year around. Walsh had fought them in France in two wars, and in Norway this time around as well. He didn't love them, but they knew their business in temperate climes and in the snow.

They knew it here in the desert, too. As always—and as dauntingly as always—they were very much in earnest. A lot of Italian units fired a few shots for honor's sake and then gave up, the men smiling in relief because they hadn't wanted to go to war to begin with. Not all the Eyeties were like that, but plenty were. Who could blame them? Fighting when you were short of aircraft and armor was suicidal, and they never had enough.

Tell a platoon of Germans to hold a hill no matter what and they damn well would, as long as flesh and blood allowed. And if the survivors did finally have to surrender, they'd spit in your eye when they came down from the hilltop, as if to say you'd only whipped them by fool luck. Bastards, sure as hell, but tough bastards.

Walsh wasn't the only soldier to feel the Royal Navy should have kept the Germans—and the Italians, for that matter—from reinforcing Tobruk. Say that any place where both sergeants and petty officers bought their pints, and you'd get yourself a punchup. *If we had Gibraltar, now . . .* the sailors would go.

They had a point—of sorts. Gibraltar had fallen to Marshal Sanjurjo's men way back in 1939. Without it, the Royal Navy had to run a formidable gauntlet to get into the western Mediterranean, and an even more formidable one to go farther east. These days, most naval support went all the way around Africa, through the Suez Canal, and over to Alexandria. Even there, the Italians had sunk a heavy cruiser with a limpet mine attached by a raider who rode a man-carrying torpedo (or maybe a one-man submarine; the stories wafting through the veil of secrecy varied).

With France back in the fight against Hitler and Mussolini, maybe things would get better. The Mediterranean was the froggies' natural naval province. They'd done a decent enough job in the narrow waters the last time around. Of course, Italy had been on their side the last time around.

Nowadays . . . Nowadays Musso was liable to grab Malta before England could take Tobruk away from him. That would hurt almost as much as losing Gibraltar had. *Well, I can't do a bloody thing about it*, Walsh thought. He might be able to help in some small way with the seizure of Tobruk—if Lieutenant Preston let him, anyhow.

A moment too late, he realized the subaltern had just said something more to him. Unfortunately, he hadn't the least idea what. "I'm sorry, sir. You caught me woolgathering there, I'm afraid," he confessed.

"I *said*"—Preston let his patience show—"that some doctors are telling us we'd be better off if we didn't smoke. As far as health goes, I mean."

"Bunch of ruddy killjoys, far as I'm concerned . . . sir." Walsh added the honorific in case Preston happened to believe the tripe he was spouting. "I might have better wind if I tossed out my Navy Cuts, but I'd be a hell of a lot grouchier, too. Can't get too many big pleasures at the front. Are they going to start begrudging us the little ones now? Wouldn't surprise me a bit." Doctors were natural-born wet blankets.

"I don't believe they're just speaking of wind," Preston replied. "If I understand this correctly, they say tobacco is bad for the health generally, and hard on the lungs in particular."

"Hmp," Walsh said: an eloquent bit of skepticism, even if unlikely to show up in the *Oxford English Dictionary*. "It'll be best bitter next, or I miss my guess." He eyed his young superior. "I don't notice *you* chucking your fags into the closest sand dune, either."

"Er . . . no." Preston had the grace to look shamefaced. "It's a funny thing. I never smoked much before I first went into combat. But in a tight spot a cigarette will steady your nerves better than almost anything, won't it?"

"Anything this side of a couple tots of stiff rum, any road." Walsh held up a hand before the subaltern could answer. "And yes, sir, I know what you're going to say. A smoke won't leave you stupid the way a tot or two will."

"Quite." Preston nodded. Then he chuckled wryly. "Doesn't seem to bother the Russians, by all accounts."

"No, it doesn't," Walsh agreed. By all accounts, the Russians drank like fish. "But then, by all accounts they're stupid to begin with."

German artillery, or maybe it was Italian, opened up just then. Walsh and Preston dove for holes in the sandy ground. As 105s burst around him, Walsh lit a cigarette. He would sooner have had the rum, but you took what you could get. And Preston was right—a smoke *did* steady your nerves.

HARRY TURTLEDOVE is the award-winning author of the alternate-history works *The Man with the Iron Heart, The Guns of the South,* and *How Few Remain* (winner of the Sidewise Award for Best Novel); the War That Came Early novels: *West and East, Hitler's War,* and *The Big Switch;* the Worldwar saga: *In the Balance, Tilting the Balance, Upsetting the Balance,* and *Striking the Balance;* the Colonization books: *Second Contact, Down to Earth,* and *Aftershocks;* the Great War epics: *American Front, Walk in Hell,* and *Breakthroughs;* the American Empire novels: *Blood & Iron, The Center Cannot Hold,* and *Victorious Opposition;* and the Settling Accounts series: *Return Engagement, Drive to the East, The Grapple,* and *In at the Death.* Turtledove is married to fellow novelist Laura Frankos. They have three daughters: Alison, Rachel, and Rebecca.